The Balance Wars

Book II
Convergence

Robert C Littlewood

For

My good friend 'Hursty' whose creative talents
have brought Menkh and Tishan to life.

The Balance Wars

Other Titles

Book 1 – Deviance

Book 3 – Equilibrium – Coming soon

GLOSSARY

PLANETS, MOONS and SUNS

Name	Meaning	Pronunciation
Tarvuli	The Mother, home planet of the Graaven peoples	**TahFOOLee**
Avlar	'Brightest' – one of the two suns of Tarvuli	**AFlar**
Colunda	'Fading Star' – second of the two suns of Tarvuli	**KoLOONdar**
Halidar	'Queen of Night' – moon of Tarvuli, the first to rise and set	**HARleedar**
Barask	'She Who Shines Coldly' – moon of Tarvuli, the second to rise	**BAHrask**
Orvasne	'He Who Waits' – moon of Tarvuli, the last to rise and set	**OrVASHhneh**

SEASONS

Name	Meaning	Pronunciation
Hordeth Gar	Season of Storms	**HorDETH Gar**
Veremis Gar	Season of Weeping	**FerEEMish Gar**
Talloch Gar	Season of Renewal	**TAlock Gar**
Carminac Gar	Season of Abundance	**KarMEEnac Gar**
Nahver Gar	Season of Waning	**NahVEER Gar**
Techmun Gar	Season of Desolation	**TeshMUN Gar**

THE SEVEN PROVINCES of the GRAAVEN EMPIRE

Name		Pronunciation
Percassia		**PearCASHeeah**
Dermoch		**DAREmock**
Voenia		**FoEENeah**
Kassarin		**KashARin**
Storluth		**SsDORlute**
Tashlak		**TARSHlak**
Crosh		**CROWsh**

THE TWELVE VASSAL STATES of the GRAAVEN EMPIRE

Name		Pronunciation
Perduvia		PearDOOfeeah
Phalandrel		FARlandrel
Lazmark		LATHmark
Murdeen		MOORdeen
Borv		Borf
Venlish		FenLEESH
Herdax		AIRdarz
Gromdesh		GROOMdesh
Derfon		DAIRfoon

PLACES and LOCATIONS

Name	Meaning	Pronunciation
Kareem Vastar	A City–State	KAReem VASHtar
Palluvia	A City–State	PaLOOveeah
Paxal	A City–State	ParkSHARL
Tekla Xemik	The Great Water Lake	TEKlah SHEMik
Ter'Malloch	Silver Water Lake	TEar MAHlok
Firma	Large island set in the waters of Ter'Malloch	FEERma
Cheptosi Gem Hallach	The Thunder Water Falls	ChepTOsee Ghem HALack
Sharana	The Black Water River	ShaRARnah
Xerfun	The Underworld	SHERfoon
Tarmech	Capital city of the Graaven Empire	TAHmesh
Camchak	River of Life	KamCHACK
Steppes of Portis	Unconquered lands to the north	PORtish
Plains of Clarist	Desert region to the far east of the Empire	CLARisht

PRINCIPAL GRAAVEN GODS BEFORE the FALL

Name	Meaning	Pronunciation
Slax Ar Terrun	Goddess of Death	**SLArx ar TERoon**
Bekkor	The Seven-faced God	**BEKor**
Bringarell	God of the Underworld	**BrinGAHREL**

GRAAVEN MEASURES of TIME and DISTANCE

Spahn	Roughly equivalent to 12 inches	**SHParn**
Talit	Roughly equivalent to one inch	**TARlit**
Persangh	A Graaven mile	**PearZang**
Chaal	A Graaven hour	**CHarl**
Dak'chaal	A Graaven day	**DAHK CHarl**
Meh'chaal	A Graaven week	**MURK CHarl**
Bach'chaal	A Graaven month	**BAHR CHarl**
Sem'chaal	A Graaven year	**ZEM CHarl**

GRAAVEN MILITARY STRUCTURE

Name	Meaning	Pronunciation
Shu Tek	Greatest of 25	**SHOO Tek**
Shu Mut	Greatest of 50	**SHOO Moot**
Shu Lan	Greatest of 100	**SHOO Larn**

GRAAVEN MILITARY STRUCTURE (cont.)

Name	Meaning	Pronunciation
Kalvak	First of 500	**KULvark**
Met Stragosh	'Little' General	**Met STRARgoash**
Stragosh	General	**STRARgoash**
Impisch	Unit of 10 000	**IMpeesh**
Impisch tarn	Unit of 1000	**IMpeesh TAhn**
Praka	Unit of 25	**PRAka**
Praka xem	Unit of 50	**PRAka SHEM**
Praka vek	Unit of 100	**PRAka Fek**
Praka haram	Unit of 500	**PRAka ARam**
Hoplex	Graaven foot soldier	**HOplecks**
Sagit	Graaven archer	**ZAYgit**
Baran Mec	Imperial guard	**BAHrarn Mek**
Zaltec	Supreme military leader	**SAHLtek**

PROLOGUE

Like some monstrous bloated spider, it sat in a web of force spun from invisible threads of power. The threads reached across vast distances of space, connecting it to all its loathsome offspring.

Its insatiable hunger was fed by lines of energy that pulsed with life essence – essence that was drawn from numberless creatures, both sentient and non-sentient, and from the very earth of a thousand worlds that had fallen under its baleful dominion.

Deaf and blind, its consciousness nevertheless was attuned to the threads of power that extended from it. Not only did these threads act as conduits for its nourishment, but they also fed back details of the worlds where it manifested its power, absorbing the knowledge of the beings it fed upon.

For years beyond count its malignant influence had spread, draining the life force of countless living creatures and rendering entire verdant worlds barren, mere chunks of rock endlessly revolving in space. Its expansion of knowledge had not diminished its complete indifference to all other life. Instead, its ability to dominate, torture, and mutilate its victims using their own beliefs and fears against them grew a thousandfold. By the power of will alone, through its offspring, it could manipulate and refashion reality, creating creatures of nightmare to further its domination. The fate of entire systems was of no concern, provided that it continued to feed. Only the torment of other creatures gave it anything akin to pleasure.

Memory it did have, and the sum total of its existence was passed on to its offspring so that there was a connectedness between them. This was not a bond based on affection or love, but of need. Its voracious appetite and indifference to all other life was a trait that was passed on, so that each of its offspring sought to dominate and consume all that they encountered. In so doing, without conscious will or power to resist, each individual offspring sent out questing tendrils of energy that were drawn inexorably to their parent. No matter the distance between them, like sought like, till the bond was established and life-giving energy flowed to the parent. Inevitably, once the life essence of the world had been absorbed the offspring's own essence was absorbed back into the parent, leaving yet another lifeless world to continue its lonely orbit.

Now the very world that had spawned the creature had succumbed to its malignancy and its poisonous form had spread across the entirety of that world, kept alive only by the energy that flowed along the strands of its web.

A disturbance.

A single, tenuous link, newly formed but burgeoning, had suddenly been extinguished. The creature turned its thoughts to the vanished link, stretching its consciousness out like a hunter following a barely traceable scent.

As its power had grown so, too, had a sense of disquiet. Its knowledge of the cosmos had expanded and it had slowly become aware that another power, beyond its ability to comprehend, had evoked a tenuous 'feeling' that was alien to it. The creature had no concept of what this vague feeling was but its knowledge base, absorbed from other beings, identified a word that gave it shape and form. That word was 'fear'. This power posed a threat that could not be ignored.

It sat and picked at the threads of its acquired knowledge. Back and back in time it went until at last it recalled the alien explorers who had, so foolishly, landed on its world. Alone and feeble at the beginning, the creature had nevertheless overcome and consumed each of the explorers, absorbing their knowledge and delighting in their terror, finally allowing just one to leave and return to its home world, carrying the seed of the creature's first offspring.

It began to stretch its consciousness beyond the mere satisfaction of endless hunger and to contemplate other possibilities.

An unexpected power. A force rarely encountered. Cloaked and guarded it was, but its vibrations showed that it had enough energy to eradicate the creature's offspring such that no trace remained.

Rage.

Such an occurrence was impossible, could not occur, had never occurred, must not occur!

Only a vague sense of where the vanished link had emanated from was left, but enough for the creature to act.

One of its offspring had enslaved a race who occupied a world that could be the springboard for an expedition to exact revenge. Malevolent and without pity, this race had worshipped the offspring as some sort of god, willingly sacrificing their own kind in offerings. Their technology was advanced: certainly, enough to seek out this new power and destroy it.

A thought was formed and transmitted through its web of power. Acquiescence was not long in coming.

CHAPTER ONE

As quickly as Menkh had disappeared from the viewing room he reappeared moments later in another area of the Complex, one that was as unfamiliar to Crixac as it was to him. Moments later Tishan, looking slightly alarmed, also appeared. After exchanging looks they peered at their surroundings. It was a massive space filled with translucent columns of white crystal that soared upwards, disappearing through the ceiling high above where they stood.

The ceiling itself appeared to be made of huge metallic plates that shimmered in a cold blue glow flowing from the columns. Through their feet Menkh and Tishan felt a strong vibration. There was also, at the very edge of hearing, a muffled sound that could not be described, yet evoked a feeling of enormous power. Menkh turned his thoughts inwards to Crixac.

<What is this place, and where in the Complex are we?>

<I know not, my friend, this place is beyond my knowledge,> responded Crixac.

The voice of the Shard entered the minds of Menkh and Tishan. <This is the tenth and lowest level at the heart of the Complex. The waters of the seven rivers converge and flow directly

underneath this location. Above you, the central tower of the Complex rises hundreds of spahn into the sky. This is the core of the weapon, the machine that the Kareems developed and which we must now reactivate.>

<To what end?> Crixac was concerned.

<You need have no fear, Tishan, Menkh, and Crixac. What was once re-engineered for destruction is now turned to defence. Its power will not only protect this world but also the sister worlds that form the planetary system that is home to Tarvuli.>

<It is that powerful?> Menkh asked.

<Assuredly,> said the Shard. <It needs only to have its satellites activated to awaken its force. That is where you come in.>

<Satellites?> Tishan sought clarification.

<There are three. Each is located on one of the three moons, and they must be activated in order. That is your mission, for it cannot be done remotely.>

<What preparations do we need to make?> Menkh asked.

Quiet laughter echoed in Menkh's mind. <You are a bonded Adept of the Red. You have your staff and possess a form that can inhabit and adapt to any environment. You need neither food nor drink. What preparation would you have, Menkh ab Dur?>

<Well, if you put it like that,> Tishan said with a tone of wry humour.

<We shall return to the viewing room. You all have a role to play, and it is as well that you understand as much as possible. It is not without some danger.>

<Of course,> said Crixac resignedly. They all were familiar with the Shard's habit of understatement.

Once again, they disappeared, leaving the room and its eerily glowing columns. They reappeared in the viewing room.

Peering at the walls around her, Tishan observed several strange, silvery craft that appeared to hang motionless in space. Her thoughts, expressed to the Shard, also entered Menkh's mind, conveying deep concern. <Things must be dire indeed, given what you have told us.>

<They are not 'dire' yet, Tishan Dar.> The Shard's voice echoed in their minds. <All is in hand, but the final steps now need to occur. This will require Menkh's and your direct involvement; you must be ready to assist in the process.>

Menkh formed a thought. <What threat do we face? If not yet 'dire', then how serious is the threat these things pose?>

The Shard's tone was measured. <The weaponry of these beings is such that they are more than capable of laying waste to whole regions of this world. More deadly still are the pathogens they carry. If these are released into the atmosphere, all life on Tarvuli will be extinguished in the most terrible of ways.>

Menkh's mind echoed with outrage. <Are these beings so intelligent that they lack a sense of morality?>

<They are merely a reflection of that which they worship, for they see the Talixit Ven as the embodiment of that which they aspire to be. To that end, they are completely lacking in anything as 'weak' as compassion or feelings for others. Even to weaker members of their own race.>

<Then they must be misshapen and ugly to look upon, as a direct reflection of their natures,> said Tishan.

<So you may think. The reality is that you would find their physical forms fair to look upon. Only their eyes give any indication of their true nature, for they are black and soulless,> corrected the Shard.

<I have seen this in my travels,> Crixac replied. <So often, that which is beauteous – even amongst flowering and growing things – conceals a deadly toxin within. Well, Shard, what must our next steps be to counteract this menace?>

<First, we must reactivate the shield the Kareems corrupted and from which they fashioned their ultimate weapon. Then we must eradicate these beings. Tishan, you will coordinate matters

here. As each satellite is brought online, so you must activate the central core located below us. I will guide you in this. Menkh, you will travel the Threadway. This forms part of your mastery as an Adept. You have done this before, albeit at our direction.>

<What is the Threadway, and how will I travel upon it?> asked Menkh.

<I could spend a lifetime trying to help you understand the Threadway and even then, you might need several more to fully comprehend it. It connects everything, everywhere. It is a manifestation of the Intelligence. Only those we choose, and bonded Adepts, may travel its paths. The Threadway leads to many places separated by time and distance – but it can be unpredictable, and you must always maintain your focus when travelling.>

<Is it like a gateway?> Crixac asked.

<No, Crixac. A gateway is a connection point between two locations. The Threadway connects all things. Anyone with understanding can utilise a gateway to travel.>

<It sounds more like travel 'between', as we did when we followed the energy traces of the enemy back to its source,> said Menkh.

<Or perhaps also like when we translocate to other places here on Tarvuli and within the City,> added Tishan.

<Certainly, there is some commonality,> answered the Shard. <But translocation requires you to be physically present on a world. You cannot translocate when journeying through space and time to other worlds and systems. Only a gateway or, if you have the technology, a ship designed for such travel will suffice.>

<And a gateway generally requires someone to set up the portal on the world or place to which you wish to travel, and they can become unstable, as I and some previous hosts have discovered to our cost,> Crixac said.

<Exactly. The arrival of the enemy on your world heralded a deviance that could lead to the complete disruption of the Balance,> responded the Shard. <None of you has yet thought of the most worrying aspect of the imminent arrival of these beings, which is further evidence of deviation.>

<What is that?> asked Tishan.

<The beings whose vessels approach are minions of the Talixit Ven. They have harnessed a power that enables them to travel the between, crossing vast distances at great speed. They cannot access the Threadway and we know that there is no gateway, save that which links Tarvuli to the Balancepoint. How did these creatures, even with their advanced technology, find the means to navigate their way? It should have been impossible. What knowledge has been passed to them by the Talixit Ven to enable this? It should have taken them at least a hundred sem'chaal to reach here – and bear in mind they had no precise understanding of your location, so quickly was the link back to the parent severed.>

<But surely with your connection to the Intelligence you already know how they have done this?> Tishan said. <And what is this parent that you speak of?>

<I am a fragment of the Intelligence, as indeed are you, Tishan Dar. Powerful, certainly, but my power has its limitations. My role here means that I am severed from the Intelligence in a way that you could not comprehend. I have no understanding of the method these creatures have utilised to journey here. My primary focus now is the protection of this world and the preservation of the Balancepoint gateway that exists here. As Agents of Balance there is some knowledge that I can equip you with, but there are some tasks you must complete yourselves and achieve in your own unique way. Foreknowledge may actually lead to failure, something that we cannot afford.

<As to your other question, the creature that tried to establish dominance here is an offspring of its parent. All its offspring everywhere establish a link back to it. The parent then feeds off the energy that flows to it through invisible lines that connect them. Eventually the offspring itself gives up its life energy to the parent, and the world upon which it established itself falls into desolation. When you, Menkh, forced the creature into the diadem, that link was severed. I anticipated a countermove. That it has been so rapid shows that whilst we worked together to deny the enemy the technology of the City and its potential access to the Balancepoint, there is still much to concern us. We must establish a convergence, a move back towards Balance. Our war has only really just begun.> The Shard's voice was ominous.

<So much for the years of peace then. I was looking forward to travelling with Menkh and showing him other worlds,> sighed Crixac.

<Rejoice then, Crixac, for you will indeed be travelling again very soon, with the added spice of unexpected obliteration giving you both that extra zest for life.> Menkh recognised the Shard's humour.

<We should have chosen the blue or white crystal, Crixac, it's our own fault,> Menkh said drily.

<I would laugh with you if I were not so concerned,> said Tishan. <I will gladly die to protect all that we have set up here in our new home.>

<Let us prepare so it will not come to that, Tishan Dar,> the Shard said. <Heed me now, we have no more time for explanations.>

No sooner had the Shard spoken than a panel opened in the wall behind them; one which Menkh remembered well from when he first came to the City. This time a glowing green crystal sat in a small depression inside it.

<Both you and Tishan have grown a hundredfold in your abilities to translocate and manipulate much that is contained within the City. Each of you have crystals that assist you in focusing your mind and harnessing their power to enact your will. Now, Menkh, you will travel far beyond the City's confines and venture into remote regions of space, albeit your first steps will only be to the moons that orbit this world. The green crystal, like the others in your belt, will assist you in focusing your will to access the Threadway. Be warned, only a bonded Adept can utilise this device. Any who try to manipulate it to their own ends will cease to exist.>

<Is death immediate then?> Tishan asked.

<You do not comprehend, Tishan Dar.> The Shard spoke deliberately. <I did not say they die: I said they cease to exist. Every atom, every particle of them, will vanish as if it had never been. All memory of who or what they were vanishes with them. No trace of them will remain anywhere.>

Tishan shrank back involuntarily with horror and Menkh's skin crawled at the mere thought of having to touch it.

<A dire penalty, indeed,> said Crixac, no less dismayed than the others.

<Better then to assume your true form, Menkh ab Dur, so that the crystal recognises you. We do not wish for unpleasant surprises.>

Menkh again discerned a tinge of humour in the Shard's voice.

<I really think I made the wrong choice in that cave, Crixac,> he said.

<Nevertheless, you did choose, and I have become quite fond of you, even if where you thought you were was not in reality a cave, nor even within this dimension. But that is a discussion for another time.>

Menkh shied away from the implications of the Shard's comment and instead, with Crixac's assistance, assumed the form that had replaced his Graaven body when he bonded with the Shard in what seemed a lifetime ago.

Tishan watched Menkh's body shimmer, divesting itself of the image of the Zaltec who was universally loved by all Graavens. An alien-looking form, covered in glowing red skin, stood in its place. It still made her uncomfortable even though she had seen the transformation before.

<Stretch forth your hand and lift the crystal. You must contact it for it to recognise you,> commanded the Shard.

Menkh reached his right hand out, gasping the crystal with three long, tapering fingers and two thumb-like appendages. Unbearably bright green light flared for a moment and then subsided to a gentle pulse. He held the crystal over an aperture on the belt he habitually wore. It abruptly vanished and, in its place, a faint greenish glow could be seen from where the crystal was now safely housed in the belt.

<What now, then?> asked Menkh.

<Now you must focus your mind, Menkh ab Dur. You wish to travel to Barask, the location of the first of the satellites. Visualise it in your mind. Crixac will assist you, and your staff, combined with the power of the green crystal, will provide the energy required.>

As Menkh focused, he noticed that both the room and Tishan, who stood alongside him, seemed to fade, becoming ghostlike and transparent. A beam of light flowed around him, lifting him so that he floated gently above the ground. Suddenly Tishan, the Complex, and the entire City were left behind as he accelerated upwards, passing through walls that had lost their power to contain him. He felt no physical sense of movement, but as before when he travelled the between, he was suspended in a beam of light. Tarvuli lay underneath him and rapidly diminished. His attention was drawn away from his home world to centre on Barask, which was rapidly approaching.

As he drew nearer to the moon's surface features began to resolve themselves. He saw vast mountain ranges and wide plains,
intersected by what might once have been riverbeds. The light of
the two suns reflected brightly off the plains, which seemed to be
composed of some white-coloured material that glinted, mirror-
like. As he floated gently down to the surface, he formed a thought
to Crixac. <That seemed to take virtually no time at all. It will be
interesting to physically walk in a place I have only seen from afar
and dreamt about.>

<I agree. The first of many more new experiences I deem, my
friend,> Crixac responded.

Menkh drank in the image of Tarvuli, its distinctive violet atmosphere aglow with the light of the two suns. He was viewing its
myriad lakes and mountain ranges from a vantage that just a few
short sem'chaal ago he would have deemed impossible. More surprisingly, he could also discern a huge body of water that occupied
a large part of the planet's surface. Its existence, hinted at by the
Xotic, was now confirmed with his own eyes and he wondered at
the depth of his ignorance of his own world.

<The more you know, the more you realise that you have much
more to learn!> he thought.

<Truly, my friend,> said Crixac, <even within my experience,
the more I understand the less I think I know.>

<Enough now,> said the Shard. <Look to the surface of
Barask. There are traps for the unwary, though nothing beyond
your power to contain. The satellite will be an array of towers,
somewhat like the Complex, but it will be shielded. You must use
your staff to locate it in much the same way that you revealed the
gateway in the Gap of Crethic.>

Menkh surveyed the terrain around him. Like glittering crystal,
Barask shone in the light of the suns. Everything around him was
covered in ice and although he felt no cold and was impervious to

extremes of temperature, he could discern the intensity of the coldness around him and the almost complete lack of atmosphere.

<I see how accurately you Graavens named Barask 'She Who Shines Coldly',> Crixac said.

<Indeed,> agreed Menkh. <I wonder how the Kareems were able to reach here and set this up. I cannot see how any creature of flesh and blood could have done so.>

<They didn't,> said the Shard. <It was Menath, Kortsan, and Tambel who established them when first they fled with their stolen crystals from the Balancepoint. They were originally set up as a defence, should any Adept seek to interfere with their designs or attempt to take back that which they had stolen. In time their use was corrupted, re-engineered by the Kareems to create their 'ultimate' weapon in secret. Only once has their power been called upon. Power that you may well recall, Crixac, before it was shut down, the last act of my predecessor. For many an age, the satellites have remained dormant. Now we shall activate them once more as a step towards convergence, and in protection of that which lies hidden on Tarvuli.>

Menkh's curiosity was aroused. <Surely Adepts from the Balancepoint could have used the gateway to travel to Tarvuli? What need of such a defence?>

<Your thought presupposes that the gateway was always present. It was not. The establishment of the gateway is a story for another time, Menkh. For now, concentrate on the task at hand.> The Shard's voice faded.

<A mystery for another day, my friend,> said Crixac.

<We are surrounded by mysteries, Crixac, but you are right, of course.>

Menkh focused his attention on their surroundings. Nothing stirred around him and he was enveloped in a frigid and total silence.

<The silence here is eerie and leaves me looking over my shoulder in anticipation of something terrible,> Menkh said.

<Yes, I can feel what you mean,> Crixac spoke quietly. <But come, let us stretch out our senses and see if we encounter anything that disrupts that feeling.>

They walked forward. Menkh held the staff before him, using it to focus his thoughts and probe the area around them. It was difficult to measure the passage of time as they walked. It felt like everything was but a dream. Only Tarvuli, visible above them, gave reassurance that this experience was real and not something imagined. Suddenly Menkh detected something.

<Do you feel that, Crixac? Just now, in this endless place of nothing, there is 'something'. I cannot put words to it.>

<Yes, I feel it too. There, just ahead.>

They climbed up an eminence that stretched to left and right in a long curve. After reaching the top they climbed down its gently sloping sides until they stood in the base of a huge crater. It was relatively flat, but intensely bright. The walls of the crater rose all around them and seemed to focus the light of the suns. Menkh placed the bottom of the staff firmly on the ground and focused all his will into it. Snaking lines of red energy pulsed out, flowing like water and splitting into many separate lines. Abruptly the lines flowed upwards, rapidly illuminating a tracery of towering structures, vague and indistinct at first but rapidly coalescing into solid reality.

The towers, of which there were several, were like the trunks of huge, crystalline trees that appeared to have grown out of the ground. They gradually grew narrower until, before reaching their majestic height several spahn above, they were pointed like needles.

<I was thinking of trees when I first saw them, but now, Crixac, I am more reminded of the stalagmites we saw in that cave.>

<Yes, I agree, but they also resemble the towers of the Complex. It seems to me that this is what we are looking for; but how do we activate it?>

<Shard?> Menkh sent out a questing thought.

<I am here, Menkh, Crixac. You must lay your hands upon the structure whilst at the same time making sure that you are in contact with your staff.>

<Is that important?> Menkh asked.

<Everything I tell you is important, Menkh ab Dur. Otherwise, I wouldn't say it.> It was amazing how much exasperation the Shard could convey in a thought. <So, if you want to live past the point where it activates, you will do exactly as I say.>

<Well, if you put it that way,> said Menkh.

<Now it is my turn to wonder if *I* made the right choice,> said the Shard, before disappearing from Menkh's mind.

<The Shard certainly gets touchy,> said Crixac. <However, let us ensure that we follow our instructions closely. I don't want to be evaporated on a cold moon and neither do you.>

Rather than making a reply, Menkh took up the staff. Holding it tightly in his right hand, he placed the fingers of his left hand on the structure, somewhat gingerly, and once again focused his will upon the strange structure before him.

Intense light erupted from the structure. Menkh's staff flashed in response, surrounding him with a blue aura that not only protected him from the pulse of energy that leaped violently from the structure like lightning, but also cushioned his fall as he hit the ground some fifty spahn away from it.

ooooOoooo

Meanwhile on Tarvuli, Tishan, guided by the Shard, had translocated to another unfamiliar place. Beneath her feet she felt again the vibration of the surging waters that coalesced and flowed under the Complex. She stood on a raised dais in the centre of a small room. In front of her, a wall that at first had been opaque now became transparent. On the other side of the wall she saw the large space below the central tower of the Complex where the Shard had taken her and Menkh earlier. She knew that she stood once more within the tenth level and that the core of the weapon lay before her.

Out of the dais at her feet a column of what appeared to be black glass arose and stopped at chest height. On the very top of the column, a perfect egg-shaped white crystal, on the surface of which were three slots, reposed.

<Harken now, Tishan Dar, this is important. Soon now Menkh will activate the first device. When he does so the crystal before you will detect an energy surge. When that happens, three filaments of crystal will emerge from the column. You must insert one filament into the egg-shaped crystal.>

<Well, it sounds simple enough,> Tishan said.

<Yes. Regrettably, the three filaments will appear to you as colourless and identical in form, although in fact one is blue, one white, and one red. Only the white filament is the correct one; insert any other and there will be a backlash.>

<Backlash?>

<A surge of energy that results as the crystal rejects the filament. The consequences of getting this wrong would likely prove fatal to you even with my intervention.>

Tishan stood in stunned silence.

<But how am I to tell them apart? Why can't you do it? Aren't you a fragment of the Intelligence? Surely your power and knowledge exceed mine?>

<I am forbidden to directly intervene. It is given to me to choose my instrument for this task, and I choose you, Tishan Dar. You have a depth of perception that you underestimate. You must follow your instincts and connect mentally with the filaments. They will speak to you in your mind. All your life, all that you have

done and learned, leads to this point. Trust me, trust yourself. You are the Guardian of the City. You were not named so as a joke.>

A maelstrom of self-doubt surged through Tishan's mind as she considered the enormity of the consequences of getting it wrong.

<What of the City and of my people and offspring, will they be harmed?>

<No. Any backlash will be contained here. This is the failsafe that the dying crystal established so that the weapon could not be activated by just anyone.>

Tishan was silent for several minutes. Breathing deeply, she nodded her head. <I am Tishan Dar, Stragosh of the Graaven Empire. I have faced death many times. I do so willingly now for the protection of my people, and for the City.>

<The time approaches, Tishan Dar. Hold to your heart and follow your instincts.>

Abruptly Tishan felt a change in the air around her; there was a definite drop in ambient temperature. She noticed, too, that the crystal had begun to glow and that, where before its surface had been opaque, it was now translucent, with bands of pale blue veins covering its surface. Tentatively she reached out her left hand and placed it lightly on top of the crystal. At once she heard music in her head. It was not pipe, flute, drum or zither. It was music quite unlike any she had heard before. Beautiful and compelling, more like a voice singing. As she lifted her hand, the music abruptly stopped, starting again immediately her hand was placed back upon the surface. As compelling as the music was, there was also an undercurrent of something else; at times the music would resonate with a sound that set her teeth on edge and caused the tendrils on her neck to flare redly.

As she drew her gaze up from contemplation of the crystal, she saw the three filaments that the Shard had referred to hanging poised above the crystal, appearing as if by magic from the structure whereon the crystal lay. Each filament had a metallic appearance and was about the thickness of a Graaven finger, ending in three prongs, which were obviously made to be inserted in the crystal itself. To Tishan's eyes they were indeed identical in form and aspect. Reaching out she touched the filament to her immediate left.

Once again, music played in her mind. This was rather discordant, uncomfortable to listen to. To her ear it was missing something indefinable, as if it were a work that had been left incomplete. Each filament was the same: different music, same feeling of discord.

Tishan stopped and thought. Placing one hand on the crystal and one on the filament to her left, the effect was immediate and stunning. A discordant, brain-numbing screech overwhelmed her senses and she desperately sought to pull her hands away. After a few moments, which felt like several chaal, she managed to pull her hand off the filament. At once the music of the crystal resolved itself to that which she had heard earlier. Gasping for breath she dropped both hands and composed her thoughts.

Obviously not that one! she thought to herself.

Resigned to what she must do, she again placed one hand on the crystal and one on the filament to the right. Even though she braced for a similar experience, she was not prepared for the horrific scream that blotted out all thought and overpowered her mind. Ten thousand tormented and tortured souls could not have expressed such a depth of horror and despair. Her mind screamed out and she briefly lost consciousness, only her connection to the crystal keeping her upright. Somehow, she managed to pull her hand off the filament, and the music of the crystal resumed.

Finally, after a long pause where she felt as tired and sore as if she had fought several battles, she stretched out her hand to the middle filament. Her eyes tightly shut, she waited for the next jolt.

It was almost immediate, but this time it felt like an electric buzz of energy that made her tingle from the top of her head to the soles of her feet. The tendrils on her neck flared again, not in alarm this time, but with a deep and satisfying pleasure. The music had resolved into a melody of complex and beautiful harmonies that was at once as satisfying and uplifting as the others had been terrifying and full of despair. With infinite care she slotted the filament into the crystal and stood back.

ooooOoooo

Menkh lay on his back contemplating Tarvuli, slowly orbiting above his head. His first coherent thoughts were aimed at the Shard. <I hate you. Probably even more than the Dorath Mar and that's saying something.>

<Nonsense, Menkh,> came the response. <You did as I told you and all is well. You won't get nearly as much as a surprise from the next one.>

Menkh felt that there was a definite undercurrent of self-satisfaction in the Shard's tone.

As he got to his feet, he could feel the ground vibrating under them. The structure pulsated with light that was intensified further by its positioning within the crater, no doubt a deliberate part of its engineering. It could have stood simply as a work of art, but it radiated an aura of menace that hinted at tremendous power. It seemed to absorb the light of the suns that shone down into the crater, storing its energy for a purpose that, at this time, could only be guessed at.

<Your thought is right,> said Crixac. <There is raw power here, contained, but lethal.>

<Come,> the Shard interrupted. <You still have two more to activate and the enemy does not tarry. Now you must travel to Orvasne and undertake the same task, though you will find that Orvasne presents a somewhat different challenge.>

<Which you, of course, will not relate to us,> Menkh said drily.

<Where would be the fun in that, Menkh ab Dur? How will you learn the extent of your powers if everything that lies before you is known to you before it occurs?>

<I feel that there is a cogent argument we could mount, but it would fall on deaf ears,> said Crixac.

<Which presumably, as the Shard entirely lacks them, would inevitably be unheard,> Menkh responded.

Laughter echoed in their minds as the Shard's presence departed and Menkh turned his thoughts towards accessing the Threadway. Once again reality seemed to shift and all about him grew indistinct. He noticed that here on Barask the lines of the Threadway could be more clearly discerned. There were a multitude of them. Ribbons of light that permeated everything and stretched off into an unfathomable distance in every direction. As he focused his mind on Orvasne, his concentration assisted by Crixac, one line of energy surrounded him, lifting him gently and speeding him upwards – presumably towards Orvasne, hidden behind the bulk of Tarvuli orbiting slowly above them.

CHAPTER TWO

The surface of Orvasne was very different to that of Barask. Instead of ice in every direction, here there were boiling pools of mud and a choking vapour filled the air. Not, as Menkh observed, that there was any 'air' to fill, which caused him to reflect, as if for the first time, that he wasn't breathing at all. Nor could he ever recall doing so when taking his current form. Interesting, yet also disturbing in a way that Menkh could not fully explain to himself.

<Menkh, concentrate!> came Crixac's sharp reminder. <We can reflect at length on your Adept form, but not at this precise moment, please.>

<I'm sorry, Crixac, you are right to chastise me. Well, let's see now.> Menkh returned his attention to his immediate surroundings. For as far as he could see in any direction, the pools of mud stretched out. At the very edge of his vision a single mountain loomed. Menkh immediately felt drawn to it and translocated whilst focusing his gaze upon it.

In the blink of an eye Menkh stood at the base of a towering cliff wall that climbed thousands of spahn into the atmosphere above him. His senses tentatively quested out, seeking the 'something' that had drawn him here. Suddenly, there it was. Amongst the rock and scree of the mountainside he sensed an unnaturally regular shape and form. Translocating once again, he reached a natural shelf, high up on the side of the mountain, where he believed the shape was located.

<Your ability to utilise your senses grows, Menkh. Soon my assistance will not be required,> said Crixac.

<Perhaps not for the mundane, my friend, but your presence calms me. I do not think you will become redundant any time soon.>

His senses had not lied. He observed the thing for some moments. Unlike the towers of the device on Barask, this was dome shaped. Grey and opaque and seemingly lifeless, perched on a huge rocky outcrop, commanding a view out across the mud plains. An array of silvery cables, the thickness of Menkh's arm, ran out from immediately behind the dome and disappeared into the face of the mountain. As he took stock of where he stood, he thought that if not for the vaporous and noxious atmosphere, the view from this point would be incredible. He felt that he could reach out and touch Tarvuli as it floated high above him.

<Well done, Menkh, Crixac,> said the Shard. <As you have observed, you are mastering the skills you will need in what is to come. Now, to the task at hand and the activation of this device. Here your staff is again required, and the focus of your will. You see a small depression in the rock shelf just in front of the machine? Stand just before it. Focus your will into the staff, and at the appropriate moment you must strike the ground at the base of the depression.>

<I'm not sure I fully understand,> said Menkh. <Focus my will to do what? And when is the appropriate moment?>

But the Shard had gone.

<Hmmm, perhaps another of the Shard's little tests for us?> said Crixac.

<That's all very well; but learning by doing when you are not quite sure what you are doing may lead to some nasty surprises, just like the last one,> responded Menkh.

<Well, let us think logically,> said Crixac. <The purpose is to activate the machine. To do so would seem to require a surge of power. Perhaps if you focus your will, with me providing assistance as required, we can generate enough force through the staff to achieve the result needed. As to the 'appropriate' moment – that would most likely be at the point where the staff has reached its maximum power; but again, I think your sense of that moment will become apparent.>

<All very logical, Crixac,> Menkh said with some asperity. <However, the application of logic in a situation where a device of unlimited power is charged to such an extent that the release of its force too early or too late may have catastrophic results, particularly to the persons who are holding the power source and standing next to a device of unknown capacity, may be superfluous.>

<It would seem that our choices are limited, my friend, and perhaps the process required to reactivate this thing is also a test in and of itself. I cannot think that the Shard would place us in a situation where there was a high likelihood of disaster.>

<Well, we can but try. If all goes awry it has been nice knowing you, Crixac.>

<Likewise.>

Whilst the exchange of thoughts was light, they carried a grim resolve. Menkh gripped the staff in both hands and held it before him. Tentatively at first, he began to focus his will upon it. Unlike when his rage had built to such a degree that the staff was a mere reflection of that emotion, this was a colder and more calculated process. His thoughts were scattered, and the energy created in the staff dissipated before it could build to anything near what he assumed would be required.

Menkh stood back, and then refocused his will. This time he did not look at the staff but instead concentrated his vision and mind on the silent grey machine. He began to see it as a silent obstruction, a living thing that taunted him with his incapacity to do what was required and that reflected his own weakness of will back at him in silent mockery. Slowly, Menkh's anger and frustration grew. He cursed the Adepts who had set these machines up and the process required to reactivate them. He cursed the Talixit Ven whose malevolent intentions necessitated the actions he must take. He cursed the Shard who seemed to give him just enough information and knowledge to overwhelm him with the quest that he was forced to take, and all the while, as his temper grew, the staff burned with an intensifying energy that blazed with a baleful green light.

Time seemed to stand still. Menkh was lost in a blaze of thought, fuelled by his anger and frustration, and it was with a sense of shock that he suddenly became aware that the staff in his hands was trembling with the energy that had built up in it. Almost as a reflex action he lifted the staff to the vertical and slammed its tip into the depression in front of him.

Three things happened. First, there was a concatenation of sound as the energy was released, a blast so huge that the rock shelf Menkh was standing on cracked and several landslides were triggered on the nearby mountain slopes. Secondly, and so quickly that it appeared to be simultaneous, a surge of green-coloured veins of energy swept up over the dome, which, as quickly as they streamed over it, appeared to be sucked into it. Finally, within a heartbeat and as the landslides continued to send boulders hurtling down the mountainsides, the grey, inanimate device began to glow with a faint blue light. In the merest of moments the light had increased in intensity. Occasionally, rippling through the blue, striations of green flickering light could also be seen.

Remarkably, at least to Menkh's mind, he still stood on the rock shelf. He had at least partially expected to be blasted into space like last time.

<Well done, Menkh!> said Crixac. <You handled that very well indeed, with hardly any need for assistance from me. Interestingly, holding the staff in the way you did seems to have enabled it to act as a more powerful shield this time.>

<Yes, well done, Menkh,> said the Shard. <Perhaps you begin to appreciate that there are some things that you must do where you cannot be told the 'how' and 'why'. The knowledge that you are assimilating from Crixac becomes available to you when you need it to assist you.>

<I am not sure what you mean,> Menkh responded. <At the beginning of that I had no idea what to do.>

<Yet, in your own unique way you did it. Unconsciously you are using the experience and knowledge of Crixac all the time. Think about that. Compared to the Kareems, your civilisation was primitive, yet now you have absorbed so much knowledge that it seems you have always had it. Think of what you now know of the planets, stars, and systems that you could not possibly have known before you met Crixac. And yet, as an internal question arises, so the answers come in response, in such a way that you do not question how you know – you just do. It is a gift beyond price.>

<Gift is entirely the wrong word,> countered Crixac. <Menkh is my host, he nurtures me in ways that he cannot even guess at this stage. A natural result of our symbiosis is my nurturing him by increasing his knowledge and, although little required given his current form, strengthening him physically and eradicating illness. No, if it is a gift, then it is a two-way giving.>

<You are right, my friend, but the Shard is also right,> Menkh responded thoughtfully. <When I reflect now on what has been said, the knowledge I have seems to have sprung from me. That I always knew it and was not told or taught by another. Without Crixac, Shard, I and all my race would be enslaved, dying or dead. There is much to be grateful for.>

<Indeed, there is much to reflect on and ponder in time to come,> the Shard agreed. <But now you must journey to Halidar to complete your task. Time moves forward: even I cannot influence that or slow it down. We will speak again once you are there.>

ooooOooooo

Tishan's mind floated inside a perfect harmony of sound that delighted and refreshed her spirit. Slowly her consciousness returned, and she found she was still standing with her hand on the white crystal, the middle filament now securely connected to it. A muted glow emanated from it and an occasional gentle pulse of light that coincided with the rhythm of the music could be seen.

<Come,> said the Shard. <That was well done, now let us see to the next. Menkh approaches Orvasne and we must be ready.>

Tishan felt herself translocate, presumably by the will of the Shard, and found herself standing on a dais in another, not dissimilar, room. Again, a crystal reposed on a column almost identical to that of the previous one. The most striking difference was the colour and shape of the crystal itself. Whereas the other was egg-shaped and an opaque white, this was long and narrow and of a shade of blue so deep it was almost black.

As before, Tishan rested her hand upon it to see what, if any, reaction or sensation might follow. Within moments an overbearing feeling of loss immediately manifested itself in her mind, accompanied by a wailing cry that carried such a depth of despair that it appeared inconsolable. It was a lament and, at its heart, a yearning for something lost.

Tishan snatched her hand away, so overcome with emotion that tears flowed freely until the feeling of grief that had arisen in her mind as a result of the contact gradually faded.

<Your own feelings of grief resonate, Tishan Dar, this magnifies the effect,> said the Shard.

<This is truly horrible. The feelings that it arouses are almost overwhelming.>

<Come, reach out to the filaments and see what your senses tell you.>

Tishan took a deep breath. As before, the filaments had appeared at almost the same moment she had laid her hand upon the crystal, and now each hung motionless, poised above the reclining crystal. As Tishan decided which to touch first, she noted almost absentmindedly that, instead of prongs, each filament ended in a series of small, tentacle-like structures, with many small corresponding holes located on the surface of the reclining crystal. Hesitantly, she put her hand on the filament to the right.

Falling. Yes, there was no doubt that she experienced a sensation like falling, endlessly, and within that sensation came a feeling that the further she fell the more remote in time and space she became. As she fell a great wave of hopelessness overwhelmed her. She was falling away from something altogether precious, though she had forgotten what it was: she knew only that it was missing. Despair then. A withdrawing into herself as she continued to fall into the void. Tishan snatched her hand away and refocused.

As she lay her hand upon the middle filament, she felt cold. In her mind she was in a dark place. Sealed off. Untouchable. She distinctly heard the dripping of water, and a feeling of disquiet grew. Something was watching her, invisible in the dark recesses of the place she was in. The feeling of something coming closer grew, and she heard a slithering sound that intensified as it approached. Abruptly she pulled her hand away. She took in deep breaths to still her heart and calm the feeling of panic that had ensued from the experience.

Finally, she reached out and touched the last filament. Silence. Deep and impenetrable. She stood within a place so vast that, other than the solidity of the ground she stood upon, she could perceive nothing else. No air. No light. No sky above, nor clouds, sun, moon or stars. No-one, nothing. An emptiness so all-encompassing that she felt like curling into a ball and crying, here in the silence. Desperately she pulled her hand away.

Once again, she stood in reflection on her experiences. Each one disturbing in its own way. Still, the feeling of loss that emanated from the crystal had a kind of resonance with the sensation of falling, in some sense a mirror reflection of the same emotion.

Placing her hand on the crystal she inwardly cringed as the wailing sound echoed in her mind and taking a quick breath, she lay her other hand on the filament to the right. The two sounds coalesced. If Tishan could have fallen to her knees she would have done so. The wailing call of grief was echoed and magnified in the cry of that which was falling away and then, abruptly, the sound began to change. It was like a shouting out to one that was lost and, beyond hope, receiving an answering call. Something precious, lost without hope of recovery, but miraculously rediscovered. The call and answering cry reached a crescendo as one drew closer to the other and then, a feeling that caused Tishan to weep tears of joy, like watching a mother find her lost child or having a beloved parent return from the brink of death, or both of those things mixed in one intense moment of euphoria.

Tishan stepped back from the pedestal and realised that, almost involuntarily, she had inserted the filament into the crystal as her emotions had whirled in a vortex of feelings. She was so overcome that it took some moments for her to recover her composure.

When she was able to fully focus, she saw that the crystal had become a more translucent blue, and deep within its surface a rainbow of colours was pulsating, like a heartbeat.

The voice of the Shard echoed quietly in her mind. <Well done, child. An even greater challenge than the last for you, I think.>

<It is difficult not knowing what to expect. That sensation brought back such feelings of desolation in the loss of my home and all that was once precious to me. Each of these is a test that affects me in different ways. Are these challenges the same for everyone?>

<No. Whilst there is certainly a test, each one is different and each draws upon the unique experiences and characteristics of whomever it is that seeks to activate the crystals. In that way it is unpredictable.>

<With the end result that failure would lead to the demise of the person undertaking the test,> said Tishan.

<As I have said. Now, we turn to the last.> With these words echoing in her mind, Tishan disappeared once more.

CHAPTER THREE

Of all the moons of Tarvuli, Halidar was the one that Menkh had always been drawn to. Not just because it was the first to rise, but there was something about the rosy colour of its surface, as seen from Tarvuli, and the way it reflected light that somehow had a calming effect on him. Now, as he descended towards it, he could see that Halidar was surrounded by an atmosphere that glowed pink in the light of the suns.

As he grounded, he noticed a vast plain of friable rock that emitted a discernible vapour into the air. It appeared this was the gas that gave Halidar its rosy glow. His senses told him that the air around him had an acidic quality which would have been instantly fatal to any of the lifeforms on Tarvuli.

Upon closer observation Menkh noticed that a wiry looking plant grew in clefts and deep crevices in the rocky surface, and that a strange, insect-like creature – about the size of his finger, with a hard, shiny red carapace and multiple legs – could also be seen sheltering within the plants.

<It seems then that Halidar supports life of its own, Menkh. Who would have thought it?> Crixac said.

<Who indeed?> responded Menkh. <All the years of looking up at this moon from within the Empire, and these creatures and plants lived out their lives while great cities grew and perished, and we fought for survival.>

<Such is the nature of Balance, Menkh, Crixac,> said the Shard. <Now to the task at hand and the activation of the final satellite.>

<I cannot see anything that actually stands out and crossing this terrain is going to prove difficult,> Menkh said.

<Then here is your next lesson, Menkh ab Dur. Focus your will and levitate above the ground. You can move in any direction you choose. The power of the staff will assist you in this, and Crixac can add in his focus. Make sure you remain vigilant; all may not be as placid as it seems.>

<Hmmm, another cryptic remark from our friend. However, the power to levitate and move will be handy,> said Crixac quietly.

<You are ever the master of understatement, my friend,> Menkh said.

<I try, I try.>

Menkh focused his will into the staff. With only a slight pause, it manifested a yellowish glow and Menkh felt as if, in some way, the staff was pushing him into the air, a comfortable spahn above the ground. Locking his vision onto a point some distance ahead, he again focused his will. He felt Crixac's focus join with his, increasing the potency of his concentration. Slowly at first but with increasing speed, Menkh flew toward the point he had selected. Menkh and Crixac were silently congratulating each other on their achievement when two things happened. First, there was a violent buffeting of the air around them as something seemed to leap up out of the ground below them, and then they were thrown with considerable force sideways for quite some distance. Menkh, having lost all control, smashed into the ground and, for the second time, lay gazing upwards into the sky above him.

As he lay prone on the ground, he realised he felt terribly weak. The feeling was one he had not experienced for a very long time. He also detected a rather unpleasant odour, a burnt smell with a chemical overtone.

<Crixac, what is that smell? It is most unpleasant,> Menkh said.

<Lie still, Menkh. I am repairing the damage to your body.>

<Damage?> Menkh tried to move, contrary to Crixac's instructions, but realised that the weakness he felt prevented him from doing so.

<Your right side, arm, and leg were badly burned. That disruption was some sort of geyser and the material expelled was not only scalding hot, it was also extremely acidic. Fortunately, we were thrown to the side a goodly distance, so we avoided further damage as the liquid splashed back to earth. Also, luckily, there is no wind at all that might have complicated things further and drifted vapour over us.>

Menkh absorbed this information. <I can't feel a thing,> he said.

<That is because I have shut down your nerve endings whilst I repair the damage. So, now we know that your current form is not entirely invulnerable to harm. Although it is remarkably adept at healing itself. If this was your Graaven form I would have great difficulty preventing permanent injury.>

<Well, that is some comfort, at least,> Menkh turned his thoughts outwards. <Another lesson, Shard?>

<I did tell you to remain vigilant, Menkh. It was not any part of my intent to see you harmed, but as Crixac has noted, you are not invulnerable to severe injury, even death.>

<Well then, might I ask for some indication of what we are looking for this time and where it might be located?>

<The device is located below the surface. Look for a crystalline dome, low to the ground. It should be quite reflective. Once you

are restored, levitate upwards. This will allow you to observe over a greater distance.>

<Very well. Crixac, how are we looking?>

<I am done. You should have no residual weakness. I have removed the block to your brain. How are you feeling?>

Menkh sat upright and looked down at his body. There was no trace of any injury and he felt as strong as he had ever done. Tentatively at first, he clenched his right fist and moved his foot, then he stood upright and grasped the staff firmly.

<Thank you, Crixac. I am feeling fully restored. Let us follow the Shard's advice and see what we can find.>

Menkh rose into the air. Slowly at first, he levitated till he floated stationary at what he guessed would be around a hundred spahn above Halidar's surface. He gazed out in all directions but could see nothing reflective in the manner the Shard had referred to, although all over the surface he saw geysers intermittently erupting into the air, violently expelling their acidic contents. He rose a further hundred, and then another fifty spahn. Finally, at the limit of his vison he spied a reflective light.

<There I think, Crixac,> said Menkh, pointing. <That would seem to be the only thing that matches the description of what we are looking for.>

<I agree, my friend. But you have no need to point it out to me. I am here with you,> Crixac replied with some amusement.

<Yes, well, old habits, my friend. Come, let's focus on that point and make our way there.>

<And let us stay at this height,> suggested Crixac. <We should be able to avoid any eruptions we might fly over, and it is good practise as well. Besides, I don't really want to be patching you up any more today.>

<Most assuredly,> Menkh responded. Focusing their combined wills, they flew with remarkable speed towards their target.

As the surface below sped by Menkh felt himself on the verge of laughter. <Well, I didn't expect it, but I am enjoying this experience.>

<I share your feelings, my friend. It is most exhilarating. Much better, if somewhat slower, than translocation.>

After what Menkh felt was too short a time he hovered over the location. As the Shard had described, he floated over a large crystalline dome that he estimated was some fifty spahn in diameter. The surface of the structure sparkled in the light of the suns, glinting like some rare jewel. Whilst it appeared to be semitransparent, the reflective glare made it impossible to see what lay beneath it.

Returning to the earth he walked around the dome's circumference. At ground level, its sides rose only a few spahn, its surface rising directly out of the surrounding terrain so that it appeared to have grown out of the earth itself. He had only walked about two-thirds of the way around it when he came across what appeared to be a narrow entryway, a kind of slot that interrupted the otherwise smooth and featureless outer skin of the dome. The slot had several steps that led downwards towards a blank vertical panel that rose from the ground, curving at the top to follow the contours of the dome. Descending the steps to some ten or twelve spahn below ground, level he stood directly in front of the panel.

<The staff again, I think?> Menkh posed the question to Crixac.

<Agreed, that would appear to be the logical choice. There doesn't appear to be any slot for you to lay your hand in to activate it. Let's try it.>

Grounding the staff as he had done earlier, he gripped it firmly with both hands and turned his mind to opening the panel. Unlike before there was no surge of energy or any other phenomenon. The staff pulsed once with a faintly blue luminescence and the door panel slid smoothly upwards, revealing a further set of steps that descended deeper below ground. Maintaining a firm grip on the staff, Menkh entered. As he did so he could now see a kind of chute that led steadily downwards. The moment he had passed through the portal, the top of the chute, some three or four spahn above his head, had lit up with a muted greenish glow, enough to light his way and ensure that he did not miss his footing on the steps.

<I can see no bottom to this, it just leads down, although it spirals to the left,> Menkh said.

<Well, my friend, let us proceed and see what we will find.>

No sooner had Menkh stepped down the first three steps than the panel slid quietly closed behind him. The silence in the chute was complete. Menkh's steps provided the only sound as they echoed off the walls around him. The effect was quite unsettling.

<Makes you wonder who or what was the last thing to use these stairs,> Crixac said contemplatively.

<Well, one would have to assume that it was hundreds of sem'chaal ago, but I think we will not get any answer to our question,> Menkh said.

Menkh continued his long descent, the stairs leading ever downwards in a steady spiral until, eventually, and after what seemed a very long time, they reached a terminus. The chute opened out to a tunnel that ran for some fifty spahn and ended abruptly at yet another blank wall. Advancing through the tunnel, whose dimensions mirrored that of the chute they had descended, Menkh stopped at the wall. Observing carefully, he saw no trace of a doorway or the usual depression that the doors of the City had.

<Well, it would appear that, once again, we must use the staff and focus on that to assist us in opening this up.> Crixac's thoughts were measured.

<Yes,> said Menkh, <it certainly has a remarkable range of functions.>

<I do not think that it is the staff alone. I had the use of it for many long years trapped inside the poor creature that was my host, but it seems to me that its range of functions actually comes from the capacity of the person that wields it. It adapts to your needs as you focus your will upon it. It is quite a remarkable device. The combined might of our wills has shown me that it can do things that I had not even guessed at, albeit I knew that it was powerful.>

<Well, hopefully we will have time together to explore the full range of its uses in time to come. I should also like to know more about how you came to wield it. In the meantime, though, let us concentrate on the wall in front of us.>

With tacit agreement from Crixac, Menkh stood at the wall and placed his right hand upon it, while holding the staff in his left. He experienced an immediate tingling sensation and luminescent lines appeared on the surface of the wall. These rapidly outlined a doorway, about ten spahn high by around four wide. Swirling patterns of light flashed across the surface of the door just before it separated into two halves, each sliding aside and disappearing into the wall.

Stepping through the newly revealed portal, they entered a room the like of which Menkh had not seen before. What appeared to be hundreds of huge, ribbed arches rose majestically in a curve above his head, meeting at a single point fifty spahn above where he stood. At this central point a concave, dome-shaped structure, which might have been the reverse of the dome that sat upon the moon's surface, hung suspended downwards, the myriad of ribs all feeding into this one section.

On further inspection Menkh realised that the arched ribs actually started at ground level like the spokes of a wheel, radiating out across the floor before rising above him. He also saw that these 'spokes' emanated from a raised crystalline pillar, around four spahn in circumference and twenty spahn high. The pillar tapered to a needle-like top which was positioned squarely in the centre of the suspended dome above it but fell short of touching the inverted dome by five spahn.

<If that is not some sort of focal point for the transmission or receival of some kind of power source, then I am a parasite,> Crixac said.

<Hmmm … I hope you noticed that I didn't make any comment on that remark, my friend,> Menkh responded with dry humour. Without waiting for a response, he continued, <In any event, I cannot argue with you, though whether that power source feeds down from the ceiling or upwards from the floor is open to conjecture. Personally, I would rather not be here when it activates.>

The Shard interrupted their internal discussion. <As to that, Menkh, Crixac, activation has already begun. It did so the moment you opened the portal and entered this room and unless you move with alacrity you will be sealed in there.>

The Shard had no sooner spoken than the door they had entered by began to close. Even with Menkh's enhanced physical capability the door had sealed completely before they managed to exit the room.

They heard a humming sound and pulsing lights of many colours emanated from the central pillar, flashing across the floor and along the ribbed vault before passing into the dome above. The dome began to glow, and the temperature in the room started to climb alarmingly.

<It's not just the temperature that is climbing, Menkh. The increasing activity brings with it a kind of radiation. Soon, I fear, it will reach lethal levels, even for us.>

<Then we must translocate out of here, and quickly. What do you think, the other side of the door we entered or back to the surface?>

<The surface if we can. These radiation levels are unpredicta-ble. The wall may have buffering built into it, but I don't think we should take the risk.>

Menkh silently agreed. But, when he attempted to channel his will into the staff, he noticed that as the temperature and toxicity within the room increased, his ability to focus was also affected. <Crixac, this is going to take both of us,> he said.

Several fruitless attempts followed, and they steadily grew weaker.

<We are missing something, Menkh. Soon we will be unable to function at all. There must be a way of doing this. If only there were some area here that was shielded.>

<Of course! Crixac, the staff! Help me focus on a shield of protection.>

In desperation they turned their failing wills on to the staff. Its reaction, though weak at first, gradually gained potency and a blue aura extended from it to surround Menkh's body. The effect was immediate and welcome. The shield protected them from the ra-diation and heat and their combined wills rapidly recovered, though there remained some residual physical weakness.

Menkh and Crixac focused on the surface above, outside the dome, and the staff flared briefly. Menkh felt a moment of disori-entation before appearing above ground and falling to the earth in exhaustion. The dome gave off a bright white light, painful even to his eyes, and the ground on which he lay trembled.

<That was a close-run thing,> Crixac said quietly

<Ever the master of understatement, Crixac,> Menkh said in response as he lay quietly recuperating.

<You both did well,> said the Shard.

<Yes, and no thanks to you,> Menkh said angrily.

<I know you are angry with me, but you must understand that I will not be there all the time to assist you. You two must work together to overcome dangers and obstacles. Your combined

power grows; you will need this and more if you are to battle what is to come.>

<And if we had not been successful? What then, Shard?> asked Crixac.

<But you were successful. I do not deal in 'what ifs', Menkh, Crixac. Now you may return to Tarvuli. Your work here is done, it only remains now for Tishan to complete the final link. Then we may turn our attention to the threat which approaches.>

ooooOooooo

Tishan felt the usual brief moment of disorientation she always experienced when teleporting. This sensation increased, she noticed, when a third party such as the Shard controlled the destination, and she was taken along as a kind of passenger. Materialising, she found that she stood in a duplicate of the previous two rooms. This time the crystal that reposed on the raised pillar before her was of the deepest red colour, its shape not unlike that of a Graaven arrowhead. As she stood upon the raised dais, three crystalline filaments arose and hung poised over the reclining gem.

Closing her eyes in concentration, Tishan lay her hand on the recumbent crystal. Immediately her mind lurched. It was an unpleasant sensation, almost like part of her body had been violently pulled away and taken to another location entirely, even though she knew she stood on the dais in a room within the Complex. She opened her eyes in surprise and felt the same lurch as she refocused on her location. Closing her eyes again, she experienced the same disorientation, even more unpleasant than the first occurrence. This time she kept her eyes closed despite her misgivings and, slowly at first but rapidly becoming clearer, a picture formed in her mind.

As her senses adjusted, she found herself standing before a huge doorway. Intricately carved door posts were surmounted by a lintel decorated with swirling patterns that seemed to move and change, so that her mind's eye could not make out if the patterns were meant to form some kind of script or whether their changing nature was some kind of alien art form, purely for decoration. The door itself was plain, devoid of any adornment. It appeared to be made of some rock-like material that gave it an aura of massive immobility. Tishan studied the doorway for some time, absorbing its features. As it seemed to be the most obvious task, she looked for some clue as to what would open the vast portal.

Steeling herself, she opened her eyes slowly. This time the transition was more acceptable. Feeling more in control of the strange sensation that accompanied the touching of the crystal, she reached out and placed her hand on the filament to the left, expecting a somewhat similar experience. Unaccompanied by any feeling or emotional response, a pattern filled her mind. She stood before the doorway but this time, a swirling pattern of colours could be seen on the door. These colours interacted with the swirling patterns of the door lintel. As the two patterns coalesced words formed and, in her mind, a deep and resonant voice spoke to her.

<And lo. She stood before the doorway, the key in her right hand and the fate of nations in her left. Rise up, mother of the world, saviour of the people. Rise up, conqueror of terror. Verily you shall be raised as a living god, and all those of your lineage after you shall be placed above all others. Your name will echo down the ages for eternity. Step forward and unlock the portal.>

Gasping, Tishan stepped back, her hands lifting upwards. She was overwhelmed with a feeling of triumph and elation. She, Tishan Dar, one-time Stragosh of the Graaven Empire, would be raised above all others, the saviour of this world and all others. Surely this must be the right filament!

Slowly she battled her emotions and fought down the impulse to connect the filament with the crystal. Taking a deep breath, she stood firm upon the dais and, touching her left hand to the crystal she raised her right and placed it on the middle filament. As she again stood before the doorway, a different pattern of colours could be seen and, as before, the two patterns coalesced and again formed words. This time a different voice, more sibilant and with a feminine timbre, spoke.

<And lo. She stood before the doorway, the key in her right hand and the fate of nations in her left. Rise up, you who would save your children. Rise up, Mother of the Graaven people. Though all other races may fall, you and those whom you choose shall be safe and protected for eternity. Loved and cherished in memory shall you be. Glory and triumph shall surely follow you. Step forward and unlock the portal.>

This time as she stepped back the feeling was less euphoric. Instead, she was filled with the need to nurture and protect her own people. She could ensure the future for all her people and keep them safe. What care did she have for others who were not Graaven? The Empire itself was founded on that notion. Then other thoughts came to her. Menkh battling the Dorath Mar with the aid of the Benshin, who were their friends. What of the Xotic, without whose support Menkh may never have found the gateway? What of Fendrax and all her brood? As she mulled over these ideas, she realised that this last test was for her alone. It was perfectly possible that any of these filaments may actually connect with the crystal and that her choice would influence the direction and outcome of what lay ahead.

Again, she stood firm, placing one hand on the crystal and her other hand on the final, untouched filament. The words came rapidly this time: an old voice, cold and bitter like an icy wind.

<And lo. She stood before the doorway, the key in her right hand, and the fate of nations in her left. Rise up, you who would sacrifice yourself for your people and races yet unknown to you. Rise up, you who would defeat the terror. Rise up in the knowledge that you will be forgotten by all except those you have spawned.

Rise up in humility and in the knowledge of your death so that others might live. Step forward and unlock the portal.>

This time Tishan stepped back so violently that she fell from the dais and landed heavily on the floor. Tears flowed down her cheeks, and she was overcome with grief.

'There must be another way! How can you place this choice before me? Do you hear me, Shard? Answer me!' she screamed aloud.

Only silence met her entreaties.

Tishan drew herself up to a sitting position and clasped her knees to her chest. She battled conflicting emotions that threatened her very sanity. Whilst she was never more convinced of the choice that she had to make, the impact of the devastating consequences of that choice was too much to bear. Never to see her offspring again. Never to look into Menkh's face or experience the shared joys of the people in their new home. Never to know what the future might have held. Sobbing, she climbed to her feet and moved forward hesitantly. Standing atop the dais, she spoke aloud, her voice throbbing with emotion, as she reached her hands out and grasped the filament that was her final choice. 'I am Tishan Dar. I make this sacrifice for my spawnlings and all my people. May the Balance be restored for all nations, and may my children live in peace and harmony all the days of their lives. Do not forget me!'

With this last exhortation she grasped the filament and connected it to the crystal.

She stood before the portal and watched as it split in two, both halves swinging open noiselessly. Beyond was a void. It felt as if the threshold of the doorway led out into space, into nothingness. A cold wind blew around her but stepping forward was like wading through a glutinous mud, each footstep taking a lifetime. Finally, as she stepped through the doorway, the void around her burst into incandescent light and she began to fall. She knew she would never stop falling, that she would be carried downwards for eternity, cold and utterly alone forever.

Then, out of nowhere, she felt as if something had taken hold of her, and her descent abruptly ceased.

<Tishan Dar, focus on my voice, come back. Focus, Tishan, do not despair. I have you!>

Tishan felt like a small child, and she cried out in terror, 'Please, Shard, do not let me fall! Do not let me be forgotten!'

<I have you, child. I will not let you fall. Come to me, follow my voice.>

Tishan mentally groped toward the sound and felt herself being lifted rapidly upwards. Feeling her body lurch, she opened her eyes and found, to her utter joy, that she still stood in the room upon the dais. For the second time she stepped back and fell to the ground in a dead faint.

When Tishan at last regained consciousness she felt remarkably refreshed, as if the ordeal she had passed through had given her a new sense of herself. Suddenly a chorus, as of a thousand whispering voices, spoke into her mind. <Hail Tishan Dar. Mother and Guardian. Adept of the White. Know that you are found worthy.>

As the words were spoken Tishan felt as if she were held by ten thousand arms, cradling and nurturing her and filling here with even greater courage and determination than she had before.

The Shard spoke into her mind. <Well done indeed, Tishan Dar. Come, see what you and Menkh have wrought between you.>

<Menkh is alright then?>

<Even now he travels the Threadway and returns to you. Come, come and see that which few eyes have ever seen.>

CHAPTER FOUR

As Menkh's facility and experience with travelling the Threadway grew, so his amazement, and Crixac's too, grew apace.

<In some ways it is like travelling between, except that in that place everything is grey and without form, between and not part of anything. But here, well, you still feel very much a part of reality. Does that make sense to you, Crixac?>

<Yes, I agree. We are part of it, yet separate from it. Slightly out of phase with everything. There is no physical sense of movement and yet we move with great speed. Focusing on something seems to slow us down somewhat as if, like a living thing, it anticipates our desire.>

<I am not so sure that it is not, in some way, alive. Once we access the Threadway it stretches ahead like a ribbon of light, a kind of highway that transports us forwards. At the same time, I feel we are protected.>

<Yes, yes,> said Crixac. <There is no sense of coldness or heat, just a comfortable temperature. Like travelling through a tunnel whose walls are invisible yet shield us from anything harmful. It is altogether fascinating. Did you also notice that when we left

the City, no sooner had we determined on our destination then all around us went somewhat out of focus and we travelled upwards at speed, passing through the walls of the Complex as if they weren't there?>

<Yes. We can both agree that it's a wondrous thing,> Menkh said. <It seems that many surprises still lie in store for us both, my friend. But come, I see Tarvuli below us and the City rapidly approaching. Let us concentrate on our final destination point.>

The Shard spoke abruptly in Menkh's mind. <No, Menkh, let me guide you down, you must join Tishan and see what work you have accomplished.>

Moments later they alighted on the floor of a room that was unfamiliar to them. No sooner had Menkh come back into phase, still in his Adept form, than Tishan stepped into his arms and held him close. Showing physical affection was such an un-Graaven thing to do that Menkh was caught off guard for a moment before he responded.

'Menkh, I am so glad to see you back safe. My experiences here have led me to appreciate all that we have and that our time in this life might be shorter than we think.'

Menkh looked deeply into Tishan's eyes and considered her words. 'Yes, Tishan. If your experiences here were anything like mine and Crixac's activating the satellites, then we must learn to make the most of every moment that we have, particularly with those we care about.'

They held their embrace for several moments before stepping apart, their eyes now drawn fully to the transparent wall that lay before them. On the other side, a pattern of pulsing energies could be seen in a myriad of colours that interacted without coalescing. They wrapped around each other and broke away again in a kind of strange dance that, whilst apparently random, was nevertheless entrancing to the eye, like watching flames in a fire.

<You stand now at the base of the central tower of the Complex,> said the Shard. <Watch carefully now: activation of the shield is imminent.>

The pattern of energies grew ever more frenetic, twisting and separating in a frenzied whirl of colour until suddenly they all converged into a single core of energy that leapt upwards. The transparent wall before them shielded the watchers from the blinding light formed by the sudden fusion of the colours. The floor vibrated with the unleashed power of the column of light. A single, focused beam of energy shot skywards from the central tower, piercing the clouds above and exiting Tarvuli's atmosphere.

Beyond sight of Graaven eyes, in the empty space above the planet, the single beam of energy was conjoined by three others that emanated from the satellites positioned on the three moons. These energies increased the central beam's power threefold, and from the point where they all combined, a golden orb of light was fashioned, which expanded rapidly outwards. Within a matter of moments, it had encompassed the world of Tarvuli, spreading further to encompass the three moons. It continued to extend outwards for a vast distance until it reached a point of stasis and halted its expansion. The muted golden glow intensified as the energy from all four sources sustained and reinforced its power as it stabilised.

From the room at the base of the tower where they stood, Tishan and Menkh had been able to observe all that happened. Like the walls of the viewing room, the walls to the left and right of them displayed what had occurred far above Tarvuli, as if they themselves were suspended in space at the moment the beams of energy intersected each other. It was impossible to find words of any kind that could even begin to describe what they had witnessed.

<Behold the work of Menath, Kortsan, and Tambel. The work of a lifetime. Originally, it was designed as a shield to prevent any

other Adepts from the Balancepoint finding them and seeking to enter their location. As it turned out, it proved unnecessary until the Kareems turned it to their own purposes. But without the additional power of the satellites, the device is unstable. It was the backlash from the use of the central beam as a weapon that brought about the Kareems' own demise, as well as those they saw as their enemies,> said the Shard.

<Surely the Adepts would have known this and could have prevented that from happening?> asked Menkh.

<Adepts live for a long time, Menkh ab Dur, but not forever. Whilst they were alive, the three cities existed in harmony: but eventually, they died. Menath was the last. Exiled by their own choosing from those of their kind, arrogant in the belief of their own power and knowledge, they had found a way to enslave the power of the crystals they had stolen for their own glorification. Menath herself disappeared. Her body was never found, and now it is so long in the past that even I cannot find any trace or clue as to what happened. For whatever reason, Menath destroyed much of the knowledge that had been archived in relation to this device, and which the Kareems and the others might have accessed and so prevented disaster.>

Crixac interposed his own thoughts. <I don't understand how it is possible that three Adepts who stole crystals and fled the Balancepoint could enter this world and not be tracked and apprehended.>

<Tarvuli is a remote world, as you know all too well, Crixac. The means by which you and your host journeyed here was lost when your host was evaporated. When Menath, Tambel, and Kortsan absconded, they left no trace behind them. Finding their location amongst countless star systems was all but impossible.>

<I am curious about the gateway in the Gap of Crethic. Is there any knowledge regarding its establishment?> Menkh asked.

<The gateways that access a Balancepoint are not fixed, Menkh,> the Shard responded. <They can and do change location, though exactly why is a mystery even to me. The gateway only appeared after the cataclysm that destroyed the three cities, so perhaps the discharge of energies was a factor. We may deduce that this is all a part of the quest to restore Balance, but neither you nor I can fully understand it, though I may have greater insight than you.>

<As you have said, Crixac, and you too, Shard,> Tishan said, <it is impossible to visualise a mountain if you have never seen one and hold only a grain of sand in your fingers to picture it. We must follow the path set for us and react to the circumstances as they arise.>

<Well said, Tishan, like fighting a battle with a force whose dispositions and battle plan are unknown to us,> said Menkh.

<Something, Zaltec, that you happen to be quite good at,> Tishan said.

<Except that the consequences of failure are too dire to contemplate.> The Shard was sombre. <But, in essence, you are right. Now we must move on to dealing with the threat that we detected prior to shield activation. Back to the viewing room – we have plans to make.>

ooooOooooo

They stood as before, looking at the ships displayed on the walls of the viewing room. The vessels floated in space, quiescent and unmoving. A slowly revolving planet could be seen beyond them, though whether it was a living world or sterile and lifeless could not be discerned.

<This is at the absolute maximum that we are able to extend our scan,> the Shard stated matter-of-factly. <As these things get closer, our view will improve.>

<They do not appear to have moved at all since last we looked. Could they be waiting for something?> asked Tishan.

<Yes, a good question. Also, there is something about these vessels that does not fit,> added Crixac. <Albeit I have been in isolation for millennia and there will have been developments in technology, but there were only two races, when last I travelled, that had the capacity to undertake interstellar voyages. These ships do not appear anything like those of the Caratys or Prenaxos. Whatever propulsion system they use, these ships are nothing like what I remember seeing.>

<How far have they travelled?> asked Menkh.

<A distance so great, Menkh ab Dur, that to relay it in Graaven persangh would be astronomical,> the Shard stated. <By some unfathomable means they have navigated to their current location. Let us say that without detailed knowledge as to how far and how fast they can move, or by what means, we can only guess at how long it will take them to reach here. They only have an approximation of our location, so the actual question is not how far but how close. Perhaps, as Tishan has queried, they are waiting for something; but I, too, sense something else, something unseen, that is associated with these craft.>

Then to the astonishment of all, the vessels simply disappeared. One moment they were there, floating in space, and the next moment they had vanished from sight.

<Have they activated some kind of shielding device? Did they discern our scanning of them?> Crixac asked.

The Shard's reaction was subdued but intense. <They travel in the between! It is as we surmised, by some means they have developed the capacity to traverse and navigate that place, a thing not deemed possible. If the Talixit Ven and their minions are able to access the between at will then the Balance will be overturned forever!>

<But surely, as part of the Intelligence, you have knowledge of these things. What they are, where they come from? Can you not tell us?> Tishan's voice rang with desperation.

<Tishan Dar,> the Shard was quietly authoritative, <you are applying a simplistic form of logic to a cosmic phenomenon. The Intelligence is not some sentient being that acts of its own volition or will give you all the answers you want. It is true that it manifests a physical, crystalline form in certain locations. Menkh chose me as a replacement for the dying crystal here in the City. That is my primary function. This is unprecedented and has only occurred as a result of what the three Adepts did thousands of years ago. I have helped you and will continue to do so as I can in your role as Agents of Balance, but there is a limit.

<In their own way the Talixit Ven also interact with the Intelligence. Do you want them to get the answers to the questions they have? Their arrival on this world was a random occurrence. If they had accessed the City, and through its technology also gained direct access to the Balancepoint, chaos would have ensued. You have averted this for the time being, but the danger is still there. You, Menkh, and Crixac must act of your own free will. You must trust yourselves and follow your instincts. Help and guidance will come, but not directly and not in the way that I am able to do here. I am inextricably linked to the City. Whilst I am 'of' the Intelligence I am now separate from it. I am sorry if this makes little sense to you.>

<You are right. I just feel so overwhelmed. Only a few sem'chaal ago I was a Stragosh of the Empire. Such unforeseen changes and exposure to a reality that still seems fantastical; I feel inadequate to the tasks set before me.>

<Child, there are few living who could have unlocked the key to the shield that now protects us, think on that. You and Menkh are both unique individuals. Self-doubt is only natural. I have great faith in you. Deal with one thing at a time and try not to speculate

too much on the what ifs. Ultimately you can only do your best. For now, you both need to rest and take stock. We cannot follow the enemy's path, as they travel in the between, but their presence will be discernible once they reappear. Be prepared to translocate back here at a moment's notice. If by some chance they manage to locate our exact position, the shield will block them. We must act quickly at that time.>

<Very well,> replied Menkh. <I, for one, will be glad of some respite, no matter how short that time might be. Tishan, why don't we make our way back to the refectory together?>

<As you wish, Menkh. However, you may wish to assume your former self, otherwise we may cause quite a stir amongst the people.>

<I was getting to that,> Crixac said. <It will take but a moment.>

Menkh's Adept form shimmered, the red skin rippling as the well-remembered Graaven form of Menkh ab Dur appeared.

Tishan smiled appreciatively. <Yes, that is much better. Come, Menkh, I feel like a walk over the causeway bridge. Meet me there.> With that remark Tishan vanished from sight. Menkh smiled and vanished as well.

Sometime later they strolled into the refectory to find that a sizeable meeting of the people was taking place. Conversation stilled as Menkh and Tishan entered. Menkh's first thought was that the meeting had been called in light of what had occurred at the Complex, and Tishan and he had already discussed what they would relate to the Graaven people to explain it.

Seated around the refectory tables, several members of the council, appointed by the people, sat a little apart. One figure stood quietly and waited for Menkh and Tishan to approach.

'Well, Ankh, as senior members of the council, Tishan and I are intrigued as to what item you have up for discussion. I, for one, did not realise that a meeting had been scheduled. Do I have anything to worry about?' Menkh's tone was jocular but there was a note of concern in the look that Menkh swept around the room.

'Welcome, Menkh and Tishan,' Ankh responded. 'On the contrary, quite a number of the people have expressed a desire to name our new home. Well, not so new now after three sem'chaal. They felt, and I must say there is general agreement, that this would be most appropriate, particularly as our spawnlings grow to maturity.'

'I agree with you all,' said Tishan. 'Was there any particular reason that neither I nor Menkh were brought into the discussion?'

Several embarrassed looks were exchanged and Horven Var stood as Ankh resumed his seat.

'It is because many of the people wished to name the City after you both. We felt that this might have been a cause for embarrassment, and that your direct involvement may have affected the debate and the outcome.'

'Well,' Menkh looked at Tishan, 'you are not far from the mark on that count. So, did you reach consensus in your discussions?'

'Indeed, we have, and your arrival here is well timed. None of us could decide on a final name and discussion was split in terms of you, Tishan Dar, and you, Menkh ab Dur, so, in the end ...' Horven paused as Ankh stood once again and spoke.

'We decided on a more neutral name but one which genuinely reflected how all of us, as survivors, feel. We wish to rename the City and call it Ta'Morin, the place of renewed hope. It is the desire of all of us and we hope that you would give your blessing to this.'

Ankh resumed his seat, and the room grew even more quiet than before, an expectant hush over all who sat there.

Menkh looked at Tishan, an intense expression on his face before he nodded to her.

In turn, Tishan's eyes swept over all before she spoke. 'Let it be known, by the will of the people, that from this day forth the new home of the Graaven race shall be known as Ta'Morin. I speak for Menkh ab Dur and myself at the honour you showed us in considering naming this place after us. However, your collective wisdom has shone forth. It is fitting for all Graavens, now living and those yet to be, that a name truly reflects the nature of the place they call home. This you have done. Is a celebration planned?'

The smile on Ankh's face was reflected on the visage of all present. 'You can rest assured that there will be such a celebration as we have not yet seen since our arrival here. We will invite our Benshin friends to share in the naming.'

'Very well,' Menkh's voice was loud. 'Let's hope that Bara Desh doesn't run out of brandy!'

In the general hubbub of the people and their conversation, Menkh and Tishan were able to forget the menace that hung over them. None of the Graavens were aware of any external threat, nor was it any part of their plans to tell them. The last thing either of them wanted was to place the burden of worry on the shoulders of people still recovering from the terror of the Dorath Mar.

'I thought this meeting may have been about something else,' Menkh remarked to Ankh in the general discussion that ensued after the announcement.

'Really? Was there anything in particular you thought we may have been discussing?' Ankh's tone was quizzical.

'Umm, well, you know,' Menkh's reply was hesitant. 'A disturbance in the City … ah, I mean, Ta'Morin. Something inexplicable perhaps?'

Ankh's eyes narrowed. 'There are many inexplicable things about Ta'Morin, as you know yourself. Most of them we have gotten used to, though I must admit, they are still a source of wonder. But no, nothing newly inexplicable. Unless you have something more specific in mind?'

'No, no nothing at all,' Menkh replied somewhat unconvincingly.

<I suggest we beat a hasty retreat; Ankh is no fool,> said Crixac, an undercurrent of humour in his voice.

<Yes, agreed,> Menkh said.

'Well, a momentous decision, Ankh. I am pleased that all is going well. Now, I feel somewhat tired after a long day, so if you will excuse me?'

Ankh nodded his head, almost speechless. His thoughts echoed in his head as Menkh walked away.

I have no idea what that was about. Something inexplicable? The only inexplicable thing is seeing Menkh at a loss for words. Not something I have experienced ever before with him. Something is going on that he his holding to himself.

Ankh's further internal ruminations were halted as Horven engaged him in a conversation, but his eyes followed Menkh and Tishan as they left.

<How is that possible, Crixac? The engagement of an enormous power that shoots a beam of light energy clear through the atmosphere, trembles the ground beneath our feet, and no-one outside of the Complex notices anything at all?>

<Well, I would think that the Shard may have had something to do with that. Is that so?> Crixac left the thought hanging.

<I would have thought that that would be obvious. We can hardly keep the current situation a close secret if we go around drawing attention to a phenomenon that nobody was expecting and that would, therefore, raise patently uncomfortable questions. Let alone increasing the fear factor to unacceptably high levels. No, Menkh, Crixac, it was within my power to cloak the activation, and I did so.>

<And we are grateful, Shard,> said Tishan. <There is enough happening without having to go into complex explanations. However, tonight's proceedings have raised a question in my mind.>

<You wish to know if I have a name, Tishan Dar? You think that calling me 'the Shard' is too impersonal?> the Shard's voice was amused but conveyed a degree of seriousness that was noticeable. <A name is a powerful thing, Tishan Dar, you should know that by now.>

<You have read my mind. I am sorry if I have caused offence,> Tishan responded quickly.

<Child, there is nothing you could do, say or think that would give me offence. No, it is a flattering thought, and until Menkh performed the choosing and underwent the bond, the reality is that I was immersed fully in the Intelligence. I was a part of the Whole and not separate from it. Only now, in Ta'Morin, as we shall now call this place, have I become more of a single entity. It is an interesting experience. So then, Tishan Dar. As it is you that have posed the question, you must select a name. What name would you know me by?>

Tishan paused. It was clear to her that the choice of a name had far deeper meaning and consequence than she had thought when she asked the question. She also realised that she could not ask Menkh for his view; the burden had been placed on her shoulders. A thousand thoughts chased across her mind but they centred on the newly adopted name for the City, which, she realised, had led to her dilemma in the first place.

<Well, we have named the City Ta'Morin, which loosely means place of renewed hope. As we have referred to you as the spirit of the City, then a fitting name, I think, would be Varnahrin, which would be Spirit of Hope. Is that acceptable to you?> Tishan's thoughts were hushed, the Shard's response unguessable.

Long moments passed without interruption. When the Shard spoke, its voice was tinged with a depth of emotion that none of them had thought to hear or experience. <It is a fitting name, Tishan Dar. From this day forth, you may call me Varnahrin. It is a powerful name, and an apt one.>

A fundamental sense of 'rightness' overtook Menkh and Tishan. <Truly spoken, Tishan Dar,> said Crixac. <I perceive that your choice of name has great meaning, though I cannot tell you why.>

<Whatever the sense is, you both need to rest. I will call you once the enemy has been located. Until then, sleep if you can.> With that, Varnahrin departed. Menkh and Tishan made their way back to the Complex and the rooms they used when they had tasks to occupy them there.

ooooOoooo

Horven sat in Bara Desh's tavern. It was Fourth Day and for every Fourth Day for the last two sem'chaal, Horven had occupied the same bench and sat quietly over a beaker of Kassarin brandy. Mareen's death had left an emptiness that could not be filled. Horven found that she could not grieve, though she had tried. Instead, there was just a vast hole in her spirit, and all who knew her had noticed that a spark had left and might, perhaps, never return. Horven had thrown herself into weapons training and physical exertion. Except on Fourth Day, she could be found in the simulation room battling multiple opponents and pushing herself to the very limits of her endurance. She still slept badly.

Her thoughts drifted endlessly. She tried, almost always unsuccessfully, not to relive the last terrible moments when Mareen had fallen. As a warrior of the Baran Mec, she had thought she was inured to death — the gods knew she had seen enough of it. But Mareen's fall had opened a wound that would not heal. She had become taciturn, and other Graavens who might have comforted her learned to avoid her and give her space.

Her thoughts were interrupted by Lerma, who had sat quietly opposite her. Lerma was not of the Baran Mec. Big, even for a Graaven male, and generally quiet and withdrawn, the flight from the capital had precluded any consideration for his admittance into the elite guard. However, there was no doubting his courage and his skill at arms. Tacitly, and without formalities, the surviving Baran Mec had unofficially adopted him as a fellow guard.

Horven did not acknowledge his presence. She did not require conversation and she kept her eyes fixed on the table before her. Her thoughts turned. Lerma had escaped Tarmech with five siblings. Four of them were warriors, and all had perished in battling the Dorath Mar. The youngest, a girl named Halika, was closest in Lerma's affections. Whether he had been charged by their parents to watch over her or not, Lerma was untiring in his efforts to protect her, even at times carrying her when she became tired.

It had been a stupid accident. Having destroyed a bridge in their flight from the enemy, Halika had slipped down a muddy slope and plunged into the river. Lerma, desperately throwing out his hand, had only managed to brush her fingertips. With a despairing cry of, 'Lerma!' she was swept away to her death. Horven would never forget the aching and gut-wrenching scream of loss that came from him as he stood forlornly on the bank. He had needed to be physically restrained from jumping in after Halika, to his own doom, and for many dak'chaal afterwards he was inconsolable and had sat adrift in his own thoughts, withdrawn from everyone. Only his ferocity in battle and a grim determination to continue kept him from complete despair.

Horven's eyes lifted from the table and looked directly into Lerma's. She was not prepared for what she saw in them. Such a depth of compassion, understanding, and shared loss, it made her take an involuntary gasp of air. Like a dam bursting under an unbearable weight of water, a sob escaped her lips and her eyes flooded with tears. Lerma's hand gripped Horven's as the bottled grief flowed out of her, a tempest of tortured emotions. Horven wept for a long time. For all that time, Lerma said nothing, but held her hand in silent sympathy.

At last, Horven drew in a shaky breath. Somehow, she felt differently. Like a violent storm after a hot day, which clears the air and makes everything fresh. Taking a deep breath, she squeezed Lerma's hand in her own. 'Thank you.'

Only two words, but with a deep sense of gratitude contained within them. Lerma nodded, smiled, stood up, and quietly left the tavern.

The change in Horven was quite remarkable and many noted that she was much more like her old self. There was still a hint of sadness behind the smile, but the smile was a more regular occurrence and her laughter, though rarer than before, was heartfelt and infectious.

Lerma and Horven took to sitting with each other. Often no words of any kind were exchanged but it was a companionable and infinitely comforting silence. It was on one of these occasions, as Horven was reflecting on the loss of Mareen, that a stunning thought and longing took her unawares.

Her thoughts turned from silent reflection to a focus on her body. She realised that it was still there. If she wished, she could invoke the Quickening. The weeks in Lerma's company and his steady presence allowed the thought to become a reality. All Graaven females could invoke the Quickening at will, though the possibility of that rapidly diminished once they had seen sixty sem'chaal. Horven had witnessed thirty-five sem'chaal. The invocation of the Quickening had an immediate physical effect. The markings on her skin, by which all Graavens had once identified their place in society, engorged and turned a deeper colour. The pores of her skin emitted an odour that was instantly recognised by Graaven males. Horven stood, her unblinking eyes focused on Lerma. Silently she folded her arms across her chest and then opened them, holding her arms wide with the palms of her hands uppermost. Abruptly all noise and conversation from others around them silenced.

Lerma's expression had turned from total surprise to something much deeper as he, too, stood. Horven had initiated the first formal steps of the Phags Par mating ritual. That she had done so had come as a total and unexpected surprise, but its initiation had sparked deeper feelings inside Lerma than he had expected. Silently, his eyes likewise fixed on Horven, he too stood, folded his arms across his chest, and bowed deeply in ritual acceptance of Horven's offer.

His voice came with difficulty due to his boiling emotions. 'You honour me, Horven Var,' he said with quiet intensity.

'It is I who am honoured. Let us meet in one meh'chaal. Shall we say dawn on Fourth Day? For some reason I think that will be propitious.'

'Then so shall it be.' Lerma made his way around the table to face Horven. Placing his hands lightly on her shoulders, he pressed his forehead to hers in the Graaven way of affection. Both Horven and Lerma found each other's presence intensely comforting.

All conversation in the tavern had stilled as the other Graavens present had quietly and reverently observed the commencement of the ritual. Now mugs rapped tables and a feeling of gladness stole over everyone.

'More Kassarin brandy,' called Bara Desh, 'to celebrate this happy day!' To which words there was general acclaim.

Horven and Lerma allowed the noise to wash over them, still in their embrace.

'May I make a request of you, Horven?' asked Lerma quietly.

'If it is within my power, Lerma, then you have only to ask it.'

'Then, if we are blessed with a female spawnling, might we call her Halika, in memory of her who was dear to me?' Lerma's voice was thick with emotion.

'So shall it be,' Horven smiled into Lerma's face. 'And if we have two, as I intend that we will, then do you object to us naming one Mareen?'

Lerma wiped away the tears that flowed from Horven's eyes as she in her turn wiped away his.

'So shall it be,' he replied.

CHAPTER FIVE

In the depths of space seven vessels suddenly appeared from out of the nothingness. Oddly fish shaped, one vessel was noticeably larger than the others. All had curious structures that extended out from their silvery, metallic surfaces, like spines on a desert plant.

The beings that occupied these craft spoke in unintelligible clicks and sounds that would have been beyond the ability of any Graaven to hear, let alone understand. They were tall and well-proportioned, though heavily boned. Long, hairlike filaments flowed down from their heads and over their shoulders, the longest nearly reaching the floor of the craft on which they stood. Each individual's 'hair' was braided in intricate patterns, with bead-like items woven into the braids that delineated their rank. An aquiline nose sat atop a generously lipped mouth, filled with small, serrated teeth. It was their eyes that drew you. Uniformly black and soulless, with a single eyelid that flicked across the surface of the eye like a sliding door. Their hands had long, tapering, webbed fingers, as if in some distant past these creatures had perhaps dwelt in an ocean. Each finger was topped with long nails that were polished and manicured to sharp points.

Their universal raiment was a cloak-like garment that sat over a loose tunic belted at the waist. The cloaks were made of a lustrous material, decorated with swirls of colour and patterns that, to their eyes, denoted their family histories and further reinforced their standing within their society – or lack of it. They referred to themselves as 'the Chosen' and had adopted the Talixit Ven as their deity. In this respect, they shared their god's values; they were only interested in their own personal advancement and that of their race. They enjoyed inflicting pain. The suffering of others was a joyful pursuit. Without exception they were cannibalistic.

The Chosen called themselves by names that reflected their own ideal of themselves. Their leader was referred to as 'Supremacy' and there was no-one on any vessel that would openly challenge his claim to pre-eminence amongst them. All, however, wished for an error that would provide the excuse to lay him screaming under their ritual knives, slicing off pieces of his flesh and devouring them, preferably while he was still living.

As the vessels emerged from the between, he turned in supressed fury on his second-in-command, a female self-styled as Hakatha, a poisonous arachnid of the Chosen's home world. His speech rapidly ascended to a frequency that indicated violence was imminent. 'Why have we re-entered normal space yet again? Do you have any idea of the importance our mission has to the Deity or what failure might mean to all of us?'

Hakatha's eyes opened to their widest extent, a sign of fear, and she quickly knelt before their enraged leader. Others of the Chosen looked on with rapt attention to see what would eventuate.

'Supremacy,' Hakatha's voice was low, consoling. 'The creatures must rest: they can only travel so far. When the weakest must stop, so do they all. We must give them more time to recover.'

'Must! Who are you to say to me that I "must"? Not so long ago, Hakatha, your family were little higher than the dirt we throw out each cycle. Do you seek to challenge me as did your forebear?'

Hakatha squirmed. She could still hear her sire's screams as they eviscerated him, albeit she had taken part in the ritual and exulted in her own advancement. She dragged herself closer and licked Supremacy's feet, a sign of complete submission.

'No, no, Supremacy, I am sorry. Might I humbly suggest that we allow more time for them to recuperate so that we might travel further this time?'

Supremacy pulled his foot away, his jewelled sandal gleaming slightly from Hakatha's spittle. His tone was still harsh but had descended from its highest range, so Hakatha knew he was somewhat mollified.

'That is better. Know your place, Hakatha.' He suddenly looked up and cast a withering gaze around the control room in which he stood. 'Remember it, all of you. We rest for ten mexil.' He prodded Hakatha with his foot as she lay at his feet. 'Did you hear me, Second? Ten mexil. A moment longer and I will eat your brains. That, at least, will give me some satisfaction.'

'I hear and obey, Supremacy.'

Turning, Supremacy walked rapidly away, passing through a doorway which slid closed behind him.

Hakatha climbed to her feet. She swore on the Deity that she would carve out Supremacy's eyes and eat them. Till then she rounded on her subordinates.

'You can stop smirking and get to your stations or I will carve a stemm sygil on your faces with my fingernails,' her voice was pitched low, and all the more menacing for it. As one, her three subordinates moved to the panels of lights that lay before them at each station.

'Make sure the inducement is ready. I want no delays once ten mexil have elapsed.'

ooooOoooo

Menkh was bathing himself after a short but refreshing nap. Although he was a bonded Adept, there were still some simple pleasures he enjoyed when in his Graaven form. Having returned from the meeting he was musing over developments with Crixac when Varnahrin's voice echoed in his mind.

<Come to the viewing room, Menkh. Our enemy has once again emerged from the between.>

Hurriedly finishing his ablutions, Menkh translocated. Tishan appeared in the viewing room alongside him. Once again, the strange vessels floated in space before their eyes.

<There is something about these vessels,> Varnahrin's voice was tinged with disquiet. <Something unseen. I sense it but I cannot discern what it is. However, the distance between them and us has diminished such that we can now pinpoint their location and act.>

<What happens if they re-enter the between before we reach them?> Crixac's question echoed Menkh's thoughts.

<Other than the frustration of causing us to wait further, nothing. But delaying further does not give us any significant advantage. Menkh, you must take to the Threadway. I will imprint the location into your mind. Once there, assuming that they have not vanished, you must deal with what you find. The enemy must not be permitted to communicate with their home world.>

<Does that include their destruction? Presuming, of course, that they do not possess the means to destroy me first,> Menkh commented.

<You must take whatever action you deem necessary, Menkh ab Dur. You may find that once you are in proximity with them, Crixac will be able to add to your knowledge. We are still at the limit of Ta'Morin's capacity to scan these vessels, and I have explained before about the limitations on my capacity to assist you. You are a bonded Adept with vast power. Use it.>

This statement was followed by silence as Menkh and Crixac reflected on what was to come.

Into the silence came Tishan's voice. <What of me, Varnahrin? What task would you have me perform?>

<Even now, Tishan Dar, an emissary of the Xotic approaches Ta'Morin. Menkh and Crixac have their task, you must deal with the news that the Xotic bring.>

<The Xotic? It must be momentous for them to have travelled here. The journey around the Mother Water is arduous,> Tishan remarked.

Menkh took Tishan's hands into his own and spoke aloud. 'You are both Stragosh and Guardian, Tishan, there is nothing beyond your capacity to deal with. Take care of yourself and our people while I am gone.'

'I have the easier task, Menkh. You go to face an unknown threat, far from home. May all our friends in spirit watch over you.'

<Come, child,'> Varnahrin interrupted. <The Xotic enter the gates. You must be there to receive them.>

Menkh and Tishan touched foreheads and lingered for a moment until, stepping back, with her eyes fixed on Menkh's, Tishan translocated and disappeared from view.

<To your task, Menkh, Crixac. Remember the power of the staff. You grow in its mastery; it may yet surprise you. Here is the location. Assume your Adept form and depart. Remember: The Balance is all.>

With the location now firmly in his mind, Menkh ascended the Threadway. Everything around him became unfocused as he phased out of reality, entering the alternate dimension of the Threadway; still part of, and yet separate from, the living, breathing world around him.

For the first time, he was conscious of speed. In the blink of an eye the world of Tarvuli had vanished from sight. Other planets and moons, suns, and clouds of gas and other heavenly bodies swept past. As they journeyed on, suspended in the stream of light, Crixac spoke. <Presumably we will appear before these craft where they float in space. I wonder if there is a way that we can use the staff to cloak our presence. An alien creature floating in front of them may give rise to a certain sense of surprise.>

<Hah! As ever, my friend, your humour understates the impact. We must assume that any surprise they feel will result in a swift response, either to attack or to vanish. Let us put our will to it and see what might be accomplished. We are invisible to them whilst we travel on the Threadway but once we are back in phase, our presence will be known.>

Menkh had only just begun to focus his mind when Crixac interrupted. <Wait, Menkh. I have a better idea. I can physically manipulate your Adept form to blend in with the background. It will be like many of the creatures on Tarvuli who change the colour of their hides to blend into the tones of the forest or the plains.>

<So, you will camouflage our presence? I like the idea.>

<Indeed, and I can do the manipulation while we travel so that when we phase back into reality it is already set,> Crixac said.

<Very well, it sounds like a good plan to me. What about the staff?>

<The staff will react to our requirements. Of itself its crystalline form would be difficult to pick up in the background of space. I do not think we need be concerned on that front.>

The passage of time was difficult to fathom as they travelled. It did not feel long before Menkh noticed that their speed was lessening, although there was no physical sense that this was the case. They flew past a sun and came to a complete stop far above a green-coloured world orbiting it. Great land masses and swirling cloud formations could be vaguely discerned covering its surface. Just beyond where they had come to a stop, the seven alien craft – previously only seen as a projection – sat close before them.

The largest of the ships assumed a central position, separated by about five hundred spahn from the others that surrounded it in a spherical formation. Each craft appeared to be at least several hundred spahn in length and girth. At close range, the weird protrusions appeared to be antennae, presumably for sensing and scanning their surrounds. Each craft had a long cable extended from the front that appeared to float in the space before them.

<Those cables, Crixac. They extend outward as if they are connected to something but there is nothing there to be seen.>

<Yes, there you have it, my friend, nothing 'to be seen'. There is something there; I can sense it, as could Varnahrin. Hmmm … let me see if I can manipulate your eyes to include a greater spectrum of light fields.>

Menkh's vision blurred and then, remarkably, he could see what before he had been blind to. Immense, jelly-like creatures, many times larger than the craft that were attached to them. Each creature was tethered to a single vessel by the floating cables, that they could now see were inserted into their bodies. Along the creatures' sides, phosphorescent blue lights pulsed slowly. Their bodies were semitransparent and long tentacles, like questing fingers, rippled in the space around where Menkh presumed the creatures' heads would be located, assuming they had one. They were the most incredible creatures Menkh had ever seen. Without fully understanding how, Menkh had the impression of vast age. The feeling of being in their presence was somehow quite humbling.

<Gathanax!> Crixac cried. <Menkh, we are in the presence of creatures of legend. They travel interstellar space, their voices echoing across the cosmos as they sing to each other, and they live for thousands of cycles. These creatures before us may be older than your home world. Rarely seen but never forgotten, they are ancient and wise and peaceful. By what cruel manipulation are they tethered to these things? It is an abomination!> Crixac's voice had taken on an intensity that Menkh had not experienced before.

<Then, my friend, we must assist them. Can we communicate with them?>

<We can try. I think we need to use the staff for this, and I believe we must lay a hand on one to channel our thoughts. These creatures do not communicate in the way that we do, or indeed like any other being. In any event, I think this would be the best way.>

Menkh gripped the staff in his right hand and laid his left tentatively on the skin of the creature closest to him. It was smooth, somewhat slick to the touch, and very cold.

Pain.

Intense pain erupted in Menkh's body. The staff flared brightly, and the pain diminished, replaced by a voice. There were no words. Only sound, a music, to Menkh's mind as if the stars themselves sang. It was ethereal and haunting, filled with a desperate sadness and echoing loss. As he listened, a construct of words manifested in his mind.

<Mother! Mother! I cannot feel you. I cannot hear you. Mother, I am lost. I am alone.>

A surge of power from the cables that were inserted into the creature's body brought an onrush of further pain. The creature's song was so anguished that Menkh and Crixac wavered on the edge of a debilitating sense of despair. Menkh desperately sent out thoughts of comfort, boosted with Crixac's assistance. For what felt like half a lifetime there was no response: and then the creature became aware. It was like a giant taking notice of an ant. Yet, as small and inconsequential as the ant was, the giant invested an intense scrutiny and hope that help might be found. The song changed.

<Will you aid me? I long to travel the timestream. I long for the voice of my kin – they, too, are lost to me. I cannot hear them. We cannot make the great song. What is existence without the great song? How will Mother grow without the song?>

<I do not know of what you speak, my friend,> said Menkh quietly, <but I can tell you that you are surrounded by your kin even though you cannot hear them. If I can unfetter you, can you return to your mother?>

<Truly? Oh yes. Yes.> In response to Menkh's assurances the creature's song changed, and hope arose in place of pain and despair. <I was trapped in the darkness. I know not how. Then these things were attached to me. Now I can only journey where they send me. I long for the time stream. Please help me!>

<Crixac, help me sense out where and how these cables are tethered. We do not want to cause any more pain and distress than we have to.>

Tentatively, with the aid of the staff, they explored along the cable insertion point. The cable ended in a spiky mass that had four distinct protrusions embedded within the creature, ensuring it could not be quickly removed. Whilst their complete purpose could not be fully discerned, it was clear that at least one objective was to cause intense pain in order to make certain the gathanax did as it was required.

<I believe we can use the staff to cut through the cable at the entry point. I am hopeful that the rest will then slide out of the body mass, though I am not sure how gathanax experience pain or if such an operation might damage them internally,> said Menkh uncertainly.

<Well, who better to ask than our friend?> responded Crixac.

They communicated their plan to the creature and, to their relief, the gathanax was confident that neither the operation of cutting through the cable, nor the action of the embedded section leaving its body, was of concern.

<Then we shall start with you and move on to each of your kin. Presumably they are isolated like you, so it may take some time to get the task done.>

<You can only do your best, but please hurry. I long to feel Mother once again and make the great song.>

It was a delicate business to cut through the head of the cable without alerting the tethered vessel that anything was amiss. It appeared that the creatures who occupied the craft had not dreamt that a third party might appear to assist the gathanax in escaping, nor was there any sophisticated device to relay the damage that was being wrought to the cables themselves. Establishing communications with the other gathanax took some time and the mental pressure mounted as Menkh and Crixac waited for a reaction from the spacecraft around them. All, however, remained quiet. Eventually the task was completed. Whilst the gathanax could not feel the presence of their fellows, their song had changed dramatically and, thanks to the communication from Menkh, they each knew that they were surrounded by their kin.

The phosphorescent lights pulsed faster and faster as the gathanax stored energy for their jump into the timestream.

<Where will you journey to, my friend?> asked Menkh.

<It is not the destination, but the journey and the song that we make. We will be back with Mother, that is all that is important. Our song will contain a warning to others of our kind across the cosmos so that no others fall into the trap that imprisoned us.>

Now the song changed again, and great emotion was vested in it. <Know that we will sing of your unselfish aid and your actions will form part of the great song. Because of that song, each of our kind will recognise and hear you. If you are in need, call to us. Your call will be answered.>

With a sound like a million voices raised in complex harmony, a great call reached out and sped across space. At the same time, the blue lights that pulsed on each creature's sides blurred into one giant flash of light and all seven of the gathanax vanished from sight. An echo of joy touched Menkh and Crixac as each gathanax became aware of the other and they reconnected, free from pain and loss once more.

<Who do you think Mother is?> asked Menkh.

<Why, I do believe it is the universe itself, Menkh. But whatever it is, I think we have made a difference here that will resound throughout the cosmos.>

Menkh turned his gaze to the vessels that still surrounded them. <Some work still to do, my friend.>

ooooOoooo

On board the Chosen vessels pandemonium was beginning to set in. Having reached the appointed time, Hakatha had ordered all ships to stimulate the captured gathanax and continue their search. When nothing happened, they realised something was wrong. In their arrogance, no device had been fitted to alert them to any external interference. This had been deemed a complete impossibility. Now the impossible had become a reality and their complacency had enabled the escape of the creatures they had so cruelly restrained and tortured. Blast shields on viewing ports had finally been opened to reveal cables floating in the emptiness of space. Moreover, the realisation that they had no means to return to their home world and were effectively marooned was not long in coming.

In the midst of this rising panic, Supremacy entered the control room on the flagship. Apocalyptic did not even begin to describe the extent of his rage. Hakatha did not see the knife flashing towards her until it was too late. The deadly blade opened her throat, splashing a yellow ichor over some of the controls. She made a strangled sound as her body slumped to the ground. Fear and horror could be seen in her opened eyes until all life energy had left them and her body lay prone on the cold floor.

Supremacy hardly noted her death or the matter that dripped off his knife hand, which he absently licked with his long tongue.

His rage had slightly abated from having removed his incompetent second, and his eyes scanned the void as he gazed through the opened viewing port before him. As he looked, a strange and alien figure appeared, glowing redly and floating in space in close proximity to where the tethered gathanax should have been.

'There! There, you blind fools! There is the creature responsible for this catastrophe!'

Surrounding crew members stared mutely. Not one was willing to respond to Supremacy's announcement, all too aware of the body that lay at his feet.

'Prepare all weapon systems! Communicate to all vessels. I want that carrion destroyed. Now!'

With alacrity the crew leaped to obey. The command was conveyed to all surrounding ships and controls activated to bring weapons systems online.

'Defensive shields?' the Chosen who was now second asked nervously.

'Defensive shields for a single alien? Are you as stupid as your predecessor?'

The Chosen, whose self-styled name was Vengeance, did not respond. Any rational argument, that a single alien who could free the gathanax was worthy of respect, went unspoken. Supremacy was not in the mood to listen to rational argument. Vengeance crossed his arms over his chest and bowed slightly, acknowledging the order.

In the meantime, Menkh noted that lights had now become visible on the vessels around him as their blast doors had opened. He also discerned that a number of the antennae were focusing in his direction.

<I think we may have upset our friends. If I am not mistaken, these antennae are part of their weapon systems. In short order, we are going to be on the sharp end of an assault by some form of energy beam,> said Crixac.

<Any idea who these beings are?> asked Menkh.

<Hmmm. Well, they do resemble a race that a host and I came across once. That was long ago and very far indeed from where we are now. They had a name given to them, as I recall. Let me think. The closest translation in Graaven would be 'Hertax im Sekkr'.>

<Eaters of flesh!> Menkh said, aghast. <That does not sound encouraging.>

<No. They were relatively primitive then but on the cusp of technological advancement. If they are vassals of the Talixit Ven, they have received help, if indeed these are the same creatures. I think only our archenemy would have any capacity to capture gathanax. Then again, the gathanax travel in family groups. You would only need to capture one to ensure that all the others are within your control,> Crixac mused. <Listen, Menkh. With the power of the staff and my abilities I can endeavour to tap into their consciousness. If successful, I can explore their background and race. I can also gain knowledge of the workings of the vessels which will be invaluable for any move we make against them.>

Menkh's response was measured. <Are you sure of this, Crixac? Will you have enough time before they commence their assault? Does what you propose make you vulnerable at all, or expose you to unnecessary risk?>

<There is always risk, Menkh. When I quest in this way, I am still connected to you by a thread of energy. We could be vulnerable to a mental attack on that front, but I judge that these creatures are highly unlikely to be capable; they lack the ability to take such a course of action. Something like an Adept? Well, that would be a different thing altogether. As to their attack, I believe you are more than capable of shielding us from their assault.>

<Very well. Is there something I need to do?>

<Just focus on me as much as you can. This will allow me to speed back to you if something untoward happens. Once I return, the knowledge I have gleaned becomes yours.>

With what amounted to the mental equivalent of taking a deep breath, Menkh felt Crixac's consciousness flow out of him. It may have been imagination, but Menkh was sure he could discern a pale golden stream of light that bound them together even while Crixac leapt away from him. The band of light emanated from Menkh and seemed to endlessly stretch, becoming thinner as the distance between them grew, but with no feeling that the line would snap. Crixac's thoughts flowed back, as if he was calling from outside.

<This is good, Menkh. Not something we should do all the time but very handy in this kind of a situation.>

It was a one-way communication, however, because Menkh's answer seemed to hit a kind of mental block which echoed in his head.

<I forgot to tell you that you will not be able to speak to me, only I to you.> Crixac's voice faded.

Menkh laughed. If that was not typical of the symbiote, to always leave some key information out! Menkh didn't like the feeling of Crixac's absence. After all this time it was uncomfortable not to feel him nearby and Menkh could not help but worry. However, it was not overly long before Menkh felt Crixac's return.

<Welcome back, my friend. How did it go?>

<Interesting. They are indeed mentally primitive, and these are the same beings I spoke of. Infinitely more technically capable but sadly very little changed from the savage creatures they were before. They have enslaved themselves to the Talixit Ven who they refer to as Deity. Their society is founded on murder and death and their leader is some kind of high priest in their noisome religion.>

<Not many saving graces then, Crixac?> Menkh asked.

<Hmmm … I am not sure. Deep inside some of them, perhaps, an unacknowledged desire for something else? I cannot say.>

<Well, the time for speculation is over,> said Menkh. <Do we move away, or do we bear the brunt of this assault?> His tone gave no hint of concern at the onslaught that might be about to come.

<Their weapons systems are powerful, but I think we need to weather the storm and then counterpunch. Do we destroy them?> Crixac responded in a tone that was somewhat quizzical. He was in no doubt that they could wipe out the whole fleet before them.

Before Menkh could respond, all seven vessels began their assault in a coordinated attack. Great violet-coloured bolts of energy leapt out from the lead antennae of each vessel; the coruscating beams intersected in moments on the exact point where Menkh hung in space. Such was the scale of the attack that an outside observer would have imagined a huge cascade of sound erupting as the weapons engaged and found their target – but in the depths of space there was no sound at all. The battle ensued in total silence with only the intensity of the light, which flared and dimmed as time passed, giving any testament to the power that was being expended.

Deep within the incandescent light and searing heat of the beams, an alien figure floated, surrounded by a radiant blue nimbus that glowed stronger and stronger in ever-deeper tones of blue.

<Interesting,> Menkh said to Crixac. <The staff is absorbing the energy and storing it, harnessing the power of the weapons being used against us and increasing its own power.>

<Yes,> Crixac responded in measured tones. <We are going to have to focus on our counterpunch. If our intention is not to destroy, then we must concentrate on crippling these vessels and knocking out their communications.>

Menkh agreed. <Once we have done that I want to see if there is a habitable planet within the vicinity that these creatures can

reach. I have no desire to kill them all, albeit they have a single-minded intention to blow us apart,> he said.

<Don't forget their plans for Tarvuli,> Crixac countered.

<I haven't. But the reality is that they will never reach Tarvuli without the gathanax, and we must suppose that under the influence of the enemy …> Menkh paused in reflection.

<You mean that, separated from the enemy, perhaps they have the chance to become different to what they are now?> asked Crixac.

<Like you, Crixac, I don't know. I just don't want to kill them. But I could be sentencing them to death anyway.>

<Well. They will at least have the opportunity to survive,> Crixac said. <That is more than they would have given us.>

While this conversation was taking place, the weapons focused on them continued an unremitting assault.

Aboard the Chosen flagship, Vengeance, the new second-in-command, spoke to the leader. 'Supremacy, we cannot continue this barrage. Energy reserves are being depleted; our weapon systems were not designed for such a continuous outburst.'

Supremacy turned a contemptuous look on his new second. 'Ceasefire then. Nothing could have survived that anyway.'

Abruptly all seven vessels broke off their attack. Supremacy slammed his fists into the console before him, incredulous, as he observed the alien figure – apparently unscathed – still suspended before him in space.

Menkh and Crixac focused their will into the staff. Crixac took the leading role, using his acquired knowledge of the Chosen spacecrafts' systems as they willed their counterpunch to render the enemy vessels inoperative.

<Of course, it has been quite some time, Menkh, so we might still end up vaporising them all.>

<That would be unfortunate, Crixac, but we can only do our best.> Despite the flippant remark, Menkh was grim.

Just as at the battle against the Dorath Mar, the enormous power of the staff was once again revealed. The light from the eruption of energy was like being next to a sun. It totally enveloped the surrounding vessels, melting away their antennae and crippling key systems on each ship. Before the light had faded, Menkh had focused on the Threadway and stretched his senses out, questing for a habitable world suitable for the creatures who occupied the currently useless vessels. One thread flared brighter as his thoughts focused. Choosing this path, Menkh ascended the Threadway to investigate.

ooooOooooo

As Supremacy turned to issue a further command, the ship was bathed in a light so intense that, with their blast shields still open on the viewing port, all the Chosen were temporarily blinded. Delicate instrumentation instantly fused, fires erupted from inside consoles as the structures within them ignited, and all weapons and communications systems were instantly rendered useless. Such was the intensity of the unleashed energy that all seven vessels, despite their size, reacted to the shockwave like toy boats in rough water. Crew members unable to anchor themselves were thrown violently to the floor.

Supremacy groped to his feet, his eyes trying to adjust back to some semblance of normality. He spoke into the chaos around him. 'I do not understand! Why does the Deity allow this to happen to us? I am a priest of the fifth circle, one of the High Set. This cannot be!'

A sibilant whisper came into his ears. 'You are a braggart and an arrogant fool. You and your kind are the ruin of us all … *Supremacy.*' Vengeance's voice dripped with scorn and loathing and the blow from the knife he wielded was expertly delivered. Supremacy felt the sting of the first thrust: by the seventh, he was dead. Vengeance allowed his rage and frustration to drive him on and he continued stabbing long after Supremacy lay in a gore-covered heap next to Hakatha.

The rest of the crew looked on, waiting to see what would eventuate. Murder and violent death were commonplace but although hands twitched and moved, knife blades remained undrawn. Such was the enormity of the predicament they found themselves in. Supremacy had failed, death was warranted and, as Second, Vengeance was, by all custom and practice, sanctioned to undertake a purge. In the expectant quiet Vengeance turned an ichor-spattered face towards those who stood by.

'Well? Take control of your teams. Assess damage and effect repairs. See if we can defend ourselves and prepare for another attack. Now!'

That the others quickly moved to obey was tacit acknowledgement of their agreement with Vengeance's actions.

'And eject this carrion into space and clean up this mess. Bring me cloths to cleanse myself,' he ordered. Turning back, he focused his attention on the alien who abruptly disappeared from view as he looked on, its intentions unknown. The Chosen were isolated and vulnerable, but they would not go down without a fight.

ooooOoooo

The Chosen vessels vanished into the distance. Although Menkh found it difficult to measure the passage of time whilst journeying through the Threadway, it did not seem overly long till he floated above a moon that orbited an immense planet. As he descended towards the moon's surface, Menkh could see vast forests with trees taller than any he had ever witnessed. Herds of animals traversed great plains and a large body of water could also be seen.

<How is this, Crixac?>

<Gravity and air will take some getting used to for them, but it's certainly habitable. Their ships contain smaller vessels so that they can transport themselves to the surface.>

<However 'difficult' it is for them, it is infinitely preferable to dying in space. Come, let us return to our new 'friends' and communicate the happy news.>

ooooOoooo

If there was consternation in the control room of the lead Chosen ship during the brief battle, it was nothing to the reactions that occurred when the strange and powerful alien simply materialised in the midst of the crew manning the damaged consoles. Surrounded by a blue nimbus of energy, its baleful gaze swept around the deck, lingering for a moment on each individual. The Chosen were frozen in apprehension. In such a unique situation no-one knew exactly how to react. Given the power that this alien had evinced earlier, the thought of any overt resistance was not one that appealed.

As the newly appointed leader, Vengeance cleared his throat and spoke. 'Who are you? What is your purpose here?'

The creature, with its glowing red skin and blue eyes, turned its full attention on him and Vengeance inwardly cringed. The alien head tilted slightly to one side and the eyes narrowed. Whether this was an indication that violence was about to erupt or a quizzical response to the question, Vengeance didn't know, but presupposing it could understand him, he tried again. 'I asked who you are and what your purpose is here.'

<Crixac, are you able to manipulate their navigation systems and set a course for that moon?>

<Already done.>

<Excellent. I must ask you how you did that when we have time.>

<Not dissimilar to when I explored this ship, Menkh, but much easier given our close proximity. Their fuel reserves are adequate though it will take several meh'chaal for them to reach it.>

The response, when it came from the alien, was disembodied. All heard the words, but none could discern how they were uttered, as the creature's mouth remained firmly closed.

'I am not here to answer your questions. You sought to obliterate me; you will observe that I have spared your lives. I could leave you here lost and disabled to die a lingering death – perhaps no more than you deserve. Instead, I offer you life. You will never be able to return home. The coordinates of a new world have been entered into your navigational system. You have enough energy reserves to reach it. It is a habitable world, although you will need to adapt to it. I suggest you start now.'

The figure began to shimmer and fade.

'Wait, wait!' Vengeance's voice was in a high register, indicating both fear and hope. 'How do we know to trust you?'

'You don't. But if I wanted to destroy you, you would already be dead. It is your choice. Choose.'

The figure abruptly disappeared.

Unseen and undetected, Menkh hung in space some distance away from the vessels. He was attuned to their communications and listened with interest to the discussion that followed. The Chosen knew that they were stranded in remote space. Without the enslaved gathanax they had no way of returning to their home world. Menkh, with Crixac's assistance, had ensured that, other than localised communications, any repairs to long range signalling of any kind was impossible. No-one would ever know what had happened to them and would suppose that they had died or become lost in the remoteness of interstellar space. Let the enemy digest that fact.

Vengeance stood looking at the space the creature had so recently occupied. 'Vermal,' Vengeance spoke to his subordinate. 'Call all leaders, I want them here for a meeting. Now.'

Vermal clasped his arms across his chest and then opened local communications to relay the command.

Soon several small vessels could be seen approaching the flagship. Undoubtedly these were the various commanders of the other craft. A faint, green-coloured light could be seen emanating from the rear of each of the small craft, which Crixac confirmed was created by whatever propulsion system they employed. In an orderly fashion each vessel disappeared into an airlock that had opened in the command craft. It was not long before they had assembled, and a heated discussion ensued.

'You may consider yourself the leader of this force, having usurped and eliminated Supremacy, but if you believe that I or my crew will follow you, then you are mistaken. To eliminate a priest of the High Set is a blasphemy that the Deity will not accept. You and all your kin will be sacrificed on the Great Altar for this.' The voice was high pitched and shrill, indicating that the speaker was in an intensely emotional state. But if she expected murmurs of assent, she was disappointed. Her comments were met with silence.

'Verrach speaks truly,' responded another. 'As priest, she should be the one to lead us in the face of this calamity. Who was this creature anyway? How are we to trust that what you say is true?'

Another voice interrupted. 'Whatever or whoever it was, it was powerful enough to disable all our ships and we were unable to affect it despite our massed fire power. So, Verrach, where was the Deity's protection and swift vengeance? I say we are beyond the reach of the Deity and far beyond concern about the consequences of aborting this mission.'

'Blasphemy!' came the voice of Verrach and two others.

Vengeance cut through the argument. 'It is clear we are in dissension. You, Verrach, Calfra, and Xarchic, invoke the name of the Deity and call for sacrifice. So then. Dimmar, Ecosha, and Falma, are we agreed on the correct course of action?'

'What actions do you propose, blasphemer? You are an abomination in the eyes of the Deity. Only those purified in the blood of the sacrificed have the right to lead here!'

A gurgling sound was followed by muffled screams and groans.

<It would seem that the Chosen have taken affirmative action,> said Menkh dispassionately.

<Yes. I do believe the blasphemers may have taken direct action to resolve the argument,> agreed Crixac.

Vengeance issued commands. 'Vermal, I think a haunch of freshly culled priest might be dispatched to each vessel to help our crews understand that the reach of the Deity has been exceeded. The rest of their carcasses you can eject. Dimmar, take a kill squad to each vessel. Any Chosen who prefer to die strong in their faith may do so immediately. I want us ready to depart in five mexil. We will relay the coordinates to all vessels and seek out this new world. There, perhaps, we will see a new order assert itself.'

'I would expect little resistance, Vengeance. Eliminate the priests and the crews will await how events turn out. Not to mention a little roast priest flesh to convince them,' said Ecosha.

Vengeance laughed without humour. 'I agree, Ecosha. Dimmar, spare no-one who you think is duplicitous. I have had enough of priests and their acolytes to last me a lifetime.'

Answering voices gave their assent and soon a single small vessel made its way to each of the other Chosen ships. Within a surprisingly short time the engines of each craft blossomed into life, and they moved off rapidly and quickly disappeared.

<So, the immediate problem has been dealt with, what next?>asked Crixac.

<Yes. I have been thinking that myself. What say you to a journey to the Balancepoint? My feelings are strong that this is where the next phase of our quest will be revealed.>

<I cannot argue with your logic, Menkh. In the light of no other ideas, I agree.>

A tracery of threads appeared around them as they focused on their chosen destination. Activating the Threadway merely required Menkh to express the earnest desire to travel to a specific location. In less than a heartbeat, the alien figure vanished.

CHAPTER SIX

ollowing Varnahrin's words in the viewing room, Tishan translocated herself to her quarters and then, after summoning Horven and Ankh, set off to meet the Xotic emissaries.

'Xotic? Here?' exclaimed Horven. 'That is some journey.'

'Yes, and given the comments Varnahrin made, their travel here can be nothing good. But we shall see.'

'Varnahrin? Spirit of the City.' Horven nodded her head. 'You have been busy, Tishan Dar. It seems very appropriate.' This statement was accompanied by a broad smile. Tishan looked at Horven as she spoke, her eyes narrowed in thought. Ankh followed somewhat behind. There was something new, something different about Horven's demeanour. Tishan realised that Horven was smiling. There was a self-contained joy about her that had been missing for a very long time. Tishan looked closer and then smiled herself.

'Horven Var, I give you joy. You have invoked the Quickening! I am so happy for you.'

'Yes, Lerma and I.' Horven paused as unexpected emotion made her stumble over her words.

'You do not need to tell me, of all people, of your feelings, Horven. It is enough to see you smile. Come, our friends approach and I see that they are accompanied by Fendrax. Let us see what tidings they bring.'

Horven, Ankh, and Tishan stopped under the permanent pavilion that had been set up to entertain the Benshin when they made their visits to Ta'Morin, and waited to greet the Xotic. Horven recognised Tlkcha and memories of their visit with Menkh and Mareen came flooding back. Tlkcha carried with her a perceptible aura of sadness, and something else Horven could not place. Three other unfamiliar Xotic accompanied her.

Tishan walked forward and greeted their guests formally. 'Welcome to Ta'Morin, dear friends. I can see that your news is heavy but please know that you are our honoured guests. If we can help you in any way, you have but to ask. Come sit, refresh yourselves.'

Tlkcha crossed her arms over her chest in the way of Xotic greeting. 'We thank you for your welcome, Tishan Dar. Though we have never met personally, Horven and Mareen and indeed, Menkh, spoke of you often so that I feel that I know you. These are my companions, Hermech, Dansha, and Kellix.'

'Welcome to you all. I see also that you bring a mighty friend with you who is not of the Xotic.' Tishan approached Fendrax and bowed low before rising slowly to look up into Fendrax's green eyes. 'Welcome indeed to you, Fendrax, it has been too long since you have visited us.'

Fendrax returned Tishan's bow and then delicately sniffed the tip of Tishan's nose. Tishan endeavoured to stay calm but even knowing Fendrax would do her no harm, it still took an effort of willpower not to tremble.

'Greetings, Tishan Dar. I see she who is called Horven standing with you. Will she greet me also?'

Fendrax focused on Horven as she approached and executed a similar bow, which Fendrax returned before drawing close to her.

'My pack was told of Mareen's fate. Haran grieves with you. He has told me to tell you that he has named the first female of his fifth litter Mareen in honour of her whom he carried, so that her name will live in our memory.'

Horven was overcome with emotion and could not find the words to convey her feelings. Instead, she bowed deeply and held that pose for a long moment as the tears ran unchecked down her face. As Horven stood upright, Fendrax touched her nose to Horven's. 'Do not grieve. Her body may be no more but her spirit lives on. She is not so far away from you, my friend.'

Horven smiled and wiped the tears from her eyes. She found comfort in Fendrax's words and, with what had happened with Lerma, felt completely whole again.

Tishan, Ankh, and Horven sat across from their now-seated guests. 'Refreshments will be here momentarily,' said Tishan. 'Please do not be alarmed by the creatures that bring them to us. They are completely harmless and you will see many of them in Ta'Morin, mostly carrying out mundane tasks of cleaning and the like.'

Tlkcha and the other Xotic smiled but they still carried that feeling that Tishan could not quite place – sadness, certainly, but carrying an undertone of something darker – and she wondered what news they brought. Her musings were interrupted by the arrival of several small, silvery, flat metal discs that seemed to float over the ground. They came to a stop by the pavilion and several armlike appendages extended from the underside of each disc. As the top of the discs opened, the appendages began to extract various containers. The Xotic were astonished and sat uncomfortably whilst the 'creatures' deposited food and drink and then, as silently as they had arrived, headed back to Ta'Morin.

'If you had not counselled us, Tishan Dar, I would have run screaming!' Dansha exclaimed. 'Are they magical creatures?'

'They are certainly invested with the Spirit of Ta'Morin, Dansha. They gave us quite a surprise too when they first appeared,' said Ankh. 'But there is always something to surprise you in Ta'Morin. We have grown accustomed to them so that we hardly notice them at all anymore.'

The Xotic exchanged looks. 'Truly Shashn spoke wisely when he told us to journey to you.'

'How is Shashn?' asked Horven. 'It would be pleasing to see him again.'

Now it was time for tears to flow down Tlkcha's face and her voice when she answered was choked with grief. 'He is dead, Horven. His last words bade us journey here, for without your aid I fear that our people may be driven from our homeland.'

Tishan, Ankh, and Horven exchanged startled looks. News of this kind touched a raw nerve with all Graavens. Although they had made their new home in Ta'Morin they all carried deep scars.

'Dead?' Horven's voice was puzzled and alarmed. 'How can this be? Was it an accident?'

'It is a long story,' Dansha said in a quiet voice.

'However long, you must tell us. You are safe here,' Tishan said soothingly.

Kellix took up the story as Horven reached across, silently taking Tlkcha's hand to comfort her.

'As you Graavens measure the passing of time it was several bach'chaal ago that Xotic messengers arrived during our Gathering. They had returned from a journey far to the south, where the Great Water which has no end marks the end of our lands. A strange people had been encountered, apparently thrown up on the shore after a great storm. By good fortune, for them at least, it so happened that a group of our people were there collecting shells that are greatly prized amongst all Xotic. These people had travelled in a strange craft, somewhat like our poctech sailers but much bigger. It had been driven onto the shore and was damaged. Some of the strangers had been injured and so they were given aid. Then, having repaired their vessel, they departed to return to their lands, which, they told us, lie many dak'chaal across the water.'

Hermech continued the tale. 'There was something unsettling about these strangers. Their faces were masked and closed to us and the aid we gave them was accepted without thanks: almost as if it were their due. When their ship left, black smoke billowed into the air and the vessel moved away without a sail, great wheels on either side of it driving them through the water.'

Now Dansha spoke. 'So it was that at the Gathering, Shashn and several more of our elders determined that we should keep a watch on the shore lest these strangers return. And return they did, only this time there were several vessels. The smoke from their ships could be seen blackening the sky long before they arrived.'

'I would that we had killed them all when the strangers first came to us,' interjected Tlkcha bitterly. 'Though it would be against all laws of Xotic hospitality.'

A silence fell over the group as Tlkcha's grief once again overcame her.

'I fear that there is great sorrow that you have yet to impart to us,' said Tishan quietly.

Dansha bowed his head in acknowledgement. 'Our people had gathered on the shore to await their arrival. What they were expecting, none can say, but long before the cursed ships of the strangers had run up on the beach, they began to shoot at those Xotic who were waiting. A great booming sound and smoke and flame erupted from their ships, and whirling spheres of metal scythed through the air, killing many of those standing there. Shashn was struck down in the first strike and was mortally wounded. Several of our people were blown to pieces in the storm of metal. In panic they ran from the shore and, reaching their poctech, set sail and moved away.'

The Graavens listened to the tale in stunned silence. Even as warlike as their own people had once been, the notion of killing people without warning, and who had succoured and supported strangers in need, was deeply shocking.

Fendrax spoke into the silence. 'I heard of what had happened. I and several of my third litter gave what aid we could but mostly we watched these people. Even such as we cannot stand against the weapons of the strangers. Now they fortify the place where they have landed. Smoke blackens the sky. They ride on two-legged creatures, the likes of which neither I nor any of my pack have ever seen. They are swift and sure-footed and range across the plains shooting game. Twice we managed to come to the aid of Xotic who had the ill luck to cross their path. I doubt not they would be dead otherwise; these strangers seem to be without pity. I agree with those here that without your aid these people will overrun Xotic lands.'

A grim look had settled on Tishan's face, one that neither Ankh nor Horven had seen in a long time. When she spoke, it was in the crisp tones of a Graaven Stragosh. 'These strangers will rue the day they spilled the innocent blood of our friends. They will be made to pay, and their arrogance humbled. I am sure there is more to tell us but for now you must rest. I will take counsel with our Graaven elders, and we will determine a course of swift action.'

Fixing her gaze on Tlkcha, her tone softened. 'All Graavens mourn with you, Tlkcha. We understand what it is to battle a foe that you do not understand and see all that you have ripped away from you. We stand with you.' She turned her eyes upon Hermech, Dansha, and Kellix. 'With all of you.'

Later, when the Xotic had been settled and with promises to meet again very soon, Tishan arranged for a meeting with the council that she and Menkh had set up. Prior to the meeting, she removed herself to the viewing room in the Complex and began a dialogue with Varnahrin.

<Were you aware of these strangers, Varnahrin? Is it not possible you could have warned us about them?>

<Hold your anger, Tishan Dar. In answer to your question: Yes, I am aware of them – but you must remember that my primary purpose is the protection of Ta'Morin and your people. These creatures offer you no threat. That they have invaded the lands of the Xotic and killed several does not affect the power of Ta'Morin or increase the threat to your people who lie safe within its protection.>

<And if I choose to turn the power of Ta'Morin in aid of our friends?>

<Your tone indicates that you think I might oppose your wishes. Tishan, I am not your enemy, nor your counsellor. If you choose to aid those you see as friends, then the power of Ta'Morin is yours to command. But ...> There was a long silence.

<But what?> asked Tishan.

<I will not countenance anything that endangers Ta'Morin. There is more here to safeguard than just your people, Tishan Dar.>

Tishan took a deep breath. <I apologise, Varnahrin. I am angry and I sought, wrongly, to vent it on you. I cannot see we have a choice; we must aid our friends. There is a question of Balance here too, I think.>

Varnahrin was conciliatory. <Then what is it you wish to do?>

<Can you show me these creatures? I wish to see them for myself.>

In response the walls shimmered and Tishan felt as if she was travelling at speed above a blurred landscape before the scene coalesced before her and drew into sharp focus. The first thing she noticed was a set of what appeared to be uniformly grey buildings that had been established well up from the shoreline. Several strange-looking vessels lay at anchor and small boats plied back and forth. In a compound a number of the two-legged creatures that had been referred to were tended by people clad in blue garments.

As Tishan's attention became more focused, the images magnified, revealing greater detail. Those in the blue garments were many and varied, some tall like the Graavens and others much shorter. These people were watched over by others who were more regular in their appearance. They were clothed in raiment of different colours, perhaps denoting their station in society. Occasionally a whip would be applied to one of the creatures dressed in blue, presumably because they moved too slowly or were remiss in some matter Tishan couldn't discern. All of those in blue had a look of fear on their faces and they appeared to try to avoid getting in close proximity to those who wielded the whips.

Those who wielded the whips were short and squat, with powerfully built torsos. They all sported long hair and their faces were hidden behind masks. They wore elaborate head gear decorated with long, colourful plumes, and some wore metal breastplates above short particoloured trousers and long boots: some black, whilst others were either brown or red.

Rows of long tube-like devices were mounted upon carriages that had two large wheels on each side. Tishan could also see that many of the strangers also carried miniature devices similar to the mounted tubes, but slung over their shoulders.

A blue-garbed worker who was being whipped suddenly ran away from their attacker. Tishan watched with a sinking feeling as several of the supervising creatures unslung the tubes they carried. They pointed the tubes at the fleeing creature and a cloud of smoke followed by a jet of flame issued from each. Around the creature the earth leapt with the impact of projectiles that, presumably, issued from the tubes. But it was clear that a number struck their intended target, one removing virtually half of the poor creature's head in a spray of blood.

The commotion was greeted with what appeared to be complete indifference from the overseers who, returning the tubes to their shoulders, gave instructions for the unfortunate victim to be dragged away by other creatures in blue. The body was simply thrown into a refuse pile that was some distance away from the main campsite. Work continued on as if nothing had happened.

Tishan was sickened at the sight. Well used to the sight of blood and the cruelty of warfare, the Graaven people had assimilated those they conquered into their empire. If there was resistance it was dealt with, but the Graavens did not employ slavery as a tool of subjugation, nor were they deliberately cruel to those they had defeated. Whilst they dealt without mercy with armed opposition, employing cold and calculated military efficiency, the empire itself was generally peaceful.

'Who are these creatures?' Tishan spoke aloud into the silence of the viewing room.

<As to that, Tishan Dar, they call themselves the Ma'Vessick. In contrast to the Benshin and Xotic, they have developed an advanced technology, but in terms of enlightenment, they are far beneath both. They care for nothing but themselves and enslave those they conquer. Come, let us look upon their homeland, which lies many persangh away over the Great Water.>

Again, the view shifted and swept across the waters. Tishan felt as if she were flying above the waves. Before long they came to a coastline marked by great cliffs covered in a dense growth of foreign plants. Creatures she did not recognise flew on great wings and cried out as they sped above the waves. As Tishan's view swept along the rocky coastline, a vast harbour and city came into view. The sky above the city was filled with black smoke and a huge river, filled with craft of all kinds, poured its oily brown waters into the those of the harbour. Gangs of blue-garbed workers could be seen loading and unloading vessels whilst others laboured to clear filth from the streets. In the centre of the city a large and forbidding temple rose up, its aspect made more chilling by the bodies which hung from dozens of gallows that were set up on all four sides of the building. Here the Ma'Vessick were cowled in yellow robes. Their features, also uniformly hidden by masks, could not be discerned and they traversed the many steps that led up to and away from the first floor of the temple proper.

A crenellated wall encircled three sides of the city and three great gates were visible. Carts and wagons of all kinds were entering and exiting the city along roads that led out into the hinterland. An army of many thousands could be seen marching out. Most of the individual troops were carrying the tube-like devices Tishan had seen, whilst the larger versions trundled along, drawn by the two-legged creatures. Still more of them carried mounted troops who sped off ahead of the marching soldiers, presumably to scout the way forward.

<Behold the city of Gahrtok, the Ma'Vessick capital and seat of their religion,> Varnahrin spoke quietly.

<How could you possibly believe that these creatures are not a threat to us?> Tishan's voice contained the thread of anger that had welled up in her before.

<Tishan Dar, think about your words. In the first place, and until now, the Ma'Vessick had no knowledge of any lands across the water. In the second, their technology is primitive compared to that of Ta'Morin. Even now they do not present a threat to us. It is not for me to make moral judgements on them – they are what they are. You are the Guardian. Whatever you determine, so shall it be.>

<And if I decide that they should be exterminated? What then?>

<Then they will be obliterated, Tishan Dar, and in your own way you will have affected a small part of the Balance. The power of Ta'Morin is yours to command.>

Tishan Dar was set back by the matter-of-fact tone that Varnahrin employed. It gave her insight into something she had not previously thought about. From these remarks it appeared that the crystal form which invested Ta'Morin was completely amoral. Somehow Tishan had perceived Varnahrin as some kind of benign force that stood for 'good'; the reality was actually very different. The capacity to wield the power of Ta'Morin to obliterate life – or indeed to set up a new empire – gave her pause. Her mind turned to consider to what extent she was actually prepared to employ that power to her own ends. It was some time before she voiced her thoughts.

<Clearly the Balance has been disturbed by the arrival of these strangers. The wanton killing of those we call friends cannot be overlooked and I will not countenance the presence of these people, who are clearly here to conquer and subdue to their own ends, on Xotic lands. That they employ slavery to subjugate and enthral those they conquer is anathema to me. Indeed, to every Graaven. So, we shall drive them from our shores, peacefully if possible – with force if we must.>

<Very well,> came Varnahrin's response. <What are your wishes?>

<You have a better grasp than I as to the nature of their technology. We need a force strong enough to nullify them and 'encourage' their return to whence they came. What would you suggest?>

The response was immediate. <A half-file of tetrans will be enough to deal with them. You will also need to transport them. We can establish a gateway. Once these creatures are driven off it can be left in situ in case any future need arises.>

<You think that possible?> Tishan queried.

<These people will not be dismayed by those of them that are now here being driven off. In my estimation, it will simply impel them to return in greater numbers.>

<Then we will deal with that after we have removed them from Xotic lands.>

<In which case, the first step is to establish the gateway that we will use.>

Tishan subconsciously nodded her head in agreement. <If she will come, I will take Fendrax and journey to their location.> Her thoughts then turned to the impending journey.

<Travel in the between would be quicker for you. Fendrax has experienced this before with Menkh so will not be disturbed by it. Besides, I have a gift for you that will enable this, amongst other things.>

<A gift, Varnahrin?> Tishan could not disguise the tone of surprise that Varnahrin's statement had caused.

<Yes. As you are Guardian of Ta'Morin it is appropriate, but it has taken me longer to locate it than I thought it would. Would you like to see it?> Varnahrin's voice had shifted from coldly dispassionate to a more playful tone. Before she could respond, Tishan felt the room around her disappear and mere moments later she found herself in a completely different part of the Complex – and, furthermore, one that was strange to her. In some indefinable sense it did not feel like anything that seemed to 'fit' with the Complex as she knew it.

A single room of huge dimensions stretched off beyond sight and everywhere she looked there were pedestals upon which strange and mysterious objects reposed. Whilst there was no discernible noise of any kind there was a palpable feeling of 'presence', as if someone or something watched over the room and took account of all that entered.

<What is this place, Varnahrin? Where in the Complex am I?>

There was quiet laughter that gave a certain whimsicality to Varnahrin that Tishan had not experienced before.

<You are not in the Complex, Tishan Dar. This place is known as the Repository of Kellen. You stand under the ruins of a city

lost so far in the past that even the memory of a memory of this place is gone from living consciousness. Yet it retains a certain power. To my mind it was one of the possible reasons why the three Adepts who fled the Balancepoint chose to come to Tarvuli.>

<What are all these objects?> Even Tishan's inner voice was hushed as she framed the question.

<What indeed? There is no-one now living who knows their function and, even if there were, there are so many that it would take ten lifetimes to catalogue them all. But there is one thing here that is most appropriate for you, and I deem something that you will need in time to come. Let me guide you to where it lies.>

Tishan felt herself moving as Varnahrin manipulated her body to float a handbreadth above the floor. Objects flashed past her as she moved rapidly through the maze of pedestals and she knew that, on her own, she would have been hopelessly lost in a few moments. Time seemed to have no meaning in that place and the room seemed to stretch on endlessly. At last, however, her forward motion stopped, and she stood before a raised dais on which rested a single piece of crystal the length of her arm. It was the deepest shade of purple, shot through with veins of black and gold. It was altogether a beautiful thing to look at.

<Varnahrin, this is a beautiful thing, but could you not have taken me straight to it when you first brought me here?>

<And where, Tishan Dar, would the fun be in that?> There was definitely whimsy in Varnahrin's voice this time. <Besides, you cannot fully appreciate this place if you don't spend at least some time travelling through it.>

<That is certainly true,> agreed Tishan as her eyes strayed to a slowly revolving set of wheels that stood, one on top of the other, with sparks of light shooting off them as they turned in opposite directions. <It is a fascinating place.>

<So, to business. You need to pick it up. You will feel some strange sensations, but nothing will harm you.>

Tishan stared in fascination at the object and, whilst it may have been an illusion, she was sure that the veins of gold and black moved ever so slowly upon its surface, changing their patterns as they did so.

<What is it? Does it have a name?>

<Oh yes. Although that may change in time to come. Behold, Tishan Dar, the Rod of Klemish. Klemish and Kellen were two of the most gifted scientists that ever lived. This artefact is one that Klemish used to enhance his abilities. Had Klemish lived during the time of your empire you would have thought him a mage, capable of astonishing and magical deeds. But now, you know better.>

<Do I, Varnahrin? Every day I am astonished by 'technology'. How is it that a city which boasted such beings lies in forgotten ruins?>

<Even such as they could not prevent the tidal waves and earthquakes that devastated their lands. You stand many persangh beneath the waves of the Great Water, the lands that once they walked upon utterly consumed.>

Tishan tentatively stretched out her right hand and grasped hold of the rod. The immediate impression was one of coldness, like it had been sitting in ice water. This was immediately replaced by warmth that radiated through her fingers. As she lifted the object it diminished in size until it was only half the length of her arm. Where before she only thought that the black and gold veins moved, now she could clearly see that they swirled across its surface, creating ever-changing patterns. Her mind felt a delicate probing as something pushed against her thoughts. It was not an altogether pleasant experience and the tendrils on Tishan's neck flared red.

<The Rod of Klemish seeks to make contact with you, child. Do not resist it, it means you no harm.> Varnahrin's voice was reassuring.

As quickly as the sensation came it went again. The swirling patterns of black and gold stabilised and the rod itself glowed with a subdued pink light. At the same time a humming sound began, growing in volume until it was loud enough to hurt the ears, before slowly diminishing until no sound could be heard, though Tishan felt a very faint vibration and a soft, tingling sensation in her fingers.

Tishan looked at the object she held in her hand. Along with its size, its shape had also altered. Now it tapered at one end and appeared capped with a metallic ferrule covered in intricate shapes that were evocative of words. But if they were a script, it was of unknown origin and indecipherable.

<Thus has the Rod of Klemish reshaped itself to fit its new purpose.> Varnahrin's voice spoke quietly in Tishan's mind.

<And what purpose is that?>

<Whatever it is, it explored your mind and adapted itself to your needs.>

<Is it like Menkh's staff then?>

<Certainly, it will have some qualities that are similar – but it is attuned to you. Menkh's staff is mysterious, even to me, as there is some quality to it that prevents my probing. However, like the staff, the rod will vanish when not required and reappear when needed. It will be your mission to explore its uses in coming days. For now, though, you may use it to return to Ta'Morin when you are ready.>

With that statement, Varnahrin's presence disappeared from Tishan's mind, and she was instantly alarmed.

<Varnahrin, come back! I don't know how to use this thing; you can't just leave me here!>

But it was immediately clear that was exactly Varnahrin's intention. Tishan fought down her initial panic at being abandoned and let her logical mind quell the disquiet. Varnahrin would not have left her if she was in danger and obviously Varnahrin believed she had the capacity to wield the Rod of Klemish. Her mind turned to the concentration required to translocate using the crystal gems she carried. She formed a clear picture of her home in Ta'Morin and concentrated on the rod in her hand. After several attempts and fighting down another surge of panic, she closed her eyes and, excluding all other thoughts, focused once more. She felt nothing, no sense of movement or sensation of any kind, so it was with some despondency that she opened her eyes – only to find herself standing in the lower room of her home in Ta'Morin. Her eyes widened in amazement.

<Welcome back, Tishan Dar.> Varnahrin's voice was light and bantering. <I am glad to see that the knowledge and experience you have gained in Ta'Morin was of use to you.>

<Thank you, Varnahrin. I do so enjoy these little 'tests' you give Menkh and me from time to time.>

Now there was outright laughter and Tishan could not help but join in.

<I grow fond of you, Tishan Dar, so I think that, albeit unknowingly, you place your own test on me. But come, there is much to do and now that you have the Rod of Klemish to assist you, travelling to the lands of the Xotic should not prove overly taxing. I have prepared the materials required to set up a gateway once you arrive. However, you will need to equip yourself for the journey; it is certain your reception will be hostile.>

<But first, Varnahrin, I must attend the meeting that I have called. Much needs to be discussed and the others must know of the arrival of the Ma'Vessick and what action we will take to nullify their presence.>

<Then you believe that all on the council will support a move against them?> Varnahrin asked.

<Most certainly. We are still Graavens. We may have been ruthless in quelling opposition, but we were, and are, unswervingly loyal to those we call friends. None of us would stand by whilst the Xotic were faced with such a threat. And even if there were some naysayers, our experience under the hammer of the Dorath Mar would be more than enough to sway their sympathies, I deem.>

ooooOoooo

When Tishan swept into the meeting, those in attendance knew immediately that there were ill tidings. She had asked Tlkcha and Dansha to attend so that their presence and a recounting of events might sway any of those who may have had doubts. The meeting with the Xotic was no secret, and rumour of invaders and the savage treatment of the Xotic at their hands had spread quickly. As Tishan had foretold, however, not one member of the council spoke against providing speedy aid to their friends.

As deliberations reached their end, Ankh stood and summarised the outcome of the meeting. His gaze swept over the other members of council, and he gave a nod to their two Xotic guests. 'Then we are agreed. I will assume the role of Head of Council temporarily in the absence of Menkh and Tishan, until one or the other returns. Stragosh Tishan,' Ankh nodded with a smile at addressing Tishan with her old Empire title, 'will immediately reconnoitre the invaders' position and establish a gateway for transporting a force to assist our friends.'

The councillors rapped the table in support.

Councillor Frmak spoke as the noise subsided. 'Stragosh, will we not take a small Graaven force to assist in removing these creatures?'

Tishan turned to Frmak. It still amazed her that he had managed to survive the flight from the capital and the privations that had followed. He was by far the oldest Graaven in Ta'Morin and was well respected amongst all the Graaven people.

'Thank you, Councillor Frmak. It is something that I have considered, and perhaps we may take a small force of Hoplex and Sagit to uphold Graaven honour. But,' she paused and looked at each person who sat at the table, 'I will not expose any living Graaven to the weapons of these Ma'Vessick until we have a better understanding of them.'

Heads nodded in agreement. The Graaven were not yet so many that they could countenance the loss of a single life without good cause, and especially not when they had a force like the tetrans to deploy.

Planning continued far into the night and final details were agreed before proceedings were called to an end.

Later, after a trip to one of the Complex armouries where she had donned protective gear, Tishan stood alongside Fendrax on the field just outside Ta'Morin where they had met their Xotic visitors. Garbed in a metallic fabric somewhat like fine chain mail that covered her from head to foot, she sparkled in the light of Avlar. She carried a pack of provisions as a precaution, lest her journey took longer than expected. Hermech, Dansha, Kellix, and Tlkcha stood close by. They looked in amazement at Tishan's apparel. With her height and the silvery aspect of the metallic suit she looked menacing and otherworldly.

Tishan clasped hands with each of the Xotic. 'It will not be long, friends. Very soon you will stand once more on Xotic lands, and these invaders will have been driven away.'

'Then there will be a great feasting, Tishan Dar, and all Xotic will celebrate,' pronounced Tlkcha. 'The Xotic will give what aid we can, though it may be little enough,' she added wistfully.

'Whatever aid your people provide, it will be most welcome,' Tishan responded gravely. She was about to add further remarks when she noticed another Graaven striding purposefully forward, dressed as she was. It was Horven Var, and it was clear that she had one intention. As she reached Tishan's position she snapped to attention and gave the salute of the Baran Mec.

'Ready when you are, Stragosh,' Horven announced.

'Your pardon, Horven Var. Ready? Ready for what?'

Neither the question nor the tone dismayed Horven one bit.

'You cannot possibly travel alone, Stragosh. I am under direct orders from the Zaltec to ensure no danger comes to you.' She admitted to herself that was somewhat of a stretch. 'Besides which, Shashn was a personal friend and so I require that the perpetrators of his murder be brought to justice under my hand.'

Tishan was both quietly amused and gladdened at the prospect of Horven's company, but she maintained the steely glare of a Stragosh. 'You require? Give me one reason why I should give permission for you to accompany me uninvited?' The tone she used had in the past caused veteran Hoplex to wither like fruit on a vine in a hot wind.

Horven's eyes, which had been focused over Tishan's shoulder, now looked directly into Tishan's. Tishan noticed a certain vulnerability that could only be discerned by those who knew Horven well.

Horven's voice changed timbre, becoming quieter and more intense. 'Because, Tishan, you are my friend and if anything were to happen to you, and I was not there to help, I could not live with myself. Please allow me to accompany you.'

Tishan was deeply touched. She moved forward to place her right arm on Horven's shoulder. 'And what if something were to happen to you, my friend?'

Horven had no answer to Tishan's question.

Stepping back, Tishan directed her voice to Fendrax. 'Are you able to carry two of us, Fendrax?'

Fendrax turned her great head towards where Horven and Tishan stood. 'You have both grown fat and lazy: even so, I believe I can bear your weight upon my back.'

'Well then,' responded Tishan gravely. 'This journey may present the opportunity for us to address both those failings.' She grinned as she looked at Horven. 'Mount up, Shu Lan Horven. Let us see if your right arm still packs a punch!'

Horven bowed formally to Fendrax and then, when the giant Tamut La knelt down, climbed upon her broad back, followed by Tishan. Grasping the Rod of Klemish, Tishan focused her mind on the location that she had selected after careful reconnoitring of the terrain via the viewing room. She had chosen a place a half sem'chaal from where the invaders had set up their camp.

The rod throbbed within her grasp and the trio disappeared into the grey void that was the between. The Rod of Klemish shone a single beam of light that guided them on and Fendrax leapt away, following it. Time moved differently in the between but, at some point, an overpowering feeling manifested itself in Tishan's mind and she asked Fendrax to stop.

Once their movement had ceased both Horven and Tishan sensed a pervasive chill, and a soft wind seemed to whisper around them, cold fingers of air setting the tendrils on their necks flaring. The feeling intensified and Tishan, without really knowing why, stuck her right hand out as if in expectation of receiving something. The Royal Diadem appeared out of nowhere to nestle in her palm.

Horven spoke out in surprise on seeing the Orb appear. 'Well, of all things. Who could have predicted this?'

'Indeed,' said Tishan. 'It is almost like it was calling to me.'

As she peered into its depths, she noticed a dark stain lying within it.

'Well, I know what that is. I cannot fathom why it should have appeared, but I cannot discount the fact that there is purpose behind it.' She passed the Orb over to Horven. 'Stow this safely in your pack. We will discuss it later when we have time and when Menkh is back with us.'

Horven had no sooner done this than Tishan asked Fendrax to resume their progress. Finally, the three of them emerged upon a grassy knoll under a cloudless violet sky. Behind them stretched the endless grassy plains of the Xotic lands, the long, orange-coloured grass stems bending and swaying in the wind that swept in from the north. Before them, the grass gave way to small, stunted shrubs and a sandy soil strewn with small rocks. Even at this distance there was a faint sound that Tishan knew was made by the waves of the Great Water ceaselessly pounding the shoreline.

CHAPTER SEVEN

Menkh and Crixac journeyed once more on the Thread-way, part of reality and yet separate from it. Menkh's attention was drawn from the contemplation of a distant swirling cloud of gas to a sudden and inexplicable sensation that seemed to penetrate his skin and fill him with an indefinable sense of wonder.

<What is that, Crixac? I have never experienced such a feeling before. Is it due to my changed form, do you think?>

<In a way,> responded Crixac. <That, my friend, is the song of the gathanax. The echoes of their voices reach out across the cosmos. Within their song lies both the power to heal and to re-new: that is why their capture and torture was such an abomination. They are truly remarkable creatures. Whilst I knew of them and of their particular gift, I have never experienced such a sensation. All sentient beings are exposed to their songs but generally it is almost imperceptible. Perhaps an unaccountable feeling at a particular time where you seem filled with hope or happiness. That is us responding to the song of the gathanax. We are all blessed by their presence.>

<Truly, we did a good thing in releasing them so that they could continue their journeying.> Menkh's thoughts reflected a sense of rightness.

For some time, they journeyed in companionable silence until Menkh said, <Crixac, tell me of the staff. How did you come by it?>

<Menkh, of all the times to ask me!> responded Crixac, surprised. <And why now, after such a time together? Is the knowledge not accessible to you from my memories?>

<I cannot explain why the thought suddenly surfaced, and yes, I have the memory. But it is always better to hear it directly from you.>

<Well, it will kill some time at the least. We are speaking of a time that is long distant in memory. As I said to you when we first met, immediately after the partial destruction of Kareem Vastar I had, by the merest chance, been able to transfer into the form that you rescued me from. Those first few bach'chaal, as you Graavens count time, were intensely difficult. Just surviving was hard as my new host was almost incapable of manipulating doorways and other necessary devices. But slowly, over time, I was able to adapt its form somewhat and I managed. One day, a number of years – or should I say, sem'chaal – into my forced isolation, the perach I had entered took me to a location that was different to the one I had wished to travel to. As my memories tell you, Menkh, I have tried and failed to find that location many times since then without success. The perach opened onto a tunnel along which were several sealed doors. All but one remained closed to me; to this day I have no idea what was housed behind any of them bar that one door.>

<Surely Varnahrin would have the answer to that?>

<I have never thought to ask. Now that you mention it, I am puzzled as to why I haven't. It seems odd that you should be asking

me questions now when you have had the knowledge, yet never sought to query what, to me, remains a mystery.>

<In any event, let us ask when the opportunity arises,> Menkh said.

<I agree,> said Crixac. <But, you know, it makes me suspect that there is some sort of a mental block in place that perhaps our remoteness from the Complex is affecting. Hmmm, I wonder ...>

ooooOooooo

The Adept Menath sat silently in isolated contemplation in that part of the Complex she had shielded. This was not only away from the prying eyes and interference of her fellow Kareems but also from the presence of the crystal that she had once been bonded with.

A black malaise had descended upon her, and her hands continuously stroked the rod of crystal that lay across her lap. Longer than her right arm and no thicker than her fingers, it had been in her possession for years beyond count. A souvenir from a small moon that she had once visited in the long-ago, when she still travelled. A world like no other, it was strangely reminiscent of the crystalline presence found in the Balancepoint and yet subtly different. She had told no-one about that world, keeping its location secret for reasons she could not explain.

An object that had fascinated and intrigued her, seemingly delicate and fragile, it had proved to be harder than forged metal and could not be broken or shattered, despite hundreds of exhaustive tests to discover its structure. Her mind over the years had focused upon it but still could not penetrate its mystery.

The world around her was changing in a way that she could not control. For a thousand cycles Kareem Vastar had flourished under her influence and that of her bonded crystal. Now that bond, slowly weakening, had finally been severed, and the shard that she had carried away from the Balancepoint pursued its own ends.

That loss alone left her bereft. Now the Kareems seemed infected with some malignant canker that slowly brought out their baser instincts and which spelled an uncertain and dark future. In Paxal and Palluvia it seemed that the same canker was spreading.

The recent passing of her siblings Kortsan and Tambel had produced a further melancholy in Menath that she could not shake. Death was expected after thousands of cycles, but even so, it had been sudden and unanticipated.

Menath gripped the crystal in her hands more tightly, closed her eyes and wept in frustration and anguish. Her thoughts were full of despair. *I will not allow myself to die! Surely it cannot come down to this?*

Strangely, after all this time, the crystal she held seemed now to call to her as her fingers sat upon its surface. An idea had formed in her mind. In her endless contemplation of the artefact she had carried away, she now perceived something that she had not sensed before. True, till now she had not managed to make contact with it, but she felt the circumstances had changed. In this moment of her direst need it spoke to her and called to her, and within that call was a promise. A promise that she would not die but would be transformed, her power transmuted and inviolate and, yes, absorbed.

Menath drew in a deep breath and made a conscious decision. There was no future for her – or none that she wished to continue with in Kareem Vastar – perhaps an unlooked-for alternative had revealed itself. She relaxed her will and her mind, and instead of trying to penetrate the mysteries of the crystal she surrendered to it. In response, black lines of energy flowed through her fingers, along her arms and across her body. Menath felt momentary panic and tried to pull away, but it was like trying to break bonds of red-hot metal. Panic flared and as it did so, a soothing and calming voice echoed in her mind, telling her to relax, that all was well. It was not death, but rebirth, and she had nothing to fear.

As Menath relaxed, the feeling of panic departed, replaced by a sense of wonder. Her perception of reality began to change; she felt her body fall away as her mind flowed into the crystal staff.

As her metaphysical self was absorbed into the crystal, her physical body began to fade, becoming ever more translucent until, within a matter of moments, it had disappeared altogether. Menath could feel no physical sense of herself. Her mind had fused with the crystal structure of the staff. In a very real way, she had become the staff. Her powers were now latent. Her transformation leached out her emotions and she found that she felt neither joy nor sorrow, sadness nor happiness. She was content and at peace and within that contentment was the certainty that a time would come when she would be needed, her powers unleashed. She waited.

Menath's disappearance was a matter of huge consternation amongst the Kareems. Searches proved fruitless and the crystal shard, in the absence of Menath, was unreachable. Theories regarding the disappearance were expounded: none gave any real insight. Over the intervening years her disappearance became a myth much embellished in the telling. Hundreds of cycles passed as the Kareems reckoned time, and the canker of hatred observed by Menath grew and spread, until the fateful moment arrived when the Kareems brought destruction on those they now saw as enemies and, in their moment of triumph, also destroyed themselves.

Within the abandoned Complex a lone surviving, misshapen creature shuffled about its empty hallways. At first, barely managing to survive, it explored the vast interior, slowly becoming familiar with its layout until a fateful moment when the creature entered a particular perach and inadvertently activated a secret key that led to an undiscovered room.

Menath sensed a physical presence, remote from her and yet so close she felt that she could touch it. A probing will, tentative and uncertain, pushed at her crystalline consciousness. Menath perceived that her time had come.

<But to continue,> prompted Menkh after several moments.

<What? Oh yes, my apologies, I was following a thought. So, when I entered that room, which I must say was really quite small, there, in a niche on the wall, was the staff. What its antecedents are I cannot really say. But its possession unlocked a number of things that, hitherto, were beyond my capacity to physically perform.>

<I find this puzzling, Crixac. The power of the staff is remarkable. Even now we are still learning. Why were you not able to manipulate it and tap into it like we do now?>

<Well again, my conjecture, but I was not a bonded Adept, Menkh, and you – that is to say, 'we' – are. The staff gave me power commensurate with my aptitude and ability. In that form my ability was limited.>

<Mayhap Frzath might have some knowledge for us?>

<Indeed,> responded Crixac, <that is a good thought. It may well be that they have information that might fill in some of our blanks.>

Silently they continued on till abruptly the space around them began to shimmer and distort. It was something that they had not witnessed before and was somewhat disorientating. They felt themselves standing on a firm surface, and the great anteroom of the Complex within the Balancepoint came into focus around them. Once more, although the ground under them was solid, they seemed to be standing above a great void. Far below them planets, moons, and stars appeared to slowly revolve beneath their feet.

Before them, Frzath and T'klath, the Kohnoor and Kohnoor Maj, bowed. 'Welcome, Menkh, Crixac. We rejoice at your return and greet you now as a bonded Adept and Agent of Balance. This is a rare meeting, indeed,' said Frzath.

'Greetings to you, Frzath and T'klath. I am honoured that both abbot and abbess should greet me. You were aware of my journeying here?'

'From the moment you and Crixac determined to travel on the Threadway. We will aid you as we can, though as a bonded Adept there is not much more we can do for you.' T'klath's voice was melodic and soothing to the ear.

'Surely, as Adepts of the blue, white, and red there must be much that you can do?' queried Menkh.

Frzath laughed with warm humour. 'It seems that at the least we can give you knowledge, Menkh, Crixac. Whilst we are all Adepts, you are a bonded Adept, and that is a very rare thing. So rare, in fact, that you are currently the only one of your kind. In you all hopes are vested with regard to the Balance.'

'The Balance is all,' echoed T'klath.

'But come, you must refresh yourself. We will meet in the same place as when first you journeyed here. Listen for the chimes and then will yourself to the room. We will be awaiting you and there will be time for your questions and to seek counsel,' said Frzath.

As Frzath finished speaking, Denith, the Adept of the blue whom Menkh had met on his previous visit, appeared at Frzath's side.

Menkh realised how much he had changed when a figure appearing out of nowhere could no longer surprise him. Turning with a short bow, Denith spoke over his shoulder. 'If you will accompany me, Menkh, Crixac, I will take you to a place where you can rest before the meeting.'

<At least he didn't disappear on us and expect us to follow him,> said Crixac with a degree of humour.

<Now that would have been interesting,> agreed Menkh.

After they had refreshed themselves and in response to the summons of the chimes, Menkh and Crixac met with Frzath and T'klath. They were accompanied by Denith, along with Morgath and Plakar, Adepts of the white and red, and acquaintanceship was renewed.

Following some short pleasantries, T'klath turned to mind speech. <Whilst we are aware of why you have come to us, it would be good to hear, in your words, some account of happenings since you bonded with the red.>

<Yes,> agreed Denith. <I, for one, would like to hear it in your own words.>

So Menkh and Crixac shared their memories of their return to Ta'Morin, the battle with the Dorath Mar, and the defeat of the Talixit Ven. Morgath in particular asked questions concerning the Royal Diadem, which Menkh had used to imprison their enemy. After listening to Menkh's responses, Morgath looked directly at Frzath and spoke aloud.

'So, at last we know what happened to the Orb of Kalash. Who could have prophesied its fate, and the use to which it was put in maintaining the Balance?'

'The Balance is all,' T'klath responded.

Frzath noticed the puzzled expression on Menkh's face.

<We apologise, Menkh, Crixac. We forget there is much here that is unknown to you. The Orb that Morgath refers to went missing when Kortsan, Tambel, and Menath fled the Balancepoint with their stolen crystals. Whether it was one of them or their followers that took it, we do not know. Kalash was a bonded Adept of the blue. The Orb was his creation, albeit in the distant past – Kalash transitioned long ages ago. As you can guess, their betrayal was not the worst of it.>

Plakar took up the story. <This is the first news of the Orb in living memory. Of course, we suspected they had taken it, but there was no proof and they had disappeared without trace.>

<But surely not beyond your ability to find them?> Menkh responded. <What of the Intelligence? There must have been knowledge of where they had gone?>

<We are guardians of the Balancepoint, Menkh,> said Denith. <It was not part of our purpose to pursue them. We also considered that this might be an occurrence that was meant to be. Current events seem to bear this out.>

<This is still confusing. Surely you – all of you, as Adepts – have the same power we do?> said Crixac, perplexed.

<No, Crixac. As we have said, none of us here, or indeed any of us who reside in the Balancepoint, are bonded Adepts. There have been none since Kalash himself, though it would appear that somehow Kortsan, Tambel, and Menath managed to effect some kind of bond with the shards they stole. Your powers are unique, not only because of Menkh's bond with the Shard, but also with your symbiotic link to Menkh. There has never been an Adept, bonded or otherwise, with your capabilities. This is not taking into account your staff, Menkh, another remarkable device and surely the work of Menath, who founded Kareem Vastar.> Denith looked around the group and saw nods of agreement from the other Adepts.

<Yes,> responded Frzath, <Menath's skill in the fashioning of devices like the staff set her apart from all others. Her pride in this ability was perhaps the catalyst for the actions that the three took later. Pride, arrogance and ability are a potent combination.>

<Well, it was our intention to enquire as to the origins of the staff and whether you had any direct information about its creator. Although we can speculate on many things, the fact that Crixac seemed to have been led in some way to the discovery of the staff in what was once Kareem Vastar may bear truth to your belief. We can discuss this later when we have the leisure,> Menkh said. <The reality is that we have averted one threat. Now we must turn our attention to the enemy proper. Crixac and I have come to seek your counsel in this. How do we battle such a power as this creature has?>

Frzath looked around the group, briefly making eye contact with each. <We have thought long and hard on this. The Talixit Ven have influence over several systems. Those whom you have encountered are but one of several races whose proclivity for power and domination and appetite for cruelty draw them together in a warped religion, with the Talixit Ven as their supreme deity. They are tools the enemy uses to vanquish and consume the worlds that oppose them. Given the power the enemy has to turn your deepest fears into reality, they are almost unstoppable. From each of the supplicant worlds their followers nurture clones which, like spoors from a deadly fungus, are then sent off into space. In a kind of suspended animation, the clones drift, randomly encountering living worlds they can consume. It was such a random event that led one of them to impact Tarvuli.>

<It seems a rather a hit-and-miss way to exert your power and influence, given the distances we are talking about,> mused Crixac.

<Those we refer to as the Talixit Ven have no concept of time as we know it. One cycle or a million means nothing to them. Consider that in the last few thousand cycles their influence has come to threaten the Balance. This can no longer be countenanced.> T'klath's response was measured but there was an undercurrent of worried concern.

<So then. How do we counter them?> asked Menkh.

<You must eradicate the one being at the centre of all this. Let me recount a story to you that will give you knowledge: and knowledge, Menkh, is power. It begins simply enough …>

ooooOoooo

Vanjika was a biologist, and a newly graduated one at that. On her first mission with the Foundation she, and the several crew and fellow scientists of the expedition, had landed on the small planet they had named Merec after one of their ancient and long-abandoned deities. Merec was goddess of dark places, and the name was apt as the planet was covered in dense and forbidding forest and swamps. They had been gone from the Foundation and their home world for quite some time. The journey here, even at light-speed, was long enough that they had each celebrated their birthing day at some point in the voyage.

Now strict protocols were in place as they gathered data on the strange new plants and creatures that occupied this place. It was through such expeditions that the Norukians had managed staggering leaps forward in technology, capitalising on the mineral wealth and other materials that they harvested from worlds like Merec. New chemical compounds had enabled cures for ailments and diseases that had, heretofore, been killers of entire generations, and the Norukians were buoyed with optimism and pride in their knowledge and increasing wealth.

Now, against all protocol, Vanjika had ventured beyond the exclusion zone Team Leader Hamast had established. She had been chasing a small insect with striking iridescent wings, unlike any she seen before. It had darted between the trunks of two trees whose greenish skin gave off a faint luminescence, on the fringe of one of the swamps that covered the planet's surface. Fortunately, as their exhaustive pre-landing testing had shown, the atmosphere on Merec was quite capable of supporting them. Gravity a little heavier, air breathable – though admittedly there was a faint taint of corruption in the air that emanated from the myriad wet places all around. Still, it was prudent to wear a tough and durable protective suit and helmet. Their vital signs continuously fed back to the mothership that orbited high above them.

As she paused in her journey past the trees and then firmly decided that she was really being completely unprofessional and reckless, she felt a light brushing sensation in her mind. It was a strange feeling, like seeing something out of the corner of her eye and getting a sudden rush as she turned to find that it was nothing – or perhaps something that looked threatening but turned out to be a tree stump or an object moving in the wind. It was even more surprising when she distinctly heard her mother's voice. 'Vanjika, it's so good to see you. It's been so long.'

As the absolute impossibility of this rose up in Vanjika's mind, a soothing and pleasant feeling dispelled all rational thought.

'Is that you, Mother?' Vanjika's voice still exhibited uncertainty.

'Well, of course, Vanjika, who else?' the voice laughed, and at the sound of that warm and cheerful chuckle all disbelief vanished entirely. 'Now, you really must bring your captain here to see me. I have found the most remarkable creature, Vanjika, quite unlike anything you have seen before. I just know your captain will be so happy and, of course, grateful to you.'

The logic of this seemed inescapable. 'Yes, alright, shall I go now?'

'Yes, yes, of course. But Vanjika, don't tell him you have seen me. Let's make it a real surprise. You know how I love surprises.'

'Well, yes, if you think so.'

'I do.'

Had the inflections of her mother's voice suddenly become just a little sterner? Vanjika recalled that her mother could be quite strict on occasions.

'Don't let me down, Vanjika. Promise me.'

'Of course, Mother. Have no fear, I will get the captain here.'

The lie that Vanjika came up with was both plausible and reasonable, and as she was rather a favourite of the otherwise stern and reserved captain, it was not that difficult to persuade him to accompany her. He left strict instructions that if he had not returned by the early dusk a party should be sent out.

Vanjika was quite oblivious sometime later to the horrific screams that came from the captain's mouth, while he still had one. She was having a lovely dream where she strolled happily with her mother, collecting plants. All the while, a black and hideous creature, covered in a fetid slime, had wrapped several tentacles around the captain's body, slowly liquifying his flesh and sucking it into its mouth, at the same time absorbing his very life essence. The captain's screams of agony and terror brought the creature to a crescendo of physical and mental pleasure. Finally, when all that remained was a slime-covered suit, the creature reflected on the knowledge it had gleaned. Far from satisfying its hunger, it had only increased it, and the need for ever-greater bouts of pleasure.

So over the coming days, with Vanjika now mindlessly under its influence, the creature absorbed all of the crew. Then, with a clone of itself safely stored aboard the mothership and using its newly acquired knowledge, it manipulated Vanjika to program the vessel to return to the Foundation. Vanjika would provide the first nourishment for its offspring. Tentatively, the creature felt the tiny filament of energy that connected them. Yes, soon its offspring would feast, and so too would its mother.

ooooOoooo

<… and so, there you have it. The very start of all this and your knowledge that there is but one bloated entity that sits at the centre. Destroy it and they all perish; they cannot live without the mother. Cut off the head and the body dies.>

Menkh spoke into the pause following these revelations. <I thank you for the information, Frzath. Whilst I have a better understanding of the creature's origins, I still cannot see how this furthers our cause.>

<It is simple enough, Menkh, Crixac,> T'klath said. <It is a much easier task to design a plan against a single powerful individual than to engage in a full interstellar conflict. With the eradication of the source, the Balance will be restored.>

<The Balance is all.> The voices of each Adept chorused as one.

<As I assume you refer to myself and Crixac, I cannot imagine that it will be an easy task to sneak up on a creature the size of a

small planet. By now its knowledge must be huge. It cannot be underestimated.>

<Nor do we. Nor do we minimise the difficulty of achieving this. The simple reality, Menkh, Crixac, is that if you, as a bonded Adept, cannot achieve this thing, then we cannot see how it might otherwise be achieved. Open war may take centuries and the result cannot be foretold.>

Menkh sat back and pondered the quest now set before them. <What think you, Crixac?>

<I think we need a distraction, Menkh.> Crixac turned his attention to the others. <You have told us of the enemy and made us aware of its minions. Is there active resistance to the Talixit Ven that might be used to our advantage?>

Frzath smiled and his gaze swept around those assembled. <Your thinking mirrors ours. Come, Menkh, Crixac – this we can show you directly.>

Mystified, Menkh stood and followed the others through the portal. He found himself standing in the antechamber, once again looking down at the floor as planets and other heavenly bodies seemed to move slowly beneath his feet. It was, he mused, like standing over a vast chasm.

<You may be slightly disorientated, Menkh,> Morgath cautioned him quietly.

Suddenly the slowly moving planets seemed to speed up. Everything beneath him blurred and then slowed abruptly. He felt a lurch even though he was standing still. Then, seeming to descend at great speed into the floor beneath their feet, they floated above several planets which had come into focus. Three of these appeared to be inhabited, the largest of them covered in immense cities. Strange flying vehicles could be seen, shaped rather like a Graaven arrowhead. These ships flew at great speed from planet to planet.

<This, Menkh, Crixac, is the home world of the Allroian Hegemony. They colonised these other planets several ages ago and their influence now spreads out across many worlds. They are basically peaceful but their economic and political influence is huge. They are powerful and, more importantly, implacable enemies of the beings you have encountered, Menkh – they who style themselves the Chosen, as well as their allies. They have been warring for centuries, but the Allroians and their allies are building for a major offensive and have developed a new technology that they hope will give them an advantage.>

<What of the Allroians themselves? Have you come across them, Crixac?> queried Menkh.

<Yes. Although when I and my host at that time encountered them, there was no hegemony. They had only just developed the capacity to travel to the other planets in their system. But that was a very long time ago. You would like them, Menkh; as a race they are quite altruistic. Although, as they resemble a kind of slimy jellyfish, their appearance can be somewhat off-putting to a humanoid.>

<What is a jellyfish?> asked Menkh. This query was followed by, <Oh, I see what you mean,> as Crixac shared his memory of them.

<Yes, they would take a bit of getting used to. Mind you,> Menkh added, <my current form would give many quite some pause if they saw me.>

Frzath's thoughts cut across their inner dialogue. <The important thing is that their attack is imminent. Here, let us show you.>

Once again, the planets around them blurred, and they hovered above an enormous construct in space. To Menkh it was like a floating city surrounded by a green haze, with huge, soaring buildings that reflected the light of a distant sun and hundreds of towers, their purpose unknown, peppering its surface. He could see many beings, some Allroian and others of different races, walking between the buildings. All in all, it was an amazing sight.

The city itself was cylindrical and the centre of it was an open space that ran its full length. As they moved closer, Menkh could see that the hole was hundreds of chaal across. The walls, if such they could be called, that surrounded the space appeared to be completely smooth, although a field of red light emanated from them so that the entire opening emitted a reddish glow.

<What is this place?> Menkh asked.

<This,> answered Plakar, <is a terminal. It was developed by the scientists of the Allroian Hegemony. If we drift back a little way, you will see what it does.>

Menkh had no words to respond, so complete was his amazement.

<Yet another surprise for you, Menkh,> said Crixac playfully, but Menkh did not respond, and so Crixac immersed himself in Menkh's sense of wonder.

Slowly the terminal changed its direction. It stopped and there was an enormous, silent eruption of red light. Several huge spacecraft abruptly appeared in the hollow centre. As soon as they had appeared the light dissipated and, other than the muted red glow that once gain lit the inner walls of the terminal, all was as it had been before. Long, tentacle-like arms now descended from what had appeared to be smooth, featureless walls and connected at various points on each ship.

Plakar smiled at the look on Menkh's face. <So, Menkh, to save you asking. This terminal is in contact with another such, though a long way from here. They align with each other and then connect. The red light acts like a gateway and, in an instant, the Allroians and their allies travel from one terminal to the next.>

<Like travelling on the Threadway?>

<Something like it and then again, nothing like it,> responded Plakar cryptically.

<What Plakar means, Menkh,> explained Morgath, <is that the Threadway connects everything, and you can travel anywhere, whereas the terminals connect each other and only travel between them is possible. The terminals punch through space and time. The Threadway sits just outside of reality, of it but not part of it.>

As they spoke, the tentacular arms retracted and each vessel began to emit a green glow from its aft section and move forward, travelling the full length of the terminal. As they neared the end, the green glow suddenly blazed and the ships leapt away, vanishing from sight.

Once again objects rushed and blurred and Menkh, Crixac, and the Adepts arrived at a point where two opposing forces were engaged in battle. Dozens of fish-shaped craft of various sizes manoeuvred through a fleet of opposing vessels. In the depth of space, no noise was heard as intense flashes of magenta and yellow light slammed into deflective shields or, penetrating the defences of some unfortunate vessel, erupted in a fiery glow on the surface of the ship that was being bombarded. Undoubtedly, the fish-shaped vessels belonged to the Chosen. Apparently outnumbered and outclassed, elliptical Allroian vessels showed fierce resistance. As they watched, one of the Allroian ships, attacked on all sides by its enemy, abruptly flared to incandescent white and blew apart. It seemed to swell like an overfilled sack before disrupting into fragments that rapidly expanded outwards. The white light disappeared as quickly as it had first appeared.

Far from attempting to break off the action, the other Allroian vessels seemed to intensify their attack, crippling a massive Chosen craft.

Without warning, and into this tangle of warring vessels, the ships that Menkh had observed leaving the terminal suddenly appeared in close proximity. Unlike the other Allroian craft, which fought independently, these new arrivals formed a diamond-shaped pattern; the largest vessel at the centre with the others in formation around it. From every vessel a lurid violet beam of energy was emitted, each beam coalescing, expanding, and growing in intensity to form a latticework of energy.

The original Allroian vessels, so closely engaged with the enemy, continued to press their attack, outnumbered though they were. Suddenly, confoundingly, every single vessel engaged in battle seemed to dissolve into a vapour that slowly dissipated into space.

<They have destroyed their own ships, their own people!> exclaimed Menkh in horror. <Is their enmity so great that victory is worth the sacrifice of their own kind?>

<Fear not, Menkh,> said Morgath. <No living being was piloting the Allroian craft, only robots.>

<They are like to our tetrans, Menkh,> explained Crixac. <I would like to see that again. It was so quick I did not catch it even with Menkh's enhanced vision.>

<That is easy to achieve,> said T'klath, who waved a hand with a sweeping motion from right to left. Then, remarkably to Menkh's mind, everything went backwards until once again the newly arrived vessels were emitting their beams of energy.

<Watch carefully, Crixac,> said Frzath.

Now things happened at a much slower speed and Menkh and the others could see that the energy had coalesced to such a degree that it seemed to shimmer violently before, by some means unknown, it was released, sweeping away from the vessels that had created it. As it moved it expanded further and further, and as the energy contacted the warring vessels they began to simply melt away. The energy ate through them as if they were paper exposed to an inferno. Then, once it had swept through all the vessels in its path, its expansion continued until it lost all integrity, and faded to nothingness.

Once again T'klath moved her arm and everything blurred before Menkh's eyes until, with some relief, they stood once more on the floor of the atrium, the planets slowly moving below them.

<So, what do you think of the Eye of Malavak?> asked Frzath with a degree of humour.

<Incredible. Something like our viewing room in Ta'Morin – but that is nothing compared to this,> said Menkh. <Though, if I am honest, travelling the Threadway is less nauseating.>

This comment was met with some amused laughter from the others. <Believe you me, Menkh,> said Plakar, <we have all experienced that feeling. It does take some acclimation.>

<Indeed,> agreed Morgath. <One or two of your sem'chaal usually does the trick!> To which comment there was further laughter.

<It is the work of a thousand lifetimes, Menkh,> explained Denith seriously. <Whilst we ourselves cannot access the Threadway to physically travel upon as you do, the Eye adapts it so we may observe events as they occur.>

<This is our opportunity, Menkh,> Frzath continued. <The Allroians will attack the nearest Chosen world with the aim of destroying the Talixit Ven clone they find there. We saw only a fraction of their strength. They have amassed a mighty battle fleet: several, in fact. With this weapon they will, for a time at least, have a significant advantage over the Chosen and the other minions of the enemy. This should provide the distraction needed to assault the enemy proper.>

<Will finding the clone be as easy as you make it sound?> asked Crixac.

<They house their deity in a temple complex where they carry out their sacrifices. This is the same on all of the worlds where their worship takes place. The temples are heavily defended, but with this weapon they should prove an easy target. The Chosen

are arrogant in their belief in the universal mastery of their god. They are in for a rude shock.>

<Then can the Eye show us the enemy itself? It would be good to get some reference to this creature and where it is located,> Menkh said.

<Certainly. The world where it abides is far from here, but the Eye can show you as much as you wish.>

<There is no possibility that it can sense our presence?> Crixac's question was said quietly but with intensity.

<None whatsoever,> Morgath replied. <Remember, we only feel like we are travelling there. We remain safely remote.>

Once again, the floor beneath them blurred and there was a sensation of travelling at speed. This time, however, Crixac manipulated Menkh's body so that the nausea was absent. After some moments, motion slowed, and they found themselves floating above a small world. Its entire surface was covered in a black substance that rippled like water when a breeze blows across it. As the planet revolved beneath them nothing else could be observed. Whatever once covered this world was completely subsumed in the rippling blackness.

ooooOoooo

The creature gorged. Myriad invisible lines connected it to its offspring and it fed. Continuously. Nothing could assuage its hunger or satiate its obscene pleasure in the suffering of other life as it was consumed. But it was not quiescent. Over the millennia, its knowledge had increased as it absorbed the lifeforce of entire races. Where before it had only focused on its ravenous hunger, now, in an entirely inexplicable way, some part of it had become 'aware', and its senses quested outwards, seeking knowledge of that which, heretofore, was closed to it. It sensed, not for the first time, that somehow it was being watched. Its rage erupted so that its body shuddered and waves of energy rippled across the surface of the world it inhabited.

<Hush now. Do not react so.> The voice was measured and soothing. The creature could not recall when the voice had started to speak, just that it did: and it reflected on this, another sign of the change that was manifesting itself inside its mind.

<Yes, yes. That is better.> The voice was soothing, calming. <We must prepare a fitting welcome for our visitors.>

The creature formed a picture in its mind.

<No. No, that is far too crude. No, we shall prepare a treat for you. Screams that will last an eternity for you to feast upon. Oh yes. What?> The voice responded to another image.

<Nothing will harm you. We will work together to create our surprise. Your knowledge and power grow. Soon you will be able to leave this place and travel. You would like that, wouldn't you?> The voice became soft and sensuous, and the creature responded like a pet whose coat was being smoothed.

The voice grew distant. <Then you and I will destroy the Balance and in the chaos that follows shall we dominate all life. Oh yes, what a time we shall have.>

ooooOooooo

<So now you know where it is located. The Threadway will take you there unobserved.> T'klath spoke earnestly. <You and Crixac can make plans on the way, but you will have the element of surprise. As you saw, there are no defences on that creature's world that could prevent a physical assault. So, theoretically, the power of the staff would be enough to totally disrupt all of the energy lines that connect it to its offspring. With those lines severed it will die.>

<Yes. You make it sound simple,> Menkh responded in measured tones. <My experience tells me it will be far from that. Up to this moment we have only dealt with the offspring. Their power

to create a living nightmare is unarguable and I can myself attest to their mental power. They are a force to be reckoned with and this creature is the progenitor of all that horror. So yes, Crixac and I will make plans: but we will also observe and try to establish something that will work. What that is I am currently unsure.>

<We will aid you as best we can, Menkh. The reality is that we have no device more powerful, or with greater capacity, than that which you already have. Yours and Crixac's combined wills and experience are formidable. We can think of no other being that has greater capacity than you to destroy this creature.>

<Very well. Then I will travel the Threadway and observe this thing from a distance. On the way Crixac and I will discuss our options. Let us hope that the conflict with the Allroians will provide sufficient distraction that we may pass unnoticed.>

Frzath and the other Adepts bowed their heads in acknowledgement. <We will observe your progress through the Eye. We have the means to communicate with you and will keep you informed with the Allroian offensive,> said T'klath.

As Menkh ascended the Threadway they clasped hands and, in what sounded like a benediction intoned, 'The Balance is all.'

Once more they travelled silently on the Threadway. Planets, moons, and suns flowed past in quick succession. Great clouds of brightly coloured gases and other phenomenon, vast and mysterious, could also be seen, either flowing around them as they passed through or rapidly diminishing as they journeyed on toward their ultimate destination. Most noticeable was when they travelled past the confines of one galaxy towards a new one. As they entered the empty space between the galaxies, it was as if they jumped over a stream from one bank to another. No sooner had they left the boundaries of one, they entered the outer rim of the next. Occasionally great ships passed them, travelling at what they assumed must be tremendous speed to an unknowable destination. All of these things fascinated Menkh.

<I still cannot fully grasp this, Crixac. This new knowledge leads me to the conclusion that the cosmos, the universe, is infinite. How then can the Threadway possibly traverse something that has no beginning or ending?> Menkh's thoughts radiated the greatest curiosity, tinged with confusion.

<I can see how the knowledge you are absorbing might lead you to that conclusion. The reality, of course, is that neither you nor I have the capacity to fully understand the nature of the universe, or indeed the strong likelihood that we live in but one of many. So, in fact, we could speak about the 'multiverse'.>

<I can barely grasp the concept, Crixac. Multiverse?>

<Think of it in this way, Menkh. We agree that there are things in life that are so small they cannot be perceived with the naked eye, but nevertheless, through the aid of our technology we know they exist?>

<Yes. Though several sem'chaal ago I would not have credited the possibility.>

<Indeed, you, and in fact, all your people, have developed incredibly in a short space of time. But follow this: if there are things so small we cannot see them, conversely, there must be things so big that we cannot see them either. Not only not see them, but completely lack the capacity to be cognisant of them at all.>

Menkh was silent for time. <Fascinating, I have never thought of that before.>

<So, following that line of thought, what may seem infinite to us may, in point of fact, be anything but. Our entire universe may just be a tiny drop in an ocean of similar universes, hence the notion of the multiverse. The Threadway sits just outside of reality. We seem to be travelling at a steady pace because of that. In reality our passage is so swift that, in terms of the passage of time, it will take virtually no time at all to reach our goal; in fact, it may be time to exit the Threadway and determine on our strategy to attack this thing.>

Menkh had barely begun to respond when several things happened without warning.

Firstly, the Threadway seemed to buckle and then shatter, leaving them abruptly floating in space. Quicker than thought, Menkh felt enormous pressure compressing his body. His staff, which he perpetually carried when travelling, winked out of existence and Menkh felt himself confined to such a degree that he could not move. More terrifying than all of this was a sensation unlike any other he had ever experienced. It was almost like fingers reaching into his body and brain. Invasive, repugnant, and defiling. An internal struggle developed as he attempted to resist, but it caused such an extremity of pain that Menkh could barely form a rational thought. He was conscious, however, of a terrible scream as the essence of Crixac was ripped from his body and left dangling before his eyes.

A voice spoke: its volume crashed into his mind and hearing it was like being cut with knives or buried under a landslide. <Arrogant and witless fools! You are nothing and less than nothing.> The voice dripped with venom and loathing. <Know this, Menkh ab Dur – you will lie trapped for eternity in a cocoon whilst everything around you dies and you are powerless to prevent it. This … thing …> Crixac's body, which appeared to be a form of light that hung suspended and immovable, was shot through with veins of darkness and a terrible scream filled Menkh's mind. <… This thing will endure an agony that will occupy a thousand years as I hang him on the Tree of Tangoreth. But your prison will not be silent. You will hear the screams of your people as they die. All that you hold dear will perish, and you will be aware of it and more. Think on this as you scream into the confines of your floating tomb – that you were powerless to save them despite your vaunted powers. Deathless, enduring nightmare. That is your fate.>

With a last despairing cry from Crixac, the presence vanished and Menkh, trapped and helpless, drifted in the cold darkness of space, gibbering on the verge of perpetual insanity.

The four Adepts had observed all that had happened and physically recoiled in horror. As one they withdrew from the Eye of Malavak.

Frzath looked intently at each individual. <We have no time to waste. You must have sensed, as I did, the power of the being that sprang the trap. We can conjecture later as to what it is, but now we must act. We cannot underestimate its capacity to track us to our location. I need not tell you the ramifications of that occurrence.>

<We are ready, Frzath,> Plakar responded. <Shall we invoke?>

The four Adepts joined hands and vanished, reappearing in the cave of crystals. In an instant they had made a psychic connection with the Intelligence. If anyone was observing the Balancepoint Complex, the mirror of that which lay at the heart of Ta'Morin, they would have beheld a wondrous sight. Slowly and majestically the entire structure rose into the air, its myriad crystalline towers seeming to compress and retract so that soon only a domed shape could be seen. Colours of white, blue, and red flashed across its surface. For a fraction of time the air seemed to ripple – and then the whole structure simply vanished. Where it had reposed upon the forest floor only a great, flattened circle, devoid of plant life remained, in mute testimony to what had occupied the space mere moments before. All trace had disappeared.

It was just in time.

An enormous shadow descended from the sky, in appearance like a massive storm cloud. Plummeting to the earth, its descent halted abruptly, and a malevolent and palpable intelligence reached out its senses, questing both the seen and the unseen. It was not long in determining that its intended target had managed to elude it. A howl of pure rage erupted in a thunderclap of such terrifying magnitude that the sides of mountains were dislodged. A shock-wave swept out from the core of the darkness and uprooted trees in a cataclysm of wind, destroying all in its path until the forest, which stretched for thousands of leagues in every direction, was totally obliterated. Satisfying its rage with wanton destruction, the shadow, like its elusive prey, also vanished abruptly, the devasta-tion left in its wake grim evidence of its power and fury.

ooooOooooo

On the world of Tarvuli, Varnahrin's consciousness flowed out-wards from its crystalline manifestation within the Complex. Genderless, ancient, and with enormous power, Varnahrin existed on multiple levels. Its essence was connected through a network of invisible channels, like the synapses of a vast brain flowing through all matter, both animate and inanimate. Its naming by Tishan Dar had been a powerful event and, separated in unfath-omable ways as it was now from the Intelligence, it had adapted to a newly discovered individuality now augmented by its new name.

Contact with Menkh and the investment of its power within Ta'Morin had wrought unexpected but interesting changes to its consciousness and, despite its newly wrought limitations, these were a source of fascination, and frustration. Varnahrin. Yes, Tishan had been clever in the choice of the name. Varnahrin was changing: whether for good or ill, only the passage of time would tell.

In the middle of this internal contemplation Varnahrin felt the psychic bond with Menkh suddenly snap shut. In that instant, Var-nahrin knew that Menkh had suffered a terrible fate and that a new power had revealed itself. There was no sense of Menkh at all, but Varnahrin did not believe that he and Crixac had been obliterated. No, the sensation would have been entirely different if that had occurred.

Whatever Menkh's fate, he was beyond Varnahrin's assistance at this time. It was likely that, given the enormity of power that this new threat must have exhibited, an attack on Tarvuli was imminent. Varnahrin had no doubt that the Balancepoint would be subject to assault as well, but Frzath and the other Adepts would have to deal with that. The consequence of their failure to do so would be dire.

Varnahrin's essence concentrated, drawing in from multiple realities, and then flowed outwards into the stream of power which emanated from the Complex. Its consciousness expanded as it shot upwards until, consolidating as a swirling ball of red energy, it floated inside the field of protection that had been established to defend against attack.

Varnahrin's senses touched many points of the screen, ensuring that all was secure. The attack when it came was ferocious. Multiple points of the barrier were impacted by an energy manifesting as an intense blackness, so that even against the backdrop of space it could be discerned. The force shield bent inwards and then violently sprang back. A flash of golden light that made the light of the two suns seem weak in comparison, was accompanied by a shattering mental scream of pain.

Varnahrin sat motionless behind the energy screen, observing silently, and as the core of blackness recoiled teased out a thread of consciousness and probed the enemy. There was an immediate and violent reaction to the probing, surprising in its intensity, and Varnahrin withdrew. It had already gleaned enough information and this new knowledge gave some degree of reassurance. This thing was connected to the enemy in ways that were intriguing.

Again, the shield was attacked, though this time with more care. The effect, however, was the same, resulting in further screams of rage.

<I see you there on the other side of your wall. You think this will save you? I will obliterate you and all the worlds that sit under

your protection.> The voice was shattering in its intensity but its power to affect Varnahrin was, at this time, the tiniest of irritations.

Varnahrin did not respond although it did allow a certain sense of smug self-satisfaction to bleed across the barrier.

<Whatever you are, I will return! Then, look to your defences!> The voice reflected impotent fury and the core of darkness vanished.

Varnahrin pondered. There was no doubting the power of the attacker. The troubling concern was that it was growing. Soon enough, perhaps, the defensive shield would prove to be inadequate. Drawing itself in, Varnahrin flowed back down the energy stream and reinvested its crystal form, lost in contemplation.

CHAPTER EIGHT

Tishan observed the terrain around her. The land on which they stood was firm underfoot and would allow for ready staging of their tetran force.

Directing her voice to Horven, she spoke. 'I think this area, now that I am actually standing upon it, is ideal. We will establish our gateway here. Fendrax, would you scout the area? It would be good to avoid any unexpected and unwelcome surprises.'

Fendrax emitted a low growl of assent and as Tishan and Horven dismounted, tested the air with her nostrils.

'I can detect the scent of those creatures the Ma'Vessick ride upon in the air. You establish your gateway. I will go forward and observe. I can do this more easily without you and they will have no sense that I am nearby.'

'Very well,' Tishan responded. 'We will await your return here.'

With a soft grunt Fendrax loped away and even though Tishan watched her from the moment she turned to leave, Fendrax was but a short distance away when she seemed to melt into the background and disappear from view.

'Now that is what I call "blending in" to the terrain. Quite remarkable, Stragosh.' Horven had reverted to Tishan's military title, given the nature of their journey. It was one that she felt comfortable with after the ingrained habits of many sem'chaal.

'Yes. Remarkable indeed,' agreed Tishan.

Carrying the cube of black crystal that Varnahrin had provided, Tishan walked a short distance away from where they had emerged from the between.

Placing the crystal on the ground, Tishan sent out her thoughts. <Are you there, Varnahrin?>

<Always, child. I have established the gateway at Ta'Morin, you simply need to activate yours. I think you will find your new toy useful for the task. Summon the rod by focusing your will upon it and then concentrate your mind and point it at the cube. You may wish to stand a little further back.>

Tishan shuddered inwardly at such a powerful artefact being referred to as a toy. However, after pacing some distance away from the cube with Horven alongside her, she lifted her hand and focused her mind on the Rod of Klemish as Varnahrin had advised. In moments, it appeared in her hand. It was still a wonder to her that when there was no requirement for it, the rod simply vanished – though where to, she knew not. Although Varnahrin had told Tishan that this would occur when she had first acquired the artefact, it was typical of the Spirit of Ta'Morin that further explanation was not forthcoming. As ever, Varnahrin appeared to enjoy the little 'surprises' that frequently occurred when information was deliberately withheld. Even so, Tishan believed that this rather annoying habit was one method by which Varnahrin ensured that both she and Menkh developed their own skills and abilities independently. She wondered, not for the first time, as to what affinities there might be between the two remarkable objects of her rod and Menkh's staff.

Pushing her thoughts to one side, she pointed it in the direction of the cube and focused all her mind upon it. After some moments, when nothing had happened, she wondered if she was doing something wrong. Just before she completely withdrew her mind from it, three things occurred all at once.

First, there was a violent rippling of the earth emanating from where the cube sat upon the ground. To Tishan's mind, these resembled the ripples water made when a rock was thrown into it. Secondly, a shock of displaced air slammed into both Horven and Tishan, which made them both reel backwards, only to be sent lurching forwards as the displaced air rushed back into the vacuum that had been created. Finally, the cube expanded outward, rapidly forming the outline of a gateway. The material of the cube flowed upward and around, like water being forced into a framework of glass, until the gateway was fully formed. In the light of the two suns, it seemed to harden into a solid mass, changing colour to a silvery metallic sheen.

'I am glad we didn't stand any closer, Stragosh, we would have been completely knocked over.'

'Yes, I recall Menkh recounting to me a similar experience when he activated the cube, so I took pains to be as far away as practicable.'

<No fun at all, Tishan Dar,> said Varnahrin mischievously. <Still, I am glad that you learn from my little surprises. The gateway is established. Perhaps you may wish to return to Ta'Morin and issue further instruction?>

<Thankyou, Varnahrin. I can hardly wait for your next surprise. Menkh and I do so enjoy them.> Tishan's attempt at sarcasm elicited no response from Varnahrin.

Turning her attention to the gateway, she and Horven walked closer. On their side of the opening, the grassy dunes and stunted trees continued on around the doorway: however, their view through the door looked straight onto the fields that stood just outside of Ta'Morin, where a group of councillors, headed by Ankh, stood, their faces carefully composed – unlike their Xotic friends, whose incredulous looks told their own story.

'Wait here a moment, Horven, while I cross over. Once Fendrax returns, we will see what she has observed.' Horven snapped a Baran Mec salute in response and then waved to those standing on the other side of the doorway.

Tishan stepped through. As before, it was initially like pushing through some resistance, akin to wading through thick mud. Momentarily it was ice-cold, and then the resistance snapped, and she stumbled through the other side, barely retaining her stance.

Ankh smiled appreciatively. 'Still takes some getting used to, Stragosh, although you did an admirable job of staying upright.' The other councillors nodded their heads with some amusement, many of them having experienced just such a passage in the battle with the Dorath Mar.

'Thank you, Ankh,' responded Tishan. 'I am sure you would have been the first to assist me had I taken a tumble,' she said, knowing full well he would have had a good laugh at her expense. She turned her attention to the Xotic who stood nervously nearby.

'You have no need to worry, my friends. Whilst miraculous, the passage across is perfectly safe – although not without its little challenges, as you will see for yourselves.'

'Verily, the power of Ta'Morin is indeed magical,' said Tlkcha. 'To travel so great a distance in but a few steps would be beyond belief were we not seeing this with our own eyes.' The other Xotic nodded their heads gravely.

'Will you return with us and alert your people to our coming?' Tishan asked.

'We will,' answered Dansha. 'It is likely that there are Xotic scouts in the area watching and they may be aware of your presence even now.'

'Good. Then if you have any belongings you wish to take with you, now is the time to gather them and we will cross back together. Ankh,' Tishan turned her attention to the councillors gathered nearby, 'summon the tetrans and have them marshalled, ready to cross over.'

Sensing the change in tone and demeanour Ankh snapped a crisp salute. 'It will be as you command, Stragosh.'

'Very well. When the time comes, I will send Horven back to lead them across. In addition, I want our force of three hundred Hoplex and Sagit ready to be deployed. You know what to do.'

Ankh smiled in response and nodded.

A short time later the Xotic had returned with their meagre belongings.

'You will find it a strange experience,' Tishan said to them. 'At first it will provide resistance to your passage, so that you must push firmly against it; but at some point, and you can never be sure exactly when, all resistance will cease and you will step out on the other side, so watch your balance. It will also be very cold, but that is only for a brief time.' She smiled encouragingly. 'Any questions?'

Nervous smiles and shakes of the head indicated that none were forthcoming so, nodding to all standing nearby and with the words, 'Follow me,' she turned and pushed back through the doorway.

This time she exited with a little more dignity than the first attempt. Behind her the four Xotic, who had no prior experience, staggered out from the doorway, Tlkcha stumbling over Dansha who had tripped upon his exiting. Horven had shot out an arm to prevent Tlkcha also falling. Shaking herself down, Tlkcha grimaced and said, 'Well, that was certainly a novel experience, but one I would be happy not to repeat.'

Tishan was about to respond when Fendrax appeared suddenly in their midst, making all of them jump in surprise. Ignoring their reactions, Fendrax spoke. 'I encountered a group of Xotic nearby. They cannot come to where we are in their poctech, but they await you, Tlkcha, and those of your companions. Follow Avlar as it descends towards the horizon. At your pace you should reach them within a single chaal.'

'You have covered much ground, friend,' observed Kellix.

'I am smoke and wind, Kellix of the Xotic. I travel unseen and unheard and the land flows under me. Hasten now, a large force of the creatures is not far. You will be safe from them in Avlar's shadow.'

Hermech spoke then to Tishan and Horven. 'Ta'Morin will not stand without our aid, little though it may be. We will return with a force of moktech sailers. Not in living memory have the Xotic sailed to war, but we do so now in support of our friends. None will say that you stood alone in our defence whilst we sat idly by.'

Tishan nodded and she and Horven took in turn each Xotic's hand in theirs. 'Fare you well, Dansha, Kellix, Hermech, and Tlkcha. We will look to your coming in the dak'chaal to come.'

The four Xotic nodded and, turning as one, jogged off in the direction indicated by Fendrax.

Tishan and Horven watched them for a short time as they disappeared beyond their sight in the scrubby terrain.

'So, to the business at hand. Fendrax, what did you see?'

'These creatures spread out like an infection. The beasts they ride are interesting. Intelligent. I brushed the minds of two or three of them, and there is a sentience there that their masters overlook, preferring the whip. They have established a main camp: it is fortified and far enough up from their original landing place to be safe from any inundation of the waters. There are several large ships out on the water. From what the Xotic have told, their encampment can be protected also by the weapons that each vessel carries. It is their minds though, Tishan Dar, which are the worst; they call themselves the Ma'Vessick, which I see comes as no news to you. These are soulless creatures, caring only for themselves. They treat the beasts they ride better than the creatures who work for them and that is not saying much. As short a time as they have been here, they have dug and delved, and black choking smoke issues from some of the buildings they have set up. To what purpose I cannot tell, but nothing good, I deem.'

'What of command? Do you see any of these Ma'Vessick who appear in charge?'

'From afar I could see that there is a grander building in the centre of their camp. If there is such a one then it is there, I would think, that you would find them.'

'So then, it would appear that it is there we must look,' said Tishan.

'But, Stragosh, you cannot possibly enter their encampment safely, even if you were to get that far unobserved.' Horven's tone indicated deep concern and Tishan reached out a hand and placed it upon her shoulder.

'Horven Var, you forget the power of Ta'Morin. I have no intention of physically walking into that place. At least not yet. No, I think that there may be another solution for us.' Here she turned her thoughts to Varnahrin. <What say you, Spirit of Ta'Morin?>

<I say,> came the almost instantaneous response, <that you should explore the further use of the Rod of Klemish. Which, by the way, might now be more accurately called the Rod of Tishan.>

<What did you say?> Tishan was stunned with surprise.

<You heard me completely, Tishan Dar. What was the Rod of Klemish has now completely acclimated to your needs. However, perhaps in honour of him that invented it, we might still call it the Rod of Klemish. It has a certain ring to it.> Varnahrin grew quiet for a moment as if in contemplation of something deeper before continuing. <Focus on your requirements and see what your rod comes up with. Of course, the results might surprise you.>

<Thank you, Varnahrin. You are as cryptic as ever,> Tishan's thoughts contained a hint of exasperation.

Once again, however, Varnahrin had gone.

'So, what did Varnahrin have to say?' queried Horven.

Tishan turned a surprised look on Horven. 'How did you know I was talking to Varnahrin?'

'Stragosh, really? After all this time, it is very easy to see when you are in communication. Your facial expressions give it away all the time.'

Tishan was lost for words for a moment but then realised that what Horven was saying must be obvious to just about every Graaven.

'And besides,' Horven continued, 'the Spirit of Ta'Morin talks to all of us, so we are all in tune with Varnahrin.'

'You mean you heard what was said?'

'No, that was a private conversation. If necessary, you already know mind speech can include others. Varnahrin speaks all the time to our spawnlings.'

Tishan realised that she had been sadly lacking in her assessment of the influence of Varnahrin and her capacity to communicate to all the Graaven people, and felt a bit sheepish as a result. Part of her expected a remark from Varnahrin to further expose her naivete but she was gratified that none was forthcoming … or was there a certain sense of smugness detectable in her mind? She pushed such distracting thoughts away to focus on the matters in hand.

Lifting the rod, she spoke to Horven. 'If this is as powerful as I believe it is, then its limitations might be down to my own capacity to wield it. The first thing is to enter the encampment of the Ma'Vessick and see if we can influence their departure without unnecessary loss of life.'

'Any ideas on how that might be accomplished?' Horven asked curiously. She was fascinated by the rod, as indeed she was by Menkh's staff. In her mind their inexplicable powers smacked of magic. Whilst she had grown used to the technology of Ta'Morin, her inability to fully grasp the mechanics of how it all worked so miraculously left her grasping for more simplistic, yet satisfying, explanations that her mind could deal with.

'Well, I don't actually know. But I am going to focus on it and just see what happens.' Even to herself Tishan did not sound confident.

'Well, while you do that I am going to cross back and see how preparations are going on the other side. Is that alright with you, Stragosh?'

'Yes, by all means, if Fendrax does not mind keeping an eye on our surrounds. I wouldn't want to be caught unawares out here.'

In response Fendrax, for all her size and might, composed her limbs and sank gracefully to the ground a short distance away from Tishan. 'Go, Horven Dar, I will watch over our friend. You may be sure that nothing untoward will occur.'

Nodding, Horven stepped through the gateway. Like Fendrax, Tishan also sat upon the ground and composed her thoughts. It was very quiet. No sounds other than the sighing of the wind through the grasses and trees could be heard, and they were almost hypnotic in their effect. Tishan closed her eyes and thought about what she wanted. Something like the viewing room's projection capability but rather the ability to allow a projection of yourself. That would be ideal. But here she was, hundreds of persangh away, sitting by herself on Xotic lands, with no idea how to go about doing this, or even knowing that it was possible. Still, the idea of a projection lingered in her mind and, perhaps in response to these thoughts, she felt a reaction in the rod. It grew warm to her touch and there was the slightest vibration. She did not open her eyes upon feeling this but rather intensified her thoughts on the idea of a projection. The rod seemed to respond. Its heat grew in intensity and the vibration she felt in her hands became more pronounced before both the vibration and the heat diminished.

She heard Fendrax grunt alongside her and when she opened her eyes, she was both surprised and elated by what she saw. There, standing in front of where she sat, was herself – or at least as perfect an image of herself as could be imagined. It was an intriguing experience to look at herself as if at another person, and her eyes swept in fascination over her torso. There were things that she had never noticed before that were revealed as an independent observer. All in all, she decided she didn't appear too bad, given the privations she had gone through.

Fendrax broke into her musings. 'Finished admiring yourself yet, Tishan Dar?' The words held amusement but were a reminder that there were other matters on foot.

'Apologies, Fendrax. You are right to scold me, but you must admit it is an interesting experience.'

'Indeed. But I am more interested in how you get your mirror-self down to the encampment. Can you see through its eyes?'

'Hmmm. An interesting conundrum. I am not sure what to do here.'

Tishan composed her thoughts and looked more closely. There was the tiniest thread, like a pale ribbon of energy, that connected her physical real self to the image. She closed her eyes and turned her thoughts to the projection. Suddenly she felt as if her consciousness had slipped into the image and she could look and see herself sitting on the ground, her eyes closed in concentration.

'Remarkable!' said the image.

'Remarkable indeed,' responded Fendrax. If Fendrax was perturbed speaking to a projection, there was no indication. 'I would suggest you spend a little time getting used to walking about in this form to see what you can do and what limitations it has.'

'That seems eminently sensible.'

Tishan went to step forward, which was much more difficult than she expected. The concentration required was immense. She focused on a tree that grew a few paces away and attempted to walk towards it. One of the first things she noticed was that she left no footprints or marks of any kind. Whilst her legs moved, her feet left no impression on the terrain. When she finally reached the tree, she could not stop herself and walked right through it. She finally halted her progress on the other side and stood for a moment, gathering her thoughts. She had experienced no sensation at all as she passed through the tree. In fact, the ribbon of energy that attached to her real self stretched out behind her, running back through the trunk of the tree.

Amazing! she thought to herself.

Varnahrin cut into her mind. <Soon, Tishan Dar you will run out of superlatives! The day passes and if your plan is to enter the camp of the Ma'Vessick, you had best get on with it. Your projection can feel no pain or any other sensation. It is merely a vehicle to carry your consciousness and assist you in communication.>

<Very well, Varnahrin, I get the message.> Tishan's response was slightly acerbic. <This does take a little getting used to.>

Even in the short time she had placed her consciousness within the projection, her facility to move and function had improved rapidly. Her thoughts were interrupted by the return of Horven, who, opening her mouth to say something, only managed a strangled gasp.

'Report, Shu Lan Horven?' The image sounded similar to Tishan but was like an echo of her voice. Horven, however, was struck dumb, turning her gaze from the projection to the seated figure.

'Fendrax, you explain to Horven, and I will go down to the campsite. It might take me a while.'

Preparing to journey to the camp, her thoughts returned to the image of the campsite that she remembered from her earlier reconnoitring in the viewing room. So it was that the second surprise manifested itself, for no sooner had the thought come than she stood on the ground immediately outside the encampment. Her surprise, however, was nothing to that of the Ma'Vessick who observed this apparition simply appear out of nothing before them.

In the first instance, all those clad in the blue garments of slaves simply threw themselves to the ground in fearful supplication. Their Ma'Vessick masters' reaction was to freeze on the spot and Tishan was able to observe them at close quarters. It was immediately apparent that, without exception, they all wore masks. These were made of some material that was capable of limited facial expression, particularly around the mouth, moulded as they appeared to be to the underlying features of the wearer. However, the overall effect was chilling. Not one of them reflected any sense of beauty but, rather, all were menacing and cold. Tishan wondered what features the masks hid and whether they were simply an affectation to terrify those the Ma'Vessick had enslaved, or some other as yet unfathomable reason.

Whilst the blue-garbed figures remained cringing on the ground, unless brutally kicked aside by their masters, the Ma'Vessick recovered quickly from their shock and surprise. Two of them leapt forward to wrestle her down, only to slam violently into each other and fall, groaning, to the ground. In response to this, several others unslung the metallic tubes they carried, and pointed them at her. She was subjected to a volley of explosive sounds, the projectiles themselves passing harmlessly through her, only to strike other Ma'Vessick standing some way off, who fell screaming to the ground.

A guttural command followed the pandemonium that these actions had resulted in and, commendably to Tishan's mind as a Stragosh, the Ma'Vessick fell back in disciplined order. They proceeded to warily keep pace with her, weapons at the ready, as she walked towards the large and imposing building that dominated the centre of the encampment.

Now she saw that a solid mass of Ma'Vessick had assembled across the pathway to block her as she approached the steps that led into the building. Though they endeavoured to grasp her or strike her down as she drew near to them, they only succeeded in injuring themselves and her progress was unimpeded.

She entered the building's vestibule, from which three doorways led off. The centre doorway was open, and a hallway led further into the building. Tishan made the obvious choice to proceed down the hallway, and arrived at a much bigger chamber. She entered through a plain doorway that four people abreast could have walked through, into a room which she estimated was some fifty spahn across and sixty deep. The floor of the room was covered in a rich carpet of a dark green hue and, unlike the hallway, which was plain and unadorned, this chamber had walls painted a universal black. The effect was unsettling. Located at the rear of the chamber was a dais surmounting three steps. A second, closed doorway presumably allowed entry and exit into the room. On top of the dais sat a large couch-like piece of furniture. It lacked any visible adornment, save for a fur pelt that lay over it and upon which sat an imposing figure. The mask on this figure had a metallic sheen, unlike the fleshy coloured material the other Ma'Vessick wore. From the top of the mask five points that looked like flames extended, and around this a deep hood disguised all other features. The clothes the creature wore were of a purple shade that shimmered in the light from skylights, cunningly set in the roof and centred on the dais. Beneath the robe, its feet were covered in shoes made from a leathery, scaled material, polished to a brilliant sheen.

Whatever emotions the creature may have felt were undiscernible. There was a palpable feeling of menace in that room and Tishan was glad that it was only a projection of herself that stood before the dais. Behind it and the couch, a single object hung from the wall. Made from some black material that seemed to absorb the light, it resembled nothing so much as a desiccated and mummified head. Looking at it made her shudder.

Guttural hissing sounds issued from the mask and slowly their meaning grew clear in her mind. The timbre of its voice set her teeth on edge. It was full of menace, albeit at first the words uttered could not be understood.

'What creature are you who dares to trespass upon Ma'Vessick territory? Speak. Or has standing in the presence of Vekan, first Prolitor of Harkan, robbed you of wits?'

Tishan stood silently for some moments as Vekan, as he had revealed himself, stirred restlessly. Barely suppressed violence emanated from him. Still, she looked at him quietly, staring into the eye slits of his mask. As he was about to speak again, she cut in with a strident and accusatory voice.

'Thieves! Murderers! You defile these lands which are not yours, but those of the Xotic. Your presence here offends me. Your stink shrivels the very grass beneath your feet.'

With a mighty roar of outrage Vekan threw himself off the dais with the intention of ripping the creature before him to pieces. Instead, he slammed into a Ma'Vessick who stood on the other side and they both collapsed in an untidy heap. In frustrated fury, Vekan beat the unfortunate creature senseless to ease the rage that tore through him. Never. Never in all his life had anyone, and particularly a filthy outlander, dared to speak to him in such fashion.

The apparition's laughter cut through him and he stood quietly, perhaps even more menacing for the violent rage he now contained.

'Pathetic fool!' Tishan's tone whipped like a lash and would have reduced a battle-hardened member of the Baran Mec to tears. 'Take heed, Vekan, first Prolitor of Harkan, as you call yourself. You and your minions have two settings of the suns to depart these lands, never to return, or you will be forcibly removed. These are Xotic lands, and you are not welcome.'

No sooner had these words been uttered than the figure simply vanished. Lack of knowing what it was, where it came from, and how valid the threat was only added to Vekan's frustration and rage. He stalked back to the dais and writhed internally at the humiliation he had been exposed to.

His eyes, alight with rage and animating his masked face, swept over the Ma'Vessick who stood in stunned silence. 'Summon Toronset! Now!'

CHAPTER NINE

Tishan's consciousness returned to her body. She found that she had developed a significant aching back from sitting on the ground but noted that she was totally oblivious of her real self when manifesting the projection.

Definitely not something one would wish to do alone. You would be incredibly vulnerable to an attack, she thought to herself.

Horven's voice interrupted her thoughts. 'Are you alright, Stragosh? You have been so still, and I just noticed you moving, which, I might add, was a considerable relief.' Horven's voice conveyed a curious mixture of scolding and concern, which on consideration was probably justified.

'I am well, Horven, and much the wiser for having experienced communicating via the projection.'

'And the negotiations?'

'I had already formed an initial evaluation having observed them from the viewing room. A few moments in their presence confirmed that view. These creatures, Ma'Vessick as they call themselves, are entrenched in their arrogance and belief in their superiority over all others.'

'Somewhat like we Graavens then, would you say?'

Tishan smiled tightly. 'Alike. Yet we were never deliberately cruel to those we conquered, nor did we ever keep other peoples enslaved. In so much as the Ma'Vessick have the innocent blood of the Xotic on their hands and their immediate response was to try to kill me rather than communicate, I chose to negotiate in the long-held traditions of the Graaven Empire.'

'You mean to say,' responded Horven gravely, 'that you threatened them with annihilation unless they surrendered?'

'Something like that.' Tishan was equally grave.

'They took it well then?'

Tishan pursed her lips thoughtfully. 'If by well you mean their leader Vekan screamed apoplectically and writhed on the floor whilst beating senseless one of his minions, then yes. Extremely well.'

Horven nodded her head. 'So, with your vast experience in high command, how would you rate the probability of them actually obeying?'

'Yes. Good question, let me see.' Tishan paused thoughtfully for a few moments. 'I would say, based on my prior experience, which you have referred to, and in consideration of what I actually said, that there is probably more likelihood of Avlar falling from the sky in the next semmit.'

Horven nodded her head, displaying remarkable control by not bursting into laughter. 'Well, you know what they say. If you want to avoid peace in favour of a war, send in a Graaven negotiator.'

'Really? Who says that?' came Tishan's quizzical response.

'I do,' and this time there was a distinct smile on Horven's face. They both laughed. After several moments of shared humour, Horven drew a deep breath. 'How much time do we have?'

'Well, considering that I gave them two dak'chaal, I imagine that they are even now preparing for a fight.' Tishan turned her attention to Fendrax who had not moved from her position and had been following the discussion closely.

'I imagine you would like me to keep an eye on the creatures' camp?' said Fendrax.

'If you would, I would be grateful. We will begin to muster our force and make ready to advance on the encampment.'

'Very well then, I will observe. No doubt they will dispatch scouts to scry out the land and see if they can locate your presence.' Fendrax paused momentarily before she added, 'Such a pity.'

'Pity?' Tishan asked.

'Yes. After all, it is a terrible thing to die alone in a strange country, never to see your home range again. But I like the creatures they ride upon. I might see if I can talk them into changing sides.'

'You can speak to them?'

'Yes, interesting, is it not? My kind have always had the ability to quickly understand the speech of others. They are intelligent creatures but hide this well in the face of their masters' cruel treatment.'

'Whatever you can do to disrupt any plans they might make would be most helpful,' responded Tishan. 'Travel safely.'

'Always.' Fendrax stood upright, shook herself once so that ripples of light from the last rays of Colunda danced over her white pelt, and then quickly disappeared into the surrounding scrub.

Tishan was about to speak to Horven when Ankh stumbled through the gateway, nearly falling but catching his balance in time.

'Ye gods, I hate that crossing. I will never get used to it.' He spoke aloud to himself but seeing Tishan snapped a hasty salute. 'All is prepared, Stragosh, we are ready to cross when you give the order.'

'Horven and I will return with you, Ankh. The light fades, and Fendrax is keeping an eye on things here. We will appoint two Graavens to watch this side and rotate through the night. Horven and I could do with a hot meal, so we may as well spend the night in Ta'Morin. We can discuss our plans and begin to deploy at the appointed time.'

'As you command then.'

With that the three Graavens returned to Ta'Morin, to be replaced by two Hoplex as night descended.

ooooOooooo

Fendrax had journeyed far into the plain searching for the Ma'Vessick scouts she knew must be ranging out in search of Tishan and the Graaven forces. She was intrigued by the creatures that the Ma'Vessick used to ride upon and drag their carts and wagons. They were intelligent creatures, which the Ma'Vessick referred to as renoth. Whilst diminutive in size compared to gonverdeem, she nonetheless felt a strange affinity with them.

Three times she encountered a lone scout. It was not difficult to 'arrange' for their mount to become completely unbiddable, and three times she had swiftly dispatched the marooned rider whilst the previously docile mounts had quietly joined her. In their turn they were fascinated by the mighty gonverdeem, sniffing her coat and tasting the air around her. She bade them keep their distance.

Fendrax became aware of a rumbling through the ground and, telling her new charges to be still, nestled low in the grasses of the plains that bent and swayed in the unceasing wind. She soon observed three Xotic craft, larger than any she had seen before, come sailing majestically past where she lay hidden. Their pettak-skin sails bellied in the wind and the Xotic crew clambered over the outer frameworks, tending to the lines that braced the sails and the tripod arrangement that held them aloft. Silently Fendrax followed.

The moktech sailers swept at speed over the plains, but as fast as they were, their speed was easily matched by Fendrax and her companions. Suddenly there was a call and the moktech changed course. Fendrax's keen eyes soon saw the cause of the commotion.

Several Ma'Vessick scouts had been spotted traversing the plain. In response to the sighting, the Xotic craft deployed into a line and Fendrax could see that suspended from fore and aft of each sailer was a large crossbow. The Xotic intent was clear, and they aimed to wreak bloody vengeance on those who trespassed over their lands.

'Quickly, my children. You must run and warn the others of your kind. The Xotic will not see you as friends yet. You must tell your brothers and sisters they must throw off their Ma'Vessick riders and get away from here. Hurry!'

Without demur the three renoth ran off to follow Fendrax's bidding and as the three Xotic sailers dropped their speed to make their attack, the renoth easily outdistanced them. Fendrax, who had swept around the scouts and the approaching Xotic, watched with satisfaction as the renoth ridden by the Ma'Vessick went wild, throwing their riders to the ground and beating a hasty retreat.

The Ma'Vessick showed courage, she had to admit. Knowing they could not outrun the rapidly approaching craft, those that still had their weapons loosed off a volley that seemed to have no effect at all. A distinct snapping was then heard as the crossbows of the Xotic launched their projectiles. One shot punched through two Ma'Vessick who stood in close proximity, impaling them together so that the shaft held their bodies as they writhed and screamed, slowly bleeding out as they slumped to the ground together. The other Ma'Vessick now turned and ran, the Xotic either picking them off or simply running them over. The three moktech circled around before coming to a halt. Rope ladders were thrown down and individual Xotic clambered to the ground to deal with those Ma'Vessick who were wounded but still living.

Fendrax revealed herself and slowly approached the three Xotic craft, to be met by Tlkcha who, disembarking herself, bowed low in greeting.

'Welcome, Fendrax. It has been long since your kind travelled the plains of the Xotic. You are welcome.'

Fendrax lowered her head and sniffed Tlkcha's face. 'I see you, Tlkcha of the Xotic. I see the magic of Ta'Morin persists and we understand each other's speech. You dispatched those Ma'Vessick efficiently. I have met three others this day who will not return to their homeland.'

Tlkcha's features were sombre. 'We kill out of necessity, Fendrax, and take no joy in it, but we will avenge our dead and protect what is ours. We are glad that you are safe.'

Fendrax dipped her head in response. Suddenly, behind Fendrax, several of the renoth appeared, galloping towards where Fendrax stood. The Xotic moved in alarm at what they first thought was an attack.

'Do not be afraid, Tlkcha, and you others: these creatures will not harm you. They, too, were enslaved by the Ma'Vessick. They are called renoth and they are intelligent and gentle animals.'

The creatures came to an abrupt halt, snorting and champing.

Tlkcha looked at them curiously. They possessed a striking appearance, with large black eyes that drew you in to their liquid depths and a greenish-yellow coat that seemed to blend in with the wild grasses of the plains. Tlkcha collected her thoughts. 'Then they too are most welcome. If they wish, they may make their home here.'

Fendrax conveyed this message.

'Thank you! Thank you!' they called out, though to the Xotic it sounded like so much piping and braying.

Fendrax told the Xotic that the renoth were very grateful and thought the Xotic lands were beautiful and much like their own homeland far away. They also asked if the Xotic would do them a further kindness and remove the harnesses and saddles that each had attached to them. This the Xotic did with alacrity, becoming quite enamoured of the creatures in the short time they had known them.

Freed now from the accoutrements they loathed, the renoth milled around happily until, as if by unspoken agreement, they suddenly bounded away.

'They are beautiful creatures; I admit to wondering what it would be like to ride upon their backs. With their permission, of course,' mused Tlkcha. Other Xotic nodded their heads in agreement.

'Well, perhaps you may have that opportunity in time to come,' observed Fendrax. 'In the meantime, I must return to Tishan. You make your way to the Ma'Vessick encampment?'

'We do,' responded Tlkcha. 'Though if we encounter more Ma'Vessick scouts we will be delayed: we will not brook them on our lands.'

'Then we will meet again soon.' Fendrax nodded her head by way of farewell and loped away.

Tlkcha watched her until, in a surprisingly short time, she disappeared from view.

'What shall we do with these bodies, Tlkcha?' one Xotic asked.

Tlkcha cast a glance over the dead Ma'Vessick scattered around them. 'Leave them for the Sky Father to deal with. We are done with them.'

Turning her attention to their vessels she ordered sails to be hoisted and, like Fendrax, they too soon disappeared, searching for more Ma'Vessick intruders, leaving the bodies to rot amongst the sighing grasses.

ooooOoooo

Plans and preparations continued in Ta'Morin. Long before Avlar had risen above the horizon on the third day, and whilst the land was still lit under the light of Orvasne, Tishan and Horven returned to the chosen site on Xotic lands.

The two guards on duty snapped to attention.

'Anything to report?' Horven asked as Tishan stood silently by her side.

'Nothing, Shu Lan. Fendrax returned briefly in the night but other than the call of wild creatures and the wind through the grass, nothing else disturbed the night.'

'Very well. Cross back and inform Ankh that he may begin to send our tetrans across.'

Saluting once again, the two guards disappeared through the gateway and shortly the first elements began to arrive. Tishan directed them to level ground away from the gateway with ample room to accommodate the half-file: some 2500 individuals once they had fully deployed.

It took less than one chaal for the tetrans to be assembled. Arrayed in five ranks of five hundred, they stood silently. A single individual stepped forward and saluted Tishan in the Graaven manner.

'I am Second of the File. What is your command?' The metallic voice of the tetrans was one that Tishan was never quite comfortable with. It had a disembodied quality which was unsettling and, not for the first time, she was glad that the tetrans were on their side.

'We will move forward. I have given the Ma'Vessick the two dak'chaal I promised, so our intention is to show ourselves to them and advance on their encampment. I believe they will attack. Remember that the creatures we face have weapons that shoot solid projectiles.' Tishan was about to add more when Second of the File cut in.

'We have been fully briefed by Varnahrin, Stragosh. We are prepared to meet them. In the event of attack do you require prisoners?'

'Those dressed in blue are not to be harmed unless it is unavoidable. If the Ma'Vessick surrender, they may be taken alive and held captive. If they choose to fight, you will oppose them, and they will suffer the consequences. We may encounter scouts on the way, although Fendrax has been out there all night, so it is likely that they have been dealt with.'

'Then we await your command, Stragosh.'

Tishan surveyed the assembled force critically. The tetrans, with their metallic and alien aspect, would chill the heart of most creatures. Gathered together near the gateway was the Graaven force that she had asked Ankh to prepare. Their faces were as familiar to her as her own and there was not one Hoplex or Sagit present for whom she would not willingly have laid down her own life to save, if required. They, too, looked formidable in the garb of Ta'Morin and had only to don their helmets to render their own aspect alien. One hundred and fifty Sagit clutched the long staves of their war bows, modified with the technology of Ta'Morin. An even deadlier weapon than before, capped as they were with an explosive force that had blown many of the Dorath Mar to fragments. The Hoplex each held a heavy mace: these, too, were imbued with a percussive force that belied their appearance.

She smiled at them as they stood awaiting her command before addressing them in a voice that had carried over many a battlefield. 'This day we march to war together in defence of our friends, whose innocent blood was spilled and whose lands these Ma'Vessick seek to take. All of us here know what that feels like. I feel pity for the creatures we face, who have never experienced the wrath of the Graaven people. Look to yourselves this day. Their weapons are deadly and not something you will have encountered. Those you see dressed in robes of blue are slaves, bound to the will of their masters and treated with cruelty. Spare them if you can. Any who surrender may be taken captive, those who choose to fight will die.' She paused. 'Will you stand with me once again?'

As one, each Graaven gave the Baran Mec salute, their right arms clashing across their chests. Words were unnecessary in that moment. Every Graaven there was a veteran of more fights than could easily be recalled and their faith in Tishan was only surpassed by that of their faith in Menkh ab Dur, their Zaltec.

Tishan nodded and faced the front. There was a thrill of anticipation that surprised her. 'Advance!'

ooooOooooo

It was mid-morning of the day that the ultimatum expired. Vekan had been expecting an attack and the Ma'Vessick had spent time shoring up their defences and deploying all available troops. It had taken Vekan several hours to get over his rage and frustration. Several slaves had paid the ultimate price to assuage his temper. If not for the intervention of Toronset, High Priestess of Harkan, his rage may have lasted even longer.

Toronset stood quietly behind Vekan as he cast his eyes over the troops. Even Toronset's calming presence could not diminish his concern at the lack of information regarding any enemy movements. Not one of the several scouting parties he had sent out had returned, adding to a growing fear that Vekan would never have admitted to any of those Ma'Vessick who had voyaged with him to this new land: that the threat, as unbelievable as it was, had real power to affect yet another triumphant Ma'Vessick conquest.

The Ma'Vessick had risen from general obscurity to dominance in a few short years. Their rise to power coincided with their adoption, as a state religion, of the worship of Harkan, although had anyone sought to recall the exact circumstances that led to this rise there would have been no clear answer. It was as if the memory of these things had been expunged from the Ma'Vessick race. The rise of this new cult had witnessed significant changes to

Ma'Vessick society, along with the eradication of any and all individuals whose beliefs did not reflect that required by the State, or indeed of anyone who spoke against the new religious practices.

The priests of Harkan had, in their turn, risen in dominance over all aspects of Ma'Vessick life. They were masters of technological development in the instruments of war and pursuit of military dominance. It was they who had shown the Ma'Vessick how to produce the weapons that allowed them to subjugate the races who occupied lands adjacent to theirs. Great factories arose, whose engines throbbed night and day, belching black smoke and polluting the land all around to feed the machinery of war.

The suppression of tolerance in place of the veneration of all things Ma'Vessick had sanctioned enslavement of other peoples, and the Ma'Vessick had profited immensely from cheap labour. The cruel and vicious treatment of those enslaved had reinforced qualities in the Ma'Vessick race approved by their religion. Ritual mutilation of their faces as an expression of religious adherence became the norm, and the wearing of masks was not to cover their horror from others but to reinforce the absence of any weak emotions like fear, love or compassion to other inferior beings. Only in religious observance, which all but the Ma'Vessick were banned from attending, were their faces uncovered to each other. The worse the mutilation, the higher esteem it brought.

Other races, like the Xotic, whom they had killed without compunction, were seen as so inferior to the Ma'Vessick that their only use was as slave labour, to be worked to death as required or simply killed if necessity or simple whim dictated. Whatever they had once been, as each new generation reached maturity, they grew in cruelty, arrogance, and pride.

Vekan felt Toronset's arm lightly touch his shoulder and she whispered in his ear. 'Calm yourself, Vekan. Nothing can stand against the firepower of the Ma'Vessick people or stand against the will of Harkan.'

'All praise to Harkan,' Vekan echoed in the ritual response to the use of Harkan's name. 'Still, I do not like it. I have placed our forces in a strong position, but this is an enemy we have not faced before. How was that creature able to enter our perimeter and hall like a living ghost and then disappear, impervious to our efforts to stop it?'

The same unsettling thoughts had troubled Toronset. Not for the last time had she rued being absent from the encampment when the visitation occurred. However, she was convinced it was no more than trickery meant to frighten them. Well, if they wanted fear, then they would be shown real fear in time to come under the knives of Harkan.

'It is all part of our master's plan. Never doubt the dominance of our race, Vekan. This is just another rabble that we will put to the sword or grind under our whips.'

Vekan grunted in response. He was reassured by Toronset, and was she not a high priestess? Vekan had been jubilant when Toronset announced her plan to accompany the expedition that he had the honour to lead. Naturally he had assumed this was a reward for his devotion to Harkan and his victories over the Par and Holim, their lands now under the heel of the Ma'Vessick.

It had all started propitiously enough, and they had easily mown down the primitive creatures they encountered. Even now the great ships that sat close in shore had their guns primed and would destroy any force that approached within range. Vekan smiled to himself. Nothing could live through the hail of projectiles that they could fire.

He looked at his arrayed forces. Five thousand veteran troops with the latest persuader firearms, their triple line interspersed with bombards, heavy artillery that could throw an iron ball one thousand paces. On each wing, two squads of cavalry. Their mounts, he noted, strangely disquieted, moved about nervously despite the whips and spurs of their riders that sought to quieten them.

'Nessa!' he called to his second. 'Send a rider to each wing and tell them if they don't settle, I will have their commanders ritually sacrificed tonight.' Vekan spoke quietly, in such a matter-of-fact manner it was enough to add an additional element of menace.

'At once, High One,' Nessa responded before running off to see the order obeyed.

Vekan nodded with satisfaction, dismissed any doubts he had, and settled down to wait for the attack he was sure was imminent.

ooooOoooo

The Graaven advance had been unremarkable. After two chaal Fendrax had rejoined them and convinced Tishan to climb up on her back for, as she explained, 'You will make an even more menacing figure and, of course, you will see further.'

Unable to counter such unassailable logic, Tishan had acquiesced and discovered the added advantage that she could easily be seen by all who accompanied her. Many a Graaven thought how like a Pohlan Kar she looked, clad all in metallic silver, the crystal rod that she carried occasionally flashing in the light of the suns, and riding on the back of the great Tamut La, the name their friends the Benshin gave to the gonverdeem.

Finally, they came to a slight rise and Tishan, commanding all to halt just beneath the skyline, rode forward to observe. Beneath her the land fell away in a gentle but steady slope of sandy soil, all the way to the Ma'Vessick encampment. Patches of a reddish coloured succulent spread like a carpet over the terrain. As yet her presence had not been detected by those waiting below and she could see at once they were drawn up for a fight. Three long lines of troops spread out across the entrance to the camp and on each flank, two units of mounted soldiers were arrayed, seated upon renoth. However, the renoth moved restlessly, despite the efforts of their riders to settle them.

'Would you like to see the first surprise, Tishan Dar?' Tishan detected a somewhat mischievous tone in Fendrax's voice.

'That will depend on the surprise. Varnahrin's little surprises can leave me a little challenged.'

'Oh, I think you will like this one. But you may wish to put on your helmet.'

'Very well,' Tishan was definitely intrigued. The helmet settled on her head and locked into place. Almost at once read outs could be seen on the inside of the clear faceplate. 'Yes, I am ready, Fendrax.'

The surprise was manyfold. In the instant that Tishan indicated she was ready, Fendrax tensed and unleashed a roar greater than Tishan thought any living animal could make. She was convinced that had she not donned the helmet she would have been deafened. Only her knees locked in behind Fendrax's head prevented her from falling off. The second surprise was the reaction of the renoth. If they had been restless before, it was as nothing to what happened after the roar. They simply went berserk. Most riders were either thrown violently from their backs or clung desperately for a time. Others with feet caught in stirrups were dragged along as, with one accord, the renoth simply charged up the long slope toward where Fendrax stood.

As they approached, Tishan could hear intelligible speech, very similar to that of the gonverdeem.

'We come, we come, blessed one! We will never return to those who held us in servitude.' As they approached, they milled around Fendrax, who stood imperiously above them all. Tishan had never seen anything like it.

'Hush now, my children,' Fendrax was commanding in the way that a parent might speak to a wayward spawnling. 'Hearken to me and quieten yourselves. You have done well and honoured your promise to me. Look behind me and all around, these are the lands of the Xotic. They welcome you and say you are free to range across them where the will of the herd leads. They will not harm you nor seek to enslave you. Go in peace.'

One renoth, larger than the others, walked up quietly and reached up to touch noses with Fendrax.

'Thank you, Mother. You and all your kind will be welcome among us. We will watch out for these Xotic and perhaps it may be that we can aid them in time to come.'

'Perhaps,' echoed Fendrax.

'Is this one on your back a Xotic?' one of them called out.

'No, this is Tishan Dar. She is a Graaven. All her people are friends of the gonverdeem and so are your friends, too.'

'Greetings, Tishan Dar,' several voices called out, but they drew back fearfully when Tishan removed her helmet.

The gem in Tishan's belt rapidly translated their speech. 'Do not be alarmed, friends. I mean you no harm. This covering is to protect me from those from whom you have fled.'

'They are cruel and vicious. You must be careful,' several called out.

'We will be. Now you should go. There will be a fight here and I would not want any of you to be hurt. Behind us, quite close by, are many of my people. Do not be alarmed; they will not harm you and they will aid you in removing the saddles that you carry. Go in peace.' Tishan had quietly issued instructions to the Graaven forces through her helmet comm about the renoth, expressly commanding that the creatures were not to be harmed.

'Thank you, Tishan Dar,' several of them called out.

As one they turned and, plunging over the dune's lip, sped off. Cries of surprise could be heard from the Graavens whilst the tetrans stood impassively as the renoth swept up to them. As with the Xotic, the Graavens found them pleasing to look at and rapidly assisted them in removing their Ma'Vessick harnesses. To Graaven ears their calls sounded like braying. In reality, they were cries of happiness, unfettered and unrestrained.

'They are so like children, Fendrax.'

'They are indeed, Tishan Dar. Though there is a wisdom about them too. Their erstwhile masters stand even more condemned to have inflicted such cruelty upon them.'

'A reckoning is coming, so let us be about it,' responded Tishan gravely.

ooooOooooo

Vekan sat on a raised dais several paces behind the arrayed forces of the Ma'Vessick. He had observed the creature that had visited them ride, on the back of a huge and savage-looking predator, over the brow of the hills that ran up and down the coast from the Ma'Vessick landing place. His initial confidence in the strength of his forces had been badly undermined by recent events and he smashed his fists in impotent rage on the arms of his chair.

Dozens of Ma'Vessick could be seen lying prone on the ground whilst others limped back toward their lines. Vekan could not imagine what had prompted the renoth to act in the way they had. He suspected the workings of the enemy but could in no way fathom how they had achieved the total defection that had resulted, nor could he begin to understand how the renoth could approach, en masse, the beast that stood so majestically on the crest of the hill. The creature was well out of range of his bombards and was too small a target for the larger guns on the Ma'Vessick ships that lay offshore. There was disquiet in the ranks, too, but the shouted commands of officers, along with a few blows, quelled it.

The Ma'Vessick had no sooner settled than the entire enemy force revealed itself, sweeping over the hill and steadily approaching their lines. Vekan lifted his scope to his eyes and drew a deep breath. This army was like none he had ever seen. A strange shimmering in the air before them could not disguise the fact that the bulk of the force marching toward him were not flesh and blood.

They walked with a strange gait, moving fluidly over the ground, like dancers moving to an unheard music. They looked to be made of glass that nevertheless had a metallic sheen – the only comforting factor being that the Ma'Vessick outnumbered them.

As they came into range the great bombards of the Ma'Vessick ships erupted in smoke and flame and the whistling sound of projectiles screamed over the ranks of the Ma'Vessick, plunging down into the advancing foe. In moments, Vekan's surprise robbed him of speech. Where he had expected a maelstrom of violence and the bodies of the enemy smashed into destruction, the projectiles seemed to make no impact at all. The only disturbance was made by those which had missed their target to left and right. There the earth was churned as they smashed into the ground and great gouts of soil were lifted into the air. Over the enemy the air seemed to compress, a shimmering which grew in intensity: and then the weight of metal fired from the ships seemed to disappear, either deflected away or, by some unknowable means, destroyed.

Now the front ranks of the enemy came in range of the smaller bombards that punctuated the Ma'Vessick troops. The bombardment from the ships ceased as the danger of their shot falling into their own was too great. All along the line these smaller weapons erupted in flame, spitting out their balls of metal into the oncoming ranks. The effect was exactly the same as with those of the larger bombards, and still the enemy came on, soundlessly and without check. No cheers or cries could be heard. The only sounds were those made by the Ma'Vessick. Vekan could sense the fear rising in the troops deployed before him. No Ma'Vessick force had ever been defeated, not since the priests of Harkan had introduced them to the technology that enabled their superiority over all other races. It was a new experience, and an unwelcome one.

Toronset moved up and stood alongside Vekan. 'Harkan will not allow us to be defeated, Vekan. As long as our people stay steady, we will win the day. I will personally join this fight.'

'You will invoke the Wrath of Harkan?'

'I carry one of his Instruments and we will sweep this carrion from the field.'

Vekan met Toronset's gaze. He had heard of the use of the Deity's Instruments and, although he never witnessed it, it soothed his fears and filled him with renewed confidence.

'Then may the will of Harkan fill you.'

Toronset nodded at the blessing. She was filled with a steely determination. At last, she was in a position to deploy the Wrath and her elevation to the Grand Circle would be complete. Her two acolytes unlocked the gilt box that the Instrument was carried in. It had been entrusted to her by Radek himself, the Grand Master of the Order, with strict instructions only to use it in direst need. This, she determined, was now.

The noise of battle increased. The enemy had moved within range of their shooting irons and the lack of any effect was causing a tremor in the lines.

Hefting the black banners of Harkan, with their silver sigillary representing power and might, she advanced, holding on to the Instrument – a long crystalline tube. As she strode through the ranks the Ma'Vessick were reassured by the sight of the sigils and the presence of Toronset herself. All Ma'Vessick knew of the Wrath of Harkan, but none had seen one of the Instruments used. She reached the centre of the line and lifted the Instrument, pointing it towards the enemy who were now but three hundred paces distant.

ooooOoooo

Tishan sat calmly on the back of Fendrax. Around her were her Graaven warriors. They had advanced behind the tetrans, some fifty paces back from the last rank and protected from the enemy weapons by the shield that the tetrans had deployed. She was reassured at the lack of effect of the Ma'Vessick weaponry, though the sound was deafening. Black smoke choked the battlefield, but its effect was limited as the constant wind from over the water dispersed it quickly enough.

As the tetrans advanced closer and closer she saw they had reached a point where they could counter the enemy fire with deadly efficiency, and she could see their energy weapons being deployed for that purpose. Suddenly Varnahrin's voice echoed in her mind. <Beware, Tishan Dar! The enemy has their own energy device!>

The warning had no sooner come than a virulent purple beam of light shot out from the centre of the Ma'Vessick line. It punched a hole though the tetran force shield and, in the blink of an eye, vapourised fifty of them. A huge cheer erupted from the Ma'Vessick line, which rapidly turned to screams of horror as the main force of tetrans activated their own weaponry. Brilliant blue lines of energy flashed out, a counter to the virulent purple light, and entire ranks of Ma'Vessick fell.

Again, the purple light flew out and another section of tetrans were consumed; however, it was fewer than before and Tishan noticed that the shimmer in the air had changed in quality.

Tishan spoke into her helmet 'Second of the File, can you hold?'

The metallic voice responded instantly. 'We have recalibrated the shield but we cannot completely neutralise the enemy weapon. The solid projectiles will cause damage but it is manageable. Our own weaponry appears ineffective against the wielder.'

'Would a distraction assist?' Tishan queried.

'Certainly.'

Tishan turned her attention to the Graavens who stood nearby. 'Harmex, I want that creature with the weapon in the centre of the line distracted.'

Harmex smiled to himself and in response to Tishan's order he used arm gestures to shake his Sagit into three well-spaced ranks.

'On my command, loose shafts and concentrate on the centre where you see that purple light,' he ordered crisply.

One hundred and fifty bows pointed skywards and released as one on the command, 'Loose!' Moments later a second wave, then a third and fourth followed, so that no sooner had the first flight reached its zenith and plunged towards the enemy than the next followed.

ooooOoooo

Toronset was jubilant. Whilst the weapons of the enemy dealt their own waves of death, the Wrath of Harkan was effective beyond her dreams and she was getting more proficient at using it.

She exulted when another section of the enemy was vapourised before her but the laugh that came to her lips was cut short by a brilliant burst of light, followed by a violent percussion of the air that drove her to her knees and totally numbed her senses. This was followed by a second and third, making her mind cringe. She could not find the will to focus on the Instrument. The sigils of Harkan were shredded and hundreds of Ma'Vessick were simply blown to pieces, gobbets of blood and flesh spraying into the air and splattering those who had managed to survive the onslaught. The terror that the Ma'Vessick inflicted on a daily basis to those they had conquered was repaid in kind in that moment.

Somehow, miraculously to her dazed mind, Toronset was relatively unscathed, albeit thrown to the ground, but so disorientated that she could not even find the strength to stand.

She felt herself pulled to her feet, not by Ma'Vessick hands, and the Instrument was torn from her grasp. Around her, what was left of the Ma'Vessick threw down their arms or simply sat whimpering on the ground. The violence of the last assault was so overwhelming that any thought of organised resistance was impossible. Toronset tried to focus on the creatures that held her fast: but her eyes could not manage even that simple a task, so it was that with ears ringing and blurred vision she was at first dragged, and then lifted and carried off. Her mind could not focus and she was unable to manage a coherent thought before her consciousness slipped away.

ooooOoooo

Tishan watched the first and second wave of shafts rain down on the enemy. As the fourth flight sprang from the bows of the Graaven Sagit, she gave the command to halt. The Ma'Vessick line had ceased to exist in the centre, and everywhere those who had survived looked on in horror and threw their weapons to the ground. Their commander had been thrown violently from his dais and lay prone on the ground. As the enemy sought to stand, they were rounded up by the tetrans and prodded toward a holding area. Violence was unnecessary: the Ma'Vessick were too cowed to offer any resistance.

Removing her helmet, Tishan rode down toward the encampment, accompanied by her cohort of Graaven troops. It appeared that their commander had survived as he, too, was pushed toward the holding area, a large pen that the Ma'Vessick had constructed to hold their slaves when required. At first Tishan was fearful that the slaves had all perished or been eliminated by their captors, but a search of the compound by her Hoplex revealed that they had been chained together and placed in a large building some distance away from where the battle had taken place.

'Shu Lan Valash, take a praka and unchain the slaves. Treat them gently and bring them to me.'

Valash saluted and, indicating those who would accompany him, jogged off.

The tetran force was busy rounding up surviving Ma'Vessick, herding them towards the holding area, and gathering up fallen and abandoned weaponry. Second of the File approached Tishan where she stood with Horven.

'Stragosh, the enemy vessels have withdrawn further from the shore. They still pose a threat but our shields will prevent any issues should they open fire upon us here. Do you wish them neutralised?'

Tishan looked out to where the Ma'Vessick ships lay. 'Maintain your shield for now. As long as they remain quiet, I will not visit destruction upon them.'

ooooOoooo

Aboard the Ma'Vessick vessels there was great consternation and a complete lack of certainty as to how they should proceed. Djormak Rell, as the Komark, commanded all the ships of the fleet, but nothing in his experience had prepared him for the shock defeat of the Ma'Vessick forces on the ground, or the complete failure of the fleet's combined firepower to affect any material damage on the enemy.

Opinions differed as to the actions the fleet must take but it was clear that any barrage from their guns, even if they were successful at piercing the enemy defences, would result in the deaths of many Ma'Vessick. In frustration Djormak had ordered his subordinates to silence. The authority and responsibility was his alone to bear. Only Lakash, priest of Harkan, dared to speak.

'Komark, you must act. The enemy have taken one of the Instruments! The wrath of Harkan must surely fall on all our heads if we do not wrest it back!'

Lakash could not keep the desperation out of his voice. He was under no illusion that he would be spared punishment, even in his privileged position as a priest. It was certain that any surviving Ma'Vessick commander would pay the ultimate price under the knives of sacrifice should they return without the Instrument. It was also clear that if Toronset, his superior, was not killed in the attack, then she was taken prisoner. Whilst those of the priesthood had the power to resist torture the enemy was an unknown force,

170

powerful beyond reckoning. Not for the first time Lakash silently cursed the arrogance of Vekan in his belief that the Ma'Vessick were utterly invincible. Toronset had fed into this arrogance in the knowledge that they carried an Instrument, should the situation require it. With such a weapon she believed that there was nothing that could stand against them, despite their almost complete lack of intelligence regarding the peoples they faced.

'We cannot fire upon the enemy without hurling death upon our own. Considering that our weapons were ineffective we have but three options in my mind. First, we sail back with news of our defeat, leaving all behind us.'

There was an audible intake of breath from those present – all knew the consequences of such an act.

Djormak raised his hand as his officers began to speak. 'Silence! I did not ask for your comments.' He paused to glare at each individual. 'Secondly, we can train our guns on the encampment and seek to destroy the enemy. If Ma'Vessick die, they can be consoled by the fact that the enemy dies with them.'

'But what of the Instrument? We must retake it!' Lakash interjected. Such was the Komark's consternation that he reached out in frustration and pulled Lakash toward him. In an instant he realised his error.

'Forgive me, Lakash, I forgot myself.'

The silence that followed was icy and the Komark endeavoured to maintain his dignity and not squirm on the spot.

'Touch me again, Komark, and I will have you dropped over the side in chains. Your status will not protect you.'

With complete contempt Lakash turned his back on the Komark and spoke into the terrified silence. 'I will accompany an unarmed delegation to parley with these people. You, Komark, will be part of the group. Of course, there is no guarantee that any of us will survive such a meeting.'

ooooOoooo

As the Ma'Vessick deliberations on board their vessels continued, Fendrax turned to look towards the south. She saw that three Xotic moktech sailers, their silver sails bellying to the wind, were sweeping towards them over the hard-packed sand of the beach.

'We have company, Tishan Dar.'

As they drew closer, the sails disappeared and the three craft came to a gentle halt not twenty paces from where Fendrax and Tishan stood. They were much bigger than the usual poctech craft the Xotic habitually used. In the bows and on the stern of each vessel, Tishan saw what appeared to be a kind of gigantic and menacing crossbow. Like all Xotic craft, they were magnificent to look upon. Cleverly designed and efficient, these larger craft had eight wheels that were elaborately carved with a swirling pattern of lines and other symbols.

Tishan dismounted and approached the first of the Xotic craft as a rope ladder was thrown down and several Xotic began to descend. The first to the ground Tishan recognised immediately. 'Welcome, Tlkcha. It is very good to see you.' Tishan held out her arms in greeting.

Tlkcha smiled in response and, after grasping Tishan's hands, bowed formally to Fendrax. 'Greetings to you once again, mighty one.' Fendrax bowed her head in response.

Tlkcha turned her attention back to Tishan. 'We are sorry, Tishan Dar, it seems we have arrived too late to assist you. It took us a long time to find a way down. Ordinarily we do not travel so close to the Great Water. This part of our lands is unfamiliar to us and not generally suitable for our sail craft, but the sand here is strong and firm, and so here we are, at last.'

'You are most welcome. It is good to see our friends and have you here with us. Fendrax has already recounted how you dispatched many of the Ma'Vessick scouts on your way here. A time for judgement draws near and as these are your lands, that judgement is yours to make,' Tishan said.

Kellix came and stood alongside Tlkcha. 'We heard the noise of battle borne by the wind; it would seem that you have triumphed over these people, then?'

'We have defeated those who were on land. Their vessels may be another matter. They are as yet unscathed and have withdrawn some further distance offshore.'

'Will they throw fire upon us?' asked Tlkcha.

'Not unless they wish to blow their own people apart, but then, I do not know their mindset or what they are capable of.'

'Other than murder or slavery?' Kellix was grim.

'Indeed,' agreed Tishan. 'However, the shield maintained by our tetrans will protect us from anything they can throw at us.'

Now all the crews of the Xotic had assembled and were looking curiously, and not without trepidation, at the Ma'Vessick encampment.

There were some sixty Xotic crew members. All were armed with a kind of long stave that had a sharpened metal blade at both ends. These they hefted and carried over their shoulders as they followed Tishan and Fendrax back to the encampment.

Upon entering the gates, Tishan saw that her orders had been obeyed and a cowed group of about one hundred individuals garbed in blue were huddled together. They cast fearful looks at the Hoplex who made up the praka that had released them. Obviously fearing the intent of their new captors, they stood awaiting their fate.

Tishan sympathised with their plight. Enslaved and cruelly treated and then forced to accompany this expedition to a new land where an unknown future awaited them, Tishan could barely imagine what they must be thinking. She looked over the group as she approached and could see that several different races were represented. Some short and squat like the Ma'Vessick, others taller and more sparingly built. These people were strikingly similar to the Xotic, albeit not as skeletally thin. Yet others had skin as black as night, with large eyes of a piercing blue and ears that were very long, the lobes touching their shoulders. Tishan wondered if she seemed as alien to them as they did to her.

'Valash, you may stand your praka down. Assist with gathering up the fallen weapons of the enemy and set them under guard.'

Valash saluted before directing orders to his praka as he strode off with them. The eyes of the captors followed their departure, and then all eyes turned back to Tishan.

'You have no need to fear me or any of those who have defeated your masters. Our quarrel is not with you. As long as you act with peaceful intent and are respectful of the ways of our Xotic friends, upon whose land you stand, no ill will befall you.'

This statement was met with a range of expressions. Renewed hope in some, suspicion in others, doubt and fear remaining with many.

'Come, is there anyone amongst you who would speak for you? We will answer questions and allay your fears as best we can.'

A babble of conversation erupted and the name Hamra could be heard on the lips of many. Eventually a figure stepped forward and bowed deeply, arms folded over its chest. Whether male or female Tishan could not tell, as its features could have been interpreted as either; however, its voice was deep and resonant and Tishan decided that it was male.

Piercing, angular blue eyes regarded her and the Xotic standing nearby and lingered over Fendrax. He was otherwise expressionless.

'The people have asked me to speak for them. I am Hamra, one-time Penratha of the Coalteaca tribes. With me are those of many races ground under the heel of those you have defeated. None of us thought to live to see the Ma'Vessick laid low. Praise to you and to those with you.' Here not only Hamra but every individual in blue bowed low, holding the pose for a long time.

Standing upright once more, Hamra spoke again. This time he directed his words to the Xotic. 'I see by the look of your people that it is to you that we must extend our deepest sorrow. We have seen our own people ground into the dirt and butchered by these Ma'Vessick. We stood by and wept as your people were slaughtered on the beach. All of us wish that we might have been able to help, but we were powerless to do so.'

Once again, every individual bowed deeply. Tishan translated the words for all the Xotic who stood by, though none could doubt the sadness and sincerity of the tone in which the words were uttered or the respect that each individual showed to those of the Xotic present.

'Will you translate my words, Tishan Dar?' Tlkcha asked, and Tishan nodded in reply.

'My name is Tlkcha. My father, Shashn, was one of the first of many to be cut down on the beach that day. The Xotic have sworn vengeance on these invaders. Know this, the Xotic people do not hold you accountable for the crimes and actions of those who enslaved you. We thank you for your words, which we see are true and heartfelt. We are a peaceful people, slow to anger or to take up arms. Heed, then, our judgement on you.' Tlkcha paused as Tishan finished translating. The words were greeted with total silence and some trepidation as to what the Xotic would say.

'Unwilling you were brought to our lands and unwilling forced to toil for the brutes who ill-used you. We offer you food and shelter, warmth and friendship. Stay willingly or depart in peace, here you are free. As long as you respect our ways, you are welcome.'

The reaction from those who had been enslaved was moving. Laughter and tears, some people hugged each other with delight, and some just sat on the ground with their heads in their hands, so overwhelmed were they.

Hamra wept tears of joy and fell to his knees at the feet of Tlkcha. 'We gave up all hope many cycles since, but,' he paused, his voice became quieter, and he looked up into Tlkcha's face, 'is it really true that you do not mean to keep us enslaved?'

Tlkcha and Kellix bent down and gently lifted Hamra to his feet. 'You need not abase yourself to us and yes, it is most certainly true.'

Tishan smiled at Tlkcha before saying, 'The magnanimity and compassion of the Xotic should be a lesson for us all. Take your people now, Hamra, go and refresh yourselves, and we will meet and talk later about the future.'

'I would accompany you, if I may?' asked Hamra. 'It may be that I can assist, and there should be one of us to witness the judgement to be passed down.'

Tlkcha nodded at Tishan in acceptance. 'Very well then, Hamra. See to your people and then join us. We will meet in their main building.'

CHAPTER TEN

Three chairs were set upon the dais in the large meeting hall where Tishan had first confronted Vekan. To her left sat Tlkcha and to her right Hamra, who sat uncomfortably but at Tishan's insistence. Around them several Graaven Hoplex and Sagit stood, along with a number of Xotic. All were armed and ready to counter any aggressive act on the part of the Ma'Vessick leader who was even now being escorted, in the chains of their erstwhile slaves, into their presence.

Into Tishan's mind came Varnahrin's voice. <Tishan Dar, it is clear from all that has happened that you were right, and I was wrong; this is not an occurrence that has happened in a very long time and reminds me that I am not invulnerable. The use of the energy weapon has revealed a power that must be countered. Until now they have been shielded but the deployment of the device in battle has changed the action we must take. Such devices cannot remain in the hands of creatures such as these and only the power of Ta'Morin can counter it. We have seen one weapon but there are several others. I have probed the mind of their priest Toronset, she who wielded the Instrument during the battle. She resisted me for a time but there was a cost to pay, which has driven her to

insanity. Given what she is, you may deem this a fitting punishment.>

<As ever, you speak in riddles, Varnahrin. You have said 'what she is' – can you clarify?>

<This priesthood of which she is a member are not Ma'Vessick. They are not humanoid at all but cover themselves in a cloak of illusion.>

Tishan found the news disturbing. <Are you saying that they are like the Dorath Mar?>

<No. They are naturally occurring creatures, but their race was eradicated by the Paxal, or so it was thought.>

<You mean *the* Paxal, those who built one of the three cities?>

<The same. Paxal was situated in the lands that spawned the Ma'Vessick. But these are a much older race. They were quite sophisticated with an inbred loathing of all humanoids, who they see as interlopers. Ultimately, they were no match for the Paxal.>

<But if they are not humanoid, what are they and where did these energy weapons come from?>

<Did you ever travel the forests of Perduvia?>Varnahrin asked.

<You know I did, if you have accessed my memories. I had the misfortune to be bogged down for several meh'chaal on campaign. Not an experience I would like to repeat.>

<What was one of the worst things about your experience?>

<You mean apart from marauding Perduvians? Let me see, the obvious answer is the insects and one particularly nasty bug that gave a very painful sting.> Realisation came in the silence that followed Tishan's response. <Are you telling me that these priests are actually some kind of bug!?>

<Let us say they are insectoids. Even for them, bug is a little demeaning. The Paxals called them the Kchk, which is a sound they make when they click their mandibles. But yes, they are using the Ma'Vessick as pawns in a wider game. They have established a

kind of religious dominance and have introduced technological advances that, whilst primitive, are no less effective, particularly when those around them do not have the same sophistication. As to the energy weapons, now that I have seen the Instrument used by Toronset, I can say that they are Paxal in origin. Though how and where they were acquired as yet remains a mystery. Toronset certainly had no knowledge. They call themselves the Hrv, by the way. The term Kchk used by the Paxals was meant to be insulting and derogatory.>

Tishan shook her head from side to side in wonder. <So, if as you say the creature is now insane, is it able to control its disguise?>

<No. But then I have teleported it back to Ta'Morin where it is safely confined for now. You can take a look when you return, I am sure you will find it of interest.>

<Droll as ever, Varnahrin,> responded Tishan. Only silence greeted her retort.

The entire exchange with Varnahrin had taken very little time. Tishan's attention became focused on Vekan as he was pushed into the room and made to stand before the dais. She felt Hamra stiffen beside her as Vekan's gaze fixed on him.

'Slave scum. You will die screaming when we have our vengeance!'

'Silence!' Tlkcha had shot to her feet and Tishan was amazed at the volume of sound that she was able to produce. 'One more word from you without invitation and it will be your last.'

There was no response from Vekan. The combination of the command from Tlkcha and a stunning blow to his head from a Xotic guard as he was forcibly pushed to the ground was enough to quell him.

Tishan looked at the blank metallic mask that hid Vekan's features, and she turned to Hamra. 'Hamra, relate to all here as to why the Ma'Vessick wear masks.'

Hamra cleared his throat before he spoke and looked around the room at those gathered. 'The Ma'Vessick practice certain religious rituals. Their masks are only removed during ceremonies in veneration of their god. Remove the mask and you will see at first hand the devotion they display to their master.'

There was something in the underlying tone that suggested Hamra knew more than he was telling, but his expression did not change and no further information was forthcoming.

Tishan turned a stony gaze upon Vekan. 'You will remove your mask or I will have it removed for you.'

Vekan reared up and was immediately restrained by two Graaven Hoplex. 'Blasphemy!' Vekan called out as he writhed on the floor. 'None may see my countenance except in worship of Harkan. Evil shall befall any who try to remove it.'

Tlkcha stood slowly and looked at the Xotic who had dealt the blow to Vekan's head.

'Derpesh, remove that mask!'

Bending, Derpesh grasped the edge of the mask and, despite Vekan's efforts to prevent it, ripped it away. A muffled scream followed this act and Vekan lay still before raising his head to horrified onlookers.

'See the depth of my devotion to Harkan, the Lord of All. You will suffer under his hand for your blasphemy!'

Vekan's face was horrifically mutilated. Whether by the cuts of knives or the application of some acidic fluids or both, his remaining features were the stuff of nightmare. A virtually lipless mouth sat under the remains of a nose. Great scars from terrible gashes were visible on one cheek whilst the other seemed to have melted, the flesh bloated and scored. Horror and pity ran counter to each other that even a creature like this should have so willingly suffered such torture and look upon it as devotion.

'Give the mask back. I have no wish to look upon him.' Tishan commanded, and a horrified silence ensued as Vekan snatched back the covering and reapplied it to his face.

'Yes, you stand in awe of my devotion and soon you will all be screaming under Ma'Vessick knives as you gasp out your pitiful existence.' Despite the reality of his situation, it was apparent that Vekan retained an unshakable belief in the pre-eminence and power of the Ma'Vessick. There was not a single observer present that did not conclude that Vekan's mind hovered on the edge of insanity.

Tlkcha leant across and spoke quietly to both Tishan and Hamra. 'Despite the madness and brutality of this creature there is in my mind a level of pity. It comes to me that the worship of a god that demands such devotion must drive any person to acts of violence and cruelty.'

Tishan nodded her head slowly. She, too, was horrified at what she had seen.

Tlkcha continued. 'Through countless nights I have dreamt of passing the judgement of death on his kind. Now I am in that position there is a part of me also that holds me back. My people have suffered much at the hands of the Ma'Vessick. Does passing the sentence of death taint us also? I wonder.'

Tishan considered her words. 'We Graaven were warlike and capable of cruelty. We learned to our cost that such acts led to even greater resistance from those we conquered. In this case, however, I would counsel that the fate that awaits these creatures when they return to their own lands will be harsher than any punishment we might choose to inflict. Let us leave it to their own to decide their ultimate fate.' This statement was received with a nodding of heads as both Tlkcha and Hamra considered Tishan's words.

Into the brief silence, punctuated by the curses of Vekan, Kellix made his way to the dais. 'A small craft approaches the shore from one of the Ma'Vessick ships. They make no hostile moves so we deem it may be that they come to parley with us.'

'Very well,' Tlkcha nodded. 'Take this creature. Keep him bound and separate from the others of his kind. Let us see what these emissaries have to say.'

They gathered on the beach where the Ma'Vessick slaves had constructed a short pier for the purposes of loading and unloading the ships. A small vessel approached. A single large metal stack in its centre exuded black smoke, whilst a subdued clatter could be heard coming from inside the vessel itself. It moved by some means that was not immediately apparent but which Tishan felt sure was associated with the belching smoke. Both the noise and the smoke stopped as the vessel was tied off and three individuals climbed warily on to the pier.

One, garbed in red and hooded, was undoubtedly one of their priests. The two others, both short and squat, had skins of a dark grey hue. They stood just above chest height of the Graaven and Xotic people and had broad shoulders and powerful builds. The priest was taller and more finely proportioned but Tishan knew what lay behind the illusion that disguised its true features. The two shorter individuals were dressed in a uniform. Each bore markings, geometric designs that were embroidered on the sleeves of the coats they wore and were likely indicative of rank. Their coats, which were nearly as dark a grey as their skin, reached down to mid-thigh, loose white leg coverings could be seen, and broad feet were encased in calf-length boots of a russet-coloured material.

Cautiously they walked to the edge of the pier, unarmed as they were. The sight of the armed foe who awaited them was augmented by the tallest and most vicious looking predator they had ever seen standing quietly amongst the group. However, before their feet even touched the ground Tishan's voice rang out. 'Halt there. You may not tread on Xotic lands. You are not welcome.'

If there was any surprise at Tishan's ability to speak their language they hid it well, although the expression on the unmasked face of the red priest was intense.

'Who addresses Djormak, Komark of the Ma'Vessick fleet?' The words were issued by the priest, while the other two Ma'Vessick stood silently.

'Who I am is no concern of yours. Listen without interruption. Those surviving of your people will shortly be herded to this pier. You will be allowed to take them back to your ships. When the last of your people has gone you will leave these shores. If you attempt to return you will be destroyed. If you attempt to fire upon the shore, you will be destroyed. Do not think this is an empty threat: your weaponry will not prevail, and your end will be both swift and certain.'

Tishan could feel the frustration and rage emanating from these creatures, particularly the priest. They were easier to read than a storm cloud in the middle of Hordeth Gar, the Season of Storms.

The priest's voice rang out. 'This is unacceptable. What of the holy relic you have stolen? We demand its return!'

Tishan could feel Tlkcha and all the other Xotic bridle at the tone, albeit they did not understand the words. The growl that emanated from Fendrax, however, was enough to inflame the markings on Tishan's skin and the tendrils on her neck flared in response, so great was its menace. Not for the first time, Tishan was glad that Fendrax was their friend.

'Tishan Dar, beware this creature. It is not what it appears to be.'

'I know what it is, Fendrax. Stay calm, now is not the time to strike.'

'If you say so,' Fendrax rumbled.

Fendrax's reaction had caused the three Ma'Vessick to retreat a few paces.

'You appear to think that this is a negotiation,' said Tishan. She smiled and let her gaze rest on each Ma'Vessick. 'This is an ultimatum. You may choose to take your people and go, or you may die. The choice is yours, but you will answer now. As to your "holy relic" – that is a trophy of war and remains in our possession. Such weapons cannot remain in the hands of thieves and murderers.'

Tishan's words had a powerful effect on the Ma'Vessick and particularly on the red-garbed priest. With a cry the figure launched itself at Tishan. Inhumanly fast as the tetrans were, they were no match for the blinding speed of Fendrax. A mighty paw flashed out, so great the blow that the body was nearly ripped in two and it flew back to crash with a sickening thud against the timbers of the pier.

'Hold, hold all of you!' Tishan shouted a command into the alarmed gathering, lest pent up anger be unleashed on the two Ma'Vessick who had leapt back from the sudden affray. Pointing her right hand, she drew their attention to the body of the priest. 'Look now upon that which was hidden.'

No sooner had she uttered the words than the mutilated body of the priest seemed to flicker and go out of focus for a moment. There was a slight shimmering of the air and there, where the body of the priest had lain, still covered in its red robes, lay the remains of a huge insect, its mandibles still clicking as its life force fled. Green ichor leaked from its terrible wounds and huge multifaceted eyes gazed blankly at the sky. There was a terrible stench of decay and before their eyes the body quickly decomposed, leaving a viscous slime.

All present jumped back in horror and none more so than the Ma'Vessick. 'Witchcraft!' and, 'Sorcery!' came from the mouths of each one, the remarks levelled at those who stood by on the shore.

Tishan's eyes narrowed. 'Do you refuse to acknowledge what you have seen with your own eyes?' her tone was incredulous.

Whilst the masks were expressionless, the tone of voice was unmistakable. 'Now do we see how we were defeated. The use of sorcery has overcome Ma'Vessick might and now by your arts you try to undermine our beliefs with this illusion, but you will never destroy our belief in the might of Harkan!'

'Then you are both fools and your people doomed.' Tishan's voice was scathing. 'You are as much slaves to your priesthood as any of those you have conquered and held in your thrall. You are convinced of your superiority in all things and yet you are only the means by which your so-called priests achieve their own ends.' Before any reply could be made Tishan pointed her right hand at the two Ma'Vessick. 'Our ultimatum stands. Take your people and depart these shores. Return at your peril. Those you have enslaved remain with us, free to do as they will and free from your cruelty.'

The Ma'Vessick spat back a response. 'Yes, we will depart, but the might of our nation will be turned against you. You may count the days till our return and your destruction!'

Whatever response they were expecting, it was not the derisive laughter that issued from Tishan's lips and which continued for some time. Finally drawing a breath, she flicked her fingers contemptuously at the individuals standing on the pier in silent fury. 'Go away, ere I lose patience. Your people will be led down shortly, be ready.'

She turned and walked off, speaking rapidly. Tlkcha and the other Xotic who had followed the exchange interpreted what was said by the tone of voice and body language. Behind her four tetrans stood guard, their baleful red eyes never leaving the Ma'Vessick even as they turned away and took the ship back to their waiting vessels.

'Tishan, what was that thing? How is it possible that those Ma'Vessick did not believe what they saw with their own eyes?' Tlkcha and the others shook their heads in wonder.

Hamra too was horrified. 'Never in my wildest dreams did I imagine that these priests were not themselves Ma'Vessick. It is the stuff of nightmare.'

'You will get no disagreement from me,' Tishan responded. 'No, they did not believe. They took it as a trick of sorcery and blamed their defeat on the use of magic arts. Believe me, Tlkcha, as Hamra well knows, they are not the sort of people that will heed the warnings given. Their arrogance and pride and belief in their invincibility, even in light of what happened here today, will lead to their return.'

'Then we must be ready for them,' said Kellix, who had been listening closely to Tishan's words.

'Indeed,' responded Tishan.

For the rest of the day, as the suns dipped toward the horizon, the surviving Ma'Vessick were led in chains to the pier and were ferried away in a flotilla of small boats. The last to be led down was Vekan himself, forcibly restrained in the grip of two Graaven Hoplex, all the while gibbering and calling vengeance on those gathered around. Finally, as the light of Avlar waned and Halidar crept into the night sky, the Ma'Vessick ships departed, the black smoke from their funnels blowing towards those gathered on the shore. The tetran force maintained the protective shield all the while to guard against treachery.

'So, for now, they are gone,' remarked Tlkcha.

'Yes. Though I deem that some, or perhaps all, of those in command may not survive their homecoming. I think the loss of their Instrument may be a cause of considerable anguish.'

'No doubt their god will be requiring appeasement,' said Kellix grimly.

'Let us be glad that it will not be us doing the appeasing,' echoed Tlkcha.

Into the night a celebratory feast was held. Varnahrin had assured Tishan that the Ma'Vessick ships continued a steady course away from Xotic shores and that, for now at least, they were safe from any invading force.

The next morning discussions were held and the future of those who had been enslaved decided. After much deliberation it was agreed that the encampment of the Ma'Vessick was sound and offered secure shelter and security. It was also a protected anchorage and therefore the most likely place that the Ma'Vessick would return to. The surrounding waters were abundant with fish and the lands adjacent to the settlement capable of raising crops. A number of those in the group were from peoples who had knowledge of boats, and both the Xotic and those from Ta'Morin agreed to aid the newcomers. As these were lands the Xotic rarely visited, none objected to the continuing occupation of the site and, indeed, there was much conjecture about opportunities for trade in time to come.

Already both sides were learning individual words of each other's language and a firm foundation for the future was begun.

'Do you not long for your homeland?' Tishan asked Hamra.

There was a pause before Hamra responded and a number of those who sat nearby went silent in reflection. 'We are ever homesick, Tishan Dar. But it is mostly for the memory of what was. Nothing could ever return to the life before the Ma'Vessick and the knives of their priests. Perhaps one day, but for now it is enough that we are free. We are in a new land and the world offers us new opportunities. It is like a dream, so whilst we are sorry for the suffering of our new friends, we also look to a future that we could not envisage when we arrived here. Though, we are fearful of the Ma'Vessick return.'

'As to that, Ta'Morin will ensure that your new home is well protected. If it is agreeable to you and to our Xotic friends, we will move our gateway closer and station a praka of tetrans here with you. I am also sure that many of my people would wish to visit you and you, in turn, would be welcome in Ta'Morin, as are our Xotic friends.'

'Your gateway is a thing of wonder, Tishan,' said Tlkcha. 'If we did not know you as friends, I, too, would think that such a thing is a work of magic.'

Here Hamra also nodded his head.

'What cannot be explained rationally within the limit of our experience and knowledge does appear magical,' Tishan responded. 'We Graavens would agree with you, Tlkcha. Ta'Morin is ancient and full of wonders and surprises, but you must never doubt our friendship and desire for peace. We will fight to protect ourselves, our friends, and to preserve the Balance.'

ooooOoooo

With Varnahrin's aid the gateway was repositioned closer to the encampment and, over the course of several meh'chaal, the fortifications were improved upon and the facilities within the camp expanded. Those who had so recently been enslaved worked tirelessly on what was to be their new home and, with assistance from their Xotic friends, access to the hard-packed sand of the beach was smoothed so the encampment could be easily reached by any Xotic who came to trade. As Tlkcha remarked one evening as they sat around a communal fire, 'All Xotic will be intrigued and wish to visit you. We are always looking for items and goods to trade and now that we can visit Ta'Morin, many more of us will come this way.'

Tishan regularly travelled between the encampment and Ta'Morin and a steady stream of curious Graavens had taken the opportunity to visit the new destination, meet its people, and stand in awe of the wide sweep of the waters. Nothing could compare with its size, and there was much conjecture as to the lands that lay across so huge a body of water.

Following the evening meal one night when Tishan was at the encampment, Hamra spoke. 'Dear friends. The turnaround in our fortunes has been so remarkable that we who were once slaves hope that we do not wake up from a deep sleep to find it was but a dream.' This remark was met with some laughter and head nodding. 'But we cannot continue to call this place the encampment: it smacks too much of those who oppressed us. No, all of us feel that we need a new name, not only for this place, but also for ourselves.'

Tlkcha nodded. The Xotic facility with speaking the tongue of the newcomers had grown markedly in the time spent working together, as indeed had their new friends' ability in grasping the Xotic language. The Graavens seemed to have a remarkable capacity for picking up both the Xotics' and the newcomers' speech in a very short time: but then, as Tishan remarked to Horven, she had no doubt that Varnahrin was responsible for this seemingly effortless ability.

'That is entirely understandable,' said Tlkcha in response. 'Did you have a name in mind?'

Hamra looked around the large room where they had gathered and saw general agreement amongst all those who attended. 'We come from many different lands which now lie under the heel of the Ma'Vessick. None of us here have seen our countries for many Graaven sem'chaal. The years passed by in despair. We cannot speculate on what has happened to any of those who were our families.' A general murmuring greeted this comment and Tishan looked around the faces in the room with sympathy.

'No. Tlkcha, you and Kellix, and indeed all of your people, have greeted us with open arms. You have not, at any time, sought to blame us for what happened to your people. Such generosity of spirit to us is remarkable. So, it is only fitting, as these lands are yours, that it is you who name this place, and in so doing, in ways both real and symbolic, allow us to rename ourselves as citizens of this place.'

A silence fell upon the room as the newcomers waited for the Xotic response. The Xotic nodded amongst themselves and began a quiet but earnest discussion. Finally, Tlkcha stood and spoke to all who were assembled.

'The words you have spoken come from the heart. As slaves you came unwillingly. As friends you have chosen to remain. Hear, then, what the Xotic have decided. I am Tlkcha and after my father, Shashn of blessed memory, Palx Mer of the Xotic people. Den Har, Sky Father, hear my words.' She turned her gaze on those seated around her. 'Stand, people of no name. Stand, people of no lands.'

Other than the sound of people standing quietly, the sighing of the Mother Water, and the crackle of the fire, not a sound was made.

'Where this place now stands is called by the Xotic Noh ir mech sah kash, the place where sky and water meet. Few Xotic travelled here in earlier times — our lore tells us that here Den Har disappears into the great waters and to travel on open water is to fall into death, so it is kocharlin, forbidden to us. Now from out of the Mother Water you have arrived. The eyes of the Xotic have been opened and we see that, whilst there is some truth in our lore, Den Har does not disappear but sits above other lands and peoples.' She paused for moment in the silence of the room. 'Your coming was bittersweet but you are not responsible for the actions of those who held you in thrall. Now do we the Xotic people cede to you all the lands that lie around this place, for as far as you may travel with the rising and setting of the suns for three cycles in any direction. The Mother Water belongs to no-one, it is yours to harvest as you see fit. But know this: though we cede these lands to you, you must care for them. Plant crops and harvest as you will the fruits of the earth and the bounty it may offer, but remember that without the land you have nothing, you are nothing. Abuse this at your peril.'

The emotion in the room was a palpable thing. Tishan and those other Graavens that were present were deeply moved at the generosity of the Xotic people. There was nothing in her considerable experience that even came close to the compassion and generosity of spirit of the Xotic.

Tlkcha spoke again. 'Let this place and all the lands around it under your control be called Xaranca. There is no word for it in your language, but its closest translation would be "new beginnings". Henceforth, you who were of no name shall be known as Xarancan.' The formality of Tlkcha's voice gave way to a bright smile, and into a tangible silence where the Xarancans, as they were now called, were trying to come up with an adequate response, she said, 'Is it time for a beaker of clshmik now?'

The weight of silence gave way to a wave of laughter that lifted everyone's spirits. The joy that had arisen at the pronouncements of the Xotic was so great that the laughter did not in any way diminish the solemnity of the decision.

Much later, after many beakers of clshmik, a Xotic beverage of particular potency, Tishan spoke quietly to Tlkcha and Kellix. 'I don't think there are any words that could express the gratitude of our Xarancan friends.'

'In truth, Tishan,' responded Kellix in a rather slurred voice, 'there are many advantages having them here. We Xotic would never have utilised these lands and now, not only will we have a new source of trade, but we also have an early warning if those Ma'Vessick seek to return.'

'Not to mention the presence of the gateway, Tishan,' added Tlkcha. 'That alone is priceless to us. Now we can visit our Ta'Morin friends whenever we will. Oh yes, so many good things arising out of the horror.'

'Yes,' agreed Tishan. 'Such is the nature of Balance. But I cannot believe that the Ma'Vessick will not return. We need to remain vigilant.'

'We will,' agreed Kellix, smiling. 'But not tonight! We still have gourds of clshmik to lighten!'

Tishan nodded her head: she had only drunk sparingly of the potent liquor. 'Then I will leave you to continue your task and wish you a good night.'

Against several small protests, Tishan left the gathering and walked down to the shore. It was a still night, although she could smell in the air that Veremis Gar, the Season of Weeping, was approaching and rain was in the offing. The Mother Waters lapped the shore and gentle waves sighed as they endlessly caressed the sand and drew back again. Lifting her eyes, she peered into the horizon. The silvery light of the three moons glinted off the restless waters and she turned her thoughts to the problem of the Ma'Vessick. Horven came and stood alongside her in companionable silence, also gazing out over the silvery waters.

'Who would have thought that a land full of strange peoples existed on the other side of these waters? Our lives continue to throw surprises and challenges at us, Stragosh.'

Tishan turned and smiled fondly at Horven. 'Indeed, and now we must find a way to neutralise this new foe, ere they return to our side. In the meantime, I want you to supervise the defences of this new place and lend these people your assistance. You may return as you will to Ta'Morin, but I need you here for now.'

Horven nodded. 'Very well. Actually, I am looking forward to learning more about these people. They are a source of great curiosity to me.'

'Good. It is also in my mind to send Drenyk and Pershivon here as well. They grow to maturity, and it will be good for them to meet these new people and lend what aid they can. You will take them under your wing?'

Horven laughed. 'I will treat your offspring as my own and teach them as much as I can. It will be good to have them here.'

'Very well,' Tishan responded. 'Why don't you spend a few hours in Ta'Morin? Perhaps Lerma may be of assistance here, too?'

'I will ask him. You know he has a soft spot for Pershivon so he may be far too gentle with her.'

'Well, Shu Lan Horven, I am sure you can sort that out!'

Laughing, Horven saluted and then strode off to the gateway whilst Tishan turned back to her contemplation of the waters, the sounds of singing and revelry echoing in the night.

<Child, you know what must be done.> The voice of Varnahrin echoed in her mind.

<They cannot be allowed to return here, I know that. A pre-emptive strike is required but I have no idea how we are to cross these waters, or the best way to affect what needs to be done. They have access to energy weapons – but do we know how powerful they are? I wish Menkh was here, he would already have a plan worked out.>

There was no response from Varnahrin and the silence caused Tishan a frisson of fear.

<Has something happened, Varnahrin?>

Some moments passed, which did nothing to alleviate Tishan's increasing worry, until finally Varnahrin responded. <Return to Ta'Morin, child. There is much to discuss.>

Tishan turned, her fear now manifest, and hurried to the gateway, following in the footsteps of Horven who had so recently passed ahead of her.

CHAPTER ELEVEN

Radek, High Priest of Harkan, stood on the topmost floor of the Grand Temple in the Ma'Vessick capital of Gahrtok. His multifaceted eyes picked out details far below where he stood in the heart of the city: details that no Ma'Vessick eyes, or those of any warm blood, could discern. Impatiently his mandibles clicked in a sign of frustration and his forelimbs susurrated as he rubbed them over the spiny ridges of each limb.

Nchk, high priestess, stood behind him observing his movements. Here in seclusion they had no need of their Ma'Vessick disguise. They stood in their true form and communicated in audible clicks and sounds that none but the Hrv could emulate.

'Not since we emerged from exile have we faced such an issue,' said Radek. 'That puling fool Vekan finally spoke the truth once we had made an example of his subordinates.'

'Yes,' agreed Nchk. 'There is something about seeing another's guts spilled on the floor that loosens the tongue. I yearn for the day we can suspend this pretence and assume our rightful place.'

'Patience, Nchk. The plan proceeds smoothly and these Ma'Vessick have been useful tools that suit our purpose admirably. Just the right degree of total stupidity and blood lust.'

'What, then, are your thoughts regarding these creatures across the water?'

'They must be neutralised. Our dilemma is that we have no knowledge of how powerful they might be and there is every likelihood that they will move to strike us first.'

'Yes. Toronset made a grave error in deploying the Instrument.'

Radek's audible tones raised an octave, a sign of fury. 'Curse her! The secret of one hundred cycles exposed in one stroke!'

'We can deploy the others,' Nchk said soothingly. 'Surely there can be no force capable of withstanding their combined power?'

'We cannot be certain.' Radek paused in thought. 'We have no option. Retrieve the others and initiate the process. Increase the sacrifices, we will need more energy. Start with that idiot Vekan and make sure he lingers. Harkan must be appeased to the fullest measure as a warning to others.'

Nchk clicked once in assent and swept from the room.

Radek's thoughts turned in contemplation of the past. The Hrv were a long-lived race and their nests had once occupied most of the lands which abutted the Great Water. Timbered roadways connected one nesting site to another and their technological advancements were superior to all other sentient creatures who had the misfortune to occupy lands adjacent to theirs. Highly intelligent, they loathed all warm bloods and slaughtered without compunction any that they encountered. Then, disaster.

Seemingly from out of nowhere, strange warm bloods appeared with a technology so far in advance of the Hrv that their arrogant belief in their superiority was dashed in moments. Within the space of but one cycle, their nest sites had been obliterated, their nurseries incinerated, and the few pathetic survivors forced to flee.

Harried by those the Hrv had themselves persecuted, only a few individuals managed to elude capture and death and escape into the uttermost wilds. Bereft of tools and any vestige of their technology, they hovered on the verge of extinction for years. Slowly, painfully, their numbers grew. Still pathetically few but safe from extinction, they gradually made a way of life that was more than just daily survival. For every trial and tribulation they faced, their hatred of the warm bloods grew.

Vague whispers of a mighty city reached their remote land. The rumours spoke of a great power vested in a place called Paxal, and the Hrv lusted after the promise of what such a technology might afford them. Then, after many cycles, all rumours stopped completely and the Hrv wondered if perhaps the time for their re-emergence might have come.

The time spent in exile was now so great that most of the Hrv thought of the lands they had been driven to as their home, for none remaining had any memory of what had gone before. Only their stories carried an echo of the calamity that had befallen them. But their hatred of all warm bloods was as powerful as ever.

Finally, a group of Hrv left their lands and began the long trek back to what was once their homeland. So many cycles had passed that all knowledge of the lands around them was lost, and so they travelled in a strange and new world. For a time, weary of endless journeying, the group settled in one place to rest. It was in that time that Radek emerged, newly hatched. He had no sooner reached maturity then the group set off once more. So it was that they stumbled across the remains of a building unlike any they had seen before.

Entering this ruin, they had encountered implements and devices that were a wonder to them. By trial and error, and horrific accidents from time to time that killed and maimed some of them, they learnt the uses of the artefacts they had found. Whilst they could not reproduce them nor fully understand their workings, they learnt how to charge them and found that they were virtually indestructible. Confident in their new-found power, they journeyed on and at last began to encounter warm-blooded peoples, who ran from them in terror, not only because of how they looked but in fear of the weapons that the Hrv used. Still, the peoples they encountered were numerous and the Hrv few, and it was only a matter of time before the warm bloods would overcome them and they would die, their newly discovered technology lost to them.

The Hrv had one power unique to their species: the ability to cloak their true forms and disguise themselves as warm bloods. Using this power, Radek went forth and lived amongst the warm bloods who called themselves the Ma'Vessick for a time, learning of their ways, and a plan began to form in his mind.

The Ma'Vessick were a primitive people with a naive and shamanistic belief in the world of spirits. They lived their lives in fear of the unknown world, a world of spirits and demons which existed for them as a part of their everyday reality. Warlike but without the means to pose any threat to their neighbours, they were the ideal instruments to form the foundation of the Hrv return to power.

One day, twelve priests cowled in black appeared by inexplicable means in the midst of a Ma'Vessick stronghold, which would later become the Ma'Vessick capital. Calling on the power of the god Harkan they slaughtered all opposition, making disciples of those left and promising them wealth and power. So complete was the domination of the Hrv that in only a few seasons they had completely established the worship of Harkan, enslaving the Ma'Vessick in a web of religious ritual and observance. The cruel mutilations they promoted as a means of worship went someway to assuaging the hatred they felt for all warm bloods, and it amused them to require the Ma'Vessick to submit to pain and disfigurement. In turn, the treatment that the Ma'Vessick dealt out to those they conquered, aided by the technology brought to them by their priests, was both brutal and savage. This was partly as a desire to inflict the same pain and suffering on their neighbours that they themselves endured, and partly to satisfy the blood lust that their priests encouraged in them.

Radek remained upon the balcony that opened out from his suite of rooms. Unobserved by any, he stood in silent contemplation of the city below, endeavouring to devise a plan to counter the threat so clearly posed by these new people. Was it possible they were some remnant of the Paxal? So many questions that had, at this time, no answer.

ooooOoooo

Tishan materialised in front of Varnahrin, where the crystal that was its physical form pulsed gently, with ever-changing colours twisting and turning deep within its core.

<What is it. What have you to tell me?> The level of consternation in Tishan's thoughts was palpable.

A chair appeared alongside Tishan's upright form.

<Sit down, child, there is much to discuss.> Varnahrin paused while Tishan composed herself. <There is no easy way to tell this. We have survived the first assault against us and Menkh has disappeared without trace.>

Tishan gripped the arms of the chair and fought for control. <Dead?> Her mental voice was tinged with barely contained anxiety.

<I do not believe so, but there is no way of truly knowing at this time. He and Crixac were ambushed, and a new enemy revealed itself. After achieving its goal with Menkh, it attacked us, but the shield held, thwarting its plans of destruction and dealing it a painful reminder that even with its great power it is not invulnerable. There is no doubt that it will attack again, but for now it has retreated.>

Tishan closed her eyes and took deep breaths, quieting her racing thoughts. <It would seem we are beset on all sides. But you say we were attacked. How is it that there was no sign of any assault? Surely such a confrontation would have resulted in some physical manifestation?>

Varnahrin's response was immediate. <But indeed, there was, child. How has the weather been of late?>

<The weather? Just the usual storms one expects as the seasons change. It is always stormy at the approach of Veremis Gar. Why, just recently there was a huge lightning display and ...> Tishan made the connection. <You mean that lightning was the result of the attack? The flashes were the brightest I can ever recall seeing.>

<Such is the power of the shield, child. But it is as well that the attack went unremarked and was easily explained. It may not be so the next time as we confront this new power.>

Varnahrin's remark gave rise to more questions. <You say 'new'. Was the presence of this enemy hidden from the Intelligence, then?>

There was a pause before the answer came. <By some unknown means, yes. Now, perhaps unintentionally, it has revealed itself. Menkh and Crixac were caught unawares but their capture created waves in the Threadway. To those who can sense it, this was enough to provide awareness. The presence of this force is powerful. It draws all negative energy towards it. No sooner had it dealt with Menkh and Crixac than it traversed the Threadway itself, speeding back along the path followed by Menkh when he left the Balancepoint.>

Tishan gasped. <It attacked the Balancepoint?>

<It would have, had not the Balancepoint relocated itself in the instant before the attack manifested. Frzath and the other Adepts achieved this in time and sent a communication to me.>

Tishan sat back. <That, at least, is a relief.>

<Yes, that is so, but it was then inevitable that an attack on Tarvuli would eventuate, so it is well that you and Menkh were able to energise our defence.>

<Will it be sufficient to hold this thing back a second time?> Tishan was matter-of-fact, the Stragosh asserting herself and coolly assessing the situation.

<Theoretically, yes, but we will have to wait and see. There are still things that we can throw into any battle, and which may give us an edge. But this being grows in strength and knowledge. I was able to learn a little more about it during the attack. It appears that this thing is some kind of alter ego of the enemy. A physical manifestation of the knowledge the enemy has acquired over thousands of cycles. How it came into being is beyond even my understanding, and my knowledge covers aeons. It sees itself as superior to that from which it sprang, yet, like the other Talixit Ven it is tied to the mother – only, in this case it draws its power from the enemy, feeding from it unlike all others.>

<If you cannot understand it, Varnahrin, then what hope have any of us? Whatever it is we must find a way to counter it, but without Menkh I am not sure what we can do.>

<There are many questions to which we have no answer, Tishan Dar. We can only take the actions that are necessary and within our power to affect. In the meantime, therefore, we must deal with the Ma'Vessick.>

<Is there nothing we can do to aid Menkh and Crixac?>

There was a long pause and the question hung in the air. Tishan fought to control her emotions. She could not imagine a world without Menkh in it.

<Child, Menkh is a bonded Adept. If he had died, believe me when I tell you that I, of all my kind, would have felt his life force passing. No, he is out there somewhere, and we must trust to his ingenuity and determination to find his way back to us.>

Tishan nodded her head slowly and reflected on Varnahrin's words. Varnahrin was right, of course, and whilst some part of Tishan would continue to worry about Menkh's fate, there was another matter that had to be dealt with.

Tishan mentally took a deep breath and ordered her thoughts, pushing her worry to the back of her mind. Varnahrin was right, there was nothing to be done for Menkh at this time but much that still needed to be done on Tarvuli. <So, we deal with the Ma'Vessick and to do that we must cross the Great Water. What is our first step?>

<Why, we are going to hunt bugs, of course!> Despite the situation they found themselves in, Varnahrin's words were playful and as close to laughter as Tishan had ever heard. <Without their priests the Ma'Vessick will be virtually leaderless. Their Hrv masters allow them some freedom of will, but it is closely controlled within their religious practices, and they are completely dominant in that area. Also, the Ma'Vessick are incapable of operating the energy weapons which the Hrv have control of, so if we neutralise them, we can mop up the Ma'Vessick. Come, I will show you what you are up against.>

Tishan felt herself being transported to another part of the Complex. She arrived before a glass screen that looked into a small room. Inside the room was a creature unlike any she had seen before. Shorter than a Graaven, it was undoubtedly some giant form of insect. Its overall outer covering was a golden colour with a shine that was consistent with polished metal. Long forearms with serrated edges were clasped under its head, the tips finishing in four spiny protrusions that Tishan assumed were its fingers. Two huge, multifaceted, violet-coloured eyes dominated a rather triangular head, with what appeared to be two smaller eyes on either side of a long, beakish snout. Its mouth was surrounded by two mandibles, which the creature clicked rhythmically, at the same time bobbing up and down in a ceaseless rhythm on two powerful rear legs that were also serrated and finished in a sharp spur just above its long and pointed back feet.

<It is quite mindless,> Varnahrin remarked. <The price of its resistance to my probing was insanity and it has remained in this position ever since.>

<Will it take nourishment of any kind?> asked Tishan.

<To what purpose? Prolonging the creature's existence would be less than merciful, it has no hope of recovery.>

<We cannot simply let it starve to death in captivity. Death on a battlefield is one thing, but it is an object of pity, and I would give an end that is as easy as possible.>

<I can reduce the air inside the room slowly. It will pass into unconsciousness and death, and will not suffer as a result. Is this satisfactory to you?>

<If there is no hope of its recovery, then yes, I would wish that, were I in a similar situation, such consideration would be given to me.>

<Very well. You should know, however, that should you be caught by the Hrv in whatever state, a merciful end will not be a remote possibility. Their hatred of all warm-blooded creatures is deep-seated, and they are capable of great viciousness.>

<So are we all, Varnahrin, I have too much experience of battlefields to think that I am any better than these Hrv. I would like to believe that I have changed somewhat since the fall, but I fear I am still capable of cruelty to those I see as a threat to my people.>

<There are many and great changes to all of your Graaven people, Tishan Dar. Have faith in yourself; all sentient life has the capacity to change, to learn and to grow if they wish it. But come, let us leave here, we have no need to watch this creature any further and I have something else to show you.>

Tishan once again felt herself transported. All around her blurred for a moment and then she reappeared quite some distance away from Ta'Morin, which she could see in the distance. She stood on a flat area of ground that was verdant with wild grasses but was free of any cultivation. On three sides, the field, which was perhaps three bowshots wide and long from where she stood, was surrounded by flowering trees whose magenta blooms gave off a heady perfume. She felt quite drowsy, wondering if the scent was the cause.

<I have not been to this place before. Why are we here?> Her thoughts were quite dreamy, and she felt that she would like to lie down on the soft grass and sleep.

Varnahrin's voice was like a dash of cold water and the dreaminess vanished. <Snap out of it, child, no-one visits this place unless I allow it, and the trees here make sure that no-one ventures too far if they do wander in. These trees are called ermax and their scent is potent. Now, attend to me. Use your rod and focus your mind upon it to reveal that which is hidden.>

<Can't you just tell me?>

<Where is the fun in that?> Varnahrin responded. <Besides, you have to learn to do these things yourself. Where you are standing is not what it appears to be.>

Tishan was going to ask how to do that but realised that Varnahrin would be less than forthcoming, and she would have to work it out for herself. She turned her gaze to the field, which appeared totally unchanged and utterly peaceful. A gentle breeze ruffled the leaves of the trees, and she could not identify anything out of place. Then it struck her. The grasses she stood amongst were absolutely still. Whilst the breeze gently moved the branches of the trees and their long, pendant shaped leaves, the grasses, soft and pliable to the touch, were completely motionless.

Taking up the rod and grasping it in both hands, she focused her thoughts and expressed the desire to truly see what was around her. At first her efforts went unrewarded, and she felt not a little foolish, but knowing that there was something hidden reinforced her determination to succeed. In frustration, she closed her eyes

and found that her mental focus increased. After several moments
of feeling nothing, she opened her eyes in exasperation. Had anyone else been present they would have laughed at the play of
emotions over her face. Exasperation changed instantly to amazement.

The grasses around her had disappeared. Instead, she stood
upon a circular field of unbroken crystal, which filled the entire
area and pulsated with colour, much like the colours that pulsed
through Varnahrin.

<Well done, child. You are the first to have stood here since
before the destruction of Kareem Vastar.>

<What is this?> Tishan asked in wonder.

<The Kareems experimented with many things. The develop-
ment of gate technology meant that the use of this machine
became redundant. There were plans to dismantle it, but they were
never acted upon. In the Kareem tongue this is an ImXin. Its function was originally for exploration. It hovers above the ground and
can travel in any direction. It is this that will carry you across the
Great Water to the lands beyond.>

Tishan looked closely at the surface of the huge, disc-shaped
object. It appeared to be quite flat, like the base of a plate, but all
across its surface there were small depressions, set in pairs. These
depressions were arrayed in neat lines. Experimentally she placed
her feet in two of them. They were somewhat larger than her own
feet, but she found that she could stand quite comfortably.

<What is the purpose of these depressions?> she said curi-
ously.

<These are restraining points. Once the ImXin is activated
they hold any travellers securely in place. You will see in due
course. Come, walk forward, you will see where the controls are
located.>

As Tishan walked she found that the surface, which looked as
slippery as glass, was in fact quite soft underfoot. She was baffled

as to how something that appeared so hard could be so yielding under her feet. As she walked forward, she noticed that there was a slight bulge in the surface of the disc, around four chaal in diameter. As she reached the centre of the bulge, the crystalline surface began to flow upwards. The unexpected movement caused her to step back abruptly and, at once, the movement ceased and the surface began to recede back into the floor.

<Do not be alarmed, child. The deck of this vessel reacts to movement. The bulge here is where you pilot the craft. Move forward once again and then stand still, you will find the experience interesting.>

<Given my experiences with you, Varnahrin, your words do not reassure me at all. But I am curious, even if it is a source of amusement for you.>

There was no answer to her comment and Tishan walked forward once more. As the surface of the vessel flowed upwards in response to her presence, she stood quite still, as instructed. Varnahrin was right: it was certainly an interesting experience. As the deck flowed upwards it entwined itself around her legs and filaments, like the fragile roots of a flower, swept upwards, delicately framing her head in a lacework of crystalline threads.

<What is happening, Varnahrin?> There was a tinge of panic in Tishan's thoughts even though she knew that no harm would come to her.

<The ImXin is interfacing with you, Tishan. Soon your thoughts and willpower will control the craft and allow you to travel.>

<But supposing I crash it or fly us into a mountain?>

<Do not concern yourself, there are built in fail-safes that preclude that eventuality. The ImXin is quite capable of preserving its integrity and of defending itself should it be attacked, as well as protecting those who travel upon it.>

<Weapons? Is it capable of attack?>

<No, child. As I said, it was primarily for exploration, but the Kareems' interest in what lay around them diminished, they grew more insular, and their population declined. Besides, they had developed gateways and the need for craft like this vanished.>

Tishan pondered the information Varnahrin had provided. <Well, it's going to cause quite a stir as people see me flying around on this thing.>

<Not at all. Only you can see it and only those who travel upon it are aware of its existence. If you flew over Ta'Morin and someone happened to look up, all they would see is a slight shimmer in the sky above them, so it is unlikely they would notice it; and even if they did, would shrug it off as a weather effect. Why don't you try it out? It would be good practise for you anyway.>

<So, what do I do?>

<What you always do: clear your mind, focus your thoughts, and command the ImXin. Try taking it up above the trees.>

Tishan looked once more at her immediate surroundings. The trees that shielded the field were to her immediate front and extended along two sides of the field, so that the gap in the trees was behind her. Her arms were completely free, and she still grasped the rod in her hand. This she now dismissed, and it disappeared from her grasp. She thought about what she wanted to do, and it seemed natural to lift her arms at the same time as she gave a mental direction to the ImXin.

She laughed in delight as the vessel lifted noiselessly. A slight sensation of weightlessness for just a moment accompanied the upwards movement and then the ImXin sat hovering above the treetops.

<Interesting technique. If you do that all the time you are going to be exhausted by the time you reach the Ma'Vessick homeland,> said Varnahrin with amusement.

<You may mock me, Varnahrin, but it helps me focus my intent.> Tishan's thoughts were laden with an amused disdain. She

thought that Varnahrin was right, and to any outside observer she would appear like some lunatic conductor of a non-existent group of musicians; but no-one could see her, and it did actually help. With a superior expression on her face, she commanded the vessel to turn, at the same time raising her right arm and moving her hand with a circling motion.

This time there was a musical sound of laughter from Varnahrin which Tishan found infectious, and she joined Varnahrin even as the ImXin spun around in time with the movements of Tishan's hand.

<You are quite right, child.> Varnahrin's words were tinged with humour. <Keep doing it that way. If it works for you, then continue; it certainly amuses me.>

<I am so pleased,> said Tishan in a tone that indicated the exact opposite. It took some time for Varnahrin to regain composure and Tishan smiled inwardly, not least at sharing humour with a fragment of the Intelligence. It was a sobering thought.

Tishan spent the rest of that day piloting the ImXin. As her confidence grew, she flew a little further afield each time. Looking down from above was a fascinating experience and she flew over Ta'Morin several times, watching her people walking the streets, all oblivious to her passage above them. For a time, she hovered over the Complex itself and watched the beam of energy issuing from the central tower. Inevitably her thoughts turned to Menkh. She prayed that he was alive and that she would see him again, safely returned once he had completed the greater task that he was embarked upon.

CHAPTER TWELVE

Menkh fought to maintain his sanity. He was completely confined within a black web of energy that deprived him of all physical movement and sensory stimulation. Entombed in an impenetrable blackness, only one sound intruded: screaming. For some time, he was not sure that it was not his own tortured cries he heard, but as he battled with all his will to establish rational thought, he realised that the screams were not his, but Crixac's, and he recalled the words of the creature that had ambushed and entrapped them both.

Slowly Menkh exerted control over himself. There was a void inside his mind where Crixac had once filled a place. He had not realised how much the symbiote had become a part of him. It was like a terrible battle wound, where an arm or a leg had been removed but the sensation of that limb remained. In conjunction with the restoration of control, a slow, burning anger began to manifest. Whether it was the build-up of this rage, or some other quality that revealed itself in times of dire need as a bonded Adept, he found he could block out the screams and retreat into another aspect of himself buried deep in his subconscious. As his thoughts retreated inwards, he strove to reassert self-belief, to reach an inner calm, and suddenly he found himself immersed in a long-forgotten memory.

ooooOoooo

Dur ab Shemma, Pohlan Kar of the Graaven Empire, sat enthroned outside his pavilion. The Royal Diadem glinted on his brow and the Mace of Office lay in his lap as he observed his army assault the last of the enemy holed up in their mountain fastness.

For the third time that day, as the war drums boomed and the blare of horns sounded the attack, his warriors were once more thrown back in bloody disarray.

'Pohlan Kar, we must send in the Baran Mec. They will break this rabble and send them reeling.' Peremon of the Shallic spoke quietly but insistently in Dur's ears. Muted agreement came from Fazor of the Persavic and Hema of the Mellish clans, themselves of the highest nobility, though none as high as that of Dur ab Shemma.

The skin markings on Dur ab Shemma's body had begun to engorge. A sure sign of his increasing wrath.

'You would have me throw the Baran Mec against … what did you call it? This rabble?' The Pohlan Kar was scathing. 'Not so much a rabble then, Peremon ab Karmic, if you would have me blood the guard against them.'

'Your spawnling Menkh is newly returned, Supremacy. Surely his skill in battle would guarantee our success?' Fazor's voice had a guarded tone and he exchanged pointed looks with the others who stood near the seated Emperor. 'Unless, of course, you think him unworthy?'

Fazor in his arrogance had overstepped himself. Dur ab Shemma turned a baleful glare on the smirking noble, who quailed at the look on the Pohlan Kar's face. The noble did not fail to notice the tendrils on Dur's neck had flushed scarlet. With alacrity

Fazor knelt in abject apology, whilst Peremon and Hema averted their gazes from Dur's face.

'You forget yourself, Fazor. Now, crawl on your knees out of my sight and be grateful I do not have you gutted and hung on a post for target practise,' said Dur ab Shemma with barely contained rage. 'Go! Return to Tarmech and hope that my displeasure has been assuaged when I return.'

Dur ab Shemma did not see the look of naked hatred that played over Fazor's features. He had almost made a fatal mistake, but the plans to dispose of the Pohlan Kar were well advanced. Even now his closest advisers administered a slow-acting poison, and soon they would be rid of Dur ab Shemma. The problem of Menkh ab Dur remained. Having him lead an attack against this entrenched position may lead to a swift resolution of that matter.

Dur ab Shemma turned his gaze away from Fazor's cringing figure. He felt slighted and his honour tarnished; perhaps there was merit in what Fazor and the others had suggested, however unworthily the view had been expressed. Dur ab Shemma spoke aloud. 'Call for the Pohlan Harac, tell Menkh ab Dur he is summoned.'

As Dur ab Shemma watched the last of his warriors limp back from the attack, Menkh ab Dur stood before him and gave the Baran Mec salute. Menkh's gaze was wary. He could see that his sire was in a temper and approaching the Pohlan Kar whilst he was in any sort of belligerent mood called for tact, lest sudden rage fall upon the supplicant.

'You have seen the results of the attacks?' Dur ab Shemma said querulously.

'I have, Supremacy.'

'You will take the Baran Mec and deal with our enemy.'

Menkh nodded his head. 'I will.'

Dur looked down upon his spawnling. His rage had diminished, and a sardonic smile crossed his features. 'You will?'

Menkh looked deep into his sire's eyes. 'I will, but I will need two chaal to mount the attack.'

Dur ab Shemma nodded once in assent. Menkh ab Dur saluted once more and turned rapidly away, summoning the Kalvaks and Shu Lan of the guard to him. Dur ab Shemma sat down once again and, raising his hand, called over Shu Lan Tishan Dar. Tishan gave a crisp salute and leant across to hear Dur ab Shemma's command.

'Shu Lan, you will stand alongside the Pohlan Harac and protect him.' As Tishan Dar went to salute again, the Pohlan Kar fixed her with a steely gaze. 'Do not come back if anything happens to him.' His voice was wintry.

'If anything happens to him, Supremacy, I will already be dead.'

Dur ab Shemma nodded in response and watched her as she saluted and jogged away to stand near Menkh. Hema ab Arkas presented a cup of Storluth brandy, which Dur accepted with a grunt. A knowing look passed between Peremon and Hema.

Meanwhile, Menkh had made his preparations. The Baran Mec were deployed in three ranks of five hundred, twenty paces apart. Behind them one thousand Sagit also stood, in two ranks of five hundred, thirty paces further back behind the last row of guards.

'You understand what I want you to do?' Menkh peered at the Kalvak commanding the Sagit.

The Kalvak nodded in assent. 'It has never been done before, Pohlan Harac, but these are the most experienced and reliable of our Sagit. They will do their best.'

'Very well. I will need your best too, Kalvak.'

'You will have it, Stragosh.'

Menkh nodded and strode to the front rank. He saw that Shu Lan Tishan had placed herself alongside him. Smiling, he pushed his helmet over the bristles that covered his head and shoulders and laced his helmet. 'Under orders, Shu Lan?'

'As ever, my Harac. My job would be easier if you stood in the last row.' Tishan's tone reflected a degree of frustration.

'You cannot lead from the rear, Tishan Dar: you, of all people, know that.'

Menkh did not wait for a response. Hefting his shield, he raised his mace in the air and called out in a strong voice, 'Baran Mec! Baran Mec! Are you with me!?' In response, a mighty clash of maces against shields reverberated and echoed off the cliff face ahead of them. No further encouragement was necessary. These were the Baran Mec, the cream of all Graaven forces, elite warriors known for their skill at arms and their unremitting courage.

Menkh's arm came down from the vertical and pointed ahead. As one, the ranks of Baran Mec stepped forward. A hissing sound passed over their heads as one thousand arrows sprang from Graaven war bows and shafts were launched at the enemy stronghold. As the guard steadily advanced, the Sagit advanced behind them, sending shower after shower of shafts arcing over the heads of the Baran Mec, pinning the enemy down. Any foe foolish enough to look above the rock walls they had erected was spitted by arrows that fell in an unceasing rain.

Menkh had closely observed the enemy positions. Great pillars of weathered rock, like fingers, rose out of the parched earth, pointing skywards. Ravines and crevasses full of tumbled boulders and scree were everywhere, and growing up out of these were dense and thorny plants, almost impossible to pass. The enemy had chosen their ground well. These were the last of the Percassian rebels that resisted the might of the Graaven Empire. Menkh inwardly admired their stoic courage in the face of adversity. Whoever their leader was, he or she was both wily and courageous. Now this was the last stand for them. The traditions of the Graavens were that all resistance was to be crushed mercilessly and the enemy obliterated. Increasingly, Menkh had begun to have doubts over this practice: doubts which were shared by his sibling Pershiva.

Now he drew closer to the wall of rocks and other impediments the Percassians had erected to break up any attack, and still the arrow storm continued unabated. It would do so until Menkh raised his mace high once more. At least, Menkh hoped that it would abate, otherwise Baran Mec would begin to die under the barrage. Already some shafts were falling short and either pinged off Graaven shields held aloft or slammed into them, so that the front ranks began to resemble the spiky head of a treloth.

At the last possible moment Menkh held his mace aloft and began to run towards the barrier of rocks in front of him. Two more showers of arrows tore into the wall ahead of him, many shattering on the rocks. It was only a matter of time for the Percassians to appreciate that the arrow storm had ceased. With a mighty roar, the Baran Mec sprang after Menkh and Tishan and swept like a tide up the rock barrier. At last, the Percassians stood, themselves loosing arrows, spears, and rocks into the Graavens as they climbed. As Menkh placed his foot onto the rocks to begin his climb, Tishan shoved him to one side, lifting her shield to deflect a large rock that one of the enemy had hurled down.

'Pohlan Harac! I must insist. You are no use to the Empire if you are dead!'

Menkh was filled with battle fury, his skin markings were engorged, and the tendrils on his neck flared. As Tishan looked into his eyes she saw the rage of battle diminish and Menkh nodded his head. 'You are right to chastise me, Shu Lan. We will let the guard clear the way.'

Already the second rank had reached the barrier and begun the climb. Judging it safer, Tishan climbed with them, covering Menkh as he, too, ascended. Individual Percassians were still being picked off by Graaven Sagit, who had closed the gap between them and their attacking forces when the opportunity arose.

As Menkh and Tishan climbed over the barrier and reached the other side, a lone Percassian broke away from the desperate fighting in front of them and came straight at Menkh. Tishan swept her arm around and knocked him off balance and Menkh's mace smashed into the enemy's head. Menkh noticed it was a female but whether unconscious or dead, he could not tell.

When the third rank of Baran Mec joined the fray, the Percassians had retreated into a tight ring. Their wounded had been dragged behind them, along with those Percassians too old or too young to fight. The Percassian soldiers fought with suicidal desperation, but the end was inevitable. Suddenly Menkh was sick of the slaughter.

'Baran Mec! Baran Mec! Withdraw! Withdraw!'

Menkh's call was echoed by Shu Lan and Shu Mut so that in moments the surviving Percassians were left alone, standing warily some twenty paces from the stationary Baran Mec, their exhaustion evident, their comrades lying dead on the ground around them. One or two Baran Mec lay motionless and some nursed wounds, but they had taken a terrible toll of the enemy and their own casualties were too few to be of any consideration.

Defiant yet despairing, the Percassians awaited their fate. They knew all too well how Graavens dealt with those who took arms against them. Their spawnlings wept but there was little comfort to be had.

Menkh stepped forward and stopped just a few paces back from the enemy line. He had left his mace and shield on the ground behind him, but Tishan Dar stood to his right and another guard to his left, ready to defend him from a sudden desperate attack. Percassian speech was very close to Graaven in meaning and intonation so Menkh was confident he would be understood.

'I am Menkh ab Dur, Pohlan Harac and spawn of Dur ab Shemma, Pohlan Kar of the Graaven Empire. Who amongst you will speak for your people?'

The Percassians looked with confusion amongst themselves until a bloodied figure stood up, with assistance from two other wounded warriors, and limped painfully to the front rank.

'I am Haraid, leader of those of our people left standing here. What do you want? Is this some Graaven trick?'

Menkh removed his helmet. 'I am not sure what it is, Haraid of the Percassians, but perhaps we might make history here today. Will you sit?' Without waiting for an answer Menkh sat upon the rocky ground. The Baran Mec exchanged looks but not a word was uttered.

Grunting, Haraid lowered himself as well and sat directly opposite Menkh.

'It seems to me,' said Menkh, his eyes never wavering from Haraid's, 'that an enemy who shows such courage and tenacity in the face of Graaven might is an enemy to be respected. Perhaps even an enemy who might, in time, become a friend.'

Haraid's expression was unfathomable. Distrust mixed with enmity and the tentative beginnings of hope.

'You are Graaven. It is not your way to leave an enemy living on the field of battle. How then would this be possible? You speak of a dream, tempting but unobtainable.'

Menkh looked about him. 'This is a hard land. Uninhabited, from what I have seen, but with good water and ground that may yet be favourable for terrax growing.' Menkh's eyes returned to Haraid's. 'Land that might be yours, given certain conditions.'

Haraid blinked with pain, but his voice was steady. 'Conditions?'

'You will swear by Bekkor that you will never take up arms again against the Empire. Further, within, let us say, three sem'chaal, you will send a tribute of three callum of terrax to our nearest garrison.'

'How would this be possible, even if we agreed? Will the Pohlan Kar of the Graaven Empire accede to your offering, or will he prostrate himself in laughter before he orders our extinction?'

'I would not make the offer unless I believed that the Pohlan Kar would agree.' Menkh's voice reflected total belief in what he said.

Haraid shook his head in wonder and laughed before grimacing in pain. 'Very well, Menkh ab Dur, Pohlan Harac of the Graaven Empire. If you can achieve this miracle, we will make a pledge before Bekkor.'

Menkh nodded his head gravely. He was convinced that the Pohlan Kar would grant what he had promised. There was much in the Empire that needed to change and Dur ab Shemma was no fool. Besides, this was barren and uninhabited land which may yet be turned into a valuable asset. Situated as it was near the Steppes of Portis, it could also act as a buffer against the savage nomads who lived there. He stood and turned to the ranks of Baran Mec gathered around him. 'Tishan Dar, you will remain with two praka to watch over our new "friends". I will send food, water, and medicines.' He turned his attention back to the guard. 'I am proud to have fought with you today. The time for killing is over.' Menkh paused. 'The time for drinking has begun!'

This last pronouncement was met with a mighty hammering of mace upon shield. A cry of 'Menkh ab Dur' rose up until it roared from every throat. The Percassians lay down their arms with a sense of wonder and not a few tears of heartfelt relief at this unexpected and unheard-of turn of events. The gaze of Haraid of the Percassians did not move as he watched the departing figure of Menkh ab Dur. Rightly or wrongly, he had committed his people to peace; only the future would tell if these Graavens could be trusted.

Far away, Dur ab Shemma heard the cries of the Baran Mec and smiled.

ooooOooooo

The memory of that conflict and what he had wrought on that day reinvigorated and restored Menkh's faith in himself. Slowly he focused his will and, tentatively, he reached out with his mind and pushed against the darkness that constrained him. At first, he could sense nothing but the lines of energy that held him fast. It was like trying to grasp a fresh-caught fish that slithered and slipped out of his grasp. His initial lack of progress did not deter him and the more he persisted, the more he began to realise that the darkness was actually the secretion of a complex series of energies that expected his efforts to fully understand them and twisted away, reforming themselves. His experimentation left him in no doubt that the prison he was trapped in could anticipate his actions and react accordingly.

Menkh maintained an unyielding focus. In the blackness of his confinement, he could not measure time. He fought down the panic that threatened to arise when he thought of his people and what they might be facing even now. The creature that he and Crixac had encountered was incredibly powerful, but Menkh had met powerful enemies before and had ultimately defeated them. So he continued to push and prod, changing his approach and endeavouring to adapt his tactics and anticipate, in his own turn, what the energies that encased him might do. Finally, after what seemed endless chaal of struggle, he isolated a single strand. Mentally he explored it and its connection to the other strands that comprised the trap. His mind teased its way between the flows of energy and for the briefest moment he opened the tiniest gap to the outside before it snapped shut.

For an endless and frustrating time, he endeavoured to open his prison, but always the energies seemed to be able to shut down the tiny cracks he established. At last, he found that he could 'twist' one of the energies and establish a kind of mental block, which enabled him to keep a tiny crack open.

217

Menkh rested. Whilst a part of him exulted with his achievement, he had to think about the next move whilst maintaining the newly opened crevice. His first step was to try and summon his staff, which had winked out of existence the moment the trap was sprung. This proved fruitless. Whether, as he hoped, the substance of the energies which bound him prevented its appearance or, as he feared, the staff had been destroyed or stolen, he gave up the attempt after several wasted efforts.

As he concentrated on his situation a new idea emerged. It had no basis in logic but was rather a feeling that, the more he concentrated on, the more right it felt. He thought about what he could do to see if he could translate the feeling into an action.

With the utmost care, he slid part of his mind out through the crevice. It was like thrusting his head into too small a gap between iron bars. Not only was there a terrible sense of constriction but there was also a palpable resistance. Then, in the last moment, he managed to push through, like an eye pushed up against a keyhole, and he could sense the outside. All around him was the black emptiness of space, a void of nothingness that he floated within.

Menkh fought back despair. Was it possible that this was a prison within a prison? He pondered this for a time. No, his senses told him that the quality of the space around him was very different. Cold and empty, yes, but it was the outside. Intuitively he formed a thought, like a shout out for help. So vast was the gulf surrounding him he felt that his idea was both ridiculous and pointless but, as he considered, there was nothing to lose, and the concentration required to both maintain the opening and his limited presence outside was taxing.

Focusing all his will, he called out for aid. He could not have explained why he did so, or how he could conceive that anyone might actually hear that call, but within the construct of the thought was the image of himself, the situation he was caught in, and a desperate plea for help. He did not, even now, fully comprehend the latent powers of a bonded Adept, but he hoped that his cry might trigger something. He maintained the call for as long as he could until a terrible pain engulfed him, the tiny crack snapped shut, and he was flung back into the confines of his lonely cell. Crixac's screams continued without abatement.

ooooOoooo

They sang. Their complex harmonies echoing across the cosmos emitted a song of joy that impacted every living creature who heard or felt it. Across the boundless distance of space, they called to one another as they journeyed where need led them. They fed on light, and the complex bonds that joined them lent power to the music that they made. Ever alert for vibrations of discord and imbalance, they travelled faster than thought on the edges of reality in the between, their song one of comfort and of hope, of new beginnings and an end to sorrow.

Above a swirling cloud of cosmic dust illuminated by a distant sun and diffracted into a rainbow of colours, a school of gathanax appeared out of the ether. For a moment, by mutual acknowledgement, the glorious notes of their song were stilled, and they attuned their sense to something else. It was a call – tenuous, barely discernible, so distant in space was it.

Bright lights that flashed along the jelly-like bodies of each individual gathanax became muted, so intense was their tuning to the vibration. In an instant, each individual knew not only who had made that call but where it was located, for in the moment that Menkh and Crixac had freed the enslaved gathanax, held so cruelly by the Chosen, the knowledge of them been passed to every gathanax family grouping and individual by those so recently released. With unvoiced and perfect consent, the school of gathanax pulsed with light and disappeared.

ooooOoooo

Menkh lay entombed. Fighting off madness had begun to take its toll, his entrapment likened to being buried deep under the earth, still living but beyond assistance. Lost in a vortex of mental pain, he had no perception when the gathanax appeared, floating around the pool of darkness that encased him.

The gathanax probed the shell with their thoughts and recoiled at its horror. Their song stilled once again, and their collective thoughts turned to the thing before them. In perfect accord, their voices began with a low susurration of sound, building layer upon layer and harmony upon harmony. Soon the volume of that sound was indescribable. The vibrations produced irresistible waves and their effect on the casing of Menkh's prison was visible as it twisted and warped. Finally, and irrevocably, the energy that bound Menkh lost all power to resist the song of the gathanax. It was utterly overcome and shred away to nothingness, leaving Menkh floating, still and lifeless.

The song changed. Its strident call lowered in pitch and volume. Its vibrations, both physical and metaphysical, were now healing, calming, regenerating.

Menkh was trapped in a living nightmare. In what seemed reality to his mind he saw Crixac being tortured beyond endurance, and the bodies of Tishan and their offspring mutilated and killed before his eyes. His own screams rose to mirror theirs. Into this horror, a voice he remembered well spoke to him. A whisper at first, it grew stronger in his mind.

<Menkh, Menkh! Come back. All is well, this is but a nightmare. Follow my voice, dear one, follow me to the light.>

<Pershiva,> Menkh called. <Pershiva, they are dead, and I could do nothing!>

<No, brother. They live. They miss you. Follow my voice. Leave the nightmare behind you. Follow me to the light.>

<Pershiva, do not leave me. I am afraid!>

<I will never leave you, I am always with you. Follow my voice.>

Menkh felt his strength returning and the horror receding from his mind. A song of joy and healing filled his mind and he felt himself flying upwards towards Pershiva's voice. At last, he emerged, and his eyes opened. It was if he was bathed in a radiant light of warmth and comfort. Around him several gathanax sang a song that reminded him of a lullaby. Within that radiant light the form of Pershiva floated and smiled at him.

'How is this possible?' He spoke aloud in a tone of great wonder.

<With gathanax, the veil between life and that which lies beyond is lifted. They called to me, and I came.>

<How can I repay them for rescuing me?>

Another voice entered his mind. Deep and sonorous, it was neither male nor female but contained echoes of both. <Your thanks are unnecessary, Menkh ab Dur, we feel your gratitude and renewed hope. You are a friend to all our kind, and we, too, work to uphold the Balance. Call us, we will aid you where we can.>

Before Menkh could send out a thought in response the gathanax disappeared, though their song lingered for a time.

<I, too, am always with you, beloved. Go now, you have much to do.>

Pershiva seemed to phase into a bright blue light, and then she too disappeared, leaving Menkh surprisingly calm in the aftermath.

Without conscious thought, and to Menkh's considerable relief, the staff reappeared in his hand. Menkh nodded to himself. Cautiously he summoned the Threadway and with his senses questing out ahead of him he turned his thoughts to the Balance-point and to the rescue of Crixac. One thing above all was in his mind: he would not see his friend exposed to torture for one moment longer than was necessary. Only together could they defeat the evil that opposed them.

Menkh travelled and a sense of urgency fuelled by his captivity and confinement ensured that he sped across the gulf of space that separated him from the Balancepoint. He was completely dismayed when, as he materialised in the place where the Balancepoint had once stood, a picture of devastation met his eyes. A vast bowl of glowing rock was surrounded by a forest of ashes. Even the sky above was flecked with lightning and a darkness covered all the land. It was apparent that the enemy had been and gone, but whether the destruction of the Balancepoint had been achieved was, to him, a mystery.

Menkh fought down wayward thoughts and concentrated. The Balancepoint was a source of infinite power and control and would not be destroyed easily. His logical mind told him that had the enemy overcome those who defended the Balancepoint, it would not seek to destroy, but rather to use the power to its own ends. Therefore, the Balancepoint would still stand and be subject to manipulation. He concluded that either Frzath and the other Adepts had themselves destroyed it, or they had a contingency plan in place. Menkh immediately adopted this thought; it was something he himself would have had in place and it was inconceivable that those whose task was to guard the Balancepoint would have left any potential threat without a counter.

As a bonded Adept he had a connection to the Intelligence that was unique. Focusing his thoughts upon the Balancepoint, he drew in the Threadway and disappeared from view. The colours of the Threadway flowed beneath him. Other worlds and moons flashed past him. He approached a blinding light that grew rapidly, until it seemed to stretch forever in every direction, and then he pierced the light and sped on once again through the blackness of space. Finally, he descended the ribbons of the Threadway, spiralling down toward what appeared to be a cloud of luminous gases and dust. As he descended, he discerned an object suspended within the heart of the cloud and, as he drew closer, he could see that it was itself a ball of even brighter light. His senses whirled, there was the briefest disorientation, and he felt himself emerge, standing upon the Eye of Malavak within the Balancepoint. Before him stood Frzath and Plakar, looks of wonder upon their faces.

<We gave up hope of seeing you again, Menkh!> The intensity of Frzath's emotions underlaid his thoughts.

<More wondrous still is how you have managed to locate us. It should be impossible,> remarked Plakar. <Not only because we have shifted several times, but we have also moved outside of reality. Currently we exist in the between and it should not be possible for anyone to find us.>

<It leaves me worried that the enemy may be able to locate us also,> Frzath added pensively.

<As to that, my friends, I cannot answer. I focused my will upon the Threadway after leaving the devastation of our last meeting place and I was carried inexorably here. Perhaps the Intelligence itself lends me aid? My burning question is how much time has elapsed since my imprisonment? Has the enemy attacked Tarvuli itself?>

Frzath and Plakar looked at each other. <As we have said before, time works differently in different places, Menkh. What may seem to be but a few moments in one place may be days or weeks somewhere else,> said Plakar. <For us, it has been several cycles of time as we measure it, but if we are brutally honest, we have had little time to consider your situation other than desperately hope that you were alive. Since the initial attack we have managed to stay ahead of the enemy and our location, as far as we are aware, remains undetected.>

Frzath offered his view in response to Menkh's voiced concerns. <As to the aid of the Intelligence, mayhap you are right. Events move apace: however, we can at least reassure you that Tarvuli has beaten off an assault by our enemy. We have been able to observe events from here. It would seem that Tarvuli is shielded

by a powerful force that for now, at least, has proved more than ample to thwart a direct attack. However long the period you were entrapped, it would seem that only several of your meh'chaal have passed in the interim. But in any event, you are here now, and you have come at need. How may we aid you further?>

Menkh felt a deep sense of relief; for all he knew, a thousand sem'chaal may have passed by and Tarvuli been reduced to ashes. Given the horrific nightmare of his experience and the screams of those he held dear, it was reassuring to know that they were, indeed, just dreams. <Tishan and I, aided by Varnahrin, were successful in re-energising a defensive shield originally established by the three Adepts.>

<Varnahrin?> Frzath was quizzical.

<Yes, Tishan has named the Shard, just as the City is renamed Ta'Morin.>

<Remarkable.> T'klath's tone was reflective, and she shared a look with the others. <I cannot recall such a thing ever happening before. A name is a powerful thing and may have unintended consequences.>

Menkh was urgent. <We may speculate on that at length but right now, I need to rescue Crixac. Without our combined wills I believe our greater task is doomed to fail. He was ripped from me by the enemy who vowed to have him screaming for eternity hanging from the Tree of Tangoreth. I need to know where that is.>

Frzath and Plakar exchanged worried looks.

<You speak of ancient lore, Menkh. The way the legends tell it, Tangoreth supported a form of life like no other. Technologically advanced, they became the architects of their own destruction. Once a verdant world, Tangoreth became a place of noxious gases, its climate and environment totally hostile to any creature of flesh and bone. Do not be misled by the word 'tree'. The Tree of Tangoreth is not like the trees of other worlds. The

legends tell us that this Tree is likely the cause of Tangoreth's corruption. Whilst the stories are unclear as to its true nature, it is evident that it is some form of malevolent force. If the enemy has indeed imprisoned Crixac there, it reveals more about the strength of its power and evil intent.>

<I have no doubt that it has done exactly what it said it will do. Where do the legends tell us that Tangoreth is located?> Menkh said.

<For that, we need Morgath. His expertise and knowledge of ancient lore is without peer.>

No sooner had the words been uttered than Morgath appeared before them in answer to a mental summons from Frzath. After being acquainted with the news, Morgath wasted no time in harnessing the power of the Eye of Malavak. Menkh felt the dropping sensation as the Eye blurred into motion. Several long moments passed as entire galaxies swept by until, at last, the speed of their passage diminished, and objects came back into focus.

Morgath responded to Menkh's unspoken question. <Yes, it is a long way away, Menkh. Even on the Threadway it will take some time to reach the location where Tangoreth is reputed to be, but as you can see, the Eye can provide us with no specific details. This quadrant of space is either cloaked or there is some kind of interference that even we Adepts cannot pierce.>

<I need not tell you to be cautious, Menkh,> said Plakar.

<I have been caught unawares once, my friends – it will not happen a second time,> Menkh responded grimly. <However, I am hopeful that this enemy of ours is so confident in the arrogance of its power it will not suspect that I have escaped or that I might reach Tangoreth itself.>

<Then you have no time to spare. If you believe that the rescue of Crixac is critical, then so be it. You have its general location fixed in your mind. We will relocate the Balancepoint shortly. Once that is achieved, we will endeavour to send a message to

Tarvuli that we are safe. Varnahrin will already know that you have returned to our reality.>

<Yes, I feel the bond though I cannot speak to Varnahrin in my mind. I was worried the enemy may have been able to manipulate our connection and follow it to Tarvuli.>

Frzath pondered Menkh's thoughts. <I understand your thinking in this, but the bond we speak of is an indefinable thing, so rare that none living have any concept of how the bond is maintained. I cannot conceive of any way that the enemy might exploit it for its own ends; but clearly it has been able to locate Tarvuli so, yet again, we have questions to which, as yet, there is no answer.>

<Then we must pursue the course of action we think is right.> Menkh paused and took a breath. <My friends, may you stay safe. Once I have rescued Crixac I will return to you – until then, may the Intelligence aid you.>

The three Adepts raised their arms and Menkh felt a soothing energy issue from them and surround him. <Go with our blessing, Menkh ab Dur. We will aid you as we can. The Balance is all.>

<The Balance is all,> Menkh echoed. As he summoned the Threadway, the features of the three Adepts glimmered and then vanished, so rapid was his ascent. The ultimate destination was fixed in his mind and Menkh sped away, faster than thought, into the unknown.

CHAPTER THIRTEEN

Menkh's staff blazed with light. He had created a protective shield that he hoped would repulse any attack that might eventuate. He was determined not to be caught unawares and although his mind was focused on his ultimate destination, his consciousness extended beyond his physical being, probing ahead for any sign of unwanted attention. If any sentient being could have observed his passage, he would have appeared like a star hurtling across the heavens. So great was the speed of his travel that entire planetary systems passed in a blur.

Eventually he knew he was nearing his goal and he slowed his movement. Things that had been blurred came back into focus and he passed above several planets. His senses indicated that they were now devoid of whatever life they may have once held. There was an emptiness around him that was not simply the emptiness of space: rather, it was a total absence of any sense of life. And yet, within that emptiness, a sense of desolation, a brooding but indefinable presence that grew ever stronger as he approached a single planet.

Menkh halted and probed the surface of the sphere. It was covered in a dense cloud of gases which, even from his height, he could see swirled violently. So thick was the mass of cloud that his mind could not penetrate it. Steeling himself, he descended.

As he pierced the maelstrom of toxic gases he was buffeted by violent, searing winds of enormous temperature. As he descended further, the density of the cloud increased, as did the pressure all around him, until it was so great that he felt like a mountain weighed him down. Finally, he reached the surface, and he hovered slightly above the ground – which was just as well as, for the most part, it consisted of almost molten rock. The clouds of gas were like a fog that totally obscured his surrounds. Still, he felt drawn by something, and he moved toward it. He could sense a presence like nothing he had ever experienced. Powerful. Malevolent. Aware.

Time meant nothing in this place. His journey forward through the obscuring clouds and violent winds was as if he floated in some never-ending nightmare, trapped but enduring. Abruptly the fog of gases parted, and the noise of the wind became muted. Although he had felt no sense of piercing a veil of any kind and the toxic wind continued to rage all around him, he had entered an area shielded from the planet's hostile environment. He floated above a black and rocky surface and was approaching a single finger of twisted rock that projected over a vast chasm. As he drew closer, he could see that the chasm itself was so deep that the bottom could not be made out. He determined the shield was like an inverted bowl for, in the distance, he could see the swirling clouds of gas held at bay far above his head and extending for quite some distance away from him. He stood within a dome but could not sense what kind of force could hold back the power of this world's fury.

Something tugged at his thoughts and his eyes snapped back to the finger of rock. There, where moments before he had seen nothing, was a shape of horror and his mind recalled a memory from a long-ago battle. They were pursuing the enemy across a vast swamp whose hidden pathways were well known to those they pursued. Inevitably in the heat of the chase they reached a point where several Hoplex had simply stepped off the precarious path of solid ground they followed and into the bogland. Frantic efforts were made to extract them but, weighed down as they were by chainmail, it was an almost impossible task. Menkh could still hear their screams as if it were yesterday, as they sank into the depths. One image was fixed in particular. Menkh had formed a kind of friendship, as much as was possible between a prince and a common soldier, with Ekkar, a Hoplex who had told Menkh his stories of past campaigns and experiences. Menkh had found them fascinating. Now Ekkar's eyes were fixed upon Menkh's as he sank into the bog. Whilst Menkh would never forget the look on his face as he disappeared, it was his hands – raised high above his head into the air, reaching helplessly towards the light, the muscles and tendons of his arms extended, and the fingers stretched out in supplication as the rest of him disappeared – that gave Menkh nightmares. That was the shape of the Tree of Tangoreth, which, of course, was now revealed to be no tree at all.

It appeared to be made of millions of panes of black glass. The 'fingers' of its limbs stretched upwards so that they appeared to brush the shield of protection high above. Its massive trunk was twisted all around and appeared to be made of many different stems that coiled around each other. The Tree of Tangoreth exuded a sense of despair that defied description whilst remaining silent and brooding.

Menkh approached, drawing ever closer. His will was tightly focused into the staff, as prepared as he could be for an attack on his mind. Menkh realised that Crixac was entombed inside this thing. As if in tune with that realisation, Menkh discerned a muted moaning, like a thousand tormented souls crying out in agony. The Tree of Tangoreth moved. A rippling sigh emanated from its many trunks as they turned fractionally, twisting together likes strands of rope.

The attack, when it came, was like nothing Menkh had experienced. Even what he had endured in the ambush seemed but the brush of an insect's wing to the assault that dropped on him like a hammer blow. The staff flared through red, yellow, and green in rapid succession and then settled into a virulent purple as Menkh fell to his knees, holding it above him like a shield. Menkh's mind cringed, such was the pressure and intensity, and he could not gather his thoughts to counter the strike. Unlike the ambush where the being that had executed it exulted in Menkh's weakness and stupidity, here there was nothing. No emotion of any kind could be felt and no attempt at communication was made. It was as if a mountain had suddenly decided to attack him. It was like being buried under an avalanche with the mountain totally indifferent to the outcome. Yet, there was something else. It was hunger: yes, that was it, an all-consuming hunger. Not the hunger of someone starving seeking nourishment, nor even a hunger fuelled by pure greed and insatiable appetite. This was something different: detached, cold, emotionless.

Menkh felt his defences crumbling. The staff quivered in his hands, and he felt that at any moment it would shatter into a thousand pieces. In desperation, Menkh reached out to the Threadway. His only thought was to escape the clutches of this thing and come up with a new strategy. His efforts failed and as his energy and mind hovered on the edge of collapse, with one last gargantuan effort of will, he reached out.

Tendrils of light coalesced around him, but rather than bearing him up and away as he expected, they seemed to flow all around him, penetrating his fraught mind. Voices came into his head in numbers too great to tell.

<We are here with you, Menkh ab Dur. Merge with us. Join with us. Drink in our energy and refocus your mind.>

Menkh had no power to answer. He merged his mind with the presence in the way that someone drowning might clutch at a branch that floated within reach.

This time there was a reaction from the Tree of Tangoreth. It was a rage so pure it felt like a physical manifestation and with it, the assault intensified.

Meanwhile, Menkh's focus and energy felt renewed. As he merged with the presence, his power grew commensurately. His will, thus reinforced, rose up to match the assault of the Tree and then, indomitable, surged. His mind wrapped around the Tree of Tangoreth, penetrating it and extending through every limb. Now he perceived that which had been hidden – for the Tree of Tangoreth was an artificial intelligence with but one purpose. Within its construct it held the life force of countless individuals who cried out in terror, forever entrapped and forced to relive, over and over again, an endless nightmare of pain and torment. To his horror, Menkh now understood that this ocean of suffering was the seat of its power.

Still, Menkh's focus grew, and he journeyed into a separate reality, created in part by the power of the Tree of Tangoreth but reinforced by the life force of those entombed within. Trapped inside their own living nightmare, each soul lingered in horror and despair, incapable of escape. Until now. As Menkh encountered each speck of life, he focused his will upon it, ripped apart the power that held it, and set it free. Each time, the speck disappeared immediately, leaving behind only an echo of elation. With each release, cracks and fractures appeared in the structure of the Tree and it began to disintegrate, faster and faster, forming a residue of black powder that fell heavily to the ground, as if each particle had the weight of a stone.

Deeper and deeper into the construct Menkh's mind travelled. Now he could feel that the myriad of voices that had filled his mind had themselves branched out in different directions and, continuing his work of freedom, Menkh felt the power to invest every limb and particle of the Tree with his mind. It was vast. Its interior space seemed to stretch on and on endlessly so that its external shape defied the reality of its internal form. At last, Menkh came to a place so deep within the Tree that it was like a crossroads, a place where many strands of power intersected.

There, suspended in space, hung a blue form. Intersecting lines of blackness pierced it, stretching the shape so that it appeared to be on the edge of being ripped into fragments. The blue form writhed in the grip of the black lines and Menkh could feel the terrible and unending torture that each line inflicted upon it.

There, at last, was Crixac. Hung as had been the dreadful promise, upon the Tree of Tangoreth.

Throughout all his training and years of experience in battle, Menkh had excelled in a calm detachment that had enabled victory after victory. As it had done in his battle against the Dorath Mar, however, Menkh's anger again became incandescent, his fury like a living force. With a single touch of his mind, he severed every last line of blackness and sent a bolt of energy surging back along every pathway. He could sense, rather than actually hear, a vast series of detonations as the Tree imploded.

Freed at last from its terrible embrace, he gently cradled Crixac in a web of light created from the staff and, drawing on his own power, drew Crixac's form back into himself, at the same time casting him into a deep and healing trancelike state.

As everything around him dissolved, Menkh sped back along a ribbon of light, withdrawing his mind and returning to his physical body. In satisfaction he watched as the Tree of Tangoreth disintegrated into a great mound of glinting black powder. Above him the shield of protection began to bulge and crack open, and the violent winds and gases began to break through the barrier which had held them at bay for millennia.

Menkh felt himself diminish somewhat as the presence left his mind and instead the colours of the Threadway took their place and bore him upwards.

<Thank you, my friends. Without your help I fear that my journey here would have had a different and less satisfactory result.> Menkh's thoughts were tinged with the horror of just what that result would have entailed.

<We will aid you where we can, Menkh ab Dur. All actions lead to a single convergence, but the result is not guaranteed. There is still much to be accomplished. We also have touched Crixac's being. He will recuperate. Be watchful, Menkh ab Dur. The Balance is all.> With that last message, the presence had vanished. Menkh floated high above the planet where he had nearly lost everything.

He was still wary. Escape from the Tree of Tangoreth and its destruction had not lessened his apprehension, lest he merely escape one danger only to be ensnared by another. Yet, as his senses extended outwards, sharpened by the power of the staff, he could sense a subtle but definable alteration in the space around him. Where before it had been devoid of anything, now there was a sense of something. Intangible but nonetheless real for that.

<You have restored Balance, Menkh. Now the promise of life renewed manifests itself.> Crixac's voice was so weak as to be barely discernible.

<My dear friend. You have no idea how good it feels to hear your voice and know that you are safe.> Menkh's answering thought was filled with a profound sense of relief.

<When we first made pact and you willingly allowed yourself to act as my host, I could not imagine what a debt I would owe you. I cannot even begin to describe the horror of my imprisonment. At first, though I sensed your presence, I believed it was just another level of torture to fuel my despair. It will be long before those memories can be pushed to one side. I did not think that my

kind could experience actual pain or fatigue, but I find now that I was so very wrong. But what of you, my dear friend? Your tale must be as harrowing. How did you escape the clutches of our mysterious enemy?>

Menkh and Crixac shared their travails, and each felt the pain of the other, and as a result their bond grew even stronger, so that they were less two entities and more one unified being.

<Who would have predicted the importance of our meeting with the gathanax, Menkh? Truly, I see the hand of the Intelligence in some of these occurrences.>

<I agree. In my own case I believe it was the Intelligence's direct intervention that was the only thing that saved me from being imprisoned with you in the Tree of Tangoreth. I cannot explain that presence in any other way. It was certainly not the gathanax; this was vastly different.>

Menkh felt Crixac shudder. <Please, Menkh, do not utter that name again, it is like having hot needles thrust into me.> Crixac's voice was tinged with horror. <Though I exult in its total destruction. No-one can say how many life essences were trapped within it, all now free, thanks to you.>

<So, we have exchanged our stories and time moves on. My thoughts are to return to the Balancepoint and plan our course of action from there. We may also be able to access more information about our as yet unidentified enemy. Your thoughts?>

<I can think of no better idea, Menkh. With your forbearance I will withdraw and rest. The experience of physical weakness is new to me, and I find I cannot sustain my thoughts any longer.>

<Do as you must, Crixac, regain your strength. We are both going to need it very soon.>

As Crixac's presence retreated, Menkh summoned the Threadway and, focusing his mind upon the Balancepoint, set off, his hopes and strength renewed now that Crixac was with him once again.

During the exchange with Crixac, Menkh had halted their journey on the Threadway. As he floated in space, threads of light energy swirled gently around him. As Menkh was about to restart the journey a thought entered his mind. It was logical and, though it might not work, he could not think of any undesirable consequence should his attempt fail. At the least he would have tested his theory and found it flawed.

As he would have done were he translocating on Tarvuli, he fixed his mind upon the Balancepoint, visualising in as much detail as possible the anteroom where the Eye of Malavak was located. He felt his staff throb with power in concert with his thoughts. Around him the Threadway, which had been gently swirling, began to spin faster and faster until the individual lines of energy blurred into one solid block of colour. The moment the colours coalesced, his senses reeled and he closed his eyes. The sensation lasted for just a moment and when he opened them, what he saw generated a combined sense of awe and satisfaction in him. He stood safely within the Balancepoint. He had crossed vast distances of space in the blink of an eye, and Frzath, who it appeared had been crossing the floor on an errand, had come to an abrupt halt, a look of stunned amazement on his face.

Having been joined in a hurriedly convened meeting by Plakar, Frzath, T'klath, Denith, Morgath, and Menkh sat in deep discussion, the thoughts of all clearly communicated with no need for speech.

<Truly this is a remarkable thing, Menkh,> Plakar observed. <None of us here were living when the last bonded Adept was alive. From what you have told us, only the gathanax can apparently travel as you have done.>

<That may be so,> Menkh responded, <but it very much depends on my experience of having been somewhere before. You cannot visualise, in the exact details required, a place you have never been to in order to journey there. Whilst it may seem that I

can travel like the gathanax, the way they navigate their journey I think is vastly different.>

<Still,> remarked T'klath, <it means that the Threadway can carry you back to Ta'Morin or anywhere on Tarvuli that you have been to in moments. It is amazing, certainly something I never anticipated and quite a remarkable discovery.>

Heads nodded in agreement.

<Let us return to a consideration of our enemy. Are there any thoughts as to who or what it may be?> Menkh posed the question to all present.

Crixac's thoughts quietly entered the conversation. <Creatures of myth reveal their living presence and it seems that things that were thought impossible now appear plausible. My experience with this being brings an echo of something ancient that tantalises my thoughts.>

<Crixac, welcome indeed,> Frzath responded warmly, his thoughts echoed by the others. <We are pleased beyond measure that Menkh was successful in securing your release. The obliteration of the Tree of Tangoreth restores Balance in that part of the cosmos.>

<It is the movements of the enemy that concern me,> said Menkh. <After the ambush, the enemy sped to the Balancepoint, and your destruction was averted by the narrowest of margins. It then mounted an unsuccessful assault on Tarvuli. Now it has disappeared. I have managed to reconnect with Varnahrin, albeit briefly. It is a relief that all is quiet here for the moment, so I will journey back to Ta'Morin. Varnahrin may have gleaned further information for us that will be critical. It seems also that Tishan is involved in some kind of war.>

<War? On Tarvuli?> Denith remarked.

<Perhaps 'war' is too strong a term,> Menkh conceded. <In any case, Tishan Dar is a masterful general. I am confident that any matters on that front would be more than amply dealt with.>

<But it is yet another reason that we should return there, Menkh,> Crixac added, and Menkh nodded in agreement.

<Very well then,> announced Frzath. <Hasten back to Tarvuli. We will monitor events via the Eye of Malavak and we will consult our archives. Clues may be found there as to the identity of the enemy.>

<Can the Intelligence itself not be contacted via the crystal cave?> Menkh queried. <Surely its knowledge encompasses all things.>

Morgath smiled. <Even as a bonded Adept, friend Menkh, there is much yet that you have to learn, and I say this in all humility. You know already that the cave you speak of is no cave in reality, nor does it even exist in this dimension. As to the Intelligence, that is not how it works. It is one of the five immutable laws that the Intelligence will not directly intervene in matters of the Balance. Its ways are subtle and unfathomable, working through seemingly random events and via sentient beings, who largely remain ignorant of the role they play in events.>

<Although, having said that, Morgath, it appears to have directly intervened with Menkh, so perhaps the immutable laws themselves are now subject to change,> Frzath mused. Morgath's face carried a troubled look as he pondered the significance of Frzath's comment.

There was silence as all digested the comment.

<If that is the case, Frzath,> Denith observed finally, <then all that we have come to understand as reliable and certain may be as ashes before the wind.> The Adepts looked at each other in acknowledgement.

<What is certain is that great changes are afoot,> said T'klath. <Our ruminating here will not change that. Our first step is to identify the enemy and counter it.>

<Given that you are moving the Balancepoint, are we able to retain communications?> Menkh asked.

<I believe so. Our next relocation will put us back in phase with Tarvuli's reality. Once this is done, we can open a dialogue through Varnahrin,> Frzath responded.

<Then I will take my leave.> Menkh smiled warmly at each Adept. <Varnahrin is aware of my return. I will speak with you all again soon. I think the final battle approaches.>

<Yes. There is a convergence of forces evident. We will aid you where we can.>

<The Balance is all,> said Menkh in farewell. He did not wait for the response but took up the Threadway and willed himself to Tarvuli.

CHAPTER FOURTEEN

Ankh stood alongside Tishan as she piloted the ImXin over Ta'Morin. He laughed with delight as she sped them around the Complex and hovered over the chasm where the waters of the seven streams, after joining together under the Complex, became a raging waterfall. A great veil of mist rose into the air, in which the light of the two suns fractured, causing rainbows of colour to dance around them.

'I would never have believed anything like this to be possible,' Ankh shouted above the noise of cascading water.

This was the second time that Tishan had taken Ankh up on the ImXin. In discussions with Varnahrin she had decided that key members of the council should know of its existence and how the use of the ImXin would be factored into their plans for the Ma'Vessick. Ankh was particularly fascinated by it.

Plans were well advanced as to the size of the force that would be taken. The council had agreed that, given the Hrv would be able to deploy energy weapons, the strike force would be almost entirely composed of tetrans. It was not deemed that a full file of tetrans would be required; indeed, once landfall had been made a gateway could be swiftly established, and reinforcements and other materials transported with speed utilising the existing gateways at Ta'Morin and at Xaranca.

Hamra had asked to accompany the Graaven force as a representative of the people and, as he had explained, he could also speak to those suffering under the brutality of the Ma'Vessick. This had been agreed and the expedition was planned to commence as soon as plans were finalised.

On the day of leaving, two praka vek of tetrans and a handful of Graavens, including Ankh, Pershivon, and Drenyk, had assembled just before the dawn and quietly disappeared through the gateway to Xaranca. Tishan translocated herself to the grove and materialised in the field of grasses that stood motionless all around the concealed ImXin. A large white shape stood slowly up and emerged from the tree line, stretched languorously before walking towards her. Tishan recovered quickly from her initial surprise and shook her head in wonder and amusement.

'Fendrax! It would appear that nothing can remain secret for long around you.'

Fendrax towered over Tishan and then brought her head down and snuffled Tishan's face – an action that Tishan still found unsettling, given the size of Fendrax's teeth – before drawing back and sitting daintily on her hindquarters with a delicacy that defied her great size.

'You could not expect that I would let a friend walk into danger without me there to prevent an unfortunate accident,' she stated placidly. 'Besides, it was Varnahrin that let me in on your plans, I cannot claim any mystical foresight. I am curious to see what it is like to fly like a bird; the first of my kind ever to have done so.'

'Well then, my friend, you must climb aboard with me,' said Tishan as she directed her focus to the ImXin that now appeared before them.

If Fendrax was surprised at the sudden appearance she gave no action that would suggest so, though she sniffed the edges of the

ImXin suspiciously before prowling around the outer edges. She climbed on board once she was satisfied with what she had seen. Accompanying her, Tishan assumed control and lifted off into the morning light as Avlar peeped above the horizon.

They climbed swiftly above the lands that surrounded Ta'Morin. There was a single flash of blue light as they pierced the protective shield that lay over the city before travelling eastwards towards the Great Water. The hair on Fendrax's back had lifted in response to the movement of the craft and she growled in a low voice, 'I would not mind this so much if I wasn't held in place. It is unnatural for one of my kind to feel fettered, though I can understand why.'

'Yes,' agreed Tishan. 'It is a strange feeling; I, too, can move my upper body but from the waist down I am anchored to the ship. But better that than a long fall to sudden death or injury.'

Tishan skimmed over the ground at great pace, above the height of the tallest fern trees. They flew over great herds of grazing animals who remained oblivious to their passage and entered at last the plains of the Xotic lands. Tishan flew higher until they could see the great stretch of the Mother Water ahead, and the ImXin flew unerringly towards Xaranca. Arriving there they set down on the long stretch of beach, several bow shots from the rapidly expanding settlement. The landing caused great surprise as the craft only materialised once it had settled onto the sand.

Several individuals approached, including Hamra, Pershivon, and Drenyk. Tlkcha was present as well, she and Pershivon talking animatedly together as they came closer, with Ankh listening and smiling at their conversation.

No sooner had the craft touched ground than Tishan and Fendrax felt themselves released. After quickly disembarking, they exchanged greetings with the others. Whilst this was occurring the ranks of the tetran force approached the stationary craft, climbed aboard, and stood rank upon rank as their feet located the depressions that were set so precisely into the surface of the ImXin.

Once the tetrans had embarked Tishan stood with Hamra and the others. 'Pershivon, you will oversee the gateway here and keep the curious away. I have left a praka of tetrans here under your command to assist you.'

She turned to Drenyk. 'Return now to Ta'Morin and oversee the reserve tetran force and supplies. Send them across to Xaranca as soon as you can. Once the new gateway is established on Ma'Vessick lands it will link to this one. I rely on your judgement, Pershivon, to send our forces across as speedily as possible. Any questions?' Pershivon and Drenyk shook their heads.

'You may rely on Pershivon and me, Mother, we know what is required.'

Tishan looked with pride at her two offspring. She knew that Menkh, too, would share that pride. Both were reaching maturity and she knew that Varnahrin was there to ensure that all was well, though that was a thought that she did not communicate to either of them.

'Be careful, my spawnlings. We cannot predict what the outcome of this expedition may be. Once the bridgehead is established, I will open the gateway. If something untoward happens, look to Varnahrin.' Her words were tinged with feelings of pride and affection and their response mirrored hers.

'Be safe, Mother. The Balance is all.' Pershivon gripped Tishan's hands and touched her forehead with her own in the Graaven way of affection. Tishan nodded and accompanied by Ankh, Hamra, and Fendrax, climbed back on to the ImXin and prepared to set off.

ooooOoooo

On the topmost level of the Grand Temple, six Hrv had gathered. Each carried an energy weapon the Ma'Vessick knew as the Instruments of Harkan. They stood in close proximity and a humming noise, punctuated by clicks and high-pitched sounds, emanated from the group as they communicated. Long, hairlike filaments extended from each head, and these reached out and touched corresponding filaments on the other Hrv. In this way they assessed the mental and emotional state of each individual. Radek was pleased. He sensed only determination and a fearless resolve, despite what might come against them.

'It is disappointing that Toronset was stupid enough to deploy the weapon and be defeated,' voiced Zapasset to the group in scathing tones. 'You were right to have a backup system of communications, Radek.'

'Yes. It was a mistake for us to entrust an Instrument to Toronset. I was ever mistrustful of her ambitions and that mistake was compounded by Lakash, her confidant. We are fortunate that the hold we have over the Ma'Vessick is so strong they didn't believe the evidence of their own eyes,' agreed Agras.

'Even if they did, their fear of the consequences of resistance deprives them of the will. Watching those who returned in failure slipping in their own guts provided a salutary lesson. Amusing for us, terrifying for them,' Zazma added.

This resulted in the wheezing sound of Hrv laughter.

'That is true, but we certainly ate well. The terror of their ending added a particular sweetness to the meat,' observed Pasrt.

Radek's voice raised above the others. 'We learn from our mistakes. Preparations are almost complete. We have reinforced Gahrtok with Ma'Vessick troops, all armed with the latest weaponry. Tshok and Verm are to be congratulated on their attention to this.'

A series of rapid clicks issued from the two Hrv so named in appreciation of Radek's praise.

'As you know, we cannot combine the weapons, due to the missing Instrument, but if we work in concert with each other, they still have overwhelming power. As we are priests of the Grand Circle, we will remain here offering up prayers to Harkan whilst our lesser priests exhort their fellow Ma'Vessick to resist any invading force. It is important that we do not get separated. Whilst each Instrument is powerful by itself, the effect of six weapons massed together must lead to victory.'

'Radek, these preparations are good, but can we trust the messages we have received from Tek?' asked Zazma.

Radek's immediate response to the question was to stand completely still and fall silent, a sure sign amongst the Hrv that offence had been taken and violence might result.

Zazma issued a series of high-pitched clicks and whistling sounds in apology. 'Great One, I meant no offence, but we place much trust in a slave.'

Radek resumed the rocking motion; to Zazma's relief, he had accepted her apology. 'You forget yourself, Zazma. You forget also that Tek successfully led forces against the Ma'Vessick before we took an active part in quelling his people. For a warm blood he is clever and resourceful. The information sent back thus far confirms my suspicion of Vekan and Toronset and her plans to achieve pre-eminence. Tek would not dare betray us or give us the lie. I hold his family in thrall, and he knows the consequence to them of betrayal: their end will not be quick.'

'Is the device you gave Tek reliable over such a distance?' quizzed Pasrt. Although they all knew that Tek had been provided with a communicator, no-one other than Radek had seen it.

'It is completely reliable and small enough that detection would be unlikely. No, I know that plans for an attack are advanced, and they will come soon. I only need now to know the how and when of it, and we can meet them with surprise on our side.'

The wheezing Hrv laughter came from each individual as they envisaged the destruction their weapons would cause. They continued to refine their plans, endeavouring to meet every eventuality.

ooooOooooo

A sudden disturbance in the small crowd that had gathered to watch the craft depart drew Tishan's attention. One figure suddenly ran forward and, approaching the still stationary ImXin, threw itself on its knees, its arms raised in supplication, and began to cry.

Hamra fixed his attention on the wailing figure and, along with Tishan, climbed down from the ImXin and walked up to it.

'Who is this?' Tishan asked Hamra.

'This is Harasah Tek, he is one of the Holim people enslaved by the Ma'Vessick. Harasah, what is the problem that you should abase yourself so and be in such distress?'

The figure of Harasah was an object of pity. Like the Xotic, he was tall and thin, but tears flowed down his face and he could barely speak. 'I am so sorry, Hamra. So sorry. But they have my family and unless I did what they told me, they said they would …' Harasah could not continue, so great was his emotion.

Tishan looked at Hamra and then the kneeling figure of Harasah. Bending over, she lifted him firmly to his feet. 'Harasah, look at me.' Tishan's voice cut through his misery, and he focused his bleary eyes on her. 'Whatever you have done, you must tell us. I give you my word that I will do all I can if your family is in danger, but it is obvious that the weight of this thing has borne you down. You know what is the right thing to do.'

'Yes, yes.' Harasah's voice was not more than a whisper, heard only by Tishan and Hamra. 'I have betrayed you all.' Fresh tears spilled down. 'I have killed my family.'

Hamra took a sharp breath.

245

'Ankh,' Tishan rapped out a command. 'We need to get to the bottom of this. The flight is delayed. Leave the tetrans on board, we shall retire to the meeting hall and discover what our friend Harasah has done.'

ooooOoooo

They sat in silence in the hall as Harasah confessed that he had been passing information on to the Hrv in relation to the preparations that were being made. Critically, he had not told them of the imminent attack, having had no opportunity to do so without detection. He showed them the device the Hrv had given him. It was no bigger than an amulet one might wear on a chain around the neck and Ankh had inspected it with interest. Now Harasah sat miserably in the centre of a circle, shivering in the aftermath of grief and guilt and awaiting the verdict of those who surrounded him.

Hamra looked around the faces and saw accord in the expressions of those who had heard the news. He stood and approached the forlorn figure of Harasah, placing his hand on Harasah's shoulder. Harasah flinched at the touch as if at the blade of a knife.

'Harasah, look at me.' Hamra's tone was gentle. 'There is not one person in this room who would condemn you out of hand for what you did. I think, in your place, I would likely have done the same. Ultimately, you could not live with yourself with your betrayal of us and it is credit to you that, despite the cost, you came forward and told us what you had done.'

Harasah's voice was hushed. 'You … you forgive me for what I have done?'

Tishan stood and fixed her eyes on Harasah's still-trembling figure. 'Stand up, Harasah, and hear your punishment.' Harasah flinched – he had expected no less, and he despaired that he would not now see his beloved mate and family again. He could only think of one punishment for his actions. In resignation he stood and faced Tishan, who stood tall before him.

'This council sets this charge upon you, Harasah. When the time for departure arrives, you will accompany us. You will join us in this fight and the task you have been allotted is to save your family and as many others as you can, or die trying. Do you accept this punishment?'

Now fresh tears spilled down Harasah's face, but they were tears of relief, bordering on joy, and he straightened his body, standing tall. 'I willingly accept this punishment. I swear here and now that I will do all in my power to save those that I can, even at the cost of my own life.'

A smile brightened Tishan's stern features. 'Good. Ankh, I believe our friend will need fitting out.'

'I will see to it at once, Stragosh.' Ankh smiled at Harasah as he confirmed Tishan's order.

In response to this the tension in the room eased. 'There is one last thing, Harasah,' said Tishan.

Harasah paused and refocused his rapidly churning thoughts.

'You must continue to communicate with the priests if they contact you. Let them know that the attack will not come yet for a few dak'chaal – that is a few days, as you reckon them – but that plans are proceeding, and you have yet to ascertain the means by which we will carry it out. That should throw surprise back in our favour. They might possibly guess the when of our assault, but the how will carry the day. But be careful, Harasah, do not let a change in your tone of voice allow them to suspect that we know of the device or of your communication with them. That is vital, not least for the safety of your family.'

'They are expecting my next communication at dusk. The Ma'Vessick generally locked us down for the night around then. I usually managed to be one of those that were let free to serve them in the evenings which meant that I could find time to be alone long enough to get a message through. I have continued this habit and they are used to hearing from me at that time of day.'

'Will it raise suspicion if you open contact with them now rather than later?'

'I do not believe so,' Harasah replied. 'This has occurred before and there are a thousand reasons as to why communications might happen at another time.'

'Very well, then find a quiet place and reassure them that the attack is not imminent. By dusk today we will be assaulting Gahrtok and no further contact will be necessary.'

Harasah nodded his head and turned to go. He paused as Tishan spoke again. 'Remember, Harasah, it is vital that you give them no reason to doubt what you say.'

Hamra watched him quietly leave. 'It is strange to me that the Hrv, as we now know them to be, would entrust a slave with communications,' he said. 'They had more than one priest of their own here, and both were of their inner circle. Surely Toronset or Lakash would have been in contact with them?'

'Perhaps they mistrust the ambitions of their own?' Ankh's question was speculative.

'In light of what happened, it would appear that the Hrv were trying to cover every eventuality, however remote the notion of defeat might have been,' Tishan responded. 'Fortunately, the information that Harasah passed on is not critical in adversely affecting our attack, so we proceed as planned. They will have some inkling of the forces we can deploy but surprise will aid us.'

There was general agreement, though none underestimated the task ahead. With no other deliberations, Ankh left with Harasah, to equip him as Tishan had instructed, and the others made their way back to the ImXin, ready to depart.

ooooOoooo

Upon the return of Ankh and Harasah the ImXin lifted once more and as those on the shore waved, it moved off, skimming the wavetops at first before gradually climbing away, disappearing from sight.

A strong wind blew towards them but its effect on their craft was minimal. They had gained enough height that the waves below seemed tiny. Occasionally they flew past flocks of strange-looking raptors who floated on enormous wings, calling out in harsh cries to each other. So great was the ImXin's speed that the flocks passed rapidly, disappearing behind them. Whether it was something to do with the shielding that the ImXin was equipped with or some other feature, it was very quiet aboard and those who travelled could easily communicate with each other.

Ankh, who was standing alongside Tishan as she piloted the craft, spoke. 'How much further do you think before landfall, Stragosh? By my estimate we have been travelling for several chaal.'

'Not long now, I think, Ankh. In fact, I believe the horizon before us grows darker, a different quality to the clouds. If I am not mistaken our landfall approaches.'

Ankh, his eyesight not what it once was, peered ahead, but the darkening aspect eluded him until Tishan drew his attention to it.

'Yes, I believe you are right. Our timing is perfect as dusk closes in.'

'I will take us down a little and reduce speed as we approach. Hamra, you might recognise some features of the land once we come into plain sight.'

Hamra nodded in response to Tishan's remark. 'My people lived on the coast of Shellimar, what you call the Great Water, but I spent time as a slave in Gahrtok when the Ma'Vessick invaded our lands. I will watch carefully.'

Now, in the distance, a great range of mountains began to take shape, their massive shoulders marching down to form part of a rocky coastline that revealed itself as they drew closer. In many places, dense growth of ferns and other plant life grew down to the very edge of the waters. Occasionally they could see that from out of narrow clefts in the mountains great, wildly foaming cataracts debouched into the Great Water, throwing a fine mist high into the air.

'It is a beautiful land to house such horror,' Ankh remarked.

'Yes, friend Ankh,' Hamra agreed. 'The lands all about are verdant and fertile. In the interior there are great areas of marsh and swamp, so many are the rivers that flow, and water is plentiful. We of the Paressi, as we call our peoples, refer to all the lands as Hardessi Sekr, the Place of Plenty. In the main we lived peacefully and the Ma'Vessick, though belligerent, were a small people and easily discounted. Then their priests came, and in a few short years all had changed.'

Suddenly Hamra pointed to a wide body of water bordered by dense forest that flowed out into a wide bay. 'There, that is the Kim Sas. Follow that river and it will take you to the city of Gahrtok.'

'Very well,' Tishan responded.

They glided well above the river; the forest seemed to stretch away in every direction, but some distance along the waterway they came to a stronghold. Here the forest had been cleared and a pier ran out into the river, alongside which a number of high-prowed craft were moored. Others moved upriver, belching smoke, each propelled by a single large wheel that churned the waters behind it.

The walls of the stronghold were all made of timber, presumably harvested from the surrounding forest, and a single high tower rose up in the centre of the fort, dominating the landscape. Figures dressed in blue could be seen scurrying in all directions. Boats were being loaded and off-loaded, and tracks winding their way into the forest could be clearly seen from above.

'This is one of many such strongholds scattered across the land,' said Hamra. 'Here the Ma'Vessick house troops to garrison the area and quell any unrest.'

'Well, to be honest, we Graavens did the same thing,' Ankh replied. 'Our practice was to annihilate those who took up arms against us. We never used slavery as a means of controlling our vassal states. In the main, providing that they lived peaceably under our rule, the peoples whose lands we conquered were assimilated into Graaven society. At least, they traded peacefully with us and to a large extent we left them alone to govern themselves.'

'Then your people are very different from the Ma'Vessick. Terror and cruelty are their main means of subjugation.'

'Do not be misled, Hamra,' Tishan added. 'We Graavens could be ruthless, and we would not tolerate any hint of rebellion. Our armies were stronger than any and we employed our Hoplex and Sagit to crush any hint of dissension. The military life was all I knew; it is only now as I look back that I can see where the flaws in our society lay. Menkh and Pershiva had great plans to reset our society, so it is ironic that their dreams have largely been fulfilled as the result of our overthrow and at the cost of so many lives.' Tishan's voice was reflective.

'It would seem that we have some things in common then, Tishan Dar,' said Hamra. 'I am also grateful, if that is the right word for such a tragedy, that your people are here to help us in our need. It would seem to me that much that is good has arisen from something that was so bad.'

'Therein lies the nature of Balance, Hamra. Though there are countless numbers of dead who might question their own unexpected sacrifice for the sake of it,' Ankh observed quietly.

Ankh, Tishan, and Hamra stood in silent reflection following Ankh's words, and watched as the river flowed under their ship as they flew silently on.

Night was falling as they finally approached the city of Gahrtok. From above it was illuminated by the light of countless lamps, and fires from troops encamped outside of the city. Their flight overhead went unnoticed and unremarked. Though the streets below them were still filled with people, there was a sense that the city was slowing as the day drew to a close. Detachments of troops moved along every street, their obvious task to patrol and warn of anything untoward. From the temple in the heart of the city a huge gong sounded, its echoes reverberating through every district, and people everywhere scurried and disappeared into buildings. Those too slow were accosted by the patrolling troops and most were given a sharp beating if they were unfortunate enough to be caught in the street as the curfew fell.

Silently the ImXin settled to the ground. All was still and quiet, except for the chatter of unnamed insects and the occasional call of some animal from amongst the trees that grew all about. Had anybody looked they would have been amazed at the sight of the tetrans that seemed to appear out of nowhere once they had disembarked from the ship. They moved quickly to set up a defensible perimeter.

Once the gateway was established and additional tetrans assembled, a diversionary attack against the city gate nearest to them would commence. Tishan and Ankh would then translocate to the temple with the tetrans from the ImXin and carry the attack directly against the priests.

They had both spent many chaal practising translocation of more than just themselves. Ankh, who was relatively new to this process, seemed to have an innate ability and quickly perfected the technique, able to translocate larger and larger groups of tetrans.

At the same time as they were perfecting their technique, their use of the viewing room in the Complex had been effective in developing plans for the assault, identifying key parts of the city that would need to be controlled. Tishan and Ankh had discussed their plans with Horven and Lerma and had selected an area that appeared to be some sort of parkland, close enough to the city with ample space to set down the ImXin and assemble their initial force. It was also ideal for enabling quick deployment of additional tetrans as they arrived via the gateway that Tishan would set up. From careful observation they were confident the area could not be seen from the city's walls and, with the gates shut fast, as per standard Ma'Vessick practice after dark, no-one would be about.

Once all their tetrans had disembarked Tishan climbed down, accompanied by Ankh and Hamra. In her arms she carried a cube of black crystal, its sides almost as long as her forearms. Moving swiftly some hundred paces away, she set the cube upon the ground. Turning to ensure that everyone stood well away she focused her will, and as the rod appeared she gripped it in both hands and pointed it at the cube, putting her mind to the task at hand. Almost at once a beam of red light emitted from its tip and, upon striking the cube, the light and energy seemed to be drawn deep inside it, the cube virtually disappearing from view as the energies were absorbed.

At first, other than the absorption of light, nothing seemed to happen. Then, suddenly, with a 'crump' of sound, a shockwave swept outwards, bending the grass in its passage and causing a stir of wind. The balance of those standing nearby was impacted and they swayed violently backwards in the wave of power, suddenly overbalancing the other way as the energy was sucked back into the rapidly forming gateway. Tishan, who had already experienced this phenomenon, was prepared, and the rod shielded her from the buffeting.

Before them now stood a doorway wide enough to allow four people to walk abreast. Within its sides and lintel an opaque mist was swirling. The mist swirled ever faster and then disappeared as if it, too, had been sucked away, and in its place Drenyk and

Horven, with Lerma at her side, could be seen peering back at them, the buildings of Xaranca visible behind them.

Tishan waved at Drenyk to commence the crossing of their tetran forces. Returning the wave, Drenyk turned to Horven, who responded with a crisp Baran Mec salute and turned aside to issue orders. For the initial phase of operations, the gateway was confined to traffic issuing only from Xaranca; in the event of matters turning against them it would only be opened back to Xaranca if retreat was required. The possibility that hostile forces might use the gateway to mount a counterattack was one of the main reasons why Xaranca had been chosen as the staging area and not Ta'Morin itself.

Tishan turned to Ankh. 'You may begin your attack, Ankh, and do take care.'

'I shall endeavour to proceed with aggressive caution, Stragosh.' Ankh spoke with an undercurrent of dry humour. 'May I say the same to you also? The world would be a lesser place without you in it.'

Tishan laughed. 'Get away with you, Ankh. We will drink a toast after this is all done. Keep in contact with me, our helmets should enable clear communications.'

Fendrax, who had been standing alongside Tishan, lowered her massive head as she spoke. 'I shall accompany Ankh. Where you are going, I do not think my frame would fit: besides, I believe my presence may be an aid to Ankh. He can ride on my back to get a better view of what lies ahead as we traverse the streets.'

'Very well, Fendrax. That being the case, you take care also.'

Fendrax gave a coughing grunt of laughter. 'I, too, will do my best.'

Without further ado Fendrax moved towards Ankh who, at her bidding, climbed up on her mighty shoulders.

Tishan turned her attention to Harasah who stood garbed in the protective gear of Ta'Morin. 'Now is the time, Harasah. Proceed as we have discussed. Once Ankh breaches the gates, two tetrans will accompany you as protectors. Make haste into the city and get to your family, free as many as you can. If they wish to join the fight, they are welcome; our tetrans will not harm any dressed in blue.'

Harasah smiled nervously. 'I will do my utmost, Tishan Dar – I mean, Stragosh,' he corrected himself.

Tishan smiled and placed a hand on his shoulder. 'You know all the back streets and alleyways, Harasah. Our attack should cause a disturbance which will draw off the Ma'Vessick troops. I look forward to meeting your family.'

'Thank you, Stragosh.' He turned away, quickly donned his helmet, and stood near to where Ankh sat upon Fendrax's broad back.

Tishan returned a final salute from Ankh, and in the blink of any eye Ankh, Fendrax, Harasah, and the tetrans of his praka vanished. It seemed only moments later that a huge detonation reverberated from the direction of the city as the tetrans launched their attack.

Tishan turned towards Hamra. 'Ready?'

Hamra nodded nervously. Of all the slaves now resident in Xaranca, only he was knowledgeable in the internal layout of the temple. It was his job to guide Tishan's force in the main assault against the Hrv. Whilst the viewing room had been excellent for overall planning, it was incapable of piercing the walls of the temple to look inside, so Hamra's role was a crucial one.

Tishan turned as the first of the reserve tetrans, accompanied by Lerma, came through the gateway. No sooner had they stepped through than they jogged away with surprising speed to reinforce the attack on the gate.

In her turn, Tishan gathered her forces around. The lead tetran carried the captured Instrument, which Varnahrin had modified for the tetran's use. Varnahrin's instructions had been explicit.

<This is a powerful weapon, Tishan. Unlike your rod and Menkh's staff, it does not need a concentration of will to initiate a reaction. A tetran will simply apply pressure to the part of the tube that sits under its arm, and it will fire. It is capable of absorbing energy from other weapons to recharge itself and, in this way, it also acts as a shield. I have increased its power, but a sustained pulse of energy will drain it quite quickly.>

<Are the tetran weapons not powerful enough to counter those of the Hrv?>

<Singly, yes. Their shields have also been modulated to meet the power of these weapons. But if the Hrv combine the force of the Instruments, the tetrans may be hard pressed. If we can use our weapon to overpower one or two, we can take theirs and add it to our weaponry.>

<Surely the Rod of Klemish will enable me to defeat them?> Tishan could not imagine any power that could overcome it.

<Certainly, as it is now, it is limited only by your force of will. But, in the midst of battle, facing simultaneous attack from different quarters, you will need the tetrans' aid. Coordinate your attack and defence and all will be well.>

Shaking off any misgivings she had, Tishan secured her helmet and, concentrating her will to include those who had been selected to form her team, translocated to the chosen location, a wide terrace on the seventh level of the temple.

Translocating a large group was an interesting experience and initially a real challenge. At first it was like trying to hold a handful of dry sand without letting it spill through her fingers and it took a deal of practise to become adept at managing it. Whilst translocation was instantaneous when alone, the bigger the group, the longer it took to make the jump: or at least it felt that way. Nonetheless, Tishan could feel the presence of all of the individuals around her that made up the group as they journeyed, even though they were physically insubstantial.

They had no sooner appeared on the terrace than the tetrans deployed, activating their shields against attack from energy weapons.

Tishan spoke into her helmet. 'Ankh, how are things progressing?'

Ankh's response was immediate, and the clarity of his speech made it feel as if he were standing next to her. 'Very well, indeed, Stragosh. The gates were destroyed within moments of the initial assault. We have deployed forwards into the city, and we are manning all the strongpoints agreed. Reinforcements are entering now.'

'Horven. How is the deployment going at the gateway?'

'Nearly all tetrans are through, Stragosh. No problem here. I will accompany the last of the file as they pass by. I will join Lerma with our reserve.'

'Very well. I am commencing our attack now.

'Hamra, which way?'

'Through this doorway.' Hamra pointed to a set of ornately carved doors that were closed. 'On the other side is a set of stairs leading up to the eighth level. We will find Ma'Vessick guards stationed around, unless they have been distracted by the assault on the gate. The ninth level is exclusively for the priesthood, no-one goes there except for those chosen to be sacrificed – and they are never seen again.'

'Well, why don't we let our friends know we are coming to visit?' Tishan rapped out a crisp order. 'Third of the File. Blow those doors apart and secure the stairway.'

The command tetran responded in the metallic, curiously detached tone that all tetrans used regardless of the situation. 'At once, Stragosh.'

CHAPTER FIFTEEN

Tishan had to admit that, as explosions went, this one was rather spectacular. The two ornate doors were literally dashed to fragments as they burst inwards from the effect of the weapon carried by Third of the File. Several armed Ma'Vessick troops who were unfortunately stationed on the other side were similarly blown apart. As Tishan stepped through the blasted doorway, she saw that their mangled body parts were spread out over a wide area around the stairwell. Pools of their blood and other remains made a grisly picture amongst the scattered debris.

Oblivious to the carnage around them, the tetran troops stood shoulder to shoulder as they advanced up the stairway, the glow from their protective shielding emanating a greenish hue. Third of the File stood in the centre of the lead group as they stepped upwards, carrying the modified weapon of the Hrv. No sooner had they reached the top of the stairs then a hail of projectiles slammed into them from Ma'Vessick guards who had arrived at the scene, drawn by the huge blast.

One tetran was rendered inoperative as a bullet smashed into its head but the remaining tetrans remodulated their shields and, other than the first casualty, no further of their number were impacted. Having effected this change, they engaged with the enemy. Short pulses of lurid red energy, which sizzled as they shot through the air with blinding speed, struck their attackers. The energy bolts penetrated metal, flesh, and stone. Those who thought themselves safe behind tall pillars were felled as the energy passed cleanly through them before hitting the Ma'Vessick who stood behind. Often a bolt would strike through up to three individuals before vanishing with a snapping sound, its energy expended.

There were no survivors. The effect of an impact, even if it were on an arm or a leg, was such a shock that death was instantaneous – there was no time even to cry out when struck. Once hit, the Ma'Vessick troops fell, lifeless, to the ground.

Several tetrans peeled off from the main group to hunt down any enemy who still hid or lingered on the eighth level within close proximity to the stairway. The remaining force made their way along an ornate passageway, passing unoccupied rooms and other hallways that appeared devoid of life. Other than the sounds of their feet as they walked, it was eerily quiet although a faint sound, a disturbance in the air, could be felt. Tishan thought it must be an echo of the clash going on in the streets far below.

ooooOoooo

Ankh stood in an alleyway that led off a broad thoroughfare knifing its way through the heart of Gahrtok. He now held all the agreed strongpoints and his forces had engaged a huge column of Ma'Vessick that were advancing rapidly in the direction of his initial attack.

Earlier Ankh had given several Graaven Sagit a severe dressing down – somewhat lessened by a knowing grin – because they had, under their own authority, stepped through the gateway and entered the city. He had placed them in several strategic locations where their arrows picked off the Ma'Vessick with unerring accuracy. As they advanced, they occasionally used the modified arrows in open areas like plazas. These exploded on high, delivering death to dozens of Ma'Vessick who, after a fruitless attempt at driving off their enemy, had retreated down the street, endeavouring to find hiding places safe from arrows and marauding tetrans. Red bolts of energy flickered down the street picking off any Ma'Vessick who showed themselves, and occasionally there was a scream as Fendrax, a prowling and unseen menace, dragged a hapless Ma'Vessick soldier to their doom.

Ankh spoke into his helmet. 'Lerma, I think we need to drive these lingering Ma'Vessick off and neutralise this sector.'

'Agreed, Kalvak. Do you wish me to join the attack?'

'No. Hold your position. Second of the File? Deploy your tetrans and clear those Ma'Vessick out. I want this roadway emptied.'

'As you command, Kalvak,' Second responded in its metallic voice.

Within moments a body of ten tetrans, their shields aglow and weapons deployed, advanced with fluid steps down the street and past Ankh's location. Ankh stepped out to observe their passing and watched as their irresistible advance pushed the Ma'Vessick back.

Two of the Sagit Ankh had addressed earlier appeared from out of the alleyways where they had been stationed. He had just turned to speak to them when a huge impact struck him between the shoulders and threw him off his feet. Ankh vaguely heard the shouts of the Sagit, and he was only dimly aware of the thud of a body, impaled by two arrows, that toppled out of a window above him and struck the ground nearby.

Helping hands lifted him to his feet as his senses reeled. Anxious voices spoke into his helmet. 'Kalvak, are you alright? You went down like a mellax had struck you!'

Ankh groped at the hands. 'Thank you, my friends. The suit took the worst of it but I feel as if every part of me is bruised.'

'Shall we clear these buildings for you, Kalvak? Might be a few more lurking,' one Sagit said.

Ankh took himself to task. It was an obvious thing that should have been done, but until now the buildings all around had been shut tight and, despite the disturbance, other than the troops in the streets, not one Ma'Vessick had ventured out.

'No. We don't have the time and bar this one, any Ma'Vessick inside has chosen to stay safe behind closed doors. No. Let us keep out of the open as best we can.'

Lerma's voice interrupted their exchange. 'Kalvak? There is another Ma'Vessick force approaching my strongpoint.'

'Can you hold them?'

'I can. But a couple of our Sagit would be helpful.'

Ankh's thoughts had come back into focus and he recognised the voice of the Sagit who had addressed him. 'Passid, collect Orvak and Kelm and run back to Lerma's position. He wants you to tickle the enemy for him.'

Passid chuckled before responding. 'With alacrity, Kalvak. Are you sure you are alright?'

'Yes, yes. It will take more than one projectile to see me off. Helk can stay with me. Besides, I can see our tetrans are returning so I will soon have plenty of company.'

Passid withdrew her supporting arm from Ankh. 'As you command, Kalvak. Come on, you two, let's go and spread some mayhem for Lerma.' The three Sagit jogged away, the readout in their helmets guiding them to Lerma's position.

Ankh walked a little unsteadily back to the alleyway, with Helk's assistance. He watched the returning tetrans and gave a quick start as Fendrax appeared out of the shadows. 'Can you not do that, Fendrax – you scare me more than the enemy.'

Fendrax's grumbling laughter made Ankh shudder.

'I am glad to see that you are still alive, Kalvak. But you need have no fear, I don't usually eat my friends.' Fendrax's laughter continued for quite some time before she again disappeared.

'For that, I, for one, am grateful,' Ankh said quietly.

'Me too,' echoed Helk in agreement.

Ankh turned his attention back to the roadway. Not for the first time he gave thanks for the protection of his Ta'Morin armour, if such a pliable suit could be called such.

ooooOoooo

Tishan's group approached the stairway to the ninth level. Here there was a subtle change to the air around them. There was a feeling of menace that grew distinctly stronger as they neared the stairwell. Whilst her tetrans were impervious to such feelings, she could imagine that no living Ma'Vessick would have willingly approached anywhere near those stairs.

Her tetrans paused to remodulate their shields, which once more emitted the greenish glow to combat energy weapons. Tishan focused on the Rod of Klemish and it appeared in her hand again.

'Ready, Third?'

'Ready, Stragosh.'

'Then proceed. Hamra, if you wish, you may stay here with a tetran for company.'

'Thank you for your kindness, Stragosh, but I am determined to see the destruction of these creatures, the fount of so much horror and sorrow to my people.'

'Very well. Stay close to me.'

They mounted the steps cautiously but, upon reaching the top and entering a vestibule whose walls were covered in strange glyphs, they found the area deserted. Other than the distant noise from the streets far below, all remained quiet; the feeling of menace, however, had increased. Directly ahead of them two huge, metallic black doors, also carved with strange and ornate symbols, stood shut before them. Tishan had the acute feeling that they would be impervious to her tetrans' weaponry. In any event, she was not prepared to waste the energy. Ordering her force to halt she stepped forward into the front rank alongside Third.

'Tetrans, prepare. I will reduce these doors, but expect an attack as soon as that barrier is down. These Hrv may have massed their weapons, so be ready.'

Third's reply was immediate. 'We are prepared, Stragosh.'

'Very well.'

Tishan gathered her thoughts and focused her will, at the same time fixing her gaze upon the doors in front of her. The rod pulsed with a swirling rainbow of colours. She felt a vibration through her hand and the colours swirled faster and faster. The rod grew hot to the touch and pressure built up in the air around them, building and building until it felt as if they were being crushed under the weight of a mountain. Then suddenly, the pressure was released, sweeping away from them in a titanic shockwave. It struck the doors, which bowed inwards like the sails of a ship billowing in a gale. Further and further they bent, until it seemed that they screamed in torment with a living voice before they vaporised. It was not what Tishan was expecting. Given the reaction of the doors to her attack, she anticipated that they would be wrenched away and thrown back into the space that opened behind them.

In the sudden absence of the doors and in the aftermath of the pulsing energies deployed, she could not see what dimensions the space beyond might be. Her attempt to peer into the newly opened space was momentary, as a huge detonation of blinding white light struck the lead ranks of the tetrans. The defensive shield buckled, in one or two paces a rent in the fabric of the shield appeared, and beams of energy struck through, looking for all the world like dappled sunlight streaming through the limbs of trees. The effect on any tetran struck by the energy was dramatic. They melted, like ice exposed to flame, but no sooner had one tetran fallen than another stepped forward to bolster the shield. The tear was repaired but it was apparent that it could not last against the power being exerted against it.

In response, Third of the File struck back with their modified weapon. Its beam of purple energy punched through the incandescent white glow that enveloped their defences, followed in quick succession by a bolt of green energy from the Rod of Klemish.

Whether from the single impact of the weapon, the rod, or a combination of the two, there was a high-pitched scream that pierced their ears, followed by a muted detonation. The incandescent white light died instantly and beyond the dazzle three black-clad figures could be seen retreating rapidly down a long hallway, whilst a fourth shape lay crumpled on the ground. An unpleasant smell of burning lingered in the air. Advancing, Tishan saw the smouldering remains of a Hrv. The aroma of the burnt body was nauseating. Near the shell of the fallen Hrv, a buckled and twisted piece of metal was all that was left of what Tishan assumed was one of the Hrv's Instruments.

'We are fortunate that, for whatever reason, only four of these Hrv managed to combine their power. I fear that had all of them been present the outcome may have been unpleasant for us,' Tishan observed.

Hamra replied in a shaking voice, 'If by unpleasant you refer to our obliteration, I agree with you.'

Tishan looked around at her remaining tetrans. Of the fifty units of her original praka sem, she had lost twenty, with a further ten units clearing out the floor below. She paused whilst her tetrans spread out around her and spoke into her helmet.

'Ankh, how are things with you?'

Ankh's response came quickly. 'All is well in hand, Stragosh. The Ma'Vessick are completely demoralised and offering no effective opposition. We retain control of all our objectives. We can hear fighting continuing in other parts of the city, but they are not our forces. It may be that Harasah has managed to free the slaves and they are taking their own action. I have been unable to communicate with him. Whether that means he is dead or there is some other reason, I cannot determine.'

'Very well. Is Fendrax with you?'

'No, Stragosh. Fendrax has, to use her phrase, gone hunting. I suspect that she may well have made her way to the fighting we can hear in the distance.'

'Hmmm. Well, I am sure that whilst the darkness holds, she will be an unpleasant surprise for any Ma'Vessick she comes across. In the meantime, hold your position and continue to try and contact Harasah.

'Horven?'

'Yes, Stragosh?'

'I want another praka haram sent into the city. Accompany them and take over from Ankh. Once you have relieved Ankh, push forward. If there is fighting going on, we need to lend support.'

'At once, Stragosh,' came Horven's reply. 'I have a reserve force mustered on the other side of the gateway. We can be there very quickly.'

'Excellent. Ankh, I want reinforcements. As soon as Horven arrives, translocate to my position and bring a praka sem of tetrans with you.' Tishan did not wait for Ankh's assent. 'Lerma, all is well with you?'

'Indeed, Stragosh. All is quiet here. I had thought that we might meet resistance from the Ma'Vessick who occupy the buildings all around, but it would appear as if they are keeping out of the fighting. Very curious.'

'Well, you know what to do if you meet any opposition. If they are content to stay in their homes, I am content to leave them there.'

'Yes, Stragosh. Shall I join Horven's attack once she is in position?'

'No, hold where you are. I want your force to control access to the city gate and hold an outer perimeter.'

Tishan turned her attention back to her own situation. She was more than satisfied with progress thus far in the city. Her mission to nullify the Hrv was yet to be concluded: and it was now clear that their power was formidable.

ooooOoooo

Harasah moved with cautious speed down one of the many alleyways that ran off the main thoroughfare into different districts of the city. Two tetrans accompanied him as protection, keeping pace with him with ease and, almost in knowing anticipation of his movements, changing direction in synchronisation with him so that their steps almost resembled a choreographed dance.

Behind him the noise of fighting grew loud, but Harasah had no doubt about the outcome. The Graavens and their mighty force were an unstoppable power and Harasah blessed the spirits that had led the Ma'Vessick to venture into the strange lands where they lived. Now all had changed, and he held a hope, deep in his heart, that their actions tonight would herald a new beginning for all his people who had managed to survive. He held his thoughts close and concentrated on his destination. He hoped that the tetran forces would draw off all the Ma'Vessick troops. There were at least two points where they would have to cross two main thoroughfares to reach the slave compound where his family were held.

He turned left down a laneway that ran past a number of silent buildings in which weapons were crafted for the Ma'Vessick elite. All was quiet. It would appear that the priesthood had invoked the curfew, which guaranteed that, no matter what the disturbance, no Ma'Vessick would set foot outside for fear of the consequences.

In many ways, Harasah reflected, the Ma'Vessick were more slaves than those they held in captivity.

Now he halted, his tetran guards coming to a complete stop the moment he stopped. Somehow, it was an unsettling feeling. Tentatively he looked out from the laneway they stood in, to left and right along a wide, well paved street that intersected the city, leading to one of the gates. The tail end of a Ma'Vessick force was disappearing over a rise to his right. He darted forward, turned left, and ran quickly for fifty paces before turning right into yet another laneway.

Dim lighting from streetlamps provided limited vision, but Harasah knew the city well, and his helmet's ability to focus on his surroundings gave amazing clarity, despite the fact that he felt claustrophobic encased inside it.

Twice more he and his guards crossed broad streets. Only once were they surprised by a squad of Ma'Vessick hurrying around a bend. The tetrans, with inhuman speed, dispatched every last one. Red bolts of energy killed them on impact, passing through one to kill another, and with no more than the merest pause Harasah and his tetrans continued on.

Finally, they came to the end of an alleyway that twisted and turned its way past two- and three-storey buildings that leaned inwards, revealing only a narrow gap of sky above. As with the rest of the city, the doors were barred and all was silent, other than an occasional muted noise from inside to indicate that the buildings were occupied. The buildings were constructed of identical materials and in a uniform pattern. Closer to the Temple of Harkan they were larger, but the pattern was repeated with dreary monotony. Here the more modest proportions reflected the lower status of the occupants. For the most part the city was kept clean by the efforts of the many slaves like Harasah, but refuse had piled up in some places, waiting for the daily round of work to commence.

The curfew still held, however, and would do so until the dawn, which, by Harasah's calculations, could not now be far off.

Once again Harasah peered out in the gloom. Directly across from him the compound and buildings that held the slaves were in shadow. Strangely, there was no sign of the customary guards posted at the entrance, which, if they were truly absent, was an advantage to him entering the compound quietly. Distant sounds of fighting could be heard from far off and perhaps it was this that had drawn the Ma'Vessick away. Even in abnormal circumstances, however, the lack of guards to those caged within was not a problem, as the slaves were not only held under lock and key and chained to their miserable sleeping pallets in the night hours but, even if capable, no slave would dare venture out. The consequences of capture were too terrible to contemplate.

Harasah removed his helmet. It was vital that his fellow slaves recognised him. As it was, the silvery metallic suit he wore and his alien-looking protectors would be enough to terrify them even further. At all costs he must convince them to escape and, hopefully, to join the fight to overthrow the Ma'Vessick.

He placed the helmet on the ground and darted across the roadway that separated him from the compound, his tetran guards loping with him.

Under a forbidding gateway, two huge metal gates were locked and barred before them. Here was the first problem, as Harasah had assumed that one of the guards would carry the keys to unlock the gates. For the first time since setting off, Harasah spoke to his tetran guards. It felt strange to be speaking to them, quite unlike any experience he could recall. 'We must open these gates, and we need to do it as quietly as possible as there are bound to be guards inside.'

The tetran to his left fixed its red eyes on Harasah and nodded once. Walking up to the centre where the two gates met, it placed a hand on the locking chain. Almost immediately the metal began to glow, and gobbets of molten metal sizzled as the chain and bar simply dissolved. In the shortest time imaginable, the tetran removed its hand and pulled the gateway open wide enough for them to slip through. 'Well, you two are full of surprises,' Harasah remarked quietly. 'Follow me.'

In front of them was a wide parade ground where the slaves assembled each morning after a sparse meal and what passed for ablutions, ready to be allocated to a work group. They skirted around the many-windowed walls that surrounded the compound on three sides. Harasah inwardly flinched at the possibility that they might be seen. However, all went well and, arriving at the doorway that was his objective, he pushed the door open and stepped inside. Ahead a small room containing a desk was lit by a torch. From this room a series of steps led both downwards and upwards.

He could feel the presence of the slaves crammed into individual cells. He knew they would not make a sound – to do so brought savage punishment.

Quietly they barred the door to the parade ground. To Harasah's mind there was only one way to do this, and he placed his faith in his tetran friends that they could deal with any hostile Ma'Vessick guards. His experience told him that guard numbers were few during the deep reaches of the night. The slaves were too intimidated to make trouble and in any event were all locked down; additionally, there was the possibility that, like the gate guards, many Ma'Vessick had been drawn into the fighting in the city.

He turned to the tetrans. 'Up that stairway and down this one there is a long hallway. Off each hallway are doors to left and right; these are the cells that house the slaves. There is no other entry or exit point other than through this room. Any Ma'Vessick guards will be stationed in the hallways. We need to neutralise them.'

The tetrans issued a single word in their strangely metallic voices. 'Affirmative.'

Advancing, one took the upwards stairway, whilst the other descended. A strange glow emanated from each of them, their shielding against any projectile weapon, and they disappeared from view. Within moments Harasah heard the discharge of energy weapons and the sudden calls of Ma'Vessick guards caught in surprise. It did not last long. Almost simultaneously both tetrans reappeared.

'Objective complete,' they intoned.

'Very well,' responded Harasah. 'Phase two, not forgetting we have two other blocks to neutralise.'

Descending the lower stairwell, he drew a deep breath and called out into the silent hallway in the biggest voice possible. 'Listen to me. My name is Harasah – some of you may know me. Like you, I was a slave. The Ma'Vessick guards are dead. Even now, allies and friends assault the city. I am here to free you. Do not be afraid. My friends will appear strange to you, but they will not harm you, only the Ma'Vessick need fear them. Join us and throw off the shackles of slavery, the time of retribution is at hand!'

At first there was no response to his message. But then he could hear the noise of people moving and a voice, full of fear, called out.

'Harasah? Is it really you? This is not a trick? It is me, Paran.'

The sound of Paran's voice was a relief. Someone who knew him and would vouch for him.

'No, Paran, it is not a trick, I promise you. Wait now and you will be freed.'

Freeing the slaves and disposing of their Ma'Vessick guards took less time than Harasah had thought, but still the night was pressing on. Many of those freed were still too afraid to leave their opened cells and Harasah wasted little time in trying to convince them that their fears were unfounded. He felt a sense of elation when, in the final block and from almost the last cell opened, Malleva stepped out. In disbelief and with tears flowing freely from them both, she stepped into his arms for a long moment. Neither had expected to see each other again and Malleva kept reaching out to touch Harasah to make certain that she was not dreaming.

'Harasah. Can it really be true?'

'Yes, Malleva. I have so much to tell you but not now. Where is our son? Where is Champa?'

Malleva pressed close in to Harasah. In a despairing tone she spoke. 'You were one day too late, husband. Only yesterday they took our boy to be sacrificed in the temple today.'

Harasah held Malleva tightly and fought down despair. 'Do not lose hope yet. Our friends even now attack the temple with the aim of eradicating the priests. Together we may yet have him restored to us.'

Malleva looked into Harasah's eyes. 'Yesterday and until this moment I was in a living nightmare. Now hope is revived in me. Lead on to whatever fate awaits us. If we are to die, it will be together.'

They took a last quick embrace and turned back down the hallway, chivvying the newly freed ahead of them.

In the parade area several hundred individuals stood, talking in low voices. Fear and trepidation there was, but also a renewed sense of purpose. Harasah had called for volunteers to join him in assaulting the Ma'Vessick. Whilst the response had been disappointing, there had been enough. Upwards of two hundred had come forward. These individuals had swallowed their fears and determined that, come what may, they would not return to slavery, preferring death with honour than continuing a life of servitude and brutality.

Several of them now hefted the weapons of the Ma'Vessick, taken from their fallen guards. If unfamiliar with their practical use, they had all seen enough demonstrations of how they were used by their Ma'Vessick masters to ensure that they could, at last, deal out punishment of their own.

'More weapons will be available to you soon. For now, we move out and allow our tetran allies to lead our attack. Have courage, my friends, the long night is coming to an end. Let us show these Ma'Vessick how their craven slaves can fight!'

This call was met with some cheers and they moved out into the city, tentatively at first but with increasing confidence as the streets around them were empty of all Ma'Vessick troops. They moved warily towards the sound of fighting with a growing determination to mete out swift justice to any Ma'Vessick they might encounter.

Too late, Harasah remembered his discarded helmet and realised that his only means of direct communication was now denied to him. As he realised that the tetrans might be able to pass on a message, the first contact began. They had come up behind a group of Ma'Vessick who were also making their way towards the noise of conflict. The tetrans had displayed their normal lightning speed and dispatched almost all of the Ma'Vessick before they had even turned around. Some of the slaves with weapons raised them, and the explosive sound of gunfire was added to the shouts of the Ma'Vessick. Whilst the firing from the slaves was erratic, some struck home and the screams of the wounded added to the general air of confusion.

In no time at all the entire group of Ma'Vessick were dead. The freed slaves were not inclined to mercy and the few Ma'Vessick that lay wounded were shot where they lay. Now there were enough weapons for all and the group, shielded by the tetrans, continued their advance into the city.

ooooOoooo

Ankh had no sooner been relieved by Horven and her reinforcements than he translocated to the temple with his tetran force. Advancing through the blown doorway they rapidly ascended the stairway to the upper level and made their way to Tishan's position easily, by dint of their helmet communications.

'Most timely, Ankh. I thought that you may have been longer,' Tishan stated as Ankh came up to her.

'You may thank Horven Dar, Stragosh. She executed her orders with commendable speed and even now carries the assault into the city.'

'Then let us make an end to these Hrv priests. Four of them proved a considerable threat. Whilst we have disposed of one, I would expect that the others will link, so our additional tetrans will be most welcome.'

The tetrans were deployed and, with their defensive shielding enhanced by the new arrivals, they progressed with measured tread into the hallway down which the black-clad priests had fled, alert for any counter move.

The silence was ominous. Distant sounds of battle could only faintly be heard as they passed by windows that looked directly out on the city far below. The muted glow of dawn light could now be seen as the long night at last passed by. Huge violet clouds presaged a violent storm, which to Tishan's mind was fitting, given the circumstances.

An air of menace grew and grew. The tetrans, oblivious to any emotional response, continued their wary advance whilst Tishan, Hamra, and Ankh found that just putting one foot in front of another was a matter of utmost will and determination. Tishan concentrated on the rod that she now almost habitually carried, throwing out a second shield around her, Hamra, and Ankh, so that the green glow of the tetran shielding was eerily enhanced by the blue light now emanating from the rod.

'It seems to me, Stragosh, that the Ma'Vessick may ultimately have been worse off than those they pressed into slavery,' Ankh remarked as he stolidly set one foot in front of the other.

'There may be an element of truth in what you say, Ankh, but I am not sure that the Ma'Vessick suffering would in any way diminish the feelings of Hamra and all the enslaved peoples here.'

Hamra's voice was grim. 'When I think of the brutality endured by all of us, I cannot but wish to inflict it back in equal measure. But I see now that the true menace lies here with these Hrv and all that they have done. I would see them obliterated and then my one desire would be to go home, back to the lands of my birth. If I were never to see another Ma'Vessick in my life I would not lose a moment's sleep. Let them reap what they have sown.'

They continued in silence until Third of the File, along with all the other tetrans, abruptly stopped before a sharp turn to the right. Ahead of them, a doorway covered in strangely hypnotic symbols stood firmly closed.

'They are here, Stragosh. There is a build-up of energy beyond those doors.'

'Send a tetran down the hallway to our right, see if there is any other entry point.'

Without acknowledgement from Third, one of the tetrans immediately set off and disappeared around the corner. The pressure of awaiting its return was for Tishan, Ankh, and Hamra almost unbearable, coupled as it was with the certainty of violence once the doors were breached.

Outside, dawn had broken and whilst the sounds of fighting could no longer be heard, it was replaced by the roll of thunder and sudden flashes as forks of lightning leapt across the sky.

'Fifteen reports that the hallway is clear. There are no other entry points.'

Tishan was about to respond with a command when Third sounded a warning. 'Beware, an energy wave is unleashed!'

No sooner had the words been uttered than the doorways in front of them burst outwards, hitting the front rank of tetrans and disrupting the shield as they deflected the doors up and over their heads, sending them smashing into the ceiling above them. Chunks of falling masonry added further confusion as the doors impacted both ceiling and walls before finally coming to a stop, fused and broken, some fifty paces behind the Graaven force.

Accompanying this violence, a wave of tremendous energy punched into the tetrans. Incandescent white light and searing heat blasted a hole in the weakened shield, vaporising the front rank of tetrans, including Third of the File. Tishan's secondary shield buckled. She felt a searing pain in her right arm before the shield reasserted itself, so that the energy wave parted like water before the bow of a ship.

Tishan's mind was dazed from the effect of the attack and the huge amount of concentration required to keep her will focused on the rod. Now, however, if it was not perceived before, the benefit of a tetran force became apparent. Any force made of flesh and blood upon surviving the ferocity of the attack would have fled in panic. Instead, a metallic tetran voice issued calm orders as Tenth of the File assumed command. 'Harmonise shielding and counterstrike.'

Tishan was sure the communication was for her benefit as tetran commands were instantaneous and without need of words. Mere moments after the devastation of the Hrv strike, the tetran response pulsed through the shattered doorway. High pitched and alien screams, on the very edge of her hearing range, announced the fact that at least one of the Hrv had been struck. Now Tishan summoned her will and a powerful beam of green energy followed the tetran strike. Further screams were heard and Tishan gave a tight smile in satisfaction.

'Tetrans, advance!' she snapped out.

As one, the surviving tetrans entered the doorway in ranks six wide and five deep, their combined shields glowing strongly. Tishan stepped through with Ankh and Hamra close behind. On the floor, several paces inside the doorway, two Hrv forms lay motionless. Their body parts had formed a gruesome splatter all about, mute testament to the power of the counterstrike, even diminished in number as the tetrans were.

'It may be that they were simply not prepared for the speed of the tetran counterstroke, Stragosh,' remarked Ankh. 'Any Graaven force would have been incapable after such a blast.'

Tishan watched dispassionately as the tetrans picked up three of the Hrv Instruments. It appeared that only one was serviceable.

'Whatever the cause, let us be thankful, Ankh,' Tishan said. She could see that they were in a large chamber, in the centre of which was a table made of some dark wood that, in the same fashion as the now destroyed doors, was elaborately carved. The table was surrounded by several things that she assumed were chairs of some sort. Certainly not ones that could possibly accommodate any living being that she knew. On the far side, three doorways exited the chamber. All three were open, revealing dimly lit stairways beyond.

'It would appear, Ankh, that our friends have exited this chamber, though whether all together or separately, we will soon find out. Tetran commander, identify yourself.'

'I am Tenth of the File, Stragosh. What is your command?'

'Send forward scouts and venture cautiously beyond those doors, see if you can determine where the Hrv have gone.'

'As you command, Stragosh.'

'Horven, Lerma. Can you hear me?'

'I am here, Stragosh,' came Horven's response. 'All resistance has collapsed. We have met up with Harasah and the freed slaves. Even now we are freeing others. Many Ma'Vessick have surrendered and they are enjoying the hospitality of the slave quarters.'

'Excellent. What of the Ma'Vessick in their homes? Surely they must have ventured outside by now?'

'According to Harasah, the Ma'Vessick are so indoctrinated that they will not leave their homes until the temple bell sounds the end of the curfew. That is usually at dawn, so it would appear that you have been distracting them.' Horven's tone suggested a smug confidence.

'Be vigilant nonetheless, Shu Lan Horven. Complacency may lead to unwanted consequences.'

'As you command, Stragosh,' Horven's response was immediately contrite and Tishan smiled. Horven was undoubtedly enjoying herself.

'Lerma?'

'As with Horven, Stragosh. All resistance is overcome. I, too, have encountered freed slaves. Those Ma'Vessick living have been put to work cleaning up those who have fallen. The dead we are placing in mounds in the barrack squares within the slave compounds. From there we can burn them or our tetrans can vaporise them.'

'Very well. Good work, both of you. Ankh and I are hunting down the last of the priests. It is hot work. I will contact you again once this has been accomplished.'

Tishan did not wait for Horven or Lerma to respond. The city was in their control and all she had to do now was focus on the removal of the last of the Hrv priests.

CHAPTER SIXTEEN

Three tetrans moved forward and mounted the stairs revealed by the opened doors. Once again, waiting for their report stretched the nerves, but it was not long before Tenth of the File communicated with Tishan.

'Stragosh, the stairway of the door to the left led to a kind of holding area in which there was a cage. There are several individuals locked within it. They appear terrified, we have not approached any closer. To the right, the stairway ends on a large balcony overlooking the city. Other than those held captive, both areas are deserted. The central stair leads to a further hallway, at the end of which is a doorway not dissimilar to those we have encountered before. This doorway is closed.'

'Then we will take the centre stairs. Recall your scout who accessed the balcony and have them join us. Tell the others to hold position.' Tishan turned to Hamra. 'Hamra, any ideas as to why there should be captives held above?'

'I can think of one purpose, Stragosh. Sacrifice. No slave who entered the upper levels has ever been seen again. I suggest that I go to them. I can assuage their fears and release them. If the tetran on guard stays with me, we can wait for you here.'

'Good. I would have suggested this myself. You should be safe enough here; hopefully we will see you again soon.'

Tishan watched Hamra mount the stairs to the captives. Having given the order, the remaining tetrans again advanced, four abreast. The central stairwell itself was easily negotiated and debouched onto another wide hallway. For all intents and purposes, it mirrored those below, save that the walls were decorated with swirls and patterns of colour that, to Tishan's eyes, appeared chaotic and without purpose. She sensed there was more to it but, if so, she was unable to interpret it.

The group formed up close to the stairway and this time Tishan would not wait for any surprises. 'Ten. We will destroy those doors but prepare for a counterstrike.'

The tetrans had been able to deploy into a compact body in the hallway, ten wide and four deep. In a combined attack, a single beam of pulsing red energy erupted from the front line and smashed into the two closed doors. For a few brief moments they seemed to resist the surge of power hurled against them before they suddenly flared into an intense red colour and burst inwards. The blast of energy, now unimpeded, streamed through the shattered entrance, followed by a bolt of energy from Tishan. Almost immediately a counterstrike of intense white light blossomed from beyond the ruined doorway and smote the front lines of the tetrans. However, the intensity was noticeably less than the first attack and this time the tetran shields held, deflecting the energy that, diverted from its intended target, blew holes in the ceiling and walls all around.

'Advance!' Tishan ordered.

By the time the group had advanced thirty paces down the hallway the intensity of the Hrv attack had diminished considerably. Suddenly two unexpected assaults were launched simultaneously from hidden alcoves to the left and right. As blindingly fast as the tetran redeployment was, they could not prevent the destruction of several caught in the fire from the surprise attack. Tishan felt herself shoved violently to one side as Ankh's voice called desperately into her helmet, 'Tishan, lookout!'

Tishan fell to the ground, her helmet absorbing the impact, her rod still tightly clenched in her right hand. She looked up and saw Ankh standing above her, any expression hidden behind the blank visage of his helmet. Time slowed. It seemed to Tishan that he stood above her for a lifetime. Punched through the centre of his suit was a fist-sized hole.

In that frozen moment of time, images of Ankh flashed in Tishan's mind. Details of interactions with him over the many sem'chaal they had served together appeared with amazing clarity as if it were but yesterday, accompanied by an aching sense of loss and sorrow. Tishan watched as his body slowly buckled and he fell to the floor, his life extinguished before her eyes. As this happened, the passage of time, which had seemed to slow, returned to normal and as Tishan stood up, she felt a sense of rage so all-encompassing that it stole all rational thought, save that of vengeance. The rod reacted instantaneously to the focus of her will. Two Hrv had been placed in the alcoves. In the ferocity of the rod's unleashed energy, they, their weapons, and the alcoves themselves were reduced to atoms in an instant.

Incoherent with rage she ran down the hallway, followed by several tetrans, a Graaven battle cry on her lips. She blasted through a doorway in a concentrated burst of power that filled the room beyond with a heat so intense the walls around them began to melt. A single Hrv stood motionless in the centre of the room. Tishan watched as it caught alight, and she exulted in its dying screams as its body shrivelled: a counterpoint to the terrible grief that her rage had pushed down. She stood unharmed within that blaze of incandescent light, like a demon out of tales of nightmare, and she exacted the last exquisite moment of pain from her enemy as it was immolated in front of her. Finally, without a word, she turned away from the destruction she had wrought, banished the rod from her hand, and returned to the hallway to kneel over Ankh's lifeless body. Silently she lifted him, tenderly removed his helmet, closed his sightless eyes, and looked into his face, rocking him gently in her arms, lost in a thousand swirling emotions.

Deep within her mind she thought she could hear a voice speaking to her. She tried to ignore it and stay where she was, locked deep in her memories, but once noticed it could not be ignored and it gradually grew louder, as if the whisperer grew ever closer to her hiding place.

<Child. You must return. The time for grief is later. Ankh is beyond all harm. He died without regret, knowing he had saved you, his dearest friend. His death was quick and painless, a fitting end for a Graaven of the Empire. Come, you are needed.> Varnahrin was gentle but implacable.

Slowly Tishan's mind returned to the present. She looked up at the surviving tetrans who stood around her and then gently laid Ankh's body on the floor.

'Your orders, Stragosh?' Despite its voice being toneless and metallic, Ten managed to convey a sense of worry.

Tishan pulled back her focus. The tragedy of Ankh's death had caught her unawares, even given her experience with sudden death on a battlefield. She drew a deep breath and mentally pushed her grief deep inside.

'Secure the temple. Bear Ankh's body away to the gateway and convey him back to Ta'Morin. We shall return to Hamra. Horven, Lerma, report.'

There was considerable relief in Horven and Lerma's voices as they acknowledged Tishan's call.

Horven spoke for them both. 'It is good to hear from you, Stragosh. All is under our control here. Harasah is with me, he has found his mate, but there is no sign of their son as yet. He was taken to the temple, so there is some hope. What of the Hrv?'

'They are eradicated.' Tishan paused and closed her eyes briefly. 'Ankh was killed saving my life in the final assault.'

A terrible silence met these words. Lerma responded in a quiet voice, full of sadness. 'That is grave news, he will be missed by all of us.'

'Yes.' Tishan fought for control of her voice. 'The end was very quick; we shall mourn his passing back in Ta'Morin. For now, hold your positions and await my further instruction.'

ooooOoooo

Much later Tishan stood upon the wide terrace of the temple where the priests were wont to address the Ma'Vessick. A crowd had gathered below upon hearing the peal of the great temple bell, and a subdued hubbub of voices could be heard as the citizens of Gahrtok became fully aware of what had passed in the night. Their fear was tangible.

Alongside Tishan were Hamra and Harasah, reunited with his mate, Malleva. Their joy was complete when they discovered that one of the survivors found locked in the cage was their son, Champa. Beyond all hope, Harasah's loved ones were returned to him and a new future now beckoned for all of the freed slaves.

The temple was cunningly designed. On the terrace a kind of speaking trumpet was set in place so that when words were spoken into the mouthpiece the voice was amplified, and the words reverberated around the plaza below. A sea of Ma'Vessick faces, veiled behind the masks they all wore, looked up as Tishan began to speak. Around them a ring of tetrans were placed in case of any aggression on the part of the Ma'Vessick; the tetrans' orders were clear as to what course of action they should take.

Tishan's voice rang out. 'My name is Tishan Dar, from the City of Ta'Morin. I am here because your people journeyed across the Great Water to the lands of our friends and allies the Xotic, and

283

there visited death and destruction upon them. This was their reward for providing succour to your people who were driven upon their shores after a storm, enabling their safe return here. Your army is overthrown, your false god cast down, and your priests eliminated.'

'We have other armies!' a voice called out from the crowd, followed by a murmuring assent from many.

'Yes, you do,' responded Tishan grimly. 'Even now, the forces of Ta'Morin, allied with the oppressed peoples you have enslaved, deal out death to those who foolishly think to oppose us. Where, then, is your false god now? Where are your priests who, by their arts, tricked you into a false belief in a baseless religion? Look about you. Every one of you has mutilated themselves as a sign of your devotion to your god, as required by those same priests. Why? See now your priests revealed to you in their true form.'

Here Ten hefted up the body of Toronset, which had been preserved in Ta'Morin, and displayed it to the crowd. A muttering sigh passed through the Ma'Vessick.

'You lie,' called out another voice. 'This is but a trick. Harkan will save us!'

Tishan nodded to another tetran who stood by, holding a huge metal image of the mummified face of Harkan that it hurled effortlessly down the temple steps that stretched before them.

'Hear me, you Ma'Vessick! Here is the false image of your god. Let him strike me down now and show you his power. Let him prove my words are as lies! I say he is false and you the unwitting pawns in a religion which held you in a slavery worse than that you inflicted on those whose lands lie around yours. Your priests were from the Hrv. Insectoids who once held sway in these lands and whose hatred of those of flesh and blood is without limit. They fed off your hatred and cruelty and feasted on the flesh of those you sent to sacrifice to your god. Yes, even your own that were sent who displeased them.'

Fear of the tetrans held some of the crowd back whilst others stood in shocked silence. Not all Ma'Vessick believed in Harkan, but all lived in daily fear of the priests and the consequences of failing to abide by the religious tenets that dominated their daily lives.

'What will happen to us? Will you now enslave us, or worse?' someone called, echoing the fear of all who stood there.

'Even should I will it, I could not place you under a worse bondage than that of your religion. Cooperate with us and you need have no fear of retribution. Your arms will be confiscated and anyone hiding weapons will be punished. Those you have enslaved are free and may depart in peace. All of you will need to take on the tasks that those you held captive previously performed. It may be, in time to come, that those you treated so brutally will trade with you and a new period of cooperation will ensue, but it will take a long time for that to happen.'

There was a rising babble of talk as the Ma'Vessick spoke amongst themselves. Several tried to shout out questions but were drowned in a rising chorus. Horven's voice cut like a whip through the noise.

'Silence!' She glared out across the plaza as the voices dwindled to nothing. 'Did you think that you could enslave and brutalise the people of neighbouring lands and there would be no consequence to you? Be thankful that you are not lying dead upon the ground and all that you have built, with the sweat and toil of others, not laid low around you! Listen and hear your fate.'

Tishan nodded at Horven and turned her eyes back to crowd. 'As of now, a ruling council will be established. In time, you will have representation on it. In the immediate term, the council will take direction of this city and ensure that there is adequate food so that you need not fear starvation. Understand that there are no slaves to perform menial tasks – they now become your tasks. All religious observances are forbidden, and that includes ritual disfigurement. The city of Gahrtok will continue, though there will be many changes and difficulties that you will need to overcome. For now, you will all return to your homes and stay there until you receive further instruction.'

'But how will you do this? There are thousands of us, faceless and unknown to you! We are many and you are few! How do we know that you will keep your word?' a strident voice called out, and once again there was an echoing cry from many of those gathered together.

Tishan turned her gaze upon the caller, hidden as he was in the crowd, an anonymous voice in a crowded sea. 'In the same way, Kremmish, that I know your name and the street where you live. In the same way that I know your mate, Hlva, and your three children, Mrc, Sila, and Harv, who live with you. In the same way that I know you are a merchant who deals in fur.'

Kremmish fell back in awe and fear as Tishan named random people in the crowd and related back to them their occupations, their family members and where they lived. The crowd grew silent, cowed by what to many was an overt act of sorcery.

Varnahrin's voice echoed in Tishan's mind. <That's given them something to think about.>

<Do you know them all, then?> asked Tishan.

<Not all. I am working on it, Tishan Dar. Soon I will be able to identify those who may ably assist us in making the changes required.>

<What about those who will do all to oppose us?>

<Them also. You must decide what you want done with them.>

<I would prefer it if they didn't wake up.>

<That is a very Graaven solution, Tishan Dar. Are you quite sure that it is the only solution?>

<I am quite sure that if they choose not to walk a new path and act to oppose the changes needed, then they are an unnecessary distraction.>

<So be it.>

<Then can you inform Ten of the identities of those who will work with us? I want them here in the morning. I will speak to them then.>

<As you wish.> Varnahrin withdrew from Tishan's mind.

Tishan stood and watched in silence as the crowd departed, some noisily calling out, with many a backward look to where Tishan stood.

ooooOoooo

Throughout the day Tishan was kept busy with a myriad of tasks. Ma'Vessick forces in the city were disarmed. Newly freed slaves had to be managed, many still digesting the news that their liberty had been restored. Horven and Lerma played a key role in organising resources to aid the departure of those who wished to leave, and reports came back all through that day as tetran forces subdued Ma'Vessick troops outside the city. Tishan barely had time for a meal, let alone any time for rest, so it was with a sense of disbelief that she saw that the night had closed in.

In the early hours of the next day, she finally managed to snatch a small amount of sleep but was up well before the dawn. She was in a small room, sitting down to her first meal in many chaal, when Horven entered, past two tetran guards who stood at the doorway.

'Stragosh,' Horven's voice was formal and delivered in the crisp tones of a report. 'It is apparent that hundreds of Ma'Vessick have died during the night. There is no clue as to the cause, they simply appear to have taken to their beds and expired. In some cases, whole families have been affected. I am worried that it is some contagion. Fortunately, there are very few Graavens in the occupying forces if that is the case. Your orders?'

Tishan wiped her hands clean and paused a moment before looking up at Horven, whose gaze was firmly pointed over Tishan's left shoulder.

'Very well, Shu Lan Horven. Your concerns may be well founded. Direct all Graaven Sagit and Hoplex still in Gahrtok to depart. Organise our tetrans to remove the Ma'Vessick dead. The parkland outside the city will be best, depending on how many bodies. Keep me updated with total numbers. Once collected, we will make preparations to dispose of them.'

Horven gave a Baran Mec salute and for a brief moment looked deep into Tishan's eyes. 'As you command, Stragosh.'

As she turned to go Horven placed her helmet on her head and then exited the room with rapid steps.

Tishan closed her eyes, gave a deep sigh, placed her head in her hands, and sat in silence.

<They did not suffer, child. To have left them alive would have ultimately resulted in further civil strife and war. All this you have averted.>

<I am not who I once was, Varnahrin. I have stood upon battlefields surrounded by the dead. I have sent enemies beyond count to the afterlife and watched without emotion as prisoners were executed in front of me and at my orders. Yet this one act makes me feel ashamed.>

<Then learn from it, Tishan Dar. The battle we are embarked upon may lead to events far worse than this. Many now living would suffer and die had you not made your decision. Take comfort from that thought.>

<I will think on it, Varnahrin.>

Varnahrin departed and Tishan continued to sit alone with her thoughts. She failed to notice the arrival of Hamra who stood quietly by for some time, watching her, before speaking.

'You are withdrawn, Stragosh. Might I assist you in some way?' Hamra's voice indicated that he was quietly concerned.

Tishan looked up and turned towards Hamra. 'I have sentenced many Ma'Vessick to death, Hamra. There was a time when such a decision would not have weighed upon my mind. I find that I am not the person I once was.'

'Whilst I cannot comprehend how you have achieved this, Tishan Dar, if I may call you by your name rather than your rank?' Hamra paused whilst Tishan gave him a small smile and a nod in acquiescence. 'I know you to be a good person. You have not experienced the brutality and callousness of the Ma'Vessick. All here in this city had some role to play in the suppression, conquest, and enslavement of their neighbours and in that sense, they are all guilty. If the deaths you spoke of remove the taint of that cruelty, I, for one, cannot but praise you for it.'

'Thank you, Hamra. Militarily it was the right decision, but I perhaps did not consider other alternatives.' She sighed and took a deep breath. 'What's done is done. I cannot change it now.' Tishan reached out and grasped one of Hamra's hands, changing the subject and pushing her thoughts – like her grief over Ankh – to one side. 'May I ask you to stay and form part of the council here in Gahrtok, at least temporarily? Your knowledge and experience are balanced by a sound mind. You do not thirst for vengeance but would see Balance restored.'

Hamra stood quietly before moving to a window that looked out over the city. 'It is strange. Just a few cycles ago if someone had said to me that I would be standing within the great temple, presiding over the defeat of the Ma'Vessick, I would have called them insane. I should run far from here and never return. My single desire was to return to my home. But …' he paused in thought and Tishan sat silently whilst he considered. 'Where would I run to? All that I once knew is gone and can never be returned.' He turned back to Tishan and smiled. 'Yes, Tishan Dar, I think I would like to be part of a new beginning.'

Tishan nodded. 'I am most pleased, Hamra. Now if you will excuse me, I must return to Ta'Morin for a short time and oversee the final farewell of a great friend.'

'I too would accompany you, if my presence would not offend?'

Tishan smiled, took Hamra's hand and disappeared from the temple, reappearing moments later before the gateway back to Ta'Morin. No sooner had they arrived than a small group of Benshin, headed by Draachnull, emerged from the gateway. If Draachnull was discomposed by the journey, he did not show it. Seeing Tishan, he walked towards her. The usual smile on his face when he greeted good friends was replaced by a look of solemnity and sadness and, reaching up, he grasped both of Tishan's hands in his own and looked up into her face.

'Tishan Dar, we were visiting Ta'Morin when the body of our dear friend Ankh was carried through. All Benshin mourn with you. We could not wait in Ta'Morin but chose instead to cross to you to offer our deepest condolences and any aid that we may be able to offer.'

Draachnull's arrival and sincerity stirred deep emotions within Tishan, and she gripped his hands, taking some deep breaths to steady herself. 'My thanks, Draachnull.' Her gaze shifted to the small group of Benshin who stood behind Draachnull. 'My thanks to you all.' She turned back to Draachnull. 'Ankh gave his life to save mine. It was very quick, had we still lived within the Empire we would have said it was a noble ending: now, I cannot but think it was a waste.'

Draachnull nodded in sympathy. 'I do not think Ankh would think that giving his life to save yours was a waste, Tishan Dar. He held you in the highest esteem and regard. Also, he gave his life to free others. All Benshin would agree that this was a worthy thing to have done.'

Tishan smiled briefly and gripped Draachnull's hands tighter. 'Would you stand with me when we say our final farewells?'

'I would be deeply honoured, Tishan Dar.'

'Good.' She turned to one side, indicating Hamra. 'This is Hamra, I do not think you have met. He was once a slave of the Ma'Vessick. Now he is free to follow his own path and has become a friend to the Graaven people.'

Draachnull clasped his hands together and then held them, palm up and open, in the Benshin form of greeting. 'Any friend of Tishan Dar and of the Graaven people is a friend to the Benshin. Hamra, I bid you greetings.'

Hamra bowed deeply. Whilst he had not understood the words Draachnull had spoken, he could guess their meaning and he returned Draachnull's smile. He had stood silently watching the exchange between the two and whilst Tishan Dar towered over the diminutive Benshin, the dignity of Draachnull's manner and bearing evoked a sense of wisdom and knowledge that more than compensated for his smaller stature. His clothing and those of his companions was fascinating. Intricately embroidered vests and leggings of supple animal skins. Calf-length foot coverings were fringed and also highly decorated. Their long, greenish-black hair was plaited with brightly coloured stones and feathers. Smooth-skinned faces of deep brown were dominated by piercing black eyes that sat above a large nose and a full-lipped mouth filled with even teeth. They were at once the most amazing people that Hamra had ever seen. Their appearance and demeanour reflected a wildness of spirit which somehow hinted at a deep and ancient knowledge.

Tishan Dar Looked at Hamra. 'Draachnull bids you greetings as a friend. Soon their language will become familiar to you in the same way that ours has. The Spirit of Ta'Morin invests all of us with knowledge, though wisdom is harder earned,' she remarked with a knowing look.

Tishan's words resonated with Hamra. For the first time he had pause to think about what Tishan had said and now he reflected upon it. Things that he previously had no cause to question before now rose in his mind. How was it that Tishan Dar could speak Ma'Vessick and his own dialect even though they had never met? How was it that, in his turn, he could understand the speech of the Xotic and they his? So natural was the understanding that his mind had accepted it unquestioningly. Now Tishan had referred to the Spirit of Ta'Morin. Was this something to be feared? Hamra dismissed that thought as soon as it had arisen. If the city of Ta'Morin was powerful then he could not but be glad of it. Everything that had happened thus far had a profound sense of 'rightness' to it. Without it, he reflected, he would still be suffering under the whips of the Ma'Vessick.

After each of the Benshin had greeted both Tishan and Hamra, they crossed back through the gateway, which had been recalibrated to allow for passage both ways. Tishan had left Lerma and Horven in control of Gahrtok, trusting their combined judgement in reordering matters satisfactorily – a task that would keep them both busy for some time to come. Then, following the departing Benshin, she too crossed back in to Ta'Morin.

ooooOoooo

Several dak'chaal passed by as preparations were made for the Ceremony of Leaving. Ultimately there had been many hundreds of Ma'Vessick who had not awakened the morning after the capture of Gahrtok and overthrow of the Hrv but, in a city of thousands, the overall number was much less than Tishan had anticipated might be the final result. The Ma'Vessick believed that some kind of illness had affected the city and Varnahrin's influence had reassured everyone that it was a passing thing and not to be feared. If any suspected that the Graaven forces had been the cause, the idea was quickly and quietly suppressed.

The suns of Tarvuli hung in a cloudless violet sky and the sound of the seven streams was a constant backdrop.

Garbed in the mail of the Baran Mec, Tishan stood silently, but not alone, in one of the large plazas that were scattered across the city. Surrounding her, a silent crowd of Graavens – virtually the entire population – had gathered to pay their respects. Whilst the Graaven population was on a healthy increase it was still not so great that they spilled outside the confines of the plaza. Many had worn the flowing garments that now marked them, to Tishan's mind, as citizens of Ta'Morin.

Others had joined them for this day. Tlkcha of the Xotic led a group of twenty of her people and a similar sized body of Benshin, headed by Draachnull, also stood in respectful silence. Before them, Ankh's body lay on a crystal plinth which appeared to have grown out of the ground. His face looked serene and at peace.

An honour guard of one hundred Baran Mec, dressed in mail and carrying the broad shield and mace that signified their elite status, stood quietly. Draachnull spoke in a soft voice to Tishan as she looked at the body.

'If it is permitted, we and our Xotic friends would like to place a gift with Ankh to aid him on his final journey?'

Tishan spoke formally. 'It is permitted, we are honoured.'

Draachnull nodded to one of the Benshin who stood with him. Forward into the silence and in full view of all gathered, Shartuk of the Shadow Hunter Clan stepped forward, along with Kellix of the Xotic, bearing a carved totem. Intricate designs were carved into a gnarled and ancient piece of wood decorated with feathers and plaited cords of the wild grasses that grew all across the plains where the Xotic dwelt. They both bowed to the form of Ankh and placed it reverently on the body. Standing back, Shartuk lifted both arms into the air.

'I send a voice in four directions. Let the words of Shartuk of the Benshin be heard throughout the lands. Our friend Ankh has begun the journey home. Let Varthansh Mek clear his way. We who were his friends mourn his passing. There is no greater tribute than to say our hearts will miss him.'

Now Kellix's voice took up the cry. 'Sky Father. Look down upon us. Our friend Ankh crosses over to you. Bear him up on the winds and carry him safely home.' Silently, Shartuk and Kellix rejoined the others.

There was not one Graaven unmoved by the words they had heard. Into the silence a mighty roar resounded throughout the plaza. Tishan and the others with her jumped in surprise. Fendrax had returned silently via the gateway, in itself a compliment to Ankh as she had previously resisted that form of crossing. The primal call of the gonverdeem seemed to pierce everyone to the very core of their being. It was at once wild and free, stirring feelings of unfettered freedom and the joy of the open plains under a bright sky; yet, for all its wildness, a poignant sense of loss echoed within it as well. Somehow it was the perfect resolution to the calls of Shartuk and Kellix.

Tishan Dar fought back her emotions and took a step forward. Upon her head, a helmet of highly polished metal surmounted by the stylised head of a mellax denoted her rank. In her right hand she grasped the Rod of Klemish, and she raised it high in the air. Taking a deep breath, she called out into the silence in a voice that echoed throughout the plaza. 'Whose body is this that lies before me!?'

A hundred Baran Mec voices shouted the response. 'It is our brother, Ankh ab Zuma.'

'Is he worthy?'

'He is Baran Mec. He is worthy!'

'How shall we judge him?'

'We shall judge him in blood. We shall judge him in courage. We shall judge him in honour. He is worthy. He is Baran Mec!'

Silence descended on the gathered throng.

Finally, in the quiet, Tishan walked to the plinth and stood before it. 'I am Tishan Dar. You have passed judgement on he that lies here. He is judged worthy.' Turning her gaze upon the body of Ankh, she placed her left hand on his chest. 'Depart in peace, brother.'

Throughout the plaza, from a thousand throats, came a wild ululation in response to Tishan's words. Raising her right arm, she pointed the rod at Ankh's body, as Varnahrin had instructed her. She was not sure what to expect, Varnahrin's penchant for surprises as predictable as the phases of the Seasons. In the empire that had been, a great funeral pyre would be lit, and all would stand until the flames had consumed the body utterly. Here, as with Mareen, that seemed totally inappropriate and Tishan could not stand to see Ankh's body immolated. Somehow it seemed a desecration.

Tishan felt energy flow out of the rod – a display of light so dazzling the eye could not see what actually happened. Within moments, in place of the body, a pyramid-shaped block of crystal stood, twice as tall as any Graaven. Appearing on one side in Graaven glyphs was Ankh's name. If one looked at it long enough, other script appeared that detailed his life and his final moments and, in concert with this, Ankh's face – unblemished and untouched by age – appeared, smiling out from inside the crystal.

This was not the only surprise. Whilst the Graavens peered at the crystal, other names appeared and other faces rose up to the surface to look out. Every Graaven who had fallen on the flight from the Empire was there. As the crowd went past the memorial stone the faces they remembered could be seen. As Tishan looked, the face of Mareen arose, her name and her life story rising with her. Tears flowed unashamedly down Tishan's face.

<What do you think, Tishan Dar? Is it a fitting monument to those who have fallen?>

<You know my thoughts, Varnahrin. I cannot express it in words. I must let Horven and Lerma know.>

<I judged the time right for such a memorial. Time enough for the pain to have diminished so that the memories would be a source of comfort and not of further grief. In essence, it mirrors the memorial that Menkh created to those who fell with Pershiva before the walls of Tarmech in the last days.>

<I have not seen it, but if it is like this, then it is fitting. I would like to visit that place and pay tribute to those that fell.>

There was not one Graaven who was not moved by what they saw, and a great celebration followed the ceremony that night as they reflected not only on the life of Ankh, but of all those who had journeyed with the survivors and fallen.

ooooOoooo

Over several meh'chaal much was achieved in the settling of Gahrtok and the reordering of the Ma'Vessick. Those selected by Varnahrin proved to be reliable and committed to the changes required. Increasingly, as matters settled into a new order, small groups of Benshin and Xotic travelled to Gahrtok, ever mindful of opportunities to trade. Some of those who had once been enslaved, like Hamra, chose to remain. They, too, were instrumental in assisting the reacclimatising of those they had once seen as their implacable enemy. Much remained to be done. The Ma'Vessick lands around Gahrtok had been pacified, the tetran forces of Ta'Morin had little difficulty in subduing those Ma'Vessick who chose to fight, and many former slaves sought to return to the lands that they called home. The aid of Ta'Morin and its allies would play a critical role in establishing a new order.

Upon their return from Gahrtok, Horven and Lerma stood silently together looking at the faces of those they had lost. As Varnahrin had predicted, most Graavens spent time looking into the memorial and used this as a way of showing their spawnlings family and those they had once called friends, so that they could have a real sense of those who had preceded them. Graavens who watched Horven and Lerma show their offspring, Mareen and Halika, the images of those they had been named for were particularly moved, not least because they bore such a likeness to their namesakes.

It was with relief, then, that as the situation with the Ma'Vessick became increasingly stable, Varnahrin informed Tishan of Menkh's imminent return. She translocated to the Complex in anticipation of his arrival.

CHAPTER SEVENTEEN

Tishan appeared in the spacious apartment that sat high up in one of the many towers that were a feature of the Complex. It was a room that both she and Menkh used on occasion when their accessing of the archives stretched deep into the night. Here a broad balcony could be accessed, which had a view that, in one direction, looked out over the mist of water rising from the cataract that poured ceaselessly into the chasm where once the other half of Kareem Vastar had stood. In the other, Tishan could look out across Ta'Morin and see, in the distance, the quadrant of the city occupied by her people.

Above her, the towering pillar of energy could be seen punching its way through banks of cloud to where it intersected with the other energies from the satellites that she and Menkh had activated. It would have been reasonable to expect that such power would be accompanied by great heat and noise but, other than a vibration she could feel through her feet, there was no other sensation. This reality did not detract from the enormous power that it manifested.

No sooner had Varnahrin greeted her than there was a shimmering in the air and Menkh appeared. For just the briefest moment, the alien figure of the bonded Adept stood there, staff in hand. In the blink of an eye the form changed to that of Menkh ab Dur, the staff vanished from his hand, and the smile she knew so well traced the corners of his mouth as he looked at her.

<Tishan Dar.> The mental projection of her name contained a depth of emotion that mere spoken words could never have conveyed. Tishan's answer of, <Menkh ab Dur,> was equally heartfelt. Silently, they clasped hands and touched foreheads, gazing deep into each other's eyes.

<I, too, am most glad to see you again, Tishan Dar.> Crixac's voice echoed in her mind.

<How glad I am to hear your words, dear Crixac, and to know that you are safely returned.>

<I echo that sentiment, Tishan. I am thrice indebted to Menkh for his rescue of me.>

<You are both precious to me,> Menkh responded. He had never once taken his eyes from Tishan's face. <You would have done the same for me.>

They stood lost in each other's thoughts for quiet moments until Varnahrin interrupted them quietly. <So, children, the time for the greeting of friends is done and your faith, each to the other, renewed again. This will be part of our weapon and our defence in the time that is to come. Now we must move on with our plans and hopes.>

Smiling, they drew apart somewhat whilst Varnahrin continued. <Into your minds I pass on the particulars of all that has occurred so that you may know and understand what each of you has had to face and overcome.>

As Menkh and Tishan processed this knowledge they turned amazed looks upon each other, both impressed at the fortitude and courage that each had shown in the challenges that they had faced.

<It occurs to me that the war against the Ma'Vessick cannot be a coincidence,> Menkh mused.

<You are right, Menkh ab Dur,> said Varnahrin. <There are ripples that flow across the cosmos and impact sentient life everywhere. This is an aspect of the nature of Balance. On Tarvuli, Balance has been restored.>

<What of this power that ambushed Menkh and Crixac? Is this a new force, or a manifestation of the Talixit Ven?> Tishan asked.

<Yes, that is an excellent question, Tishan,> Crixac said.

<I have pondered this myself.> Varnahrin's thoughts were speculative. <There are five immutable laws. The Intelligence by its nature will not directly intervene in matters concerning Balance. But, in the battle with the Tree of Tangoreth, it would appear that there was some form of direct intervention. Although your bonding with me, Menkh, and my subsequent separation from the Whole was not completely without precedent, this direct action is unheralded.>

Menkh's question was one that each of them had. <Frzath and the others also referred to these laws: but what are they and what happens if they are broken?>

<The immutable laws hold the fabric of time and space together, Menkh. The first immutable law is that travelling backwards through time is proscribed. Such travel would completely disrupt Balance, and chaos would ensue.

<The second immutable law of Balance should be obvious. Every action taken elicits an opposite response in order to sustain Balance. A being dies, a being is born. A planet explodes, a new planet comes into existence, and so on. These things are happening continuously and simultaneously. The Intelligence manipulates the Balance subtly in order to preserve it. The arrival of the Talixit Ven on Tarvuli and their potential access to a Balancepoint was a deviance that threatened the nature of Balance itself. In creating you, a bonded Adept, to destroy the Talixit Ven, and in separating

me from the Whole, I believe we may have triggered an unanticipated opposite reaction. Your purpose is to preserve Balance. If I am right, there has come into existence an opposing force whose purpose is to destroy it.>

<Are you saying,> Crixac thoughts reflected a deep concern, <that there may be a mirror of Menkh in existence right now and it was this that ambushed us?>

<Not precisely a mirror of Menkh, no: but an opposing force, yes. And yes, that is exactly what I am saying.>

For several long moments no thoughts were exchanged as they each grappled with the consequence of Varnahrin's comment.

<Are there any other immutable laws that are in jeopardy?> Tishan was horrified by Varnahrin's supposition, but her curiosity was aroused.

<You are not yet ready to grasp the other immutable laws. Knowledge of them and why they are necessary is, for the unenlightened, potentially disturbing. Over time you may come to realise what they are as your understanding increases. Even Crixac, whose knowledge and understanding eclipses all on this planet, has only a tentative grasp of them.>

A statement Crixac did not try to refute.

Once again, they stood silently for some moments, digesting this information. Finally, Menkh formed a thought. <If we assume that you are correct, then why has this being not renewed its attack on Tarvuli? It obviously elicited, albeit unwillingly from my mind, knowledge of this place and the Balancepoint, and it must surely have knowledge of you, Varnahrin, and of what you are. It travelled in the blink of an eye to the location of the Balancepoint and, had it not been for Frzath and the others looking through the Eye of Malavak, it may have been breached.>

<It has not renewed its attacked, Menkh, because it would appear that it has thrown its might against the Allroian Hegemony. That much I have learned from Frzath during the time of your

return. It also knows of my existence, though what I exactly am as yet remains a mystery to it, and the nature of our defences it has yet to fully understand. It seems to have reached a conclusion that a renewal of the assault now would be thwarted and its own destruction a possibility. No, its might is now arrayed in favour of its allies, but I suspect a deeper plan still. If this force feeds off the Talixit Ven, then its power will continue to grow until it becomes strong enough to mount a successful assault on Tarvuli.>

<But why would it bother? Surely the link from here to the Balancepoint is disrupted?> Tishan was confused.

<Because, Tishan Dar, I am here, and I am an incalculable prize to it. Through me it will tap into power the like of which has never been seen.>

<Then it would seem logical that we should aid the Allroians and disrupt the connection of this being with the Talixit Ven whilst Tarvuli is relatively safe. Can you give guidance in this, Varnahrin?>

<No, Menkh, I cannot. Any decisions taken must be made by you three here. I will protect Ta'Morin and by extension those who now sit within its sphere of influence. I can provide no direction to you in these other matters. The reasons should be obvious to you.>

<Yet, you aided us in the fight against the Ma'Vessick,> Tishan observed.

<I provided you with some of the means to affect a successful campaign and provided you with access to the Rod of Klemish. The rest was your doing, Tishan Dar, as were all the decisions with regard to your attack. Subsequent actions to eradicate Ma'Vessick religious fanatics was on your request. I have provided you with information as to the possible source of this new threat and its alliance with the Talixit Ven against its enemies. What you do now is up to you. The resources of Ta'Morin are yours to command. In

addition, you have Menkh's staff and your rod, two of the most powerful artefacts in existence.>

<Yes, that rod you carry. It is somewhat like my staff, though smaller, of course.> Menkh's thoughts held an overtone of curiosity.

<The Rod of Klemish.> Crixac's tone was incredulous. <A lost relic of an ancient civilisation. There is some information in the Complex archives, but it is little enough. The Kareems unearthed some remains in the early days of the City and the Rod of Klemish is referred to. If this is indeed the object, I can see it does have some qualities similar to the staff. I wonder if the staff also has some link to this ancient race?>

<I cannot help you with your question, Crixac,> Varnahrin responded. <Whilst the rod yields to my probing, the staff is closed to me. Why this is so is open to conjecture. Suffice to say that, as you have experienced, they are both immensely powerful.>

Over several chaal they remained in conference, discussing their options and a plan of attack. Finally, with the deliberations ended and a coherent strategy agreed upon, they set in motion the initial phase to ensure that all remained well during their absence.

After several meh'chaal they had achieved their goals, having ensured that the Graaven Council, Ankh's position now filled by Lerma, would continue to manage things in Ta'Morin. Horven had agreed to oversee Gahrtok and the running of Ma'Vessick affairs. Drenyk and Pershivon had proven exemplary in maintaining relations with the Xotic and Benshin and monitoring the passage of curious travellers and traders through the various gateways that connected distant parts of Tarvuli.

It was with a sense of accomplishment that they met one evening in the Complex.

<So,> Menkh summarised the outcome of their meeting, <Ta'Morin will be effectively managed by the council. Horven will retain control of Gahrtok and the governance of the Ma'Vessick,

aided by Hamra. Pershivon and Drenyk will help oversee Xaranca and the gateways. Our tetran forces are more than adequate to help manage matters if unforeseen strife arises with the Ma'Vessick.>

<Yes. Horven has demonstrated an amazing capacity to administer day-to-day matters with intelligence and skill. I foresee no issues with the Ma'Vessick,> Tishan replied. <As to the council, whilst Ankh is a huge loss, Lerma demonstrates a quiet authority, and I have to say that your former steward, Majek, has grown into his new role and has gained the respect of the others. Your one-time servant has come into his own, Zaltec,> Tishan remarked with some humour.

<Who would have thought it?> Menkh responded. <Of course, being in my company over many sem'chaal obviously had a beneficial effect,> he added, tongue in cheek.

<I think Majek would suggest that it was the other way around, my friend!> said Crixac.

General laughter followed this observation and Menkh spoke aloud, 'All too true, Crixac!'

The moment of laughter passed as they turned their attention once more to the task ahead of them.

<So then.> Tishan summarised their course of action. <We travel first to the Balancepoint.>

<Yes,> said Varnahrin, <Frzath and the others will have news and, as we have discussed, I believe that you, Tishan, must seek to directly communicate with the Intelligence, as did Menkh, if you are to succeed.>

<Very well. From there Tishan will go to the aid of the Allroian Hegemony, and I will focus on the Talixit Ven. Let us hope that Tishan's intervention will be unanticipated and turn the conflict in our favour.>

<We must not underestimate the danger,> counselled Crixac. <Our enemy is powerful, as we have experienced. It is vital that

neither the rod nor the staff fall into its hands. We all know what must happen if this were to occur.>

Tishan and Menkh looked at each other and nodded.

<Go then, my children. All will be well here; we must strive to achieve equilibrium. The Balance is all.>

With the voice of Varnahrin echoing in their minds, Menkh summoned the Threadway, he and Tishan ascended, and they disappeared from Ta'Morin, bent upon their quest.

To Be Continued …

Acknowledgements

My father was the first person who said to me that, in life, it isn't what you know but who you know that is important.

I have held this as a constant throughout my life and the writing of this novel has been no different.

My wife, Marilyn, has ever been my rock through good times and bad and who, throughout the past thirty-five years, has been my constant support no matter what I have endeavoured to do. Without her steadying presence this book would have remained an unfulfilled ambition.

To Ian Andrew, who has given so unstintingly of his knowledge and experience, both as a published author and as a friend and mentor on this journey, my deepest and enduring thanks.

This Work is dedicated to these amazing people. Thank you for being in my life.

About the author

Robert C Littlewood was born in London in 1957, emigrating with his parents and sister – all now deceased – to Australia in 1964.

Prior to completing a Bachelor of Education at Murdoch University in 1992, he undertook many different jobs. After attaining his degree, he worked as a state schoolteacher for a number of years before leaving teaching to take up other interests, including semi-professional work as an opera singer.

Robert is married with three grown children and resides in Bunbury in the south-west of Western Australia.